∞ ∞ ∞ ∞ ∞ ∞

Greater love hath no man than this, that a man lay down his life for his friends. John 15:13 KJV

∞ ∞ ∞ ∞ ∞ ∞

THE FIRST & LAST POLICE CANINE

The first to sense the hostility of a suspect,
The first to react to protect his master.
The first to enter where danger lurks.
The first to detect the hidden intruder.
The first to take action against violence.
The first to sense his master's joy.
The first to know his master's sorrow or fear.
The first to give his life in defense of his master.
The last to be forgotten by those who work with
others like him. They know him as a "partner",
not just an animal.
(author unknown)

∞ ∞ ∞ ∞ ∞ ∞

Greater Love Hath No Man

By

Richard Allen Wade

Eureka Publishing Company
Cape Coral, FL

Customer Reviews

The Original "Boss"

Boss Is Really Worth Reading - This was such a heartwarming book. I just could not put it down. You can really feel the emotion in the story of the characters and even the dog, Boss. Since I am a dog lover and owner, it really hit home for me. Well written and cannot wait for the sequel. ~ Joan Ryder

Touching story. I enjoyed the fact that the print is larger than normal and very easy to read. I recommend it, especially for dog lovers. ~ Sharon Graham

Great novel! Easy reading! Keeps your interest throughout the entire book. Can't wait to see if there will be a sequel to it!!!
~ Healthier Living

Five Stars - Great story, good writing!!!! ~ Caryl Anderson

"Gray Island"

Loved It! Quick read! - I couldn't believe how much I enjoyed Gray Island. Just a simple story about a simple way of life and the rewards of being industrious. I really enjoyed it!!! I'll have to order your new one immediately. ~ Healthier Living

Gray Island Will Make You Stop & Think! - I read this story by Richard Wade a while back and it is very good. Tells the story that everyone can understand and it speaks the truth. A must read for everyone! ~ Joan Ryder

Gray Island - This is an interesting story with lively characters working diligently to obtain, what we refer to as the "American Dream." It is especially pertinent for understanding what is happening in the economy of the U.S ~ Janie

Between the years of 1914 and 1916, two privately owned dogs from London were Baltimore's first unofficial police dogs. Two Airedale Terriers, Luxe, owned by Mr. Jere Wheelright, and Morpheus, owned by Dr. Henry Barton Jacobs, were offered to Baltimore City Police Department to be used as needed.

On December 18, 1956, Commissioner James M. Hepbron started an experimental program with two dogs. The first dog, "Turk," a two-year-old black and silver German Shephard was handled by Patrolman Thomas McGinn. The second dog, Major Von-Gruntz, Major, to his fellow officers, a two-year-old German Shephard was handled by Patrolman Irvan Marders. By the middle of January 1957, 14 dogs and 14 officers were chosen as potential candidates for the program. The dogs and handlers were trained until March 1, 1957, then put on the streets on Friday and Saturday nights. On April 17, 1957, after the success of the experimental program, Commissioner Hepbron went before the Mayor and City Council to request that the K9 Corps become a permanent fixture in the Baltimore City Police Department.

What started as an experimental program would bring Baltimore City Police Department to eventually have "The Best K9 Unit in the United States." The training that the dogs and handlers received would later be called "The Baltimore Method." This method of training consisted of the dogs being taught to be more sociable, allowing them to do public appearances. The program also required that the dogs must live in their handler's home with them. Up until "The Baltimore Method" was put into place, the dogs were trained to be aggressive and had to be kenneled when off duty.

For more history on the Baltimore City K9 Unit, please visit **http://baltimorecitypolicehistory.com**

Dedication

We'd like to send out a very special thank you and a salute to the men, women and K9 officers of the Baltimore City Police Department.

This book is dedicated to service dogs of all kinds and the people who work with and love them.

This book is dedicated to the police dogs that put their lives in jeopardy each time they report to the scene of a crime with their human partners. It is dedicated to the dogs that are called to the places of disaster whenever they are needed to search for the living and the dead.

This book is also dedicated to the dogs that have shared their lives with me.

VI

Special Thanks

First, I want to thank God for allowing me to be here and to be able to bring joy, even if just a little, to every person reading this book.

For Boss, I would like to thank Martha Ann Wade and Weldon Dobson for their help with proofreading, editing, and computer work.

For Baltimore Blackie, I would like to thank Martha Ann Wade and Melissa Ann Fisher for their help with proofreading, editing, and computer work.

For the combination of the two books to make up Greater Love Hath No Man, I would like to thank Martha Ann Wade and Melissa Ann Fisher for their patience and understanding through the entire editing and proofreading process. I thank you both for all the effort and compassion you put into helping me bring these books to life. Original cover art (watercolor) by Michelle Carver. Inside art (charcoal and pencil) by Melissa Fisher. Cover layout and design by Melissa Ann Fisher.

VIII

Table of Contents

Boss

Book One (Revised)

BOSS

Jack was under the influence of the anesthetic. He seemed to be dreaming that someone was calling him.

"*Jack, where--you? Can't---find---you.*"
"*I'm here.*"
"*Where---you?*"
"*I'm not sure. I think I'm asleep.*"
"*I---scared.*"
"*Who are you?*"
"*Boss.*"
"*Boss?*"
"*Yes---Jack. Come---get------me.*"
"*I can't, Boss. I don't think I can get up.*"
"*I---can't---. Jack, what------going---on?*"
"*I don't know, boy.*"
"*Afraid---Come---get.*"
"*I will, Boss. Hang on boy, I'll be right there.*"

The odd dream drifted away; Jack was fully unconscious once again.

BOSS

Prologue

Many thousands of years ago, on the chilly morning of a day lost in the mists of time, a small group of primitive men came upon and killed an injured she-wolf. They began to remove her skin, knowing that her thick fur would help keep their children warm during the coming winter.

As they worked, one of the men heard the whimpers of her orphaned pups coming from her nearby den and went to investigate. Perhaps out of kindness, or possibly out of curiosity, he decided to let them live. He quickly wove a crude bag out of tough dry grass and tucked the four small creatures inside. He carried them back to his communal home in a cave at the base of a cliff. He had no way of knowing how his actions would affect both species for ages to come.

It may have been that he only wanted to show the pups to his mate and children before they too would be killed for their life-sustaining flesh. It's also possible he planned to feed the pups the scraps of future kills until they grew large enough to provide clothing for his family.

Whatever his intentions were, as the pups grew, he became emotionally attached to them and they formed a partnership. The half-tame wolves joined the man and his tribe as they wandered through their perilous world in search of food and shelter. From the loins of those wolves sprang the many different breeds of dogs that we later humans, through programs of selective breeding, have developed to provide aid and companionship to us in the many facets of our own lives.

BOSS

Chapter 1

The police car moved slowly down the dimly lit street. It was not the normal marked car that was driven by most officers. To anyone who happened to be out and about at this late hour, it would appear to be just another other private automobile moving through the neighborhood.

The driver of the car, K9 Police Corporal John "Jack" Randall, peered through the windshield and out of the lowered left side window. He was looking for anything that might tip him off to where burglars the had gone.

He was slender with dark hair and eyes and still in good physical condition from his military service of a few years before. He stood exactly six feet two inches tall and weighed one hundred seventy-three pounds when dressed in his uniform.

The huge black German Shepherd on the seat beside him was eager and alert. Weighing well over one hundred pounds, he was larger than the average dog of his breed by a good twenty-five pounds. Most of the other officers in the Baltimore City Police Department referred to him simply as, the Boss. Jack was proud to have him as a partner.

A gun store had been looted. There was a much better than even chance the bad guys weren't even out there; he was almost certainly too close to the store. The thieves were probably miles away by now.

Most robberies of this type were made by professionals who already had an order in their pocket for the stolen merchandise before it was taken. They usually planned for a heist to take place in an area where they weren't known, in case they were seen by any of the locals or one of their victims. This job probably wouldn't involve the type of thieves who broke into a store in the middle of the night to steal things they could peddle for a few dollars to their buddies the next day. You never knew, though.

The burglars seemed to have been targeting "smart" rifles that were simplified civilian versions of military weapons. They also took many regular rifles, handguns and several cases of ammunition, along with all the night vision goggles they could find.

The alarm had gone off at the gun store almost an hour ago. Police cars had raced through the night with sirens wailing and lights flashing to get to the scene of the crime.

When the first officers arrived, the thieves were already gone. The tools they used to break through the iron grating and side door were found lying just inside the entrance point. They would be dusted for fingerprints, just as the rest of the crime scene would be, but that would probably be a waste of time. Thieves who stole large numbers of guns were usually too smart to leave fingerprints. It was surprising they had even left their tools behind. The crime would probably be solved by police department detectives if it was ever solved at all.

Jack and Boss had been farther away than the first responders and didn't arrive until the other officers had been on the scene for almost fifteen minutes. When they got to the store, they were immediately sent to search through the surrounding neighborhoods to look for signs of unusual activity.

His communicator hummed; it was one of the first responders.

"Jack? Have you got anything?"

"Nothing, Bill."

"They're sending the chopper over. It should be in the area in a few minutes."

"Why are they sending the helicopter? These guys aren't on foot. They took way too many guns to carry in their arms. They're probably in the next county by now. What good is a chopper going to do?"

"None, more than likely, but you never know. It's probably been a quiet night for the pilot and the D.O. wants him to stay busy."

"Keep me posted if you hear anything helpful from the pilot."

"Will do. We might not be dealing with real smart guys. The bright ones usually don't leave their tools behind."

"That's true; I'll keep that in mind. I'll let you know if I see anything that looks suspicious."

"Right, Jack. Just be sure to stay on your toes and be careful. This job could involve local people. Some of them can be just as dangerous as the professionals."

"Ok, ten-four."

Jack reached over and stroked Boss's shoulder.

"Do you see anything, boy?"

The dog snorted. There was a strong bond between him and his handler. There were times when Jack believed Boss understood everything he said.

"We're probably on a wild goose chase, but we'll look around for a while. Then we'll go back to the store."

Boss snorted again.

Jack turned the car down another side street. He had the driver's side window all the way down and the passenger side window part of the way down. It was a late summer night, so they were both comfortable. The houses that lined the streets were old and shabby and were obscured by mature trees and bushes that had not been kept trimmed. It was not what most people would call a good neighborhood. Still nothing.

Ten minutes later, he was ready to return to the gun store.

"I think we're beating a dead horse, boy," he said.

Suddenly, Boss's ears perked up. He jerked his head toward the right side of the car.

"What is it, boy? Did you see something?"

Boss moved to the passenger side window and let out a low growl. He scratched at the door handle.

"What is it? I don't see anything."

Jack talked to his K9 partner as much as some men talked to their wives. He moved his head back and forth as he scanned both sides of the street. He turned a corner to the right and proceeded slowly through the neighborhood as Boss became more agitated. He stopped the car.

He spoke into the communicator. "Bill?"

"Yeah, Jack."

"We may have found something. Boss is getting worked up."

"What is it?"

"I'm not sure. I've got an older model white van. It's parked beside a shed behind a dark house and it looks like the side door of the van is open. There's no light on in it and none in or around the shed. I think I'll drive around to the back and check it out. It's too dark back there to see much more from here."

"Where are you?"

He checked the computer screen on the dash.

"I'm at 4941 East Nathan Street."

"Ok. I'm going to send backup, just in case. I'll have headquarters send a drone to check it out before you go in."

"It's probably nothing. I wouldn't even worry about it if Boss hadn't alerted. Don't worry about the drone. We'll look the place over and be done before it can get here."

"I'm sending another officer now. Why don't you at least wait until he gets to you?"

"Because Boss needs to take a leak and there are a lot of bushes back there. I'm going to drive around the block. I'll come in behind the house and get out and walk so I can get a better look at the shed. I won't park right next to it. If there are problems, backup won't be long in getting here."

"OK, hardhead. Just be careful and stay on the radio. If you've found the guys that did this, from what we're seeing here and the number of tools they left behind, there are at least two of them."

Jack turned his headlights off and pressed his right foot gently onto the accelerator. He cautiously drove toward the end of the block to where he could turn down the next street and approach the shed from behind.

He stopped two houses away from the shed and flipped the switch that would prevent the car's interior light from coming on. He opened the car door and stepped out; Boss was immediately at his side. He quietly closed the door so there would be no noise. His charcoal colored uniform made him almost invisible in the darkness.

"Let's go look at that shed, boy," he said quietly.

Jack began to ease across the yard. He carried a large black police issue flashlight in his left hand; he did not turn it on. He unbuttoned the flap on his holster with his right hand and pulled out his semi-automatic service pistol. He took off the safety. There's no sense in being stupid, he thought to himself. It was too quiet, even for this late hour.

Boss was on high alert.

"Stay with me boy, take your time," Jack said quietly. "It'll take a couple of minutes for my eyes to get used to the dark. There are a lot of bushes and other places for someone to hide."

He cautiously approached the shed at a back corner where he could see both the open side door of the van and the side of the shed. There was an open door in the shed beside the van, but nothing moved inside.

He heard a twig snap behind him. "Alert, Boss!"

Boss was already whirling to the rear just as a crowbar came whistling out of the darkness toward Jack's head. Jack instinctively lurched to one side. The bar struck a glancing blow. He felt the impact and staggered as lights twirled momentarily inside his skull. It was then that he heard the scream.

The scream was always the same. It was the cry of a now terrified man who hadn't seen the huge black dog at his side. Boss's teeth were clamped onto his arm and he was being violently shaken. The steel bar thudded to the ground.

Jack shook his head to clear away the dancing stars. "Hold him, boy," he yelled.

From inside the shed came a blinding flash and the roar of a large caliber pistol being fired. A bullet zipped past his head. Jack dropped to his knees and fired back, twice. He didn't expect to hit anything in the darkness. The flash from the muzzle of the gun had blinded him and he was trying to buy some time until his eyes adjusted to the dark. He rolled to his right and crouched behind the trunk of an ancient oak tree. It would provide cover until he could see again.

He punched the button on his communicator and yelled, "Shots fired! Officer under fire!" The locator inside of the device would bring other officers to his exact position.

He directed his voice toward the hidden shooter, "Drop your weapon and come out! This is the Baltimore City Police. You're under arrest!"

"Screw you, cop! You ain't nobody! You tell your friggin' dog to let go of my friend!"

Boss had pulled the first man down onto the ground and was continuing to shake his arm. The man screamed again as he struggled with the snarling dog.

"He won't let go until I tell him! Throw me your weapon and come out!"

The man inside the shed was not backing down. "I can see where you're hiding! You make your dog turn my friend loose or I'm gonna blow your head off and then I'm gonna kill him!"

"You hurt that dog and you won't be walking away from that shed! You'll be carried out in a bag! There are other officers and a chopper on the way! Come on out of there! You might as well make it easy on yourself!"

"No way!"

"Throw out your gun and come out or I'm going to tell my dog to take your friend's hand off!"

Another scream came from the man who had hit him with the crowbar, then the cry, "Do what he says! This dog is killin' me!"

"Alright, cop! I'm comin' out! You make that dog of yours turn loose of his arm!"

"Throw out the gun, first! I'm not telling him to do anything until I see your gun on the ground and your hands in the air!"

"I'm comin'. Here's the gun." There was a thud close to Jack's feet.

Jack could now see somewhat better. His eyes were adjusting to the darkness.

"I see the gun! Come on out with your hands up! Boss, hold him!" The first man screamed again as the dog tightened his grip. Things were looking up; he could hear the wail of a siren in the distance.

The man on the ground screamed, "We gotta do something and get out of here! There are more cops on the way!"

"I am doing something! We've got to get that dog off you, first!"

The hidden man walked from inside the shed with both of his hands held up high over his head. Jack turned on the flashlight and directed the beam into the man's eyes.

"OK, cop, I'm here. Now, call that dog off!"

Jack stood up. "I will, as soon as you turn around and put your hands behind your back so I can put the cuffs on. Then, I'll call him off."

"OK, but do it fast!" The man began to turn his back and lower his arms.

Jack reached for the handcuffs on his belt. His blood chilled as he heard an ominous laugh come from behind and felt the cold end of a gun barrel being pressed against the back of his head.

"Surprise, wise guy. I bet you're not feelin' so smart now, are you?"

There are three of them, he thought to himself. How could I have been so stupid?

The second man yelled, "Quick! Kill the cop and shoot his friggin' dog! We gotta get out of here!"

Jack heard the click of the hammer being pulled back. He swallowed hard. There was nothing he could do. Backup would not arrive in time to help them.

Suddenly, there was another blood-curdling scream followed by the roar of the gun being fired closely behind his left ear. Jack's head rang from the report and he was momentarily deafened. The bullet missed.

"Boss! Good boy, Boss!"

Chapter 2

The instant the third man's gun thundered, the other two men fled on foot. Jack picked up the pistol the third gunman dropped when Boss grabbed the assailant's arm. Then he told Boss to release. When the backup car arrived on the scene, the officer inside the vehicle jumped out and handcuffed the gunman who was still there, while Jack and Boss pursued the two that had run into the darkness.

The officer had to perform an ugly chore since Boss's teeth had made a mess of the shooter's wrist. It was almost as if he had been punishing the man for attempting to hurt Jack. The officer handcuffed the suspect and then applied a tourniquet.

The first man Boss had taken down was not difficult to locate since he was losing a lot of blood from his mangled arm. Boss had little difficulty in trailing him; the blood smell that was hot in his nose led him to where the man had taken refuge inside an unlocked car that was parked on the side of the street. He didn't have a gun when he was apprehended, which was understandable; Boss had clamped down hard on his right hand and wrist and he wouldn't have been able to hold one if he'd had it.

He was weak from loss of blood and there was little fight left in him. Just as Jack was pulling the injured man from the vehicle, another car arrived bearing two more police officers. He turned the suspect over to them.

The man who had fired at Jack from inside the shed was uninjured and more difficult to apprehend. Jack didn't know it, but he had picked up his gun before running into the darkness.

He knew the neighborhood well and moved quickly. Boss tracked him to a darkened house, where he had stolen an expensive bicycle from the backyard. The bike enabled him to put more distance between himself and his pursuers.

The police helicopter, which had finally arrived, located him almost a mile away. When the suspect heard the chopper, he realized the pilot was searching for him and doubled back on his trail. After almost an eighth of a mile, he turned the bicycle to the right and moved diagonally away from where he thought Jack and Boss were.

However, there would be no escape. The helicopter had heat-sensing instruments on board and the pilot was in constant contact with Jack. When Jack and Boss were within a few yards of the man, the pilot turned on his huge spotlight and centered the suspect in its beam.

Boss took the frantically pedaling burglar off the bicycle with a soaring leap. For the third time that night, the massive dog tasted the blood of yet another criminal who had tried to harm his partner. A stolen handgun was tucked under the shooter's belt. Except for the one spent shell that he had fired at Jack back at the shed, it was loaded with hollow point bullets that were known on the street as "cop killers".

∞ ∞ ∞ ∞ ∞ ∞

The next afternoon, Jack and Boss arrived at headquarters an hour before they were scheduled to begin their shift so Jack could finish his report on the incident.

The Duty Sergeant, who was busy talking on the telephone, handed him a note as they walked in. It read, "Go see Captain Harrison."

Jack knew he was going to have a long day. The Captain was going to be climbing up and down his back for what he'd done last night. He had gone in without backup and had almost gotten himself and his dog killed.

Jack knocked on the Captain's open office door and stepped inside. Boss walked at his side.

"Good afternoon, Captain."

"Hello, Jack. We need to talk about last night. Close the door and take a seat. Hi, Boss."

Boss whined and perked his ears. He liked the Captain, but he knew there was something wrong because of the tone of his voice.

The Captain was all business. "First things first; before we get started, how's your head?

"The medics checked it last night; I'll just have a knot for a couple days. No big deal."

Mark Harrison was a good K9 officer when he patrolled the streets. He'd been partnered with a legendary German Shepherd named Heffner when he was first transferred from regular police duty to the K9 Department. Heff had been killed in the line of duty during a shootout in a hostage situation, but not before he'd helped save the lives of a young mother and two children. He had been buried with full Police Department honors.

Harrison's second dog was named Einstein. Most of the officers who knew him said it was because he was so intelligent. Harrison and Einstein served together for almost five years until 'Stein was badly wounded during a standoff with bank robbers. After the veterinarians mended his body, he was retired from duty and was sent home to live with Harrison.

When 'Stein was wounded, Harrison decided not to partner again with another dog. Since he had served so well and had such good rapport with the other K9 officers and their dogs, he was promoted to Captain and placed in charge of the K9 Department.

Military drill sergeants had nothing on the Captain. He could chew a man out with the best of them. Jack knew he had a difficult few minutes ahead of him and tried to make the experience a little less unpleasant for both men.

"Cap, before you start in on me, I know what you're going to say. I'm not going to try to make excuses. I did a dumb thing last night. I was thinking the perps weren't from around here. I was sure it was a professional job. There were a lot of "smart" rifles, handguns, regular rifles and ammo was taken. They also took the time to grab every box of night vision goggles in the place. Because of that, I thought it was professionals who robbed the store. I didn't think it was just some local goof-offs trying to make some quick money by stealing guns close to home. I didn't believe I'd find anything when I checked out that shed. But still, I should have waited for backup before I went in."

"You're right. It was a stupid thing for you to do and I should chew your tail off about it! You acted like a rookie! We have drones to check out places like that before we go in! From what you told the other officers and I read in their reports, if Boss hadn't saved your butt, again, you'd have a bullet in your head and you'd be stretched out in the coroner's cooler right now! The Boss would be having a lot of trouble with that, wouldn't you, boy?"

Boss whined and licked his hand. The Captain had a soft place in his heart for the big dog, just as he did for all the dogs under his command.

"I know, Cap. I've been thinking about that. I doubt he'd still be here. Once I was down, they would have killed him."

"That would have been a terrible loss to the P.D. and to me. I don't want to lose any of my men or dogs because of a stupid decision like the one you made last night."

"I learned my lesson the hard way. I won't be doing anything like that again."

"You can bet your sweet stripes you won't! If you do and I find out about it, you'll be walking a beat for the next six months! Jack, you and Boss make a heck of a good team. You're good at what you do and he's an exceptionally smart dog. Most of the guys around here think he understands everything you say to him and they also believe you understand just about everything he tries to tell you. But, he can't do your thinking for you and he won't always be able to save you. When it comes to a situation like you were facing last night, you should use your head for something other than a target."

Jack relaxed slightly and tried to steer the conversation in another direction. "You're right, Cap. I think he's the most intelligent dog I've ever worked with. When I was in the Army in Iran, I worked with two other great dogs, but neither of them could hold a candle to him."

The Captain took the bait. "You know," he said, "I still can't believe the Iranians launched that nuke at Israel and were so unprepared; they couldn't get the other half dozen they had into the air before they were blasted into dust. How the Israelis knew where they all were, is beyond me. If Iran had destroyed Israel, the U.S. probably wouldn't even have gotten involved. We'd have just raised cane afterward with their United Nations representatives. There wouldn't have been a reason to get involved, except to honor an agreement with a non-existent country."

"Yeah, I know. Iran's a big place, so it is kind of surprising that the Israelis knew where all the missiles were. We lost a lot of good people over there and so did the Israelis. If we hadn't had superior technology and so many good dogs to help us, we might still be at war. Maybe I give the dogs too much credit, but they were a tremendous help when we had to do all that house to house fighting. The Iranians were scared to death of them, especially at night. I think they were more afraid of the dogs than they were of us."

"I can believe that. I know how well dogs work too, you know. I'm glad it's all over. Not all the Iranians were our enemies. The way politics work and with the Ayatollah out of the picture, in another few years, the Iranians might become one of our closest allies in that region."

"It doesn't make any sense, does it?"

"No, at least it doesn't to us. I guess the politicians can handle it."

"Yeah, the way they do such a great job of handling everything else. The only good thing that came out of the war for me was, I got to work with those two dogs. They were both great soldiers. I lost the first one, Canyon, when a sniper who was trying to take me out, hit him instead. I worked with the second one for almost a year. His name was Kelly. He wasn't much more than a pup, but he was the smartest dog I ever saw. He saved my tail a dozen times and saved the lives of a lot of other soldiers and dogs who were working with us. He was almost as smart as Boss and we had a tight bond. It broke my heart when I was forced to leave him over there. I tried to bring him back to the States with me when I was discharged, but my C.O. wouldn't allow it. He said Kelly was U.S. Government property and didn't belong to me. I tried to buy him from the Army and get him sent to me after I got back home, but when I did, I couldn't find out anything about him. It was like he just disappeared or something. I guess he probably got killed after I left."

Jack continued, "He was a great dog, but even he wasn't like Boss. A lot of the time, I don't even have to tell Boss what to do. It's as if he's already thought it out. He should have held on to the arm of the first guy he grabbed last night; he was trained to do that. I didn't tell him to release. When I heard that gun click behind my head, I thought it was all over. It seemed like Boss knew he should let the first man's arm go and try to grab the other guy's wrist and yank it before he could pull the trigger. He didn't make a sound until he had that jerk's arm in his teeth. How he did it so fast, I'll never know. He saved my life. That gun was buried in the back of my head. It's not the first time he's saved my butt, either."

"I know. I read all the reports the K9 officers turn in."

"My life was flashing before my eyes. After I got home last night, I started thinking about the war again. The fight in the darkness brought it all back. When I got out of the service and came back home, all I could think about was finding Kelly. I was never going to be around another gun again as long as I lived. Before I went into the Army, I used to go deer hunting with my Dad out in Western Maryland, but I wouldn't even do that anymore. I think my Dad started believing I was a wuss. I was home for quite a while before I started thinking about how the bad guys were doing all the winning here in the city. No matter how much I wanted to stay away from trouble, I knew I had the training to help do something about it. Then I started reading about the K9 Department and thinking I might like to work with dogs again. As they say, the rest is history. Boss and I have been together for almost two years."

"It's been a good history too, Jack. You and Boss are our best team. You've been a credit to the entire police department. You have half the crooks in the city believing they're going to have to go into a different line of work. Some of our officers were losing hope before you joined the P. D. and hooked up with your dog.

You've both been an inspiration to the rest of us and we're beginning to take the streets back from the bad guys."

"Thanks, Cap. As far as the other officers believing I know what he's thinking; they're right about that. Boss is special. I've worked with dogs for a long time and I can read their body language pretty well, but it goes farther than that. I know there's no such thing as extrasensory perception, but sometimes he makes me wonder. It's like, he tries to tell me things and I understand what he's saying. I understand him and he understands me. He's a heck of a dog and we do make a good team."

Boss whined and put his paw on Jack's knee. Both men laughed.

"See?" said Jack.

"Yeah, I do. I needed to caution you about taking too many chances, because you do. But, that's not the only reason I told the Desk Sergeant to give you that note. There's more I need to talk to you about."

"Oh? What else did I do wrong? Or was it Boss?"

The Captain smiled. "Neither of you. I'm supposed to select a K9 team for a slot in a special federal government program and you were specifically mentioned. What we talk about from now on does not leave my office. Is that clear? It's Top-Secret."

"Sure Cap; I understand completely. I thought I was through with the government when I left the Army. Except for the dogs, I was glad to be done with it."

"I'm supposed to feel you out to see if you might be interested in taking part in an experimental program they're working on. I should tell you, I'm not too fond of the idea. It sounds like a lot of hoo-doo to me, like most of the crap they come up with."

"What is it, Cap?"

"I don't know much about it, but I'm going to tell you everything they told me. They've been watching you."

"This sounds serious."

"It is. They watch just about everything people do nowadays and they can keep just about anyone under surveillance. The terrorists made all the extra security necessary. Because of them, nobody has the expectation of privacy that we used to have. Things got even worse when the FBI caught that anti-Semite U.S. Senator helping the enemy during the war with Iran."

"Yeah, I know. I'd like to get my hands on him. I still can't believe he got off with only a year in prison. The way the system works, that jerk probably collected all of his back pay when he got out of the pen and is drawing retirement."

"Yes, I imagine he is. But, let's get back to what we were talking about; the special program. Don't look so worried. I think the reason they're interested in you is because you've been doing so many things right."

"What do you mean?"

"You were talking about your second dog in Iran. He's one of the reasons they're interested in you. The officers in your unit saw the tremendous rapport you had with him. They thought it was well beyond the ordinary bond most K9 soldiers have with their dogs. He didn't disappear or get killed; he just refused to work with anyone else and wouldn't eat for a while after you were shipped home. From what I was told, he would barely drink water for a couple of days when you left. In a bone, dry place like that, it does sort of make you wonder, doesn't it?"

"Dang, Cap, why are you telling me this? I felt terrible when I had to leave him over there. Now, you're telling me he suffered after I was gone?"

"I'm just telling you what I've learned since I've been talking with the feds about their program. I've worked with dogs too, Jack. I don't like to think about them hurting. You know what it did to me when 'Stein was wounded."

"I know. I'm sorry."

"Kelly's happy now. Since he refused to work with anyone else, one of your officers asked for permission to take him home to Connecticut when he was transferred back to the States. I'm sure you know, the military usually euthanizes service dogs so they don't have the expense of shipping them back here when they get through with them. The Army not only let the officer bring your dog home, it paid for both of their plane tickets. He's still living with the officer's family. The Army kept an eye on both of you after you got home. You and Kelly must have been a very special team to arouse your Commanding Officer's curiosity so much. You have to be good with dogs or you don't get into that outfit in the first place."

"I don't know that I've ever done anything exceptional. I just did my job to the best of my ability and I've always gotten along well with dogs. They like me and I like them."

"Yeah, I feel the same way about them. They're good people who just happen to wear permanent fur coats. I was told the Army tried to convince you to re-enlist and become a K9 instructor after you were sent back, but you didn't want to."

"Why would I? I did my job as well as I could and so did my dogs. Plus, it wasn't quite that simple. They wanted me to put in another year over there before I could come back. I almost got killed for the Army. I would've been dead several times over if my dogs hadn't saved me and one of my dogs did get killed. So, how did they reward us for our service? When my enlistment was up and I was coming home, they wouldn't let me bring my dog with me and they wouldn't sell him to me. I don't like working for an outfit that treats people and animals like that."

"I understand why you felt that way. I would have too. Anyway, this is what I've been told. A few months ago, the C. O. you served under in Iran saw a picture of you and Boss in a news article about the two of you taking down a couple of armed robbers. He sent an email about it to a friend of his who oversees the research program I told you about. The friend is the Army officer who has been in to talk to the Chief and me about you. He's the person who told us about what happened to your dog after you left Iran. He's read your service records and knows how effective you've been since you've been working with Boss. He's interested in both of you."

"Oh no, Cap. We're not going into the Army, not for any reason."

Captain Harrison grinned. "Don't worry about that, you don't have to. From what I understand, it's not so much the Army that's interested in you. It's the program's research scientists."

"Why?"

"Wait until you hear the rest of it. If you don't like what I'm about to say, you walk right back out my office and we'll never talk about it again."

"Ok, but I'm through with the Army. As far as I'm concerned, I feel like I'm doing a better service for my country right here in the K9 Department than I could anywhere else. There's nothing the Army has to offer that would interest me."

"What would you say if I told you there were experiments going on concerning that extra sensory perception thing with Boss that you were talking about?"

"I'd say I'm not surprised. The Government is constantly wasting money on things like that. Weren't they doing that way back in the 1960's and 70's and again a couple of times since then? Didn't they attempt to enhance it with drugs?"

"I think so, but this is a little different. Let me run some history by you. For a long time, doctors have been putting medical devices into peoples' bodies. They began with pumps that helped people with bad hearts. That didn't work very well, so about seventy-five years ago, they started implanting pacemakers and replacing hearts. For about the last forty years, they've been putting implants into the brains of deaf people that help them to hear. They've also come up with technology that has enabled most blind people to be able to see. These days, you almost never hear about anyone being totally blind. When I was a kid, a lot of people were blind. There are other great things going on. For quite a while now, they've been putting implants into people to help them control artificial limbs."

"I know about that, Cap. They put them on people and place electronic controllers in their heads. I have buddies who lost legs in battle who can walk because of them."

"Fifty years ago, that was just a pipe dream. Now, if you lose an arm or a leg, they just stick a new one on you and away you go."

"Some of the guys I served with are living pretty normal lives because of them."

"Did you also know they've been putting implants into the brains of stroke victims who've lost the use of their arms and legs? A surgeon places one into a healthy area of the brain and over a period of time, a crippled person can train his mind to use the implant to control his body. People are walking around fine today, where just a few years ago, they'd have been permanently paralyzed."

"I've read about that."

"I'm going to cut to the chase. This is 2037, not 1937. Scientists are working on something new. Medical implant technology is becoming more advanced every day. The government's researchers want to try putting implants into the heads of K9 cops and their dogs. They think it will make them become much more effective."

"What? Are you suggesting I do something like that?"

"I'm not suggesting anything. I'm telling you about this program and asking you if you'd like to get more information about it, that's all."

"Why would they want me, specifically?"

"I believe it's because of your record and how well you worked with all of your dogs. Jack, we've worked with dogs for a very long time. For thousands of years, we used them to help us find food for ourselves and our families. We've trained them to tend to our herds of sheep and cattle. The Germans began using them very effectively in the military during both World Wars. Our dogs saved thousands of American lives when we began using them ourselves in our military in World War II. In 1956, we started an experimental program here in Baltimore for the training and use of dogs for police work. We developed one of the finest training programs for handlers and dogs anywhere on the planet. It worked out so well, police departments all over the world have followed suit. Now, the feds want to try to take it to another level with their new technology. I believe, since they know how good you've been with your dogs, they want to use you and Boss to help test the implants."

"The whole thing sounds like science fiction to me."

"It did to me when I first heard about it. But, if it's possible, it does make sense."

"So, how is it supposed to work?"

"Someone else will explain the technical details to you. All I know are the basics. They want only the most intelligent officers and dogs for their program. That cuts out a lot of cops right there, you know. Probably finding the right dogs will be easier than finding the right cops. After you pulled that stunt last night, I'm beginning to wonder why they want you." Captain Harrison smiled.

"That's funny stuff, Cap. You should go on television. What else do they want?"

"There must be some risk involved. They only want single officers without a lot of close family ties. They probably stipulate that in case there are unforeseen problems. Most K9 cops are married, so that requirement eliminates them."

"Ok."

"They also want to use ex-military people who've worked with dogs under fire. They think they might have better self-control in a crisis."

"That makes sense."

"There's also this ESP thing you were talking about. The researchers believe it might be better to work with men who have a closer relationship with dogs than others have been able to achieve. A stronger rapport, if you will. Like you have with Boss and had with your dogs in Iran."

"I don't know if that makes me more qualified than any other unmarried police officer that gets along well with dogs. Don't they have enough single K9 soldiers in the military that they can force to volunteer?"

"I wondered about that, too. I don't know, maybe they are going to use some of them. From what the officer who came in here said, you and Boss are exactly the kind of team they're looking for. You're single, your mother died years ago, your father passed away last year, you have no children and you're an only child without many relatives. You've worked under fire with dogs, both in the Army and in our police department. You have a strong sense of duty. You're smart and so is Boss. You seem to have a strong sixth sense about dogs, more so than many of our other K9 officers. So, you fill most of their requirements. You joined the P. D. so you could help our city. Think about how this program could benefit everyone involved, if you decide to go through with it and if it actually works."

"I don't want anything put into my head, even if I become disabled and actually have a need for it. I'm sure Boss wouldn't want that either. I need to chew on this for a few days. Is that ok?"

"Of course. If I was considering doing something like this, I'd want to think about it for a while, too. Jack, from what I was told, these implants they're talking about won't go deeply into the brain. They only lie on the surface. It's supposed to be a relatively simple operation to put them into place and they can be easily removed."

"Cap, why would any sane man want to get involved with something like that?"

"I don't know why you would, but I'll tell you why I might consider it if I were younger and wasn't married with a family; it's because I love dogs. I've always loved them since I was old enough to pull their ears. They're trustworthy, they're loyal and they give you one-hundred percent, unconditional love. A dog will give up his own life to save yours. It's hard to find those qualities in people. Maybe the implants will help us learn more about why they're like that."

"I still don't want to do it. I don't see how it will help us with police work."

"The officer said it will give the handler a better picture of what the dog is experiencing. In other words, if you have this done, you can send Boss out on a search and can sense some of what he sees, what he smells and what he hears. He becomes a sending unit, you become a receiver. Think about how much more we could accomplish if we could do something like that. How many lives could be saved in battle? How many bad guys could be stopped before they hurt someone else or commit another crime? Your dog sees things better at night. He smells them when they're half a mile away and he hears them when you can't. If we could tune into his senses, can you imagine how much better off our military would be and how much better we could fight crime right here in this city?"

"I'd never have thought anything like that would be possible."

"Neither would I. But, I think it's worth consideration if it can be done without harm to the person or the dog. Maybe it's feasible with today's technology."

"It still sounds awful risky to me."

"Then, there's the other thing to consider. I've always wondered what it is that dogs see in us that make them love us so much. Maybe if we could see what they see, hear and smell, we might be able to understand more about them. Maybe we would become better people and learn to deserve all that love and devotion."

"Cap, until now, I didn't realize just how much you cared about your dogs."

"I've had some good dogs too, Jack."

Jack saw the tears that welled in the eyes of the older man.

Chapter 3

Two weeks later, Jack and Boss left Baltimore in their police cruiser for the short trip down Interstate 95 to the Pentagon in Washington, D.C. Jack had told Captain Harrison he'd decided to listen to what the Army had to say. The Captain arranged a meeting with the officer that had talked with him about the program. His name was Lieutenant Colonel Joseph Meyer.

When Jack and Boss were escorted into the Colonel's office, he turned out to be not at all what Jack expected. He was a slightly overweight, bug-eyed man of about forty years of age who did not carry himself in a military manner. He wore military issue glasses, had narrow sloping shoulders and his back seemed to be slightly bent. His appearance gave the impression that he'd spent most of his life sitting in a chair while reading books or staring at a computer screen. For some reason, this was reassuring to Jack.

After they shook hands, Colonel Meyer invited him to sit down. He then pushed a button on his intercom and spoke.

"Miss Jamison, please bring our guests something to drink and something for them to snack on. They look like they could use a bite to eat."

Jack objected, but not strenuously. "That's not necessary, Colonel. We already ate."

"Nonsense, Corporal Randall. You've done me the favor of coming this far to hear what I have to say; the least I can do is to make you comfortable while you're here."

Jack had the feeling that the colonel had said the same thing many times before to others he was trying to put at ease.

"Thank you, Colonel. We didn't have time to eat a good breakfast this morning. I picked up a couple of sausage biscuits for us from a drive through window before we left Baltimore. We worked the evening shift last night and wound up getting home much later than we expected."

"I imagine police work isn't always exactly timed to an eight-hour shift."

"No sir, it's not."

Just then, Miss Jamison came into the room bearing two trays and placed one of them on the desk between the two men.

The Colonel must have left orders for food to be ready for them immediately upon their arrival. Jack was pleased to see that the tray on the desk held two plates and two cups of steaming hot coffee. On each of the plates was a large breakfast sandwich.

Miss Jamison was an attractive, sandy-haired young woman who appeared to be in her early to mid-twenties. She was tastefully dressed in a white blouse and a light blue skirt with matching high heel shoes. Jack had talked briefly with her before entering the Colonel's office. She spoke with a slight southern accent.

She carried the other tray to a side table. It held an open can of premium dog food, a bottle of water, a plate and a bowl for Boss. She asked Jack for permission to say hello to the big dog.

With his approval, she bent down and patted Boss's head. He immediately liked her. She seemed to know exactly the right spots to scratch behind his ears. She spooned the dog food onto the plate and poured the water into the bowl. She placed both on the floor in front of Boss. Then she asked the Colonel if anything else was needed.

"That will be all for now, Miss Jamison."

Miss Jamison excused herself and left the room. Colonel Meyer took a plate from the tray on the desk and picked up one of the cups of coffee.

"I didn't have time for breakfast, either," he explained. "Please help yourself, Corporal Randall."

They talked about the weather as they ate. When they finished, Boss let out a huge yawn, stretched out on the floor and closed his eyes.

Colonel Meyer started, "Corporal Randall, I'm sure you didn't come all the way down here this morning to make small talk. From what I understand, you've known something about our project for a couple of weeks. Your Captain told me he'd briefed you on our implant program and what we need from our volunteers. If you're here, it must mean you're at least considering becoming involved in what we have planned."

"That's true. I haven't made up my mind about any of this, although I have been giving it serious thought. I want to know exactly what's involved before I commit to anything."

"Of course you do. Any man would be concerned about somebody tinkering with his brain."

"That's probably my biggest concern. I know a little about what's involved and I've been assured everything is completely voluntary. I can back out at any time up until the day of the surgeries and I can have everything removed from our heads after the procedures, at any time I choose. That wouldn't be your call, it would be mine. Is that correct?"

"Your information is correct, Corporal Randall. May I call you, Jack?"

"Of course, sir."

"Thank you," said Colonel Meyer. "Jack, let me tell you about what we have planned. After you hear me out, you may decide to walk out of my office and forget everything we've talked about. Whatever you decide, always remember, our program is Top-Secret. You will never discuss it with anyone who isn't authorized to talk about it, under penalty of federal law. This involves national security. We don't want our enemies to even dream we might be able to accomplish some of the things that we've done."

"I understand. That's fine with me, sir. I can keep a secret and Boss can't talk."

"Good. First, we're looking for a small, select group of K9 officers and dogs. We want the officers to be young, single men who are in good physical condition. We want men and large dogs for our program because their brains are physically larger. We want the dogs to be young and in their prime. Since dogs don't live as long as people, we want them to be mature, but not older than five years or so. We want younger dogs so we'll have many years to observe them after surgery. You fill the bill and so does your dog."

"Boss is almost four years old."

"I know. Let me tell you about our safety arrangements. Before we would do any kind of implantation surgery, we'd run tests, a lot of them. They're necessary when we're putting things into the body, especially the brain area. We must be sure there won't be any adverse reactions. First, we do allergy tests. We'll administer a local anesthetic and put tiny samples of every type of material we use to construct the implants under the skin of your upper arm. They'll be removed after the tests. They'll lie just under the surface of the skin, so removal will be easy and painless. If you should turn out to be allergic to any of the materials, we would find out within a week or so. If you were, you would be disqualified from our program."

"I understand why that would be necessary. What about Boss?"

"He'd get the same allergy tests. In fact, he'd receive almost every type of physical test that you would. If either of you should be allergic to any of the components, that would disqualify both of you, since we need you both for our program. You don't have to worry about us doing something underhanded, like saying either of you was not allergic to something if you were, just to further our research. We're not going to spend tens of thousands of dollars to implant something into you or your dog that might cause harm to either of you. For us to succeed, we need you both to be in excellent health before the surgery and for a long time afterward. One thing is for sure, if there is anything wrong with either of you, we'll find out. You'll receive the finest physical examinations our medical people can perform, even if it's only to find out we can't use you."

"That's reassuring."

"Once we're satisfied that you both are physically and mentally viable, we'll implant the electronics. The sensors that will be placed into your heads are tiny, so minuscule, they wouldn't be picked up in a body scan if you were going through an airport security area. They must be small so they don't put any pressure on the brain. The sensor tips will be placed on the surface of your brain, not down into it. This will result in easy removal if you, or we, were to decide to reverse the procedures at some time in the future. There will be very little metal of any type that will touch the brain. An electronic receiver would be implanted into the back of your neck. It is also very small, about one-fifth the size of a dime. It would be connected to the sensors by tiny wires. Boss would have a transmitter placed into the back of his neck that is the same size as your receiver."

"Before you go any further, I need to ask you something. I should have asked before now. This all sounds well planned, but honestly, there is something that concerns me. When I enlisted in the Army a few years ago, I was promised a lot of things that never materialized. I was also promised that a lot of things wouldn't happen and they did. Why should I trust you?"

The Colonel smiled. "That's a good question. Let me reassure you, this isn't an Army program. I am in the Army, but I've been assigned to this program because of the interest the Defense Department has in the military applications of the implants. The research is entirely civilian and is funded by the U.S. Government, not the Army. You'll be a well-paid, civilian volunteer with no obligation other than to let us check up on you and your dog from time to time, so we can observe how both of you respond to your implants when you go back to work. We'll do our best not to intrude in your lives. We want your police department to benefit from this program, just as much as we want to gain information that will help us with our research. We won't be successful if either of us does something stupid, like lie to each other. If we're successful, and we're sure we will be, your police department will benefit greatly and everything we learn will be applied directly to our military. This is a good way for you to continue to serve your country while remaining a civilian."

"I'm certainly not against doing something that would help my country, Colonel."

"That's the spirit. I'm hoping you'll help us. We have something special in mind for you and your dog. We've recently had a breakthrough in the computer chips that we use in the electronics. We can now put a transmitter as well as a receiver into each of you that may make it possible for you to use your mind to send simple commands to your dog."

"You can't be serious! How would that work?"

"The electrical impulses from your silent commands will be picked up by the sensors on your brain and sent to the electronic implant in your upper neck. The chip in the implant will convert the electrical impulses into data and send it on to Boss. The chip in his implant will convert the data into information he can understand and send it to the sensors on the surface of his brain. The process is reversed when his sensory impulses are sent to you."

"That's incredible! I never imagined anything like that was possible."

"We've thought it would work if we could design and produce a chip that would interpret the data correctly. We believe we've done that. You've been in battlefield conditions. Can you imagine how much more effective you and your dog would have been if you could have transmitted silent commands to him while he was many meters away from you? What if you could have understood some of the things he was sensing? We believe this will benefit us, both on the battlefield and in crime-fighting situations here at home."

"We're not talking about ESP or anything like that, are we? I thought all of those experiments were history."

"They are. We're talking about science, not magic."

"How many other teams are going to be involved in this program?"

"As I said before, a select few are being chosen. We'll only implant a total of twenty teams. There are several reasons to keep the numbers down; the main one being security. Captain Harrison and Chief Hampton are the only people in your police department who know anything about our program. The only other people who know, other than the research scientists and those of us from the government who are supervising the program, are the chiefs of police and department supervisors of the K9 teams that have been selected. The individual teams are being chosen from various police departments across the country. For security reasons, only one team will come from any single police department. We can't have officers sitting around comparing notes about our program where they could be overheard."

He continued, "If you're agreeable to what we're asking of you and if you and your dog are physically viable, we would like for the two of you to be one of only four teams to have the new transmitter/receiver combinations implanted. The other sixteen teams will get what we originally planned. Those officers will be implanted with receivers only and transmitters will be placed into the dogs. We'll begin evaluating the results we receive from both types of implants in about six months. Once we know which type is best, we'll begin putting them into another small group of volunteers. We'll also begin implanting a few members of our military. This will give us a tremendous advantage over criminals and enemy combatants. Our program may take a few more years to bring to full fruition, but it will be well worth the effort. I was enthusiastic about the first type of implants we were going to use, but I firmly believe that with the addition of our newest chips and transmitter/receiver combination, we'll be able to accomplish much more than we originally thought possible. I hope you decide to work with us, Jack. You're a special person and we need you for our program. You and your dog could help us make history."

"I'm not sure I want to be involved in something brand new like this. What if something goes wrong? We're the ones who'll have to live with the side effects if there are problems."

"I know and I fully understand your concern. Let me go on so you'll have all the information you need to make a well-informed decision. Each team's implants will be tuned to a separate radio frequency. This will prevent the signals from one team interfering with signals from another."

He continued, "The process is fairly simple; a general anesthetic will be given to both of you and you'll both be implanted at the same time. The electronic part of the implant will be placed in the back of your neck, just under the skin and above your hairline. The incision required to place the unit is less than half an inch long and will only require one stitch to close. We won't risk using a metal staple which could possibly damage the electronics while you're healing. The resulting scar won't be visible once your hair grows over it. Both the sensors and the wires are made of an alloy that is very supple and almost weightless but has greater tensile strength than spring steel. They are smaller in diameter than a human hair and because of the alloy they are made of, will never corrode. The alloy is a better electrical conductor than either silver or copper. The sensors will be put into place by drilling tiny holes into your skull, so only the tips will touch your brain. They're gold plated and there is nothing in or on them that could possibly damage brain tissue. The wires running from the sensors to the transmitter/receiver will come up through your skull and be threaded under your scalp to the back of your neck. The wires serve a dual purpose; not only will they carry signals back and forth from the transmitter/receiver to the brain, they'll also serve as an antenna."

"How would the implants be put into Boss?"

"The exact same procedure would apply to him. If for any reason, you, or we, should decide to have the components removed, the surgeons will simply reverse the implantation process. It would be almost as easy as making a tiny slit on the back of the neck, removing the electronics and pulling the wires and sensors straight out from under the scalp. It wouldn't be quite that simple, but almost. If we would ever need to replace a transmitter/receiver, all that would be necessary would be administering a local anesthetic and making a small incision in your neck. I know all this is a lot to absorb at one time so if you have questions, now is a good time to ask them."

"How do you power something like that? Wouldn't it be necessary to replace batteries from time to time?"

"That's another good question. No. The electronics are small and require very little power. They'll run on the electrical energy produced by your own body. They could be there for the rest of your life and never need any other source of power."

"I don't know, Colonel. I don't believe I'm convinced. I'm having a hard time believing you can do something like that and not have any effect on the brain."

"Not too many years ago, you'd have been absolutely correct. Researchers have been working in programs that have been leading up to this one for a long time. As far back as twenty-five years ago, scientists were putting implants into the brains of rhesus monkeys that had been surgically paralyzed. The monkeys were then fitted into pneumatic suits that were connected to the implants. The monkeys learned to move around by using their minds and the implants to control the suits. More recently, our researchers began putting our sensors and receivers into chimpanzees and sensors and transmitters into dogs that were trained to accept the chimps as companions."

"How did that work out?"

"Not well the first time we tried, but things went better with each succeeding attempt. We believe the chimps are experiencing some of the things the dogs are sensing. Chimps are one of our closest relatives in the animal kingdom, so observing their reaction to the implants has been tremendously informative. But, they can't talk. Some of our chimps can use simple sign language, but that can't tell us everything we need to know. When we began using electronics with the latest microchips and had no new problems, we knew we were ready for the next step. We need human volunteers. Scientists and surgeons have been implanting things into people for well over fifty years with only minor problems, Jack. We're just taking another step forward. It should be a giant step."

"May I ask why you don't just use military people and their dogs for this? Wouldn't it be better to use them so you'd have more control over your program?"

"We could, but people come and go in the military. Some sign up with intentions of making it a career and change their minds after they're in a while. We need volunteers who will be working and living with the same dogs for many years to come. We believe K9 police officers fill that requirement better than our military members."

Jack laughed. It seemed to break some of the tension he was feeling.

"Darn, Colonel. I feel like I'm being asked to be one of the world's first human robots or semi-mechanical men. I'm not sure which I'd be. I'm going to have to think about this for a while. I'm not saying no, I just want to think about it for a few days. It's a little overwhelming. I think I'm more spooked about having something touching my brain than anything else."

"I'm glad you feel that way. If you were willing to rush right into this, we'd probably disqualify you for being too impulsive. Let me ask you a question. Are you on duty tomorrow?"

"No. Captain Harrison arranged for me to have the next four days off. He says this program could be very important for all of us if I should decide to go through with it." Colonel Meyer should have already known the answer to that question. Why did Jack suddenly feel troubled?

"He's right. This could be one of the most important steps we've taken for our military and law enforcement in the past twenty years. How about I set you up with a nice hotel room and have the government take care of the bill for it and your meals for the next few days? You can enjoy some of the sights around D.C. while you mull this over. You probably don't get to do that sort of thing very often on a policeman's salary. That way, if you have any more questions, you'll be right here in the neighborhood where I can answer them for you. My wife is out of town and I don't like to eat alone. Let's have dinner together tonight."

"Thank you, but I don't know about that, Colonel. I'll need to think about it for more than a couple of days. What would we do about Boss? Most hotels don't allow dogs and I'm not going to put him in a kennel. I brought an overnight bag with a few things in it in case I needed to spend the night here, but I wasn't planning on staying longer than that."

"Let me worry about that. I believe the taxpayers can afford to buy a couple of shirts and pairs of slacks for you if it's necessary. I'll arrange for a room for the two of you and I think we can keep your dog entertained if you're not with him every minute. If necessary, I'll get him a Service Dog pass so he can go right into the restaurant with us. I'm sure he's very well behaved."

"Of course, he is. He's better in a social situation than most kids."

"It's settled then." He pushed the button on his desk "Miss Jamison, can you come in here for a minute?"

"Yes, Colonel. I'll be right there."

Miss Jamison entered the room.

"Miss Jamison, I need to ask a favor of you. Are you available to work some overtime?"

"I think so, sir. How long would you need me?"

"I need to show Corporal Randall around town for a day or two. Would you be available to do some sitting at your home if need be?"

"I think so. He looks like a gentleman to me."

"I was referring to the dog, Miss Jamison." He grinned.

Miss Jamison blushed. Her rosy cheeks made her even more attractive. "Of course, you were, sir. I didn't misunderstand."

Colonel Meyer smiled. "Good. Thank you, Miss Jamison. That will be all. Jack, let's make some plans."

Chapter 4

Jack drove his car to the hotel where Colonel Meyer had arranged for them to stay. The taxpayers were more than generous; it was a very expensive hotel. He carried his overnight bag to their third-floor room, took a quick shower and put on a fresh pair of slacks and socks. Then he stretched out on the bed for a nap with Boss at his side.

At 5:00 o'clock, the room telephone chirped. He touched the screen.

"Mr. Randall?"

"Yes?"

"I'm sorry to bother you, sir. There is a Mr. Meyer here at the front desk. He asked me to call you and tell you he will be waiting for you in the lobby."

"Thank you. Please tell him I'll be right down."

Jack slipped on his shoes and put on a dress shirt. He slid a light blue necktie under his collar and took his dark blue blazer from the closet. He and Boss left the room and walked to the elevator. He ran a comb through his hair as the elevator lowered them to the first floor.

Colonel Meyer was waiting in the lobby. He had changed out of his uniform.

"Are you ready, Jack?"

"Yes. Now, what do we do with Boss?"

"We'll take him to Miss Jamison's apartment. Then, we'll go eat."

They walked outside. Jack thought they would be riding in Colonel Meyer's private car, but there was a large, black four-door sedan and a driver waiting for them at the front entrance. The driver held the passenger side doors open for them. Colonel Meyer took the front passenger seat while Jack and Boss slid into the back.

The driver pulled away from the entrance of the hotel and onto the street without instructions. Within minutes, they arrived at a well-maintained apartment building on a quiet side street.

"I'll go up with you to Miss Jamison's apartment to drop off Boss. He'll be just fine with her. She seems to have a way with dogs. I made reservations for us for 6:30. The restaurant is nearby, so we'll have time for a drink or two at the bar before our table is ready," said Colonel Meyer.

∞ ∞ ∞ ∞ ∞ ∞

Almost nothing was said about their conversation earlier in the day during dinner. Jack tried to bring up the subject, but Colonel Meyer frowned and said this was not the time or place to discuss business.

Jack was glad he was not paying the tab when they finished their meal. Everything he had seen on the menu was very expensive. When they finished eating, Colonel Meyer paid the bill. Their car was already waiting for them beside the entrance when they walked out of the front door.

"What would you like to do now, Jack? Want to hit a night club or go see a show?"

"Thanks, Colonel, but honestly, I'm not much on night clubbing. I'm very tired. We had a long shift last night and didn't get to sleep until almost dawn. Then, we had to jump out of bed after only an hour or so and drive down here. If it's all the same to you, I think I'd like to go get Boss and call it a day."

"I notice you include your dog in almost everything you say. You usually say we, instead of I."

Jack smiled. "Boss is family to me. We're always together, so I find myself talking to or about him all the time."

"That's good, Jack. I know most K9 police officers live with their dogs and feel that way about them. That's another reason we decided to ask you to help us instead of using a soldier. Military men usually have more of a temporary attachment to their dogs."

"They don't always want it to be that way, Colonel. I'm glad you understand that I have to include my concern for Boss's health and well-being in my decision."

"I do. If you're going back to your hotel, I'll have the driver let me out at my club. I'll tell him to take you to Miss Jamison's apartment so you can pick up Boss. Then, he'll drop you off at your hotel. He'll still have plenty of time to get back to the club before I'm ready to leave."

"That's fine with me. I'm sorry I don't feel up to joining you tonight."

"Don't give it another thought. How familiar are you with our D.C. tourist attractions?"

"I was here a few times when I was in my teens, but I wasn't very interested in them back then. They'd probably be more interesting to me now, though. Why do you ask?"

"Oh, it's just a thought. I need to go out of town tomorrow and there won't be much for Miss Jamison to do at the office while I'm away. How about I give her a call and ask her to take the day off and show you and Boss around? I can have my calls and messages automatically forwarded to me. You can use this car and driver so you won't have to worry about traffic or parking. Would that be something you might enjoy?"

"That would be nice, but I wouldn't want her to lose a day of her salary."

"I'll see to it that she gets paid. She's a hard worker and deserves a day off with pay occasionally. It will give her a well-deserved break and help take your mind off what we've been talking about. Once you and Boss get a good night's rest and have a little fun tomorrow, you can think about our program. What do you say?"

"I think I'd like that and Boss could use a day off, too. He seems to like Miss Jamison."

"Consider it done," said the Colonel. He pulled his phone from his pocket and made the call.

Afterward, the driver dropped Colonel Meyer off at his club and drove to Miss Jamison's apartment. When they arrived, he said, "Take as long as you want, sir. I'll be waiting right here when you're ready to go back to your hotel."

"I won't be long. I'm tired."

"Whatever you say, sir."

Jack took the stairs to the apartment and rang the doorbell. Miss Jamison opened the door with Boss at her side. The big dog jumped up to greet him. Jack patted him firmly on the head and shoulders.

"Thanks for looking after Boss. Was he good?"

"He was better than good. He's a beautiful animal and was very well behaved."

Jack laughed. "I guess that's what he is, but he's been my partner for so long, I've come to think of him more as a person than an animal."

"I can understand why. According to what the Colonel tells me, the three of us will be spending tomorrow together. Is there anything, in particular, you'd like to do?"

"Maybe just see the sights. You know, go to the Washington Monument, the Lincoln Memorial, things like that. It will be nice to be outside with Boss this time of the year when we're not working. Oh, and you too, Miss Jamison."

"I think we'll all enjoy that. I haven't had a chance to go to any of those places for a while. Would you like to see the Smithsonian?"

"I would, but we'll have a trouble getting in with Boss."

"No, we won't. He's a Service Dog, so there shouldn't be a problem with things like that. If there are, I'll call the Colonel and he'll fix it. He has a lot of pull."

"Then, yes. The Smithsonian sounds nice. I don't know if Boss will enjoy it as much as we will, but we'll do it anyway."

"I think anything we do will be fine with him. I don't know how he knew you were coming back, but when you were a couple of minutes away, he went to the window and scratched at it and whined until your car pulled up in front of the building. Then, he went to the door and waited until you walked in. I'm sure he'll be happy tomorrow as long as he's with you."

∞ ∞ ∞ ∞ ∞ ∞

Morning dawned bright and sunny. It looked as if it was going to be one of those perfect weather days the residents of Washington, D.C. so rarely enjoy. Jack dressed quickly and took Boss out for his morning walk to do his "business". After he was through, they went back to their room so Jack could shower and shave.

At precisely 8:00 o'clock, the telephone chirped. When he answered, the desk clerk informed him his driver was waiting. Jack and Boss took the stairs to the first floor and walked out to the car. He was surprised to see Miss Jamison already sitting in the front seat. She handed Boss a large dog biscuit when they got in. The dog thanked her with a wet lick on the back of her hand.

"I thought we'd have to pick you up, Miss Jamison."

"Nope, I'm ready to go. Let's get some breakfast and then we'll see the sights. From now on, when we're not around the office, please call me Heather. Miss Jamison sounds way too formal if we're going to be enjoying the day."

"I'd like that. Call me, Jack."

∞ ∞ ∞ ∞ ∞ ∞

The day turned out to be fun. Heather and Boss acted like old friends. They visited the Lincoln and Washington Memorials and then had lunch at a hot dog wagon on the Mall. Despite Jack's earlier misgivings, they had no difficulty entering the Smithsonian with Boss.

That evening as the driver pulled up to her building, Heather turned to Jack. "Will you and Boss please come up to my apartment for a few minutes? There's something I'd like to talk to you about."

"Sure. I'll ask the driver to wait for us."

They took the elevator to Heather's floor. She unlocked the door to her apartment and they walked inside.

"Jack, do you mind if I ask you something?"

"Not at all."

"Colonel Meyer would not want me to be talking to you about this. I hope I'm not violating my security clearance, but I need to ask. You seem like such a nice guy and you don't have to be involved in his program. Why are you taking part in it?"

Jack frowned. "I'm not sure. I'm not certain I'll go through with it, but if I do, I think it's because I might get a better understanding of what makes Boss tick. There's the other thing, too. I don't want to sound like I'm trying to be some kind of hero, but if everything works the way the Colonel says it should, Boss and I will be able to help catch more bad guys and save a few more lives."

"I can understand that. But, to have doctors go messing around with your brain? I don't care how safe it's supposed to be, what if something goes wrong? It's possible, you know."

"The Colonel says everything is perfectly safe and I believe him. Medicine isn't like it used to be. If I don't like the results, I can get everything removed from our bodies whenever I want."

"I don't know everything that goes on in the Colonel's program, but I can't help hearing things around the office. Just remember, he really wants to make this program work. He is, after all, in the Army. The Army expects him to get good results. What if that doesn't happen?"

"I'll have the implants taken out."

"I hope you're right. Please think long and hard before you commit to it."

"It sounds like you're trying to warn me about something."

"I just want things to work out well for you and Boss. I hope you give it a lot of thought before you make up your mind."

"Don't worry, I will. It's not just me I have to think about. It's Boss, too."

Heather walked over to the coffee table and picked up a pen and a piece of paper.

She said, "I'm going to give you my private cell phone number. I'm probably not supposed to do that, but I'm going to anyway. If you decide to go through with the program, we'll probably be seeing more of each other. If you don't, I want you to have my number."

"Thank you. I'd like that."

She wrote her name and phone number on the paper and handed it to him.

"I think you should go now. The driver is waiting. He does report directly to Colonel Meyer, you know."

"Then, Boss and I will say good night. Heather, has this new procedure been tried before on other K9 teams?"

"I can't answer that. I'm not allowed to. You can ask the Colonel. I'm not supposed to talk about anything that goes on in the office. I've probably said too much already."

Chapter 5

Jack took almost two weeks to make his decision about the surgery. When he called Colonel Meyer and told him he would agree to the procedure, the Colonel phoned Chief of Police Hampton and told him. The Chief informed Captain Harrison and the Captain immediately pushed through the paperwork which would assign Jack to temporary duty with the U.S. Government. Jack would continue to receive full pay while he was with Colonel Meyer.

Jack was given the address of a small federal medical facility in Washington, D.C. and was instructed to be there with Boss the following Monday morning at 9 A.M.

When they arrived, Colonel Meyer met them at the front desk at precisely 9 o'clock and walked with them to another office, where he had Jack put on the Army payroll as a "Special Projects" consultant.

"You can always use the extra money. You're not paid nearly enough by your police department to compensate you for what you're about to do for us. I take care of my people," he said.

Physical examinations began right away on both of them. Boss complained during the blood tests. It hurt Jack to know it was his decision to take part in the program that was causing his dog to be put through the discomfort.

Tiny chips of the materials the components were made of were placed under the skin of his upper left arm and under the skin of a shaved spot on the Boss's left shoulder. While the doctors waited a week for the allergy test results, extensive physical examinations were performed on them both. After a week passed with no negative effects, the doctors decided they were not allergic to any of the components and removed the chips.

Most of the tests were relatively painless. Tiny electrical sensors were placed under the skin of their necks during one session while researchers satisfied themselves that they each produced enough electricity within their bodies to power the micro transmitters and receivers that would be implanted.

It was necessary to find out if either of them had sustained any damage to their central nervous systems during their service with the police department. The doctors placed needles into various locations on their bodies. The needles transmitted data to a computer so the experts could analyze the results. While this was necessary, it was also very painful to both Jack and Boss.

Each test produced satisfactory results, as did the brain and body scans both had to endure. After the brain scans were performed, Jack spent several hours with a psychoanalyst who tested him for emotional and mental problems.

Once the doctors were satisfied both Jack and Boss were mentally and physically acceptable, other preparations began. The most uncomfortable procedure they had to endure was when small pieces of bone were removed from their hips. They were given local anesthetics, but that didn't seem to relieve the pain.

The bone fragments would be frozen until they were needed on the day of the surgeries. The surgeons would grind them up during the implantation procedures and mix them with a non-toxic, fast setting adhesive. The mixtures would be used to refill the tiny cavities in their skulls the surgeons would have to make to insert the sensors. Almost instant healing would occur. This would ensure there would be no movement of the sensors once they were put into place.

Specially trained teams of surgeons were assigned to each of them and they were moved to the small secret research hospital where the surgeries would be performed. Colonel Meyer wanted the procedures to be done on both Jack and Boss simultaneously.

∞ ∞ ∞ ∞ ∞ ∞

Colonel Meyer was giving Jack some last-minute information before he was wheeled into surgery.

"Well Jack, I guess there's not much more to be said. When you wake up, you shouldn't feel much different from how you do right now. You'll have some tenderness around the incision on the back of your neck and around the incisions on the top and sides of your head. There won't be much pain. You won't even need prescription painkillers. An aspirin or two should take care of it."

He continued, "We'll have to shave all your hair off, but it'll grow back quickly. Before you leave us in a few weeks, we'll have our barber tidy up the new growth. You keep your hair short anyway, so nobody should notice anything different about you. Boss must lose more of his, we can't get around that. We'll give him a good trim before you leave so the short hair on his head and neck won't be so noticeable. He'll be in the room next to you for his part of the implantation procedure and we'll be able to put him with you in the recovery room as soon as we're through your surgery. We don't want him to be stressed by being away from you any more than necessary. We'll have identical procedures going on at the same time on Corporal Hamilton and his dog. You'll all wake up together in the recovery room. I'll be monitoring everything in another room on closed circuit screens."

Corporal Hamilton and his dog Drake had been selected as the second of the four K9 teams to receive the new type of electronics. They were from the New York State Police Department.

"Thanks, Colonel. I'm about as ready as I'll ever be. How long has Boss been asleep?"

"About fifteen minutes. His surgery takes a little longer than yours. I'll be watching and recording everything while all of you are under anesthetic. I'll also be recording what goes on as you wake up in the recovery room. We never know what will be important to us, so we like to have audio and visual records of everything. After you wake up, we'll keep you here for a couple of days before moving you back to our other facility. The four of you will recover and be observed there until we're ready to release you back to your police departments."

"Then, let's get on with it."

∞ ∞ ∞ ∞ ∞ ∞

Jack was under the influence of the anesthetic. He seemed to be dreaming that someone was calling him.

"*Jack, where--you? Can't---find---you.*"

"*I'm here.*"

"*Where---you?*"

"*I'm not sure. I think I'm asleep.*"

"*I---scared.*"

"*Who are you?*"

"*Boss.*"

"*Boss?*"

"*Yes---Jack. Come---get---------me.*"

"*I can't, Boss. I don't think I can get up.*"

"*I---can't---. Jack, what------going---on?*"

"*I don't know, boy.*"

"*Afraid---Come---get.*"

"*I will, Boss. Hang on boy, I'll be right there.*"

The odd dream drifted away; Jack was fully unconscious once again.

∞ ∞ ∞ ∞ ∞ ∞

"Are we ready to wake up?"

Jack was half awake. Who is this? Whoever she is, she's entirely too cheerful, he thought to himself.

"Come on, wake up. You've slept most of the day away."

Jack opened his eyes. He was looking straight at the huge chest of an obese middle age blond nurse who was standing beside his bed.

"OK, I'm awake. I think."

"Good! We can't have you lying around here all day, can we?"

"I sure am sleepy. How did it go?"

"Everything went fine. Your surgeon should be here to see you in a little while. Can I talk you into taking a sip of juice?"

"Yeah, I think so. Where's my dog?"

"He's right here beside you. He woke up a few minutes before you did. He's fine. He'll be a little sleepy for a while, just like you."

"Good."

In the curtained cubicle beside him, a man began to yell. He sounded panicked.

"Drake? Drake! Where are you, boy?"

The nurse moved quickly into the next cubicle to see what was wrong.

"He's right here, Mr. Hamilton. He's right here beside you."

"I want to see him! Something funny is going on!"

"He's right here. He's been awake for a couple of minutes. "I'll push back the curtain so you can see him. Don't worry, he's fine."

"Yeah, but I'm not sure I am. Something's wrong! I'm hearing things!"

"Nothing's wrong with you, Mr. Hamilton, and nothing is wrong with your dog. You're both fine. You're just waking up from the anesthetic and you're still a little groggy and confused. Now lie back, you're getting yourself all worked up. You don't want to upset your dog."

Hamilton began to scream and thrash around in his bed. He was becoming incoherent. Jack couldn't see him, but he could hear the commotion become more violent as the man attempted to get up. The nurse tried to hold him down as he continued to struggle. Drake began to bark and pull against the straps that held him on his gurney as he tried to go to the aid of his partner.

Two men in green surgical gowns rushed into the room. Each carried a syringe in his hand.

The taller of the two, who seemed to be in charge, looked worried. "What's going on, nurse?"

"I don't know. He woke up a couple minutes ago and began to panic. He's too strong for me to control and the noise he's making is upsetting his dog."

"We'll take care of it. We'll let him sleep for a while. We'll have to put his dog back under, too. I don't want him to keep fighting those straps. He might hurt himself."

The room soon became quiet once again.

"Nurse?"

She came quickly to his side. "Yes, Mr. Randall."

"What the heck was that all about?"

"It's nothing for you to worry yourself over. That happens sometimes when a patient wakes up after surgery. They're still groggy and sometimes they'll go into a brief panic because their minds aren't clear. He'll be alright when he wakes up again."

"I've never heard of anything like that happening."

"It doesn't very often, but it does occasionally. It's nothing for you to worry about. You're doing fine."

"I'm not worried about me, but that noise had to upset Boss. How soon before I can see him? I don't want him to be afraid."

"I'll pull back the curtain so you can see him now. He's right here on a gurney beside you."

She pulled back the curtain that separated him from his dog.

"Boss?"

Boss was still strapped down and was lying on his left side. He raised his head and looked over at Jack and whined once, quietly.

"It's ok, boy. Don't worry. Just lie still. We'll be up and around in a little while."

Boss lowered his head. Jack remembered the dream.

"I sure had a funny dream, boy. You were there."

Boss growled. He seemed to be lying almost unnaturally still. He must still be drowsy. The memory of the dream began to slip away from Jack.

Colonel Meyer walked into the room.

"Good! You're both awake! How are you feeling?"

"I'm fine and Boss seems to be ok."

"Are you having any pain?"

"Actually, no. That's a nice surprise. I thought I'd be sore somewhere, at least in the back of my neck."

"The Marcaine is preventing that. It was injected into your wounds while you were still asleep. Your dog got some, too. He should be feeling just as good as you are. I told you that you'd be ok. You'll have a little tenderness there for a couple of days, but not much. Are you still sleepy?"

"Just a little. I'm awake, but I still feel a little groggy and very relaxed."

"Good. I think we can move you and Boss to your room right away. Nurse? Can we do that?"

"I don't think so. The surgeons will want to see them before they're moved. We should let them rest here a little while longer."

"Don't worry about that. Call your orderlies and let's get them moved to their room right now. I'll get their surgeons to go there to see them."

"Ok, if you say so, Colonel, but they might not like it. They usually come to the recovery room to see the patients before they're sent to their rooms. I don't want them yelling at me about it."

"You let me worry about that. I'm not going to have my people lying around in a noisy recovery room when they could be more comfortable somewhere else. That's the reason we give them private rooms. Call your orderlies."

"Yes, sir. I'll tell them to take Mr. Randall to his room as soon as they get here. Then, they can come back for the dog."

"Colonel?"

"Yes, Jack."

"What's going on with Corporal Hamilton?"

"Sometimes patients wake up after surgery and are a little disoriented. I'm sure he'll be fine when he wakes up again. We may have to keep him lightly sedated for a couple of hours."

"That's good. I was a little concerned."

"There's nothing to worry about. I'll make sure Hamilton's alright after I get you and Boss moved to your room. I'll have the doctors stay with him so they'll be here when he wakes up the next time. He and his dog will both be fine after they sleep a little while longer. I take care of my people. Jack?"

"Yes?"

"I heard you mention a dream. What were you talking about?"

"Dream?"

"Yes. Just after you woke up, you said something to Boss about having a dream and that he was there."

"Did I? If I did, I sure don't remember."

"I'm sure it was nothing. The anesthetic makes us say strange things sometimes. Here are the orderlies; let's get you to your room."

Colonel Meyer's prediction was true. Other than some slight swelling in the back of his neck and some tenderness where the stitches on his head were located, Jack felt very little discomfort.

Within two days, he and Boss were moved back to the facility where the original examinations had taken place. They were put into a ground floor room with a window that looked out onto a private park. The park had a high fence around it and was only accessible from the research building.

Except for the hospital bed, the room was furnished much like an expensive hotel room. The room they had when they were receiving their physical examinations had not been nearly as large. They could get out of bed within hours of their arrival, but Colonel Meyer said they shouldn't leave their room until they recuperated for a few days.

Jack felt almost perfectly normal. He assumed Boss felt the same way. He was soon allowed limited movement around the facility, but only in the small wing of the building where they were lodged and the park that adjoined the building. Colonel Meyer asked him to stay close to their room because he and Boss might be needed at any time for examinations.

Their recovery continued exactly as the Colonel said it would. Within a few days, the slight swelling had gone away and the surgical stitches were removed.

Boss would disappear from time to time. Jack thought it odd because the dog usually stayed close by his side. He was surprised Boss was allowed so much freedom. Dogs usually weren't so welcome in medical facilities.

∞ ∞ ∞ ∞ ∞ ∞

Colonel Meyer was his usual cheerful self. "Jack, my boy. How are you?"

"I'm the same as I was yesterday when you left and the same as I was two hours ago when you were here. I'm getting antsy.

Boss and I aren't used to lying around like this. When can we go home and get back to work?"

"As soon as we're sure you've both completely recovered. We need to observe you for a while so we can be sure neither of you suffered any injury during the surgeries. It's just precautionary. We think it wise when any kind of procedure is performed that involves the brain. Sometimes problems don't show up for a few days. It won't be long, so enjoy yourself. Watch television, read a book, watch some movies, listen to some music. Who knows how long it will be before you get another paid vacation like this one on Uncle Sam's dollar?"

"I wouldn't exactly call this a vacation, although it really hasn't been all that bad. It's been more boring than anything. Boss and I are both getting tired of having nothing to do. We're used to a lot more action."

"I'm sure you'll be getting all the action you want when you return to duty. We're as anxious to get you back to work as you are to be there. In the meantime, I have a surprise for you."

"Oh?"

"Someone is here to see you. You can come in now, Miss Jamison."

Heather entered the room. Boss trotted over to her side and put his head up for an ear scratch. He looked strange. His cleanly shaven head and neck had given him an unnatural appearance. The stubble that was beginning to grow back was making his head itch.

"Hi, Boss. Hello, Mr. Randall. How are you feeling?"

"Perfectly well, Miss Jamison. How are you?" He remembered to use her surname in front of the Colonel.

"I'm fine, thank you. How is Boss getting along?"

"He's doing well. He looks like he's happy to see you."

"I'm glad to see him. I wish I had more time to visit, but I can't stay long. The Colonel has a full afternoon of work lined up for me back at the office. I just wanted to pop in and say hi and to wish you both well. I'll try to stop in again before you go home."

"That's very kind of you. Thank you."

Colonel Meyer spoke. "You and Boss seem to have made a good impression on our Miss Jamison. She's asked about you several times."

"If we did, it's probably more Boss's doing than mine, Colonel."

"Perhaps. He is a handsome fellow. Miss Jamison, will you be sure to make those calls for me as soon as you get back to the office? They're very important."

"Certainly, sir. Mr. Randall, it's been nice seeing you again. You too, Boss."

She scratched Boss's ears again before she left the room. Boss whined when she left.

"Colonel? What happened to Corporal Hamilton? You haven't said anything about him and I've been wondering how he did. I haven't seen him or his dog around."

"We removed the implants. We had a problem with one of the sensors in his dog. The surgeon placed it slightly to the side of where it should have been and it was causing some sort of electrical feedback in Hamilton's receiver. I assure you, that doctor will never work for me again."

"Is that what caused him to panic?"

"No, that was the anesthetic. He was not agitated when he came around the second time, but he wanted us to go back in and remove the electronics from him and his dog. I promised we would if he wanted us to, so we did. It's a shame it didn't work out, but a promise is a promise. We'll have to find other volunteers to take their place. They'll go back to New York in a few days and be home before you even leave us. They'll soon return to duty. After a month or two back on the job, he'll forget all about this little episode."

"I'm sorry that didn't work out for you. It looks like everything is fine with Boss and me, though."

"It is. We couldn't have wanted better. The next step is for us to get the two of you back to work so we can find out how our implants are going to perform."

"We're ready right now, aren't we, boy?"

Boss whined and licked his hand.

Jack smiled. "Colonel, we're not used to spending so much time together without something to do. We're usually working. I think Boss has enjoyed lying around with me and being told how handsome he is, but, like I said, we're both ready to hit the road."

"You'll be doing that in just a few more days. We want to get you back on duty so you can work on this connection we're expecting. Are you receiving anything from him yet?"

"No, nothing at all. I've tried directing my thoughts toward him several times, but he hasn't reacted. I must admit, I'm a little disappointed. I was hoping something might be going on by now."

"So were we, but we didn't think a lot would be occurring right away. The brain takes a while to learn how to use new tools. It may not be a quick thing, but we believe it will happen. Let me know the instant you start receiving anything from him. The transmitter/receiver units are brand new technology and we don't know exactly how everyone will respond to them. In the meantime, can you put up with us a while longer?"

"Sure Colonel, whatever you say."

"Good! I'll see about getting you and Boss some lunch brought in here."

Chapter 6

Exactly two weeks later, Jack and Boss were released from the research facility. Both were extensively examined and tested before being given a clean bill of health. Scans had shown perfect placement of the transmitter/receiver units and sensors into each of their bodies.

The doctors determined it would be safe for Jack to drive back to Baltimore. He and Boss were given permission to return to work the next day and would be on light duty for the following two weeks. By then, all the tissues in their bodies would be completely healed.

They walked out of the building and got into their police car. They were almost to the Baltimore/Washington Parkway when he received the first message.

"Jack?"

What was that? There was a tingling in his head, something almost imperceptible. There was also some vertigo.

"Can you hear me?"

Jack pulled the car to the side of the street. He looked at the communicator that was clipped onto the sun visor. It was not turned on.

He looked over at Boss.

"Give me a second, boy. Something strange is going on."

"Jack, it's me. I'm trying to find out if I can communicate with you."

"Me? Me who? What the devil is going on?"

"Don't be afraid."

Jack looked around. Was there a hidden receiver somewhere in the car? Was this another test the Colonel was pulling on him?

"Calm down. It's ok."

"What do you mean, calm down? Your voice is coming from inside my head. Who's speaking?"

"Calm down and look around. Do you see anyone?"

Jack struggled to regain his composure. He could feel his heart rate shoot up as adrenalin began to flow into his blood stream. He tried to slow his breathing. What was going on? The tingling sensation began again.

"No, I don't see anybody."

"Yes, you do."

"No, I don't. Colonel? What are you doing? Is this another one of your tests?"

"It's not the Colonel. Look at me, Jack."

Boss was staring at him. He put out his paw and touched Jack's hand.

"It's me. It's ok."

"Colonel, you can tell your people you got through to me. I can hear you."

"It's not the Colonel. It's me!"

Boss touched Jack's hand with his paw again.

"Screw this. You never said anything about you being able to talk to me through this thing!"

"Jack, please. It's me, Boss!"

"Yeah, right. I'm turning the car around and coming back. I want these things taken out of our heads immediately! I never agreed to anything like this!"

"Come on, listen to me. It really is me. I wouldn't lie to you."

"What?"

"I'm going to touch you on the leg. Then, I'm going to touch you again so you can be sure it really is me. Afterward, please try to talk to me by using your mind."

Boss reached out and touched his thigh, then touched him again.

"This can't be happening!"

"Good! You're coming through loud and clear! It is happening, but it's ok. It's not going to hurt you."

"Hurt me? I'm not afraid of it hurting me. I'm afraid I'm losing my mind."

"You're not losing your mind. Just take a few seconds to calm down. Then, we'll talk about it."

"Talk about it? Talk about it to a dog that can't possibly be talking to me?"

"Just take a minute and listen. I believe I'm thinking with both of our brains. The procedures locked our minds together. You can hear what I'm thinking and I can hear what you're thinking."

"I can't believe this!"

"I've always been able to understand some of what you were saying, but not like this. As soon as I woke up in the recovery room, I could understand everything you were saying and most of what everyone else was saying around us. It was a little fuzzy at first. I think that was because of the anesthetic, but it kept getting clearer. It was a shock to me, too. I didn't realize I could talk to you then. Afterward, I was afraid to try."

"Boss, I can't accept this. It's not possible!"

"If it's happening, it must be possible. I've had since the operation to think about it."

"Then, why didn't I know? Why didn't you talk to me before now?"

"Because I was afraid. Colonel Meyer and his people were watching us all the time. If you had reacted like you are now, they would have known and they would have killed me."

"No, they wouldn't. I'm supposed to tell the Colonel when the implants begin to work. He's not going to believe this!"

"You can't tell him, Jack. Not if you want me to stay alive."

"Of course, I want you to stay alive. Why would you say that?"

"You don't know what happened to Drake and Corporal Hamilton."

"I do know. The Colonel had the surgeons take the implants out of them."

"He lied to you."

"Why would he do that?"

"He's in the Army and running a civilian research program. Doesn't that sound strange to you?"

"I hadn't given it much thought. Why would he lie about Hamilton and Drake? He said they reversed the procedure and sent them home."

"*Think back. Remember when Hamilton woke up? He was panicking.*"

"*I know, but they put him back under and the Colonel said he was fine after he woke up again.*"

"*He wasn't.*"

"*How do you know?*"

"*I was there. I saw the Colonel talking to some of the research people in the recovery room after the orderlies took you out. The Colonel made the nurse leave the room while they were talking about what was wrong with Hamilton. They had been watching all of us wake up on their monitors. After you were taken out, they gave Hamilton and Drake shots to wake them back up. Drake began to talk to Hamilton and Hamilton panicked again. Hamilton told the Colonel that Drake was talking to him. They gave Hamilton another shot and knocked him out again and began to discuss what they could do to find out how Drake could make Hamilton hear him. They were very excited about it. One of the things they talked about right away was cutting up Drake's brain. I began to realize how I could understand what everyone was saying and knew I couldn't let them know about it. I assumed I could talk to you, but I couldn't chance to try until we were away from them.*"

"*My gosh, Boss! You must have been scared to death!*"

"*I was! The Colonel sent Hamilton and Drake back to the research facility right away and put them into another wing of the building so you wouldn't know they were there. The doctors kept Hamilton sedated off and on for almost three days. Every time he woke up, Drake would try to talk to him and he would panic. He thought the surgery had damaged his brain and he was hearing voices that weren't there. I saw them several times after they were brought in. Remember when I'd go out of our room?*"

"*Yes?*"

"*I was snooping around and trying to hear what the Colonel and his people were doing in the other rooms. I did my best to make sure nobody saw me and I kept track of the Colonel so I could be in our room every time he was with you. Jack, the research people killed Drake.*"

"*Nonsense.*"

"*They did! I saw him after they were through with him! They rolled him out of a room on a gurney and left him in the hallway for a few minutes before they took him to another part of the building. He was dead. They had cut the top of his head away and his brain was gone!*"

"*Why would they do that?*"

"*So they could find out how he was communicating with Hamilton.*"

"*That's crazy. It just doesn't make any sense.*"

"*They didn't kill him right away. After we were there for a couple of days, they took him into a room that was full of test equipment. They strapped him onto a table and opened his neck and ran electricity through the transmitter to the sensors on his brain. When they were finished, they closed him back up. The next day, more people came to the facility to watch and they did it again. Then, they put him to sleep and did it once more. They did that day after day. When they were finally through with him, they killed him and took out his brain and sent it to another part of the building to be cut up for tests!*"

"*Hamilton wouldn't have let that happen.*"

"*They never asked him for permission. They didn't take the sensors out of Hamilton's head and they didn't let him go home. He's still there. I could always smell him in one of the rooms and hear him each time they took Drake away. They were torturing his best friend and he couldn't do anything to stop them. I believe he was feeling everything that was happening to Drake. His screams were awful. They strapped him down and gagged him, but I could still hear him. There were always doctors in his room while the others experimented on Drake. They hooked their electronics up to his implant and tried to read the data Drake's implant was sending to him. Hamilton said Drake was pleading for him to help him, but they wouldn't let him. It was awful. He kept begging them to let him go to Drake.*"

"*I'm so sorry, Boss. I didn't know.*"

"*I couldn't try to contact you. I couldn't risk it. I knew they could pick up the radio signals from the implants. If they changed the frequency on their receiver, they'd have been able to know I was sending to you. I wasn't certain I could contact you, but I had to wait until now to try. I had to ignore you when you tried to contact me. It's a good thing for us they were concentrating on Hamilton and Drake."*

"Surely they won't continue to experiment on Hamilton. He won't be strong enough emotionally to endure it. Nobody would."

"His mind is almost gone. He just couldn't take what they were doing to Drake. They're planning on bringing in another dog and putting the implants they took out of Drake into him. They want to see if Hamilton and the new dog will establish a connection. He doesn't have to be sane for them to do that. That's not the worst of it. Drake heard them talking about what they were going to do to him before they began their experiments. He transmitted everything that was said to Hamilton. Hamilton finally realized Drake was talking to him and they both understood everything the research people were planning. They heard them planning it and they heard Colonel Meyer order it! So did I!"

"Hold on, Boss. I've got to think for a minute and try to understand all of this."

"We should go. We don't know how far these implants send radio waves before they're too weak to be picked up. We're not that far away from the research facility and Colonel Meyer might have someone spying on us right now. If they are, they'll think it's strange for you to be parked here on the side of the road for so long. Are you able to drive while we think about this?"

"I hope so."

"Then, let's get moving. Don't use your voice to talk to me. He may have had something put inside the car so he can hear what's being said. Turn on the police radio. Maybe that will help hide these signals."

"Ok."

Jack pulled the car back onto the highway and drove slowly. He didn't trust himself enough to push the car all the way up to the speed limit.

"Jack, we can't ever let anyone know what's going on between us. We're part of a clandestine research project. Colonel Meyer owns us."

"No, he doesn't."

"He does. I learned a lot while I was snooping around. I heard him talking to some men from the Central Intelligence Agency. They're part of this and you know what those people are capable of."

"How do you know what the CIA does?"

"I have access to all of your thoughts and memories, the same as you do with mine. Until now, the Colonel hasn't had any real success with what he's been doing. I'm sure Hamilton and Drake were the very first to be able to communicate with each other at this level; except for us and he doesn't know what we are capable of. The electronics weren't available to make this happen, but now they are."

"This is supposed to be a good thing. Except for us being able to talk to each other, it's what he's been trying to do. It just turned out better than he hoped. I don't understand why he did all that to Hamilton and Drake."

"There have been four more K9 teams that have had the same procedures we had since they operated on us. Three weren't able to communicate at all, but one could. He's doing the same thing to that team that he did to Hamilton and Drake."

"No!"

"Yeah. Now, you see the problem. The Colonel is treating the three teams that can't communicate the same way he's treating us. They'll be allowed to go home.

"This just doesn't make any sense. He said he wanted to get K9 teams out on the street with the new electronics. Why would he be treating his successes the way he is?"

"It's not a program to help law enforcement and the military. He lied about that, too. I heard him talking to the CIA people about it. They've been putting a lot of the agency's money into this research. They've been hoping to eventually make implants do something like this, but they didn't realize how close they were to success. This is the result they've had in mind all along. Once *they get the bugs worked out of the new electronics, they want to put implants into teams of people. If they can do that successfully, a person can be in one location and someone in another place will be able to experience everything that's going on around the first person. They're hoping one day to be able to access the remote listener's implant to make both audio and visual recordings of the information. The Colonel couldn't care less about us or the K9 Department. To him, we're just lab experiments!"*

"Why would he use K9 police officers and dogs for this? All he'd have to do is get volunteers from prisons and abandoned dogs from dog pounds to use in his experiments."

"He had to use us. The Colonel told the Congressional committee that gives out the bulk of the funding he's doing the research to help K9 police and K9 military teams become more effective. They weren't told the CIA is involved. When the implants are perfected, the committee won't know. They'll be told they don't work. The implants will be used by the CIA to gather information and the committee won't even know about it."

"How do you know all these things?"

"Colonel Meyer and the people he was meeting with weren't as careful as they should have been. If I could get close to where they were, I could hear and understand everything that was being said. It's a good thing there weren't a lot of people at the research facility. I could slip around without being caught. If I'd been seen, they would have taken me back to our room and complained to you and you would have made me stay there."

"This is spy stuff!"

"That's exactly what it is. Colonel Meyer is working for the CIA while using the Army as cover. He's been lying to you about a lot of things. He's been doing this to other people and dogs with the old electronics for several years. A lot more teams will be getting the new electronics right away. We're one of the first teams to receive the new implants and we're his first big success. Hamilton and Drake were too, of course."

"I still can't believe you're talking to me. I haven't had time to think about this like you have. You said the Colonel was going to

let us and the other teams that couldn't communicate go home. Why?"

"I heard him talking about that. Most of the implants are sending radio signals the way they're supposed to. He thinks it takes longer for most people to be able to teach their brains to use new tools. The researchers believe the new technology will never work on some of the teams because of physical differences in the dog's brains. Those teams will never be bothered. The Colonel will be staying in touch with all of us. If he finds out any team becomes able to communicate, he'll want to know exactly how and why. That team will be picked up and taken back there for experiments."

"He couldn't just kidnap us."

"Sure he could. He has the CIA to help him. Think about what he did to Hamilton and Drake and what he's doing to the other team. You're a man. His people might not kill you and cut you up to see why we're able to talk to each other, but they would do experiments on you. They couldn't let you go after they were finished. My problem is, to them, I'm just a dog. They'll want to shoot electricity through me and cut me up like they did Drake. You can't let that happen, not if you love me, Jack."

"You know I love you, boy. I wouldn't let them do that."

"You wouldn't be able to stop it. Hamilton couldn't stop them from torturing and killing Drake. If Colonel Meyer decides to dissect Hamilton's brain, Hamilton won't be able to stop that, either. Just like the third team can't stop what's being done to them. From what I heard the Colonel say, that team can't communicate as well as Hamilton and Drake could, but there was some contact between them."

For several miles, the voice inside Jack's head was silent.

Then, *"What do we do, Jack?"*

"You're right, boy. We can't let them know. Colonel Meyer said these things can stay in us forever if we choose to leave them in. Right now, he thinks they're not working. If they don't work, there's no reason for him to bother us. We'll do our best to go about life as normally as we can. When he asks me if I'm getting anything from you, I'll just say no."

"Do you think you'll always be able to keep him convinced they don't work?"

"I hope so. He doesn't know we have a reason to keep him in the dark about it. Unfortunately, he'll keep on doing this to other officers and their dogs. I wish we could do something to prevent that, but I don't see how we can. We can't fight him and the CIA too. If we try, we'll wind up right back in his research facility."

"The scientists will keep doing this to more teams until they get better at making the implants work. It may take a while, but they'll learn to interpret the radio signals that are being sent back and forth between us. We'll have to be very, very careful."

"We will be. They're not cutting you up, Boss; not for any reason." He grimaced. "It sure doesn't look like things will ever be the same for us, does it, boy?"

"No, it doesn't; and to think, until only a few short weeks ago, I was just a regular police dog."

Chapter 7

Jack and Boss had been back on regular duty for almost six months. It was good to be in familiar surroundings doing police work. It gave them a feeling of security. They both realized they'd never have complete security if Colonel Meyer was observing them. They were hoping that in time, he might lose interest if he believed their implants hadn't worked.

He called every week on Thursday afternoon. He always asked the same questions. Was Jack receiving any signals from Boss or did Boss seem to understand any of Jack's commands better than before?

Jack's answer never changed. He was disappointed. It seemed to him that occasionally he might be able to smell food a little better or his hearing might be a little sharper, but other than that, there was nothing different from before they had the procedure. Maybe he was imagining he was experiencing those things because he was hoping to. He just didn't know.

He reported that Boss might possibly understand his commands a little better, but he'd always seemed to understand them very well before the surgery. Boss seemed to have developed a taste for a couple of different kinds of food other than what he used to eat, but that wasn't unusual for a dog. There was nothing he could say with certainty that was any different.

His reports seemed to satisfy Colonel Meyer. He always said the same thing before he hung up; "Don't worry about it, just keep on going about your normal routine and be sure to call me the instant you feel like something is occurring that is out of the ordinary."

So far, it appeared the Colonel had no idea the experiment had succeeded.

As time went by, they stopped worrying so much. Jack always tried to remember to talk to Boss vocally in the same terms he'd used before they received the implants in case they were being watched.

Jack's sense of smell and taste had changed dramatically. Sometimes, it was almost as if he could taste the very air around him. Since their two brains were now working as one, he could hear much better than before and his night vision had greatly improved. When he and the Boss were on night shift, he could search a forest or darkened warehouse almost as well as he could during the day. He could now smell and hear suspects when they were long distances away.

The two of them were not to be deceived when they were hunting for hidden lawbreakers or lost children. What one could sense, the other experienced at the same instant. He could now smell hidden contraband almost as well as Boss. He had to constantly be on guard so no one would suspect these things and they were not always easy to for him to cover up.

Jack used to like his hamburgers and steaks cooked to medium well. Now he liked them rare and bloody and not quite hot all the way through. He had lost his appreciation for certain foods. Some he used to enjoy no longer appealed to him, while others he liked much more than before. He stopped drinking soft drinks and drank mostly cold water or milk with his meals. For some reason, he still enjoyed his morning coffee and a cold beer from time to time.

He could smell female dogs when they were in heat. Most women used to smell good to him, now they smelled wonderful. He was occasionally repelled by a woman who wore too much perfume.

He constantly had to sort things out in his mind. He was always asking himself, was he using his own mind or was he using Boss's? At times, it was all very confusing.

He didn't enjoy some of the changes that were occurring. There were times when he and Boss had to break their connection so each could pause to absorb sudden new sensations without having their senses become overloaded.

Boss was enjoying most of his newfound ability. He liked the way he was now seeing and understanding the world. He was no longer limited by what his dog brain could comprehend. He was observing the world through Jack's eyes, ears, and mind. Although he was never able to enjoy spicy foods because of his keen sense of smell, there were many other kinds of foods that he began to enjoy. Some types of music were delightful to him and he could now see in full color.

In the evenings when they were off duty, if the sky was clear, Boss would insist they drive to the local park where they could have an unobstructed view of the sunset. He would stare at the horizon until all the colors were gone. To Jack they were nice, but to Boss, they were breathtaking.

"Are the colors really that spectacular to you, boy?"

"You have no idea. I can't believe what I've been missing my entire life. How can it be possible this has always been there and I've never been able to see it as well as I can now?"

"Our eyes are different. There are things in my eyes that let me see the colors, just as there are things in yours that let you see better in the dark. Now that our minds are working together, you can see colors and I can see much better in the dark."

"There are never two days when it's the same. It changes all the time while I'm watching it. If I look away from it, when I look back, it has changed. If I look away again and look back, it's different again. It does something to me down deep inside that I can't explain. It's wonderful."

"I've always enjoyed watching a sunset. I had no idea just how magnificent it would be for you."

"If you had decided not to have the implants put into us, I would never have been able to see this. For me, this alone is worth all the other things we've had to worry about where Colonel Meyer is concerned. I could never go back to the way things were before. I love you, Jack."

"I love you too, Boss."

Chapter 8

It was 8 o'clock on a Wednesday evening. Jack and Boss were relaxing on the big living room sofa while watching television. Boss was lying in his most preferred position, on his side with his head rested on Jack's thigh.

Jack found most television shows to be mildly entertaining, but Boss loved to watch them. He especially enjoyed any program which featured animals. It was one more thing he'd never been able to appreciate before what they'd come to call, "the change".

He was particularly amused when a performing dog appeared on the screen. Any images of a cat being chased by a dog were highly entertaining to him, especially if they involved a small dog chasing a large cat. Jack had to caution him from time to time not to howl so loudly and disturb the neighbors after a particularly funny scene. Boss might not have had a sense of humor before, but he certainly seemed to have one now.

The phone buzzed. Jack picked it up and touched the screen.

"Hello."

"Hello, is this Jack Randall?" It was a woman's voice; it sounded familiar.

"Yes, it is."

"This is Heather Jamison."

"Heather?"

"Yes, Jack. How are you?"

"I couldn't be better. This is a nice surprise. How are you?"

Jack looked at Boss and lifted his eyebrows. The dog was already listening to the conversation.

"I'm fine. I was afraid I might not have the correct number or if I did, you might be on duty. I almost didn't call."

"It's good to hear from you. I'm just sitting here on the sofa. Boss and I are watching television."

"How is he?"

"He's great. He's been gnawing on a ham bone. I think he's about to fall asleep."

"I hope I haven't caught you at a bad time."

"No, not at all. We're on day shift this week. We're just relaxing. We're probably going to turn in pretty soon."

"I'm driving up to Baltimore this weekend. I'll be staying with family for a few days and I was wondering if we might get together for dinner one evening while I'm up there. Would that be ok?" She sounded nervous and unsure of herself.

"I, uh, I think so. I mean, sure, great. That sounds like fun." Boss had risen to his feet and was staring at him. Did he sense danger?

"Are you sure? I wouldn't want to impose."

"No, it wouldn't be imposing at all. We'll be glad to see you again. Actually, I think we'd really like that."

She laughed. "I notice you said we."

He grinned. "Yeah, I'm used to saying that."

"Are you working this weekend?"

"I think I'm working Sunday and I never know exactly how long a shift will last. How long will you be in town?"

"I'm driving up early Saturday and I'll be leaving on Wednesday morning."

"Do you have any plans for Saturday afternoon or evening?"

"No, not yet."

"How about we meet sometime Saturday afternoon? You can call me when you're getting close to Baltimore and we'll make plans about where to have dinner."

"That sounds good. I know it's been quite a while since I last saw you and Boss, but I've been thinking about both of you off and on since you were here in Washington. I thought, what the heck, I might just as well give you a call since you didn't seem to be interested in calling me."

"I've thought about calling you several times. I was concerned that maybe you wouldn't want to mix your personal life with work projects if you know what I mean."

She laughed again. "I understand. I really shouldn't, but I thought I might since I'll be in your area and I don't know anyone around there except my cousin and her family. They've only lived in Baltimore for a couple of months."

"I'll look forward to having dinner with you. It gets kind of lonely around here with nobody much to talk to, except Boss."

Boss's ears twitched as he grunted.

"I'll call you about the time I get to the Beltway, ok?"

"Great. I'll talk to you then."

"It's nice talking with you. Say hi to Boss for me."

"I will. See you Saturday."

"Bye."

"Bye."

Jack slowly and thoughtfully touched the off spot on the screen.

Boss was pacing the floor. *"Why is she calling now?"*

"I don't know, boy. Hearing from her surprises me as much as it does you."

"Do you think she's coming to spy on us?"

"I'm thinking about that."

"Colonel Meyer has to be wondering why our implants aren't working, especially if he's been putting them into other officers and dogs and getting better results."

"I know."

"How do we handle this? What if he is sending her here to check up on us?"

"I'm not sure she'd do that, but it is strange that she's calling us now after so much time has gone by. It's been at least six months since we last saw her at the research facility. Let's think about this for a few minutes."

"Why didn't you just tell her we have to work all weekend?"

"I thought about that. It's too easy for the Colonel to check to see if we really do. If I lied to her and she is being sent to spy on us, it would have made him suspicious."

Boss had not understood the concept of deception very well when he first began to understand human conversation, but he'd soon learned that it was sometimes necessary.

"So, we have to go through with this?"

"Yes, boy. I think so. I don't see any way around it."

"Then, I think you should see her and I won't. We might do something wrong without knowing what she's looking for if we're together. We're used to communicating with each other without talking; she might see something going on between us that we wouldn't even notice."

"That won't entirely work, either. We could get by with that when I go to dinner with her, but if she has been sent here to spy on us, she's going to want to see us together. She seemed to like you a lot. If she isn't spying, she'll probably still want to see you. You are a good-looking rascal and she likes dogs. If she specifically asks to see you and I don't let her, she might think I'm purposely keeping her away from you."

"I didn't think about that. When she comes, we're going to have to be careful."

"I know."

"If we all must be together, I think we should break our connection whenever she's around. That way, you'll have to talk to me with your voice, not your mind. I won't talk to you unless it's necessary. If I see she's trying to do something to trick us and you're not catching it, I'll alert."

"I don't see any other way. I only have one problem with that, boy. When this connection first started and it was new to me, I was alright when we shut it off for a while. But, now that we've been doing this for so long, I feel like there is a part of my mind missing when you're not in it. I don't know how to describe it other than to say, when you're not in my head with me, I feel lost and extremely lonely."

"I know, Jack. It's the same way I used to feel before we got the implants when you had to go somewhere and I couldn't go along. You could be gone for five minutes and it would seem like an eternity to me."

"Now I know how you felt. You're right. If we're going to pull this off, we'll have to break our connection while she's with us. I think we'll be fine."

"There's another small detail that you're not thinking about."

"What's that?"

73

"You really liked her when we were in Washington, didn't you?"

"Yeah, boy, I guess I did."

"I did, too. It could be a problem."

∞ ∞ ∞ ∞ ∞ ∞

Jack and Heather were sitting in a crowded seafood restaurant at the Inner Harbor in downtown Baltimore. They had just begun to eat a pile of Maryland style steamed crabs. It had taken almost thirty minutes for them to be seated and they had spent that time having drinks at the bar. They now had the crabs and two glasses of cold beer sitting on the table between them.

Jack cracked a claw with his wooden mallet. Some of the clear liquid insides splashed across the table onto Heather's freshly ironed pink blouse. He grabbed a napkin and tried to wipe it away.

"I'm sorry. These things are really juicy."

She laughed. "Don't be. I knew that would probably happen when I suggested we order them. I haven't had them for a while and I thought it would be fun. I'll pay you back in kind, sooner or later."

Jack smiled. Heather was nice to be with; small talk came easily to her. It had been a long time since he'd enjoyed the company of a woman.

"So, how is business at the office?"

"Just like it always is. People are constantly running in and out and coming up with big ideas that usually won't work."

"How is Colonel Meyer?"

"He's well. I don't see as much of him as I used to. He's usually out of the office. I think he spends most of his time at the research facility. He keeps my phone buzzing, though. Just because I don't see much of him doesn't mean I don't hear from him. He keeps me very busy."

"He's called every week since we left there."

"I know. Jack, do you mind if I ask a favor of you? Let's don't talk about Colonel Meyer and his program while I'm here. I'm not supposed to. Besides that, it's been quite a while since I could get away from the office and not think about my job."

"That's fine with me. Time has flown by and since nothing happened with the implants, I've pretty much forgotten about them. Boss and I have been so busy at work, I haven't had time to think about them. If I didn't get the calls from the Colonel every week, I probably wouldn't think about them at all."

"That's good Jack, maybe better than you know. I wish we could have eaten somewhere that Boss is welcome. How is the big guy?"

"He's busy being Boss, doing dog things, thinking dog thoughts, I guess. I don't imagine he's very happy with me right now. He's probably lying in front of the door, waiting for me to get back home. I don't leave him alone very often."

"I'd like to see him while I'm in town. Would that be ok?"

A tiny alarm bell went off in Jack's mind.

"Certainly. He'll probably remember you. He liked you."

"I thought he did. I liked him too. He's a good boy, so beautiful."

"Yeah, he is. I wish he was here. I miss him when he's not at my side. We have a knack for getting into some nasty situations on the job and he's saved my butt many times. A lot of the bad guys he's pulled down would love to get even with him. They'd have to go through me to get to him, though and I'm sure they know that."

"It's a dangerous business that you're involved in."

"Well, don't worry about it too much. Nobody can hurt either of us while we're together."

"I know. That's the way you K9 guys are. He looks out for you and you look out for him."

"Yep."

"I hope I'm not being too forward, but after we finish eating, could we go back to your place a few minutes so I can say hi to him?"

"Our place is a mess. I'm not used to having company and Boss is not the neatest guy around. You might be shocked."

"I know how you single men live. Seriously, would it be alright?"

"Of course; let's don't rush, though. He'll be fine while I'm gone and these crabs are really good. The beer tastes even better."

She laughed. "There are a lot of them. We shouldn't have ordered so many. We'll probably have to take some of them home with us. Before we leave here, let's get a couple of hamburgers for Boss. No ketchup or mustard, just some mayonnaise, meat, and bread. Would he want cheese on them?"

"He'll like that and he loves cheese. We'll have to ask the waitress to tell the chef not to cook them for too long. He likes them medium rare."

Jack couldn't tell her he didn't enjoy crabs nearly as much as he used to. Since Boss's sense of taste now affected his own, the seasoning was much too intense for him. He would rather have had the hamburgers. Heather could take any leftover crabs to her cousin.

He flashed a quick message to Boss.

"She's coming; I couldn't get out of it."

Boss shot back, *"I know. I was listening. I don't think you wanted to get out of it."*

∞ ∞ ∞ ∞ ∞ ∞

Boss was waiting just inside the front door, the way a good dog was supposed to. He acted happy to see Heather, but not too happy. He acted more excited when she pulled the cheeseburgers out of the paper bag.

"Oh Jack, he's even more handsome than I remembered. How are you, boy? Do you remember me? Are you glad to see me? Sure, you are."

Jack laughed. "Don't get too pleased with yourself. He probably smelled the burgers on you when you walked through the door and got wound up about that. He's a big bum. He'll want you to go out and get him another one in about five minutes."

Boss shot him a dirty look.

Heather giggled. She had no idea Boss had just turned off the television when he heard Jack's car pull into the driveway. Boss gulped down the first cheeseburger and took the second from her. He trotted to a corner of the living room to lie down and began to eat, just as any other dog would have.

"Have a seat on the couch, but watch out for dog hair. I keep telling him to clean it off after he sleeps on it, but he ignores me. I'll get us a cold drink. My mouth is still burning from those crabs. What would you like? I think we have cola, root beer, ice water, I think there's even a beer or two in the fridge."

"I think I'd like just a small glass of ice water to sip on. Those crabs really filled me up."

"Yeah. Me, too. I'll have the same." Jack was glad she wanted water. He preferred it.

He filled two glasses with ice and water and walked into the living room and handed one to her. Boss had climbed onto the sofa and stretched out beside her so she could scratch his head.

"Look, he does remember me. I knew he would."

"I'm sure," he laughed. "Just don't forget to bring him another cheeseburger the next time you come."

The visit went well. Jack found himself not worrying so much about what Heather's real mission might be and Boss began to relax. Jack turned on the television after a few minutes and put the volume on low while they talked.

It was almost midnight before Heather asked him to take her back to her cousin's home where he'd met her earlier in the day. She was overly tired since she'd had a long week at work and not gotten much sleep on Friday night.

Boss went along when Jack drove her home and stretched out in the backseat of the car. Jack parked in front of the house where Heather was staying and the two of them got out and walked her to the front door.

"I had a wonderful evening. I don't get out much."

"Neither do I. I had a good time and I think Boss really enjoyed your visit."

"I like him so much; he's such a good dog. I hope you don't mind, but I'm going to be forward again. I'm not going home until

Wednesday morning. Could we get together one more time before I go back?"

Boss nudged his thigh.

"I have to work tomorrow and Monday. I'm not sure about Tuesday."

"Oh, I see. That's a shame. I thought you and Boss liked me."

"I do like you and so does he. Can I be honest with you?"

"I hope you always are."

"As much as I'd like to, I'm a little reluctant about seeing you again. The Colonel warned me that his program is Top-Secret and that I shouldn't discuss it with anyone who isn't authorized to talk about it. I like you, but I don't want us to get into a situation where he might feel we're compromising his research."

"I wouldn't want to do that, either. I'm not sure it would be a problem for him, though. Do you know, when I told him I would be spending a few days in Baltimore, he suggested we get together for dinner? I'm sure he'll ask me how things went when I get back to work."

Boss pushed his nose hard into the palm of Jack's hand.

"That's nice to know. I don't see how the two of us getting together once more before you go back could compromise his program, but he might think it would."

"Let's do it, anyway. I'll tell him we had dinner a couple of times when I get back to work. If it's a problem, I'm sure he'll ask me not to do it again."

"Ok, that sounds reasonable. Let me check my schedule tomorrow. If I'm off Tuesday, we'll all spend the afternoon together and then we'll have dinner. I'll call you when I find out. If I'm off, could I make a suggestion?"

"Sure."

"Unless you're prone to more seafood or a big restaurant, let's go where we can eat outside and Boss can come along. I know a place on the water just outside of the city where we can get some burgers and eat while we watch the sunset."

"I'd like that, very much." She reached up and kissed him on the lips, hurriedly, almost bashfully, and went inside the house.

Jack and Boss walked back to the car and slowly drove away.

"Well, that seemed to go ok."

"I don't know, boy. Maybe I'm getting us into something that might be tough to get us out of."

"You like her a lot, don't you?"

"Yes, I do. If she wasn't so nice and so pretty, it would be easier for me to push her away."

"I like her, too. It was good of her to think about bringing me the cheeseburgers. But, you heard what she said about the Colonel."

"Yeah, I did. I got your warning shot. I felt like, if I was too evasive about seeing her again, that might make him suspicious if he is using her to spy on us. That's why I suggested we go someplace where I could take you. I think we should play this out and see what happens. If the Colonel is using her to check up on us, maybe me being so agreeable about seeing her again and having you with me will throw him off track. He's only human and he knows how attractive she is. If I didn't react to her like any normal man would, he might get suspicious about that. Dang, boy! She smells so good!"

"She does. Jack, you know I feel the same things that you do, right?"

"Yeah."

"I could feel you getting worked up when she kissed you good night. It affected me too."

"I know. I never expected that."

"Neither did I. I could also tell you were getting worked up a couple of other times during the evening."

"I guess I'll have to lay off the beer when we get together Tuesday."

"That's probably a good idea."

"Colonel Meyer is going to be calling me on Thursday. If he doesn't ask about Heather visiting us, I'm not going to mention it to him."

"Do you think that's a good idea?"

"I hope so. Maybe he'll think I wouldn't do that if I had something else to hide."

79

Chapter 9

Early Tuesday evening, Jack drove to a restaurant situated on the low bank of a lazy tidal river just east of Baltimore. The place was locally famous for its fine food and service. There was a window on the side of the building where they could get food without having to go inside. The grass had been recently mowed along the riverbank and there were picnic tables close to the water where they could eat.

When they arrived, Jack ordered hamburgers, fries, and drinks at the food to go window and carried them to a table under an ancient oak tree where they could watch the sunset. Jack had brought along a bowl so Boss would have water to drink.

The day was cool, but not so cool as to be uncomfortable. Heather took a bite out of her hamburger and began to chew.

After swallowing, she sighed and said, "This place is so beautiful. If I lived in a house right here under this tree, I don't think I'd ever go anywhere else. Someone would have to deliver my groceries to me."

Jack laughed. "It's beautiful now, but it gets cold here in the winter. I've been here in January with Boss when we were working on a couple of breaking and enterings. The wind coming off the water would almost drop you to your knees."

"I can imagine."

"Have you enjoyed your visit with your family?"

"Yes. Unfortunately, I have to be back to work on Thursday morning. I wish I could stay for a few more days. I'm really enjoying being with you and Boss. I know D.C. isn't really that far away, but I wish it was closer so we could get together occasionally. Am I being too forward again?"

"No. I'd be lying if I said I wasn't attracted to you. I think you know that I am. I'd like to see you again, but like I said the other night, I'm not sure the Colonel would like it. It may be a good thing that we don't live closer together."

"I guess that's a bridge I'll have to cross when I come to it. I won't hide anything from him. If it's not a problem, would you like to go out with me again?"

"I would. I should warn you, though, I don't date very often. I've only gone out with a couple of ladies since Boss and I started working together. It seemed like they either didn't like him or were afraid of him. Boss and I are a package, we go together. Maybe if…"

At that moment, a scream pierced the air from the direction of the carryout window where they had picked up their burgers not five minutes before. Jack's head snapped around at the same instant Boss reacted. A man was running away from the window with a pistol in his hand, no, two men with pistols. His trained eyes quickly took in the four-door getaway car that was waiting for them in the sandy parking lot and he heard the excited driver begin to race the engine up and down. The car could get no closer to the robbers without crashing through a low fence that was made of long wooden poles.

Jack reacted without thinking. "Try to get the tag number!" he yelled to Heather as he leaped away from the table.

He ran toward the parking lot to intercept the two men before they could reach the safety of the vehicle. Boss was faster. As he ran, Jack pulled the semi-automatic pistol from his shoulder holster that he was required to carry, even while off duty. The men were almost a hundred feet from him, going away at an angle. He would not make it to them before they reached the car.

"Baltimore Police! Stop and drop your weapons!" he yelled.

The nearest man slowed and pointed his gun over his shoulder. He pulled the trigger as he ran. Two bullets zipped over Jack's head, high, nowhere near him. The people who were seated along the riverbank scrambled to find cover behind trees and picnic benches. The picnickers who couldn't find anything to hide behind began throwing themselves onto the ground.

The nearer man continued to run with his gun pointed back over his shoulder. The robber who was closest to the car stopped suddenly and turned around. He leveled his gun and fired three times past his accomplice at Jack. This time the slugs came closer, but still high.

A silent command shot from Jack's mind, *"Take the closest one, boy."*

The black snarling flash clamped his teeth onto the first shooter's arm before he could fire again. The man screamed as Boss pulled him down. A high-pitched howl emanated from his throat that was almost inhuman.

A thought shot back from Boss, *"This idiot shouldn't have brought a gun to a dog fight!"*

Jack focused his attention on the second man who was once again running toward the car. He continued his pursuit.

"I'm with the Baltimore City Police Department! Stop and drop your gun!" he yelled at the shooter who was almost to the car. The man shot again, this time over his shoulder.

" Jack! You have to stop him before he hits one of those people. He might hit Heather!"

The driver's side front window of the car came down and a hand slid out. It was wrapped around the handle of a large caliber semi-automatic pistol. The gun roared, twice. The bullets came closer to Jack. This guy could shoot straighter.

The second robber was almost to the car.

"One more chance!" Jack yelled as he ran.

The man stopped, turned and pointed his gun at Jack. Boss gave out a tremendous growl and leaped away from the first shooter. As he ran to dive through the open side window, he struck the second robber a glancing blow on his way by and knocked him to the ground. He took the hidden gunman's hand and wrist into his gaping jaws as he disappeared into the car.

The second gunman raised his pistol again as he jumped back to his feet. Jack's gun roared and his bullet tore into the robber's upper right side. The man pulled the trigger of his own gun as he slammed to the ground. The bullet flew harmlessly over Jack's head.

Screams and growls were emanating from inside the car as the vehicle began to roll forward. Jack rushed to the two men who lay bleeding on the ground and kicked their still smoking guns away. Then he moved swiftly to the driver's side of the car and pointed his own weapon through the open window at the pair struggling in the front seat.

The driver's gun had flown out of his hand and into the back seat when Boss's teeth clamped onto his wrist. Jack reached through the window and slammed the gear shift lever into park. The car stopped moving. He yanked open the front door and pointed his gun inside once again. The driver was screaming and flailing his body about as he tried to get his hand and wrist out of the Boss's mouth.

"Let him go, boy."

Horrible growls were continuing to emanate from Boss's throat.

"No, Jack! This jerk was trying to kill you! I should tear his heart out!"

"Calm down; you have to let him go. I've got him covered."

Jack's hands were shaking so hard, he could barely hold his weapon. The rage that filled Boss was taking over his own mind, almost overcoming his sense of reason. If he hadn't had all his military and police training on self-control…

"Officer, you have backup. We have the other two covered. You can call off your dog."

Jack was breathing hard as he looked over his shoulder. A man dressed in civilian clothing was standing over a wounded robber. He was holding a badge in his left hand. His right hand held a gun that was pointed at the man that Jack had just been forced to shoot.

"Who are you?"

"I'm Sergeant Brady from the Baltimore City Police Department and that's Officer Bowman over there putting cuffs on the first guy your dog took down. You need to get him out of the car and control him. If you don't, he's going to rip that guy's hand off. I'll report what just happened to the dispatcher and have her send an ambulance."

Brady turned to the people who were beginning to gather around the two men on the ground as he reached for his communicator.

"Everybody get back! This is a crime scene," he yelled.

Jack could feel the rage that was emanating from Boss begin to subside, but he continued to clench the driver's wrist in his jaws.

"*Let him go, boy, we're finished here.*"

Boss reluctantly let go and stood over the man, growling.

"*Come on, boy, back off.*"

Boss jumped out of the car onto the parking lot. Jack dragged the man out and shoved him, chest first, against the side of the car.

"Spread your legs and put your hands behind your back!"

It was then he realized, except for when he had screamed at the robbers, this was the only spoken order he had given during the entire incident. He hadn't once given Boss a vocal command. He hoped Heather hadn't noticed.

The other two officers were off duty and inside the restaurant having dinner with their wives when the first shots rang out. They ran out of the exit door just as Boss released the first shooter's arm. They heard Jack identify himself as a Baltimore City Police Officer and order the robbers to drop their guns. They pulled their own weapons and ran toward the man on the ground just as the big dog lunged for the hand of the shooter inside the car.

They saw him slam into the second shooter and ruin his aim a split second before disappearing into the vehicle. If he hadn't knocked the man off balance, Jack wouldn't have had enough time to get off an accurate shot and the outcome of the gunfight would almost certainly have been different. The officers had not been able to react quickly enough to bring their own weapons to bear. The entire incident had occurred in a little less than thirty seconds.

Jack asked the officers to take charge of the three men while he and Boss walked over to see if Heather or any of the people in the picnic area had been injured. The adrenaline in his system was still causing his hands to shake.

Heather was standing a few steps away from their table and clutching a small child that had tried to run toward the parking lot during the melee. She released the child to his grateful mother.

Jack looked around. No one except the robber had been struck by the gunfire. He grimaced as he tried to smile at Heather.

"Well, if the Colonel wasn't going to hear about us seeing each other before, he's going to hear about it now."

Her face was ashen and she was crying. Adrenalin had also been pumping through her body.

"Jack! I've never seen anything like that in my entire life! I was so afraid! Those men were shooting at you!"

Jack tried to produce another smile; this one was a little better. He took her small hand into his own.

"I know. It happens like that sometimes."

"But…but…Jack! They were trying to kill you!" She began to sob.

"I know. It's ok. It's all over now. You need to sit down. Your legs are shaking."

He gently led her back to her seat at the picnic table. He kicked at their two hamburgers that were now lying on the ground beside the one Boss was eating when the shots rang out.

Boss stuck his cold nose into her hand. The hand was wet with her tears.

"Oh, Boss!" She leaned over him and put her face into the fur between his ears and began to cry harder.

Jack put his hand on her shoulder.

"Now, now. Take it easy. Take a couple of deep breaths and try to calm down. You'll be alright in a minute."

Her shoulders began to shake less, but her hands continued to tremble.

"I know things like this went on, but I never knew how quickly they happen and how loud gunshots are! You could have been killed!"

He pulled her back to her feet and took her into his arms.

"Yes, I know, but I've been trained how not to be killed and so has Boss. The bad guys don't get the same training that we do. They can't shoot as straight and none of them have friends like him."

"Thank God, they don't!"

"I'm going to talk to the witnesses and I'll have to help the other officers. More officers will be arriving to take our statements. Will you be alright by yourself for a while? I'll leave Boss here with you."

"Yes, I guess so."

"Heather?"

"What?" She had picked up her purse and was searching inside for a tissue.

She was still sniffling. Darn, she is so pretty, he thought to himself.

"You were a witness to all this. You'll have to testify in court about what you've seen unless there are plea bargains or these guys decide to plead guilty. That's probably not going to happen. Do you understand? The investigators will take your statement and sooner or later, you're almost certainly going to have to testify. Like I said, the Colonel is going to hear about it."

"I believe he thought we'd have a nice visit, but I'm sure he wasn't expecting to hear about anything like this," she said.

Boss stared at him and shot him a silent alarm.

"*Yeah boy,*" he said silently, "*I guess that's the bridge that we'll have to cross.*"

∞ ∞ ∞ ∞ ∞ ∞

The man Jack was forced to shoot had been taken to a hospital where he was undergoing surgery. He would live, but it would take him many weeks to recover.

The other two men had been taken to the same hospital where surgeons were now working to repair the damage Boss's teeth had done to their arms. All three of the men were under guard and would remain in custody until they could go before a judge and ask for bail to be set. Jack didn't understand why the men had risked so much to steal the small amount of money that was in the carryout window cash register. He let the thought go and explained it to himself the way he always did; when a crime is being planned, the criminal mind doesn't always think things through to a logical conclusion.

Jack would write up his reports in the morning. He'd be temporarily relieved of patrol duty and given a desk job while the episode was being investigated by the B.C.P.D. It was standard procedure when a suspect was shot.

The two off-duty officers had nothing but good things to say about Boss. Both men told Jack they'd never seen anything like him in action. Jack was proud of his partner. He couldn't tell them Boss had been making his own plans during the entire shootout. Officer Bowman told him he was going to put in for a transfer to the K9 Department as soon as possible. It didn't get much better than that.

Heather had calmed down and answered all the questions the investigating officers had asked as well as she could. Things had happened quickly and she couldn't remember everything she'd seen, but if necessary, she'd make a good witness in court.

It was well past midnight when Jack and Boss walked her to her cousin's front door.

"I guess our date didn't turn out exactly as we planned," he said.

"No, it didn't. I never realized how a simple thing like going out for a hamburger could cost someone their life. Now, I'll have to worry about you and Boss when you go to work every day. I guess I didn't understand how dangerous your job actually is until I saw it with my own eyes."

Jack smiled. "Don't worry about it too much. That kind of thing almost never happens. We're usually bored to death while we're at work. We spend most of our time doing public appearances to promote the K9 Department, looking for lost kids, things like that. I spend more time in a courtroom or doing paperwork than I do chasing bad guys."

"I know, but what happened today was unbelievable. Most people never see anything like that in their entire lives. Once was enough for me."

"I feel that way all the time, but we can't let the bad guys take over the world. If Boss and I and the other officers didn't do what we do, people wouldn't be able to walk down the street in broad daylight. The world is full of people who are trying to have normal lives, but there are bad people out there who'd steal everything the good people work for if they had half a chance."

"I know, but why does it have to be you?" She began to tear up again.

"It has to be somebody, Heather. Boss and I have had the training and experience to do it better and more safely than most other people."

"I understand why you do it. It just became way too up close and personal for me today."

"It gets like that for somebody, every day. I'm just one of the people who can help make it happen a little less often. I wouldn't walk away from what I do and neither would Boss."

"I know. I guess I'll just have to get used to the idea."

She bent down and took Boss's huge head into her hands and kissed him on the forehead.

"You'll take good care of him, won't you boy?"

Jack could feel Boss's pleasure in his own mind. Boss licked her hand and placed his paw on her knee.

She looked up at Jack.

"You're very fortunate to have a friend like him looking out for you. I'm going in now. I'm exhausted. I don't know how you do this every day. Will you stay in touch with me, Jack, please?"

"You know I will. Now, go inside and try to get some sleep. Hopefully, you'll never have a day like this again as long as you live. Will you call me when you get back to D.C. so I'll know you're alright?"

"I will." She reached up to him. This time, her kiss lasted much longer.

Chapter 10

The call came from Colonel Meyer on Thursday, just as they knew it would. Jack expected the conversation would be longer than usual and he was correct. As soon as the phone buzzed, Boss raised his head and gave Jack a penetrating stare.

"Hello."

"Hello, Jack? This is Colonel Meyer."

"Hi, Colonel. I was expecting your call. It is, after all, Thursday."

"Yes, so it is. How are you? I understand you've had a couple of days that were somewhat out of the ordinary."

Jack laughed, trying to keep the tone of the conversation as light as possible.

"You could certainly say that."

"I understand you and your dog kept Miss Jamison very entertained while she was visiting her family in Baltimore."

"I don't think the word entertained quite describes what happened while she was here. She's probably still shaking."

"From what she's been telling me, she received quite a scare."

"She did. I wouldn't blame her if she never sets foot around here again."

"She told me about what happened when she came in to work this morning. She has nothing but the highest praise for you and your dog."

"We only did what we've been trained to do. Things usually don't get quite that intense for us, but when they do, we have to be ready. We had help from a couple of off-duty officers. Things might not have turned out quite so well if they hadn't been there."

"According to her, they did little. They just handcuffed the robbers after you and Boss took them down."

"She was pretty overwhelmed, Colonel. She's giving us more credit than we deserve. She had never seen anything like that before. It was a little more exciting than a regular day at the office but not much more than that."

"I think you're being too modest. It's good to know officers like you are on the job."

"Thank you, sir. I appreciate that."

"Jack! He suspects something!"

"She told me that after Boss took down the first shooter, you were in trouble. She said you had two men shooting at you at the same time and you were just a few steps away from them. She said Boss knocked one of them down while he was going for the gun hand of another man who was shooting at you from inside a car. She believes if Boss hadn't done that, you might not have been able to take the other shooter out before you were hit. She said it looked like Boss intentionally knocked the man down so you'd have time to use your weapon. What's your take on it?"

Boss was beginning to pace back and forth. *"He thinks he's on to something! I can feel it!"*

"I think it's just one of those fortunate things that happen that lets an officer walk away from a bad situation. Boss has been trained to take down anyone who is firing at his handler. He went for the gun hand of the man who had fired last, probably more out of instinct than anything else. The other shooter was standing between him and the one in the car. Boss sideswiped him as he went by."

"It looks like he would have taken out the closer shooter."

"That's probably what most dogs would have done. The two men were close together and Boss must have had his mind focused on the last one who fired. I was locked on the closest man and ready to fire. By then, the other officers were almost on top of us with their weapons drawn and ready. If Boss hadn't hit the guy, one of us would have taken him out before he got a shot off at me."

"It sounds like it was a near thing. Well, that's what they train the dogs to do. I'm glad there was a good outcome and nobody was hurt except the robbers. After all, we do have a rather large investment in the two of you. Is there anything new to report to me about our regular business?"

"No, not since the last time we talked. I surprised you haven't given up on us by now. I feel like I've let you down."

"No Jack, you haven't. Edison had many a failure before he invented the working light bulb, but ultimately, he came up with the light bulb. I'll come up with my own bulb in good time. I would like to meet with you soon if you aren't too busy. When will you be available?"

Boss shoved his head into Jack's thigh. He was shaking his head back and forth.

"Jack, I don't like what I'm picking up. Be careful."

"When do you want to meet? I'm a little tied up for the next few days, Colonel. I'm working on my reports about the incident and I have to meet with the Department of Public Affairs, more than once I'm sure. I was off duty when the shooting happened and so were the other officers. Not being on duty makes the situation a little more complicated. I'm sure you know that whenever an officer fires his weapon and someone is injured, the officer is relieved of regular duty until there is an investigation to make sure he was acting as he should have. I won't be on regular duty, but I'll still have to work and be available to answer questions whenever I'm needed."

"I'd like to get together with you as soon as you can arrange it. We've had a few developments that I need to talk with you about. How about this? I'm going to be at Fort Meade next week on Thursday morning for a meeting. Is it possible for us to have a chat Thursday afternoon if I drive on up there afterward? Could you arrange for us to have a private room at the police department?"

Jack felt Boss's relief. They would feel more secure at the office.

"There shouldn't be any problem arranging that."

"Will 2 o'clock be ok?"

"Certainly. I'll ask Captain Harrison to tell Public Affairs not to set up anything for that afternoon."

"That should work out well. Oh, I almost forgot."

"Yes?"

"Miss Jamison said if I spoke to you today, to send her best to you and Boss."

"Please thank her for me and tell her I said hello. Colonel, I did consider that you might not want us to see each other socially. I hope this won't cause any problems for you."

"I'm glad to know you thought about me when you made the decision to see her. But, you did it anyway."

"Yes sir, I did. I hope I wasn't out of line."

The Colonel laughed. "Actually Jack, I suggested to her that she visit with you while she was in your area. She's very attractive, isn't she?"

"Yes sir, she certainly is."

"Don't worry about it right now. Maybe we'll talk more about it when I see you. Ok?"

"Yes, sir. I'm looking forward to seeing you again."

"Goodbye, Jack."

"Goodbye."

"*What do you make of that?*"

"*I don't know, boy. I guess we'll learn more when we see him next week.*"

"*I'll be with you?*"

"*Yes. He knows we're always together.*"

"*Maybe you should talk to Heather before he comes. She might know what he wants to talk about.*"

"*No, Boss. If there are problems, we don't want her in the middle of them. She doesn't know anything about our connection and I want to keep it that way. There's no sense in dragging her into this. I won't talk to her again until after we meet with him unless she calls me.*"

"*You're right, that's probably the best thing to do. I don't believe she was sent to spy on us. I didn't pick up any deception in her when she was here.*"

"*Neither did I. I hope we're both right.*"

"*I'm glad the Colonel wants to meet at the office. I was hearing things in his voice that I didn't like.*"

"*At least here, we'll have a fighting chance if he insists we go back to Washington. I'd do my best to talk our way out of going.*"

92

I've kept a good bit of cash stashed away at home in case we ever needed to make a run for it. We probably wouldn't get far, but we'd try. Who knows? They may have put tracking devices into the transmitters."

"I don't think so. I believe we'd be able to know if they did."

"We'll go about our business just like we always do until we learn more from the Colonel. We have to get through the Public Affairs investigation. Those guys we took down will get lawyers and cause us plenty of headaches. You chewed up those jerk's arms pretty bad, boy, and I did put a slug into one of them. Their attorneys will be saying it's our fault their clients got hurt."

"Yeah, I know. It sucks to be them, doesn't it? Let's go get something to eat.

∞ ∞ ∞ ∞ ∞ ∞

The following Thursday afternoon came all too soon. In the days before the meeting, Jack discretely prepared in case they'd have to attempt an escape from the Colonel. He told himself he was probably just being paranoid, but they both felt the need to be prepared for anything.

He withdrew money from the bank and added it to the cash he kept hidden in the back of a drawer in his bedroom. He didn't take out all his money in case his account was being monitored. A closed account might trigger a response from the Colonel that they didn't need. They would only try to run away as a last resort.

Most people used debit or credit cards for purchases, but they would need cash. If they did have to leave, he wouldn't be able to use his cards. That would be the fastest way to let Colonel Meyer know where they were. They knew they had little chance of making an escape. The CIA was too powerful and most forms of public transportation would be constantly under surveillance. A young man traveling with a huge black dog wouldn't be hard to find.

Jack used some of the cash to buy two bus tickets to Niagara Falls. He bought the extra ticket for Boss in case some driver might object to him taking a large Service Dog aboard a bus without paying.

He had no car of his own and stealing a police car would only get them arrested that much faster. Trying to rent a car wasn't the answer; rental car records could be too easily checked by computer. Airports would be even more closely monitored than bus stations. Anyone trying to board a plane with a huge black German Shepherd would stick out like a sore thumb.

A bus or taxi would be their only possible means of escape. If they could get an eight or ten-hour jump on anyone who was looking for them, it might be possible to get to Niagara Falls before they were picked up.

If they could make it that far, they'd mingle with tourists and try to get across the border into Canada. After that, they'd have to play it by ear. There were still relatively uninhabited areas in the interior of Canada where they could hide. They would have to disappear for a long time, but Jack was prepared to do whatever was necessary to protect Boss.

∞ ∞ ∞ ∞ ∞ ∞

They had lunch before Colonel Meyer arrived. When he appeared, they walked together to Captain Harrison's office. The Captain had agreed to let them meet there privately when Jack requested its use.

Jack pulled two chairs away from the desk and offered one to the Colonel as Boss yawned and stretched out near his feet and closed his eyes, just as any other dog might have done.

"Would you like a cup of coffee, Colonel? It's good. People make jokes about cop coffee, but we need the good stuff when we work late hours."

"I'm sure you do, but thank you, no. I drank enough coffee today at my other meeting to last me a week. I don't have a lot of time. I must get back to the office to do some work before I can go home tonight and I'll have to fight the traffic all the way there. I'm sure you've been wondering why I wanted to talk to you."

"Yes sir, I have."

"There are several reasons. First, I should ask you if you've had anything new happen between you and Boss."

"No, I haven't. I've about given up on it."

"So have I. We've been trying our experiments, when you consider all the animal experiments and our human trials, for many years. We've had some success, but not what we'd hoped for. Our animal program worked out better than our human experiments. We were hoping for a lot more communication between the K9 teams than we had between our chimps and their dogs, but that mostly hasn't happened. We really thought we were on the right track with this. I still think we are, but things haven't worked out quite how we thought they would."

"How far have you gotten?"

"We're to the point where a few of the handlers actually could get into the minds of their dogs on a limited basis. You reported how you believed your sense of smell was better and that Boss might understand your commands a little more."

"That's correct, sir."

"Some of our volunteers reported the same type of things. Most of them reported no effects at all from the implants and have gone back to work at their respective police departments. We're staying in contact with them, the same as we have with you. Some of the other officers had things happen that became very disturbing for them. A few had problems eating because their sense of taste had changed so drastically. Some had their sense of smell become so acute, they were sickened by any strong odor. A couple of the officers almost starved because they couldn't eat. There were changes in vision, things like that. We've had more troubling developments. Some of our volunteers became paranoid or schizophrenic. We've had to institutionalize a few."

"I had no idea things like that were going on."

"You wouldn't since I haven't told you about it and you haven't been experiencing them yourself. We've also had problems with some of the dogs. Some almost stopped eating and became emaciated. A few starved themselves so badly, they had to be euthanized. Others became extremely aggressive and had to be put down. We couldn't understand why these things were happening to some of our volunteers, while others experienced no effects at all."

"I'm beginning to feel concerned, Colonel. What if Boss or I started having problems like that?"

"Most of these things began occurring shortly after the volunteers and their dogs received the implants, so we don't believe that will happen. However, we can't be certain of that."

"What do you suggest I do?"

"Let me finish, then you can make up your own mind. I'll tell you what I'd like for you to do before I leave."

"Ok. Can I ask a question at this point? Why didn't you just remove the implants from the men and the dogs with problems? Wouldn't that have worked?"

"We did. We tried that on all our subjects that were adversely affected. In some cases, it completely reversed the effects. In others, it didn't improve the negative effects by very much or at all."

"You assured me there wouldn't be problems. You said that everything was perfectly safe."

"I know and I'm very sorry about that. At the time, I believed it was. We had done so many animal tests and everything indicated success! Unfortunately, it didn't work out the way we would have liked. All I can do now is to try to help our volunteers as much as I can and continue to monitor the situation."

"I don't know what to say."

"Jack, I've had to do some things I'm not very proud of. I felt terrible about having to put down the dogs that were starving or becoming aggressive. Since they had to be killed anyway, I told our researchers to dissect them. I didn't want that to happen, but we're trying to learn things that could help our police and military and dramatically improve our national security. We're trying to understand why the implants are not operating the way they're supposed to. I know you probably disagree with me, but I believe some things are more important than the life of a dog."

"The life of my dog is the most important thing in the world to me, sir."

"I know it is. Like I said, I don't feel very good about some of the decisions I've had to make. But, if I hadn't made them, someone else would have."

"I'm sure you're right about that. Why are you telling me all this?"

"Because we're having other problems that I believe you should know about."

"You're scaring me."

"This has nothing to do with the safety of our program. You're aware of the money trouble our country has been experiencing. Back around the turn of the century and for a couple of decades afterward, our national leadership made some stupid decisions for our country. Many of our state and city governments did the same. They began to reward indolence and punish success. They put half the country on welfare and food stamps and tried to give all those people free health care. They opened our borders and let anyone who walked across come into the country and gave most of them free government benefits. They passed such restrictive tax and environmental laws, we lost most of the bigger businesses, at least the ones that could afford to move away and operate in other countries. Our energy policies were a joke. The government restricted oil production and our foreign trade balance got completely out of hand. Because of the overzealous economic legislation and environmental restrictions, it became extremely difficult for small businesses to survive. Jobs dried up. A few years later, inflation and recession hit us at the same time and ran unchecked for years."

"I know about all that."

"By the time we started wising up and electing better leadership, most of the damage was already done. We had borrowed far too many trillions of dollars from other countries and were drowning in debt we couldn't repay. We were trying to operate an economy on service and food industry jobs while we threw trillions of borrowed dollars into social programs. Our "cradle to the grave" social policies just didn't work. They were far too expensive. Then, all the money we spent on the war with Iran put the final nail in the coffin. We're not the super power that we used to be. We let both China and Russia overtake us and India isn't that far behind them. We've had to get used to being a second rate economic and military power. You have to deal with it yourself. You drive around in a five-year-old police car that's held together with spit and hay baling twine."

"I know, but what does that have to do with Boss and me?"

"To conduct research like we're doing costs a lot of money. I'm sure, if we'd had the success we expected, we'd have no problem continuing to get the money we need from the federal government. But, we didn't, so our funding is being cut. It's not completely being shut off, but we're losing a lot of it. I'm not involved just in implant research; I'm also in charge of other things that I can't tell you about. I have to move money from some of our less successful programs to our more successful ones. We won't be able to continue putting money into our implant research, at least not as much as before."

"He's lying, Jack. Watch out!"

"So, what about us?"

"When you came into our program, I promised you I'd take care of you. I intend to keep my word. You and Boss were one of our very first volunteer teams where both the handler and the dog received transmitters and receivers. Thankfully, you've had no ill effects. You both may go for the rest of your lives without experiencing any. But, we're not certain of that. The human brain is a strange organ. In many ways, it remains as much a mystery today as it was a thousand years ago. You may never have anything happen to you, but it's possible you could begin experiencing negative effects from the implants five minutes from now."

He paused for a moment and then continued, "I brought you into our program and promised you, not only safety, I promised you if you wanted the implants removed at any time, I would make it happen. I might not be able to do that if you wait too long. The funding for surgery may not be there. I would like for you and Boss to come back to Washington and have them taken out right away to try to ensure that you have no problems in the future."

"Jack, he's lying! He's not telling the truth about the problems with the implants. He's lying about them and he's lying about the money he has to work with. It isn't being cut off. He's trying to scare us. He suspects we can communicate like Hamilton and Drake and we're hiding it from him. He wants to trick us into going back to D.C. so he can experiment on us."

"The ball is in your court. Do you want them taken out or do you want to leave them in? You don't have to decide today, but you must decide quickly," said Meyer.

"Why the special interest in me, Colonel?"

"Maybe it's because I know you're a good person and very important to your police department and your community. Maybe it's because Miss Jamison has taken a special interest in you and your dog. Maybe it's because a lot of good officers volunteered themselves and their dogs for our program and I had to let some of them down. Let's just say it's all the above and I'd like to make it up to you for any stress or discomfort I've caused you. If you want the surgery, it will be done."

"He's lying!"

"So, I have to make up my mind about whether to keep the implants and risk later complications or have them removed and have a lower probability of problems developing in the future?"

"That's exactly what I'm saying."

"Neither choice sounds good to me. There could still be problems during the removal process. If you were me, what would you do?"

"I'd have them removed as quickly as possible. I can make arrangements to have them taken out sometime next week."

"I'll think about it, but I believe I'll leave them in. If they haven't caused us any problems by now, they probably never will. You said they could stay in there forever without causing infections or things like that, right?"

"As far as we know, that is correct. But, if you do that, I think you'll be making a mistake. Who knows what could happen five days or five years from now? Do you want to take that chance? If it was me, I'd have everything removed as soon as possible while there is still enough funding available to do it."

"Thank you for being candid with me, sir. I believe there are times when it's better to let sleeping dogs lie, no pun intended. I may be making a mistake, but I think I'll leave them in place."

Colonel Meyer stood up to shake Jack's hand and say goodbye. He was scowling as he left the room.

Jack looked at Boss. *"Do you think we're off the hook?"*

"No."

"What do you think about what he said? I have as much or more faith in your instincts than I do my own."

"There was always an undercurrent in his voice. I don't trust him at all. I felt that he was being truthful at times, but the rest was hogwash and constant deception. I'm certain, if we walk back into that place, they'll keep us."

"He couldn't just make us disappear. There would be too many questions."

"Of course, he could. He can do anything he wants after we're back there. You could "accidently" die during surgery and he can keep me for just about any reason. I'm only a dog, you know."

"It wouldn't be that easy. He'd have to do a lot of explaining about why I died and why you weren't returned to the police department."

"Explaining? There would be no reason to believe he wasn't telling the truth and you have almost no family to ask questions. The Baltimore City Police Department wouldn't like what happened, but there wouldn't be a proper investigation because of the money shortages the Colonel was talking about. He'd fake some paperwork and substitute a body in a sealed coffin and it would be buried. Meanwhile, you'll be locked up somewhere at the facility and I'll probably already be dead and dissected and nobody will be any the wiser. As far as me not being returned to the police department, the Chief doesn't have the clout or the money to fight the federal government about things like a misplaced dog."

"What do you think we should do?"

"He wants us now. You know we really can't run. If we try to disappear, he'll be certain we're communicating with each other and come after us all the harder. We won't be able to get food or transportation without being caught. There are cameras everywhere, so the bus tickets won't work. If we did get to the border with Canada, we'd still have to go through a checkpoint to get across. The people they send looking for us will have on the special glasses with face recognition technology that officers wear when they're searching for fugitives. All they'd have to do is look at you and they'd get instant verification that you're who they're looking for. Can you imagine how easy it will be to find a man with a big black German Shepherd? Yeah, he'd get us."

"Maybe he'll leave us alone since I told him I want to leave the implants in place."

"That just won't work. He wants us now and he'll come and get us."

"What do you suggest?"

"You're not going to like it."

"I won't know until I hear it."

"We're going to have to tell somebody."

"Who can we tell? There's no one who would believe me. Anyone I'd tell would think I was one of the people who is always seeing flying saucers and little green men."

"We're going to have to tell someone who would believe us and try to protect us."

"Who would do that?"

"The Captain might."

"Boss, I just shot a guy. The Captain would pull me off duty if I tried to tell him about this. He's a good man, but he's also a stone-cold realist. He didn't get promoted to Supervisor of the K9 Department because he's prone to believing in fairy tales."

"Think about it. He knows about the program, he just doesn't know how successful it has been."

"Yeah, but if I tried telling him we can talk to each other, he'd have me put into a padded room. You'll wind up working with another cop."

"Not if we can prove it to him."

"*How would we do that?*"

"*Call him and tell him the meeting with the Colonel is over. I'll explain what I have in mind while he's on the way back.*"

Chapter 11

The Captain was soon seated in the comfortable office chair behind his desk.

"So, how did your meeting go with the Colonel?"

"I'm not sure, Cap. There's something I need to talk to you about. Before I do, would you please do me a small favor? Call one of the men and ask him to take Boss out of the room and take him for a walk outside of the building."

"Sure, but why?"

"I'll explain once they're gone."

"Ok. I'll call Johnson in the Records Department. He's good with dogs and he could probably use a break."

The Captain picked up his phone and called the man. Johnson was a computer technician who Jack usually only saw when he walked out of a back office to get coffee. He came into the Captain's office and was asked to take Boss for a walk. They left together.

Moments later, Jack began to explain.

"I'm sure you remember how the Colonel's program was supposed to work."

"I do."

"What if I told you he had something different done to Boss and me and it succeeded beyond his wildest dreams?"

"I'd say that was wonderful. Was that what he wanted to talk to you about?"

"No. He doesn't know about it. I've been afraid to tell him."

"Why?"

"I'll explain that in a few minutes. In the meantime, would you humor me with a little experiment?"

"I suppose so. What kind of experiment?"

"I want to demonstrate to you just how well the implants work."

"I'd love to see that. Every time I've asked you about them, you told me they didn't work at all."

"I'm sorry I had to tell you that. First, call Johnson's phone and ask him to tell you exactly what Boss is doing. Don't tell me what he says; just write it down on a piece of paper. I'll do some writing while you're doing that."

"Why is this going to show me how the implants work?"

"I'll explain when we're through."

"This doesn't make any sense."

"It will. Before you call Johnson, put on your headphones so when you talk to him, you'll be certain I can't hear what he's saying."

The Captain did as Jack requested. When Johnson told him what Boss was doing, he laughed and began to write on his notepad.

"Is there something funny?"

"Yeah. What do I do now?"

"Ask Johnson what Boss is doing, again."

The Captain asked the question. When Johnson replied, he rolled his eyes at Jack and began to write again. Jack made his own notes.

The process was repeated six more times. Jack then asked the Captain to have Boss brought back to the office. In less than five minutes, Boss was back at his side and Johnson had gone back to his desk.

"Ok, I did what you wanted. Would you explain why you asked me to do that?"

"Yes. But before I do that, we'll run down the list of the things Boss was doing and you can compare your notes to mine. The first time you asked Johnson what Boss was doing, he was jumping up and down and spinning in circles on his hind legs. Is that correct?"

"That's almost exactly what I wrote down."

"The next time, he was lying on his back while he was biting at Johnson's right shoe. Correct?"

"Yes."

Jack read his list of things Boss was doing each time Captain Harrison had spoken to Johnson. They all were unusual. His list compared almost exactly to what the Captain had written.

The Captain exclaimed, "This is wonderful, Jack! Why didn't you tell me about this? Why didn't you tell Colonel Meyer? Are you able to see what Boss is doing through his eyes? When the Colonel first explained his implant program to me, I thought you might be able to use some of Boss's senses, but I had no idea anything like this was possible."

"You don't know the half of it."

Jack began to explain to the Captain about what had happened to them at the research facility. He told him about what had happened to Corporal Hamilton and Drake and the other K9 teams. He also told the Captain about Colonel Meyer's involvement with the CIA and what the agency had in mind for the implants.

Captain Harrison was incredulous.

"So, you're telling me, you can tell what Boss is seeing and doing, even when he's not with you?"

"Yes, but, it's not as simple as that. We can communicate with each other, talk to each other in our minds. They put different devices into us than the ones Meyer told you and the Chief about. They're brand new technology that only a very few K9 teams were supposed to receive. At least that's what they told me. I don't believe now that it was restricted to just a few officers and dogs. I know it's hard to believe, but we've been talking to each other since just after we left the research facility."

"You're telling me, Colonel Meyer kept Hamilton prisoner and killed his dog for research and has been implanting the new electronics into other volunteers? You also believe Hamilton may have been killed and his brain dissected so Meyer and his people could find out why the implants worked so well on him and his dog?"

"I'm not sure Hamilton was killed, but the rest is true."

"You're certain of this?"

"I'm as certain as I would be if I had seen it myself."

"But, you only heard about Hamilton, Drake and the other K9 team that was held prisoner from Boss..."

"Yes. Boss doesn't lie. When we first started talking to each other and he was trying to understand people, he couldn't comprehend why we sometimes deceive each other. At least, he didn't. He had to come to terms with it right away."

"So, you," Harrison looked down at Boss, "and the Boss, believe Meyer is trying to trick you into going back to Washington, where his people will perform experiments on the two of you?"

"Yes. That's what he was doing here today. He doesn't know Boss saw everything that was going on with Hamilton, Drake and the other teams and told me about it. If he was aware I knew about that and his CIA friends, he wouldn't have let me walk out of there with that kind of information."

"Jack, it's not that I don't believe you, I'm just having trouble grasping all this. A cop and a dog who can talk to each other! It's like something straight out of a science fiction movie! It's mind boggling!"

"I know, Cap. The first-time Boss talked to me, I almost wrecked the car."

"Do you think it's happened with many of the other officers who are in the program?"

"I don't know what went on after we left Washington. It's possible this could all be a mistake. Maybe the Colonel's surgeons accidently stimulated something in our brains that they didn't intend to when they operated on us and Hamilton and his dog. I guess it's possible that lots more officers and dogs are communicating. If that's happened, it could be why Meyer is coming after us. I just don't know; I'm only guessing at this point. What I do know is, Meyer will do anything to further his research. On top of that, he's is working with the CIA. You know as well as I do what those people can do. They're pretty much a law unto themselves."

"You talk to Boss and he talks to you. I just can't seem to get past that."

"Yes. It's like Boss and I each think with both of our minds. They were locked together by the implants. I can't explain to you exactly how or why it works, but we just showed you that it does. That's why Boss did unusual things while he was with Johnson. He planned it, Cap. It wasn't my idea."

"I believe you. If anyone else was telling me this, I'd be sure they were losing their minds. If I didn't already know about the Colonel's program and what he told me he was trying to do, I probably still wouldn't be able to believe it."

"I understand, Cap. I wouldn't believe it either."

"I don't know how, but we're going to have to bring someone else in on this. You're right. If the Colonel has been doing these things and suspects you and Boss can communicate with each other, he'll do everything he can to get you back down there. If the CIA is involved, once you're there, neither of you will be coming back. If they're pulling Meyer's strings, I won't be able to protect you by myself. I'll assure you, though, those butchers are not going to kidnap one of my officers and cut up one of my dogs without me doing all I can to stop it."

"What do we do?"

"I want to do a demonstration for the Chief. He's known about the Colonel's program as long as I have, so he may be open minded about this. If I can convince him about what's happened, I think he'll go to the Mayor. They've been buddies since they were in high school. The Mayor is a very smart man. If we can convince both of them, maybe between the three of us, we'll be able to come up with a way to protect you and Boss."

Boss walked over to the Captain and placed his paw on the Captain's knee.

"He understands every word you're saying, Cap, but even the three of you might not be able to stop it. If the Colonel uses the words national security..."

"I think we can come up with a couple of ideas that might slow down your Colonel. After all, if what you say is true, he's still not certain you and Boss can communicate."

"Boss sure thinks he is. The Colonel believes it wasn't a coincidence that Boss knocked the shooter down last week that was trying to take me out. He tried to convince us today we should have our implants removed. We think he's just trying to get us to go back to the facility on our own so he doesn't have to take us there by force."

"You can't go back to his chamber of horrors."

"Yeah, we know. What now?"

"We'll do the demonstration for the Chief. You'll have to stay here in my office while I take Boss to see him. The Chief will want to be sure you weren't just seeing what he was doing through the implants and believed he was talking to you. I'll get Boss to do his show and this time, I'll record what he does. The things I'll ask him to do will require thinking on his part. Afterward, I'll have you come get him and the two of you are going to go home and wait there. I'll have an officer drop me off at your house after the Chief and I are through. Then you and I, and Boss, of course, will make some plans. I'll leave my car here in case Meyer's people are watching it to see where I go when I leave the office. I don't want to take any chances. If the CIA is involved, we can't be too careful. You can drive me home after we're through talking this evening and I want both of you to spend the night at my house. We're going to have to find a safer place for you and Boss to live for a while."

Chapter 12

Three hours later, Jack and Boss were waiting at home when an unmarked police car pulled up out front. Captain Harrison opened the passenger door and stepped out. The car drove away as he walked up to the front door of the house and knocked.

After looking through a side window to make sure Harrison wasn't being followed, Jack walked over to the door and unlocked it. He relocked it when the Captain entered.

"Did you have any luck with the Chief?"

"Some. We'll have to meet with him tomorrow morning. The Chief said the Colonel's experiments sound like some of the things the Nazis used to do to their prisoners in Germany during World War II. He said nobody is going to use our officers and dogs for what is certainly, illegal research."

Boss walked over to him and placed his paw on his knee and stared into his face.

The Captain's throat tightened and his voice became husky. He looked deeply into Boss's eyes and said, "Don't worry, boy, you aren't going to be on anyone's operating table if I can do anything about it. I'm not sure exactly what, but I'll do everything I can do to protect you and Jack. The Baltimore City Police Department has resources of its own and a few friends in high places."

He turned to Jack. "Can I use your bathroom? I haven't had a chance to go since before we met in my office today. I'll tell you exactly what the Chief said when I come back out. It's not all good."

"Sure Cap, straight down the hallway to the second door on the left."

"Thanks. I know where it is"

He left the room. Jack turned to Boss.

"Well boy, it looks like we're going to be able to stop worrying so much. Who knows? The Colonel may not have been plotting anything, anyway."

At that instant, the front door crashed open and there was a loud pop. A red dart appeared on Boss's left hip. The dog dropped to the floor. His front feet twitched once and then stopped.

The sudden loss of the mental connection with Boss momentarily staggered Jack. He reached to his side for his service weapon and whirled toward the door. It was too late. A man stood at each side of the front door with a gun pointed at his chest. The guns were laser sighted; red dots were centered over his heart. His head cleared as adrenalin began to flow through his veins.

"What do you want? What did you do to my dog?"

Jack's eyes narrowed as Colonel Meyer walked through the front door. He was not dressed in his uniform.

"Hello, Corporal Randall. I guess you didn't expect to see me again today."

"No, I didn't. Who are those men and what have they done to Boss?"

"They're my men, of course. You don't have to worry; they haven't done anything serious to the dog. They only knocked him out. He'll wake up in a little while when he's safely caged in my van and on his way to Washington. You'll be coming along with us. We have a lot to talk about."

"We're not going anywhere with you."

"Of course, you are. I guess I should tell you, I'd rather you're in one piece when we get back to Washington, but it doesn't really matter one way or the other. Your heart isn't necessary for my research. The only thing I really need is your brain. Hamrick, take his gun."

The huge man who was standing by the left side of the door walked over to him and took his pistol. Colonel Meyer reached under his jacket and pulled his own sidearm from a shoulder holster and pointed it at Jack.

"Meyer, you lying piece of crap!"

The Colonel laughed, but his eyes hardened. "I think it's the other way around, Jack. I don't know why, but you've been lying to me. I've been nice to you. We could have done this the easy way, but you didn't want to. You couldn't just take me up on my offer to have the implants removed, so now we'll do it the hard way. You can walk out of here ahead of me or you can be carried out, like your dog."

"You're a disgrace to your uniform!"

Meyer laughed again. "You belong to the United States Government once again, just as you did when you were in the Army. We need you. Since we began using the new chips, we've done the surgeries on over twenty K9 teams. We weren't expecting what happened to you, but since it did, we have to know why. We could only make four teams able to talk to each other and they can't do it very well. We need to know why a few teams can communicate when the others can't.

Jack decided to act as if he didn't know why Meyer was there. "Why do you have to take our implants out?"

"We aren't going to. That was just a story I made up to get you to come back to D.C. without making trouble."

"But, why?"

"After hearing Miss Jamison's story, I began to wonder if you and your dog were able to talk to each other. These two men have been following you since then. I called you to set up a meeting to see what you would do if you felt threatened. You withdrew most of your money from your bank and bought two bus tickets. It was easy for me to find out about that. Then I came to see you, to try to get you to voluntarily go back to our research facility. You refused. I brought a small piece of technology along with me today, Jack. It's set to the frequency you and your dog use. After I walked out of your Captain's office, I went to the men's room and turned it on. You and your dog had quite a conversation after I left you. I don't know what you were saying, but I do know you were talking to each other. I knew then I had to come and get you. I think you've been communicating with each other since before you left Washington."

"I don't know what you're talking about."

"Of course, you do. I'm not wasting any more time explaining things to you. The two of you are coming with us. Hamrick, pick up the dog and carry him out to the van and lock him inside the cage. Mullins, stick your gun right up against Corporal Randall's spine and walk him out to the van. Try not to bump his head too hard when he gets in. Let's go. Jack, I'll be right behind you and Mullins."

The two men began to do as they were ordered. Hamrick placed his gun in its holster and walked over and removed the tranquilizer dart from Boss's hip. Then he picked the dog up and moved toward the door. It was a struggle for him; Boss was a heavy burden, even for someone as heavily muscled as Hamrick.

The man Meyer had identified as Mullins moved to Jack's rear. He pushed the barrel of his weapon into the small of Jack's back and shoved him toward the door. Meyer fell into step behind the three men and the unconscious dog.

"Hold it! Stop right there; none of you move!"

Everyone froze in place.

"Now, big man, put the dog on the floor. After you do that, the three of you turn around slowly with your hands in the air. Slowly, I said!"

Captain Harrison had almost finished relieving himself when the front door had burst open. He opened the bathroom door slightly and watched until he felt he could come out without endangering Jack or Boss. He stepped out of the bathroom with his service weapon drawn the instant the three intruders had their backs turned to the hallway. It was pointed directly at Colonel Meyer.

None of the men moved.

Meyer recognized the Captain's voice. "Well, it's your Captain Harrison, isn't it, Jack? How are you, Captain? It's nice to have a chance to chat with you once again." He smiled.

"Cut the crap, Meyer. My gun is pointed straight at your head."

Most of the smirk left the Colonel's face. "Captain, I'm telling you right now, you're interfering with a national security issue. I'm sure you understand, that takes precedence over whatever concerns you might have. Can we pause before this gets out of hand and talk for a moment?"

"We don't have anything to talk about. Like I said, have your man put the dog down and all of you put your hands in the air and turn around. Jack, when they do, take their weapons. Make sure you get all of them and don't get in the way in case I need a clear shot."

None of the men moved. Hamrick and Mullins had been well trained.

Meyer spoke again. "Harrison, I'm warning you, you're messing with something you don't know anything about. You don't want to get involved. This is much bigger than you or your police department."

"I think I know what's going on. You're trying to kidnap one of my men and his police dog. I don't care who you are or who you work for. You don't do that to one of my officers, not if I have anything to say about it."

"You don't. We have a gun pointed at your officer's spine and you can't move fast enough to prevent him from being shot. If the bullet doesn't kill him outright, he'll be a cripple for the rest of his life. You have a gun pointed at me and you'll probably be able to hit one or two of us before we get you. So, it appears we are at an impasse. Can't we talk about this? I'm sure, once you understand the situation, you'll let us walk out of here with your officer and his dog."

"I believe I already understand the situation. You intend to take my officer back to your research facility where you can experiment on him. You want to take his dog back so you can cut him up. Does that about cover it, Colonel?"

Meyer began to understand. "So, Randall told you all that, did he?"

"Yes, he did."

"It was the ravings of a man with severe mental and emotional problems. Surely, since you've heard them, you can understand why we have to get him back to our medical facility. We discovered just a few days ago, he suffered a serious brain injury during surgery when we put his implant in place. Since then, he could have gone berserk at any moment. If that had happened, his implant would have triggered the dog and he would have done the same thing. He honestly believes that he and the dog can talk to each other. Do you know what a liability they've been for your police department? That's why I'm taking them back to Washington. I want to get them the treatment they need and try to repair the damage. I feel terrible about what has happened."

"Nice try, Colonel. It won't work. Boss heard everything about your little deal with the CIA and what you did to Corporal Hamilton and his dog before he and Jack left your little chop shop. He passed it on to Jack. And now, I know about it and so do the Chief and the Mayor."

Meyer's voice hardened. "Then, let me tell you what will work. Do you think I was so stupid I would come in here without backup? I have this house surrounded. It's time for you to drop your weapon and raise your hands."

"Again Colonel, that's a nice try. You're bluffing. If they're out there, why don't you call them in? No? I didn't think so. You didn't come here with more men. You didn't think you'd need them. You expected to surprise Jack and knock his dog out and get them out of here in thirty seconds. Now, let me tell you why all of you are going to walk out of here and leave him and his dog alone from now on. Maybe you're thinking I just happen to be here on a social visit. I'm not. Jack spent some of the afternoon explaining to me what happened to him and Boss and what has happened to other officers and dogs at your butcher shop. I believed him."

"So, what did that accomplish?"

"I took Boss with me to see Chief Hampton afterward, while Jack waited in my office. You filled the Chief in on your program last year, too, remember? Boss showed the Chief what he could do. Then I sent Jack and Boss home. I spent the rest of the afternoon with the Chief and the Mayor before I had an officer bring me here. The Governor will be the next to know. The Mayor is setting up a meeting with him as soon as possible. You think you can get away with kidnapping Jack and his dog and that you might even be able to get away with taking me with you, but, there's just one little problem with that; both the Chief and the Mayor know I was coming straight here and that I was being brought here by one of our men. If anything happens to us, the Governor's people will be knocking on your door the first thing in the morning. The Governor is friends with some important people in Washington. You shouldn't have met with Jack in my office today, Colonel. It was a stupid thing to do."

"That won't matter, Captain. Let's go back to where we began; to national security."

"We can't."

"Why not?"

"Because, if I was worried about that, I'd have already let you walk out of here with my two friends. That's not going to happen. You've heard of newspapers, Colonel? There are still a few of them around, you know. Everything they print goes straight onto the internet."

"What about them?"

"They have a nasty habit of printing things that cops and governments don't like. The newspapers wouldn't have paid any attention if Jack had gone to them with his story about your research. They'd think he'd lost his mind. I had trouble believing him myself, at first. But, I can assure you, if you manage to get by me and the three of us turn up missing tomorrow morning, that won't be the end of it. After the Chief and the Mayor tell the Governor about you, they'll all go straight to the press. They'll provide records to prove Jack and Boss spent time away from regular duty on temporary assignment to you. The records show they spent that time at your facility and had several weeks of light duty for medical reasons after they came back. That might add a little weight to the Mayor's story, wouldn't you think? If the press printed that, it would flash around the world on the net in say, six or eight hours?"

"Maybe," said Meyer.

"Maybe? A story like that would call attention to your little program that you wouldn't like. Like, maybe someone in another country might start believing it's possible to put implants into people's heads and do a little spying of their own. There are at least a couple of countries that have more advanced electronics than we do."

The big man holding Boss was beginning to suffer under the weight of the dog. Meyer had begun to perspire. Drops of sweat appeared on his face.

"They wouldn't go to the press, Captain. They wouldn't do that to their own country."

"They would if they were forced to. Do you want to start raising those hands or do I keep talking?"

"Keep talking."

"I'll make you an offer. From what I just heard you say, you have plenty of other men and dogs to experiment on. From now on, you leave Jack and Boss alone. I don't want you to bother them in any way. If anything ever happens to either of them, like they should disappear for some reason, the Chief and the Mayor and I will go straight to the press. The Governor will back us up. We might even be able to help the other officers and dogs that you've been screwing around with. That's something we'll all have to think about too, won't we? If the press doesn't believe us, they'll still print something, even if it's just to have a laugh at our expense. You wouldn't like that, would you? My offer to you is simple; you walk out of here with your men. You forget about my officer and his dog, we all stay quiet about this and everybody will be happy."

"I can't do that."

"I think you can and you will. After you leave, you better hope nothing bad ever happens to Jack or his dog in the future. You wouldn't want one of them to get hurt on the job and have me start thinking you might have had something to do with it, would you? You have bosses too, Colonel. You're tied in with the CIA. I doubt they'd be happy if they were to find out it was you who screwed up their secret program by letting word about it get out to the press. You might do a little disappearing act of your own. That's exactly what will happen if you ever bother Jack and Boss again. Do you want to raise those hands now?"

Meyer began to slowly raise his hands. He ordered Hamrick to lower Boss to the floor and ordered Mullins to remove his gun from Jack's back. Afterward, they reluctantly raised their hands.

Jack took their weapons.

"Meyer, you can put your arms down. Turn around very slowly and look at me," said Captain Harrison. "You other two, keep your hands in the air. Do we have an agreement, Colonel?"

"It appears you have me at a disadvantage. I'll make the agreement with you, but, you tell your Chief and Mayor that none of you will ever speak of this again except among yourselves. You will not let a word about our program get out to the press. We'll leave your officer alone from now on, but if I ever hear a whisper about any of this in the media, I promise you, we'll come for him and the dog. Then, it will be a matter of national security and enough of us will come to get the job done."

"You have a deal. Before you go, there's one other thing I want to make sure you understand. I don't care who you are or who you know; I don't ever want to see you in my city again. If I do, something bad might happen to you. I don't like you. I don't like people who mistreat my officers and dogs and I don't like to think about what you've been doing to the other K9 teams. I'd love to get a crack at you when nobody was looking. If I ever see you in my city again, you might have an accident. Do I make myself perfectly clear?"

"Yes."

"Good. Now, take your men and get out of here."

"Can we have our guns back?"

"No. We'll keep them as souvenirs. You'd like for us to remember you, wouldn't you, Colonel?"

"The best thing for you and Randall to do is forget you ever met me. I'd suggest you both stay out of Washington, Captain. People have accidents there too, you know," he snarled.

"I've heard about that. You won't have to worry about me coming down there, I can't stand the place. There are too many snakes like you around for my taste!"

Meyer and his men left the house. Jack and Captain Harrison watched through the open doorway as the van doors slammed and the engine started. The vehicle pulled away.

"Whew!" said Jack. "Thank God you were in the bathroom. If they had come in a couple of minutes later…"

"I know. We might all be in the back of that van headed for Washington. My bluff might not have worked once they had the drop on us. Look at my hands. They're both shaking."

"Bluff?"

"Yeah, bluff. The Chief didn't believe everything I told him, even after he watched Boss do his thing. He wants me to bring you and Boss to his office tomorrow at 9 A.M. so he can talk to all three of us. I wouldn't have got us that far if Colonel Meyer hadn't also talked to him about using you and Boss in his program. That's why I told the Colonel to stay out of Baltimore. I don't want to take a chance on him and the Mayor bumping into each other at some social function and comparing notes. I just threw the Mayor and the Governor into my story to scare him. The Chief said it would take a miracle to convince him to go to the Mayor with a story like this, no matter how well they know each other. Maybe it'll be easier to persuade him when we tell him what just happened. Let's not worry about that right now, Boss is beginning to stir. We need to make sure he's alright. Jack, you look terrible. Your face is as white as a sheet."

"Cap, remind me never to play poker with you!"

Chapter 13

Just after 8 o'clock the next morning, Jack's phone buzzed. He tapped the screen. It was Heather and she was crying. He touched the screen again so he could see her face as they talked.

"What is it? Why are you crying?"

"Jack, I've just been fired!"

"Fired? Why?"

"I don't know. Colonel Meyer told me he would be seeing you yesterday. When he came into work a few minutes ago, he walked past my desk without saying a word. I went to his office and took a cup of coffee to him and said good morning. When I asked him how his meeting with you had gone, he threw the cup at me. It barely missed me. It shattered on the wall behind me and hot coffee went everywhere. He started screaming at me and told me I was fired. He told me to get out of the office immediately!"

"He didn't hurt you, did he?"

"No, but he wouldn't even give me time to get my things from my desk when I left. He called security and had two men escort me from the building. They only let me take my jacket and my purse and they searched them before they'd let me leave. I don't know what I did wrong. What happened yesterday, Jack? I don't understand."

"I can't explain Heather, at least not right now."

"He told me not to try applying for a position in another office. He told me I'd never work for the United States Government again as long as I live. What did I do wrong?"

"You didn't do anything wrong. He's angry about something that happened here yesterday and he's taking it out on you."

"What happened?"

"There's too much to go into right now."

"What am I going to do? I've had a government job since I got out of college. I've worked for Colonel Meyer for over two years. I've never caused any problems and I've always been a good worker. Why would he say I wouldn't be able to get another government job?"

"You should go home and try to calm down. He can't just fire you for asking how a meeting had gone. You should apply for unemployment benefits right away. I think you should also talk to the Human Resources Department about getting another government job. Meyer is steamed because of something that happened here, but he should come to his senses in a day or so. If he has any sense of decency at all, he'll treat you fairly. What happened here yesterday had nothing to do with you and he has no reason to fire you. Just let him cool off for a while."

"Do you think that will help?"

"I honestly don't know."

"If it doesn't and he blocks me from getting another government job, I don't know what I'll do. Good jobs in the private sector are almost impossible to find."

"I know. Let me think about this for a couple of hours and I'll call you back. I had no idea what happened between Meyer and me would cause you problems. Will you be alright until then?"

"I think so. I'm almost home."

"Good. I'll call you sometime this afternoon and we'll talk about this. There's something I have to do in a little while and I can't get out of it."

"I won't do anything until I hear from you. Jack?"

"Yes?"

"I miss you."

"I miss you too, Heather."

∞ ∞ ∞ ∞ ∞ ∞

Promptly at 9:00 A.M., Jack, Boss and Captain Harrison walked into Chief Hampton's office. The Chief welcomed them, a trifle woodenly, Jack thought. They exchanged pleasantries and Captain Harrison told the Chief about the attempted kidnapping of the prior evening.

"You've got to be kidding me! Meyer thinks he can get away with something like that? Kidnapping one, maybe two of my officers, along with one of my dogs?"

"He didn't expect me to be there," said the Captain.

"Still, he actually tried to grab Randall and the dog and haul them back to Washington against their will? They're Baltimore City Police Officers, even the dog. He's not going to be pulling that kind of crap in my town! Captain, when you came here yesterday and told me your wild story, honestly, I thought you'd been out in the sun too long. Now, I'm not too sure. I think I'm beginning to believe you. I guess I do need to talk to the Mayor about this. He's going to think I'm out of my mind, the same as I thought you were out of yours yesterday, but I'm going to tell him anyway. Maybe he'll listen to me after he hears about the attempted kidnapping. It'll help that I've known about Meyer's program for a long time. Take Corporal Randall and Boss and go back to your office and wait there until I call you. I'll need you all to come to the Mayor's office later today, I'm sure."

"You know," said the Captain, "if there are any repercussions about this, Meyer is going to yell national security."

"I don't care what he yells. He won't be yelling about national security if he thinks word of what he's been doing down there might leak out to the press. I'm glad you hit him with that."

"I didn't plan it that way. It was just the first thing that popped into my mind. I was trying to buy us some time until I could get that gun away from Jack's back and get a clear shot."

"It was the best thing you could've done. We need to keep a lid on this. If you had shot one of those goons, there'd be the devil to pay."

"I know. We'll go back to my office and wait until we hear from you."

They walked out of the Chief's office. Upon their return to Captain Harrison's office, Jack informed him about his involvement with Heather and the earlier phone call from her. The Captain was concerned.

"Do you think Meyer might try to use her to get to you?"

"What do you mean?"

"He may have fired her so it wouldn't look bad on him if she disappears in a day or two. He could have her kidnapped and use her to try to force you to go back to D.C."

"I didn't think about that. What should I do?"

"How do you feel about her?"

"I like her, a lot. So does Boss."

"I think the sensible thing for you to do is call her and tell her to put a few things into a suitcase and come up here, immediately. If he decides to grab her, we can't do anything to prevent it if she's down there. Tell her to get up here right away."

"When should I call her?"

"Right now; it may already be too late."

Within moments, Jack was speaking to Heather.

"Heather, this is Jack. Do you trust me?"

"Yes, I do. Why do you ask?"

"I need you to do something and don't ask any questions. I want you to throw a few things into a suitcase and come up here right now. Don't wait. Go to a crowded restaurant near my place and get something to eat and stay there until you hear from me. Don't leave, even if it's a police officer or someone you know from work unless you have me on the phone and I say it's ok. Can I trust you to do that?"

"Yes, but why? You're scaring me."

"I want you to be scared. This is important. Don't wait, do it right now. Ok?"

"I will, but why can't I go to your place?"

"It's not safe. I don't want to tell you where to go in case our phones are bugged. When you get near my house, I want you to find a crowded restaurant, call me and tell me where you are. I'll have a police car nearby and I'll get it to you as soon as I hear from you. You'll be brought to where I am. If you're in a public place, it will be harder for someone to harm you. Don't leave the restaurant with anyone, officer or otherwise, until you talk to me. Will you do this for me?"

"Yes, Jack. I'll leave here within ten minutes. Why do I have to leave right away and be so careful?"

"I'll tell you when I see you. I can't leave here and I can't do anything to help you until you get to Baltimore. Don't speed, but get here as quickly as you can. If you have problems while you're on the way, call me instantly."

"I will."

He tapped the screen and broke the connection.

"I hope all that isn't necessary, but when you're dealing with people like Meyer, you never know," said the Captain. "It's better to be safe than sorry. If we hadn't had that run in with him yesterday, I'd think we were being overly cautious."

∞ ∞ ∞ ∞ ∞ ∞

In less than two hours, Jack, Boss, and Captain Harrison were sitting in the Mayor's office with Chief Hampton. The Chief had already explained to the Mayor all he knew about the Colonel and his research, the situation concerning Corporal Hamilton and his dog and the results of the experiments on Jack and Boss. He'd also told him about the attempted kidnapping of the prior evening and the Colonel's involvement with the CIA.

Mayor Arnold Pembroke was a huge man, thick around the middle of his body and neck. The extra weight he carried did not conceal his considerable intellect. He asked Jack to explain all he knew about the secret program and he and Boss were asked to demonstrate their abilities once again.

Afterward, Mayor Pembroke broke a brief silence.

"Chief, if I hadn't just seen this with my own eyes, I wouldn't have believed it."

"Does it really stretch the imagination that far? It was just a matter of time before scientists could do something like this. We've been placing implants into people's heads and bodies for a long time."

"Why would we use this kind of technology to have dogs talking to us? You'd think if we could do this, we'd use it to have people silently talking to other people, not dogs."

"It does make sense to use the technology in this way. It could have good law enforcement and military applications. Colonel

Meyer told the Congressional committee that originally funded the program that the implants were to be used by police departments and the military in their K9 units. It's possible he may not have even been working with the CIA at that time. We don't know when they took over the research. They may have recruited Meyer after he was already with the program for a while."

"You're probably right. Now the next question is, what do we do to protect Corporal Randall and his dog? They'll never be safe if the CIA is involved and this Colonel Meyer told them about why he was coming to Baltimore yesterday. Since he wasn't certain they could communicate with each other until then, he may not have told the CIA. Now, he'll be afraid to tell them. Still, I doubt he'll leave Corporal Randall and his dog alone. They're too valuable to him. He probably began making plans about how to retake them as soon as he cleared the city line. Whatever we do, we'll have to keep it to ourselves. Do you know what kind of political football this could be? There's no telling how many people in Washington are involved. We can't go to Governor Thomas about this and there's nowhere else to go. The Governor is a good man, but his primary concern is his political future, first, last and always. If he thought he could get any brownie points by turning Corporal Randall and his dog over to Meyer, he might do it. I don't believe he would, but it's a possibility."

"Those are my thoughts, too."

"We have another complication," said Captain Harrison. He explained about Heather.

"Let me think about this for a moment," said the Mayor. He turned toward the window and stood there gazing out at the city for several minutes.

Finally, he turned back to the three men and the dog.

"Corporal, from what I'm being told, your dog understands everything I say. Is that correct?"

"Yes, sir, he does."

Pembroke smiled. "As serious as all this is, I'm intrigued. I talk to my own dog when I'm at home. I've always wished he could understand me better and that I could comprehend what he tries to tell me. I would love to be able to hold a conversation with the old boy. You know why I'd like to be able to do that, don't you Boss?"

Boss walked over to the Mayor and placed his paw into his hand. The Mayor scratched the dog's head.

"He says to tell you, he does, sir," said Jack. "He understood everything you said."

"Good. Hopefully, anyone who would want to harm either of you might overlook the fact that he can do that."

"The men with Colonel Meyer didn't. The first thing they did yesterday was to dart him and knock him out."

"Yes, but they were with Meyer. If other men come without him, they might not know Boss can think and plan ahead. That could be an advantage. Corporal, what would happen if you were unconscious? Would he still be able to use your mind?"

"I don't believe so, but I'm not certain. He can while I'm asleep, but I don't know what would happen if I was unconscious. I had trouble reacting yesterday when they knocked him out. It really slammed me."

"That's something to keep in mind."

"We will, sir."

"Getting back to this Miss Jamison; didn't I read something in the newspaper recently about you and Boss being involved in a shootout?"

"Probably, but it was no big deal. Boss and I had the day off. Three guys tried to rob a carryout window while we were getting a bite to eat and we took them down."

"Wasn't there a young lady with you? Was she this Miss Jamison that Captain Harrison is talking about?"

"Yes sir," said Jack.

"We might be on to the answer to our problem. I hope she gets to Baltimore safely."

"Why would that help?"

"Weren't there some children caught in the crossfire?"

"No. There were some people in the area who were eating and there were a few kids with them, but none were ever between the shooters and me. Heather did grab one child to prevent him from running toward the parking lot where some of the shooting took place, but all the rest of the people were either taking cover behind trees and picnic tables or on the ground. All of the shots the robbers fired went well over their heads."

"No, they didn't."

"Yes, they did."

"Listen to me, Jack. This Colonel Meyer might be able to get his hands on you despite everything we do. If he meets secretly with the Governor and asks him to give you up, the Governor might do it. If Meyer and the CIA lie and say you and your dog are national security risks and the Governor didn't understand the situation, you could be history. You and Boss would just disappear and nobody would ever know what happened to you. You're a relatively unknown Baltimore City Police Corporal and to everyone else, Boss is just a dog. But, what if you were both big heroes? We may be able to use that press idea Captain Harrison dreamed up, only in a different context. I'm going to call every friend I have at every television station and newspaper in the City of Baltimore and tell them about the shooting and about all the lives that you, Boss and Miss Jamison saved."

"Why?"

"If Boss saved some kids from almost certain death, the news media would be full of it. They know their audience loves it when a dog saves a child. It would be on every television news program and in every newspaper in town and it would be all over the internet. What if Miss Jamison helped Boss pull several of the children to safety, right in the middle of a gun battle with bullets flying everywhere? That would be an even bigger news story. The public loves tales about dogs saving children. The only thing that would make it better would be if a woman was helping the dog save a bunch of kids while a lone police officer was involved in a life and death gun battle with several robbers. Meyer might be able to get away with kidnapping an unknown officer and his dog, but I bet he wouldn't be so eager to grab a famous hero police officer, his hero K9 Police dog and his hero girlfriend. If the three of you disappeared and Captain Harrison and the Chief and I went to the news media then, our story would get major coverage."

"But, that's not what happened, sir," said Jack. "Heather did grab one of the kids, but the child was never even close to getting between the shooters and me. It wasn't the easiest takedown Boss and I have ever done, but it wasn't the hardest, either. Boss took two of them out of action while I nailed the third. We're no more heroes than any other officer and dog that find themselves in a situation like that."

"Nonsense, my boy, you're being far too modest. But, that doesn't matter. The media will love you for it. Is this Miss Jamison pretty?"

Jack blushed. "Yes, sir, she's very pretty."

"That will make it even better. The media will love that, too. They owe me some favors and they're always looking for the next big story. We'll give it to them."

"But, sir, that robbery happened several days ago."

"That won't matter. The story was just overlooked by the press for a while, that's all. The more I think about this, the better I like it. The world needs heroes to look up to; they inspire the rest of us. I'm also thinking about the good publicity it will give to the B.C.P.D. and the City of Baltimore. If this comes off the way I think it will, you and Boss and Miss Jamison will be safe from now on. This Colonel Meyer will think more than twice before he tries grabbing you and Boss again and he won't be able to use her to get to you. You'll simply not be worth him taking the gamble of having his program exposed. He won't like it, but he'll eventually get used to the idea. You and Boss will probably have to spend a lot of your time doing public relations appearances with Miss Jamison and things like that for a while, but you've done them before. Somebody has to do it and it might as well be you. If you don't go along with this, we may not be able to protect you. There's also another angle. Governor Thomas would love to be the President one day, or at least a United States Senator. Once he sees the three of you on the news, he'll want to do public appearances with you. He might get more mileage out of something like this than he would by giving you up to curry favor with the feds. We won't even have to tell him about what Meyer wants with you. Boss, make him understand. This is probably the only way the three of you will ever be safe again."

Boss grunted. *"He's right, Jack."*

"I know, boy, I just don't feel right about taking more credit for that arrest than we deserve."

"Mr. Mayor, what about Heather? She may not go along with this," said Jack.

"I imagine she will, once she understands the gravity of the situation. Does she know about this connection you have with your dog?"

"I don't believe she does. She knows about the implant program, but she has no idea anything ever came from the experiments on Boss and me. We didn't want her to be caught in the middle if Colonel Meyer ever came after us. We thought the less she knew about it, the better."

"That's understandable. The first thing we'll have to do is get her here so she'll be safe. Then, I'll call my media friends and ask them to do me a favor. They'll get the first shot at a big story and some of them will enjoy making heroes of the three of you. They have to print something in their papers and the television stations have to put interesting things on their news shows. A hot item like I'm going to give them may even get them national exposure. To sweeten the deal, I'll owe them each a favor. They'll like that."

"We have to get Heather here safely. That's my biggest concern right now, sir" said Jack. "We're not in a romantic relationship, but Colonel Meyer doesn't know that. He might not have thought about using her to get to me yet, but it won't be long before he does. I don't want to see her get hurt."

"None of us want anything like that to happen. Call her and find out where she is. We need to get her here as quickly as possible."

Jack pulled his phone from his belt and spoke into it.

"Heather."

She answered on the second ring. "Jack?"

"Yes. Where are you?"

"I'm on Interstate 95, almost to the Baltimore Beltway. It took me longer to get here than I thought it would. Traffic is heavy."

"Can you tell if you're being followed?"

"I don't think I am, but I really haven't been watching for anyone. What's this all about?"

Mayor Pembroke motioned for Jack to hand the phone to him.

"Miss Jamison, this is Mayor Arnold Pembroke. Corporal Randall and I will explain everything to you very soon. Right now, I'd like to arrange for some of my police officers to intercept you. One of them will drive you here and another will bring your car along. Will you please do that for me?"

"Yes, if Jack says it's alright. He told me not to get into a car with anyone unless he says it's ok."

"That's fine, Miss Jamison. Here's Corporal Randall again. Explain to him where you are and I'll have my officers' rendezvous with you."

He handed the phone back to Jack.

"Heather, it's ok. Where are you now?"

"I just turned south onto the Beltway."

"Get into the slow lane and turn on your four-way flashers. Drive about ten miles per hour under the speed limit and keep going until you see police cars behind you. The Chief is giving the order for them to find you right now. They'll pull you over to the side of the highway and you'll be brought here where we'll explain everything to you."

"Ok, Jack. I hope you have a good explanation for all this. You've really frightened me."

"I do. I'll see you in a little while, ok?"

"Ok. I'm going to get off the phone. Traffic is heavy and I have to get to the slow lane. If I have any problems, I'll call you back."

Almost an hour passed before Heather was escorted into the Mayor's office by a patrolman. The Mayor thanked the officer and dismissed him.

Then he turned to Heather and said, "Miss Jamison, you know Corporal Randall and his dog, Boss. I'm Mayor Pembroke. The other two men are Chief of Police Hampton and Jack's K9 Department Supervisor, Captain Harrison."

"Yes, sir. Mr. Mayor, what's going on? I've had a very strange day."

The Mayor grinned and a twinkle came into his eyes. Jack was beginning to understand why he received so many votes from the women of Baltimore, regardless of his girth.

"I'm sure you have, Miss Jamison. It's about to become a lot more extraordinary. Captain Harrison, please go with Miss Jamison into one of our private meeting rooms and take Corporal Randall and Boss with you. Have them explain to her about their amazing abilities. Chief Hampton and I have a few reporters to call. Once you're through talking, all of you come back to my office. We have a lot of planning to do."

∞ ∞ ∞ ∞ ∞ ∞

Jack had feared Heather might have difficulty accepting the fact that he and Boss could speak to each other through the electronic implants. He was also afraid she might find their abilities to be unsettling or distasteful. He could feel that Boss was jittery, too.

When Jack finished telling her about what the implants had done to them, the big dog walked to where she was seated and put his head on her lap.

She scratched his ears and said, "I thought there might be more going on between the two of you than you were letting on, but I had no idea it went this far. After some of the things I've heard in the office, it makes sense. Can you really talk to each other? Just like I'm talking to you right now, except in your heads? Boss, can you understand everything I'm saying?"

Boss whined. He placed his paw into her hand and slowly nodded his head.

"Captain Harrison, you believe this, too?"

Captain Harrison chuckled. "I do. At first, I thought Jack was losing his mind, but, yes. I believe it."

"I'm not having as much trouble accepting this as you might think. I've heard things I wasn't supposed to around the office and I've suspected Colonel Meyer has been attempting to do

130

something like this for a long time. I just didn't know he'd been this successful. I was only allowed into the research facility a few times while I worked for the Colonel and some of those times were to see Jack and Boss while they were recuperating from surgery. There have been a lot of other officers and dogs undergoing surgery, too. Jack, how much does the Colonel know about you and Boss being able to communicate?"

"He knows enough to try to kidnap Boss and me and take us back to Washington to perform experiments on us. If Captain Harrison hadn't been at my house yesterday evening and used his gun to prevent it, Boss and I would be Meyer's prisoners right now."

Heather looked startled. "So, that's what this is all about. Is that why he fired me this morning?"

"Yes. I'm sorry that happened to you, but it is. He obviously became enraged when you asked about us. That's why we wanted to bring you here. We couldn't take a chance on you being hurt. He might have tried to kidnap you to use you to force Boss and me to go back to the research facility. The Mayor and the Chief are working on a plan to protect the three of us right now."

Heather turned back to the Captain. "Thank you for protecting them from the Colonel. They can't go back there. I have a Top-Secret security clearance and I'm not able to tell you what I know, but if he wants them enough to kidnap them, they are in great danger."

"Boss found that out while we were recuperating before I even knew we could talk to each other. We're not going back," said Jack.

"What do we do now?"

"We go back to the Mayor's office and see if he's had any luck with the press. He'll have to tell you about his plan. It's a little too embarrassing for me to talk about."

They walked back to the office where Mayor Pembroke explained his plan to Heather. She agreed to everything he proposed. Just before they left his office, the Mayor walked to his window and folded his hands behind his back. After several minutes, he turned to them.

He said, "Before you go, I want to explain to all of you exactly how I feel about this situation. Throughout history, there have always been men like this Colonel Meyer, who abuse the authority that is given to them. We read about them in history books. They fooled their followers into believing that what they were doing, they were doing for the common good. But, in truth, they and the people who helped them were only looking for ways to enrich themselves and gain power. Their names and faces changed, but the methods were always the same. Their pathways to success were littered with the broken bodies of the maimed and the dead. Meyer is of their ilk. He sees himself as someone who is performing a necessary task, someone who is doing a job where the ends justify the means. It doesn't matter to him how many people or animals die along the way. He's an ambitious and dangerous man, more so now that he has run into what he sees as a roadblock on his way to achieving his goals. I wish there was some way to stop him, but I'm afraid we will not be able to do that. I'll have to consider it a success if we're able to keep the three of you out of his hands. I wish I could do something to help the other men and dogs that are in his clutches, but unfortunately, I don't see any way to do that. If he's controlling this program and exerting so much power, he's certain to have allied himself with other, possibly much more dangerous men."

Chapter 14

Mayor Pembroke's friends in the media responded with fervor and their narrative quickly outgrew his expectations. The story of Corporal Jack Randall and the heroic police dog, Boss, broke on the local 5 o'clock news programs. Reporters, who had raced to the scene of the shooting to record their stories, described how Boss saved the lives of several children and innocent bystanders, while he and Corporal Randall fought three crazed gunmen to a standstill.

Heather was portrayed as the beautiful young woman that dodged bullets in an open parking lot, as she helped Boss rescue children who were caught in the crossfire between Corporal Randall and the desperate robbers who refused to surrender. The story became more embellished with each retelling as the different branches of the media competed to satisfy a public hungry for more information about the shootout.

There were additional developments the next day when several eyewitnesses came forth to give interviews. They told reporters how Corporal Randall and his brave dog had withstood a hail of gunfire and fought with the robbers as Heather snatched children from the very jaws of death.

Some of the children who had been on the riverbank were interviewed. They told how Miss Jamison had run between the shooters and the officer and his dog and pulled them to safety while using only her body to shield them from the flying bullets.

Two of the witnesses had managed to capture shaky video recordings of the event on their "smart" eyeglasses. Police investigators had not been told about them.

Television stations quickly bought the legal rights to the recordings and broadcasted them to the public along with the interviews. Heather could be seen pulling a child to safety. The struggle between Jack, Boss, and the robbers was also shown. The videos were edited to make the incident seem even more terrifying than it had been.

It didn't matter that what the witnesses said were gross exaggerations of the truth. The local media forwarded the stories to national and international news agencies as quickly as they could be recorded.

Something unusual occurred that didn't find its way into the news broadcasts. Lawbreakers that had been taken down by Jack and Boss during other arrests began to boast about the scars on their arms and hands where Boss had clamped his teeth into their flesh at one time or another. It quickly became a badge of honor among the criminal element in the City of Baltimore to have had your arms marked by the huge police dog.

Almost overnight, Jack, Heather, and Boss became media sensations as their images began to appear in news magazines, social media and on almost every television news show across the nation and around the world. Reporters, cameramen, and photographers waited outside of buildings and hid behind trees to record their every move.

Requests for interviews with the three heroes became unmanageable for the Baltimore City Police Department. The Mayor called a press conference at the courthouse, where Jack and Heather were interviewed by the media as Boss stood at their sides. Members of the press were also invited to a special dinner where the three of them were to be honored. It would be held at the new Civic Center in downtown Baltimore.

At the dinner, Jack was officially promoted to the rank of Sergeant and Boss was promoted to Corporal. Both Jack and Boss were presented with Medals of Honor by the City of Baltimore. The City presented Heather with a gold medal for her bravery during the incident and she was asked by the Mayor to take a position with his office as Goodwill Ambassador.

Civic organizations began making requests to have Jack, Heather and Boss appear at gatherings where more awards and certificates of merit would be presented to them. They began a seemingly unending series of personal appearances to promote drug awareness, public safety and other problems the police department had to deal with daily.

As Mayor Pembroke had predicted, Governor Thornton Thomas seized upon every opportunity to be at their sides to proclaim his personal friendship with the newly dubbed "Trio of Heroes" whenever awards were being presented. He was quick to recognize how much the national attention they were receiving would help satisfy his political ambitions when he ran for higher office in the future.

Mayor Pembroke was facing a strong opponent in the next election. His appearances with Heather, Jack and Boss and the resulting favorable publicity assured his re-election.

Chief Hampton was pleased with the number of requests for less well known K9 officers and dogs to make public appearances when Jack and Boss were not available because of scheduling conflicts.

The police department's budget was increased as large monetary grants were made to the agency by both the state and federal governments. The unexpected windfall was welcomed by the underfunded Chief of Police and he used it wisely. Crime statistics began to drop.

Captain Harrison's budget was increased. He immediately requested that more officers be hired and assigned to the K9 Department as quickly as dogs could be trained for them.

∞ ∞ ∞ ∞ ∞ ∞

It seemed everyone except Colonel Meyer had benefitted from the news stories. He did not take it well. He fumed silently for hours on end as he paced the floor in his office, but he knew his hands had been firmly tied by the Mayor and the media. Jack Randall and his dog would have to wait for another day.

Chapter 15

As the weeks ticked by and media attention began to fade, Jack and Heather's friendship blossomed into love and Boss was delighted. He had become more devoted to Heather with each passing day. She returned the love of the huge dog.

The three were constantly together. It seemed only natural that Heather should move her belongings from the apartment she rented in downtown Baltimore to the home that Jack and Boss shared.

The evening before Jack planned to ask her to make the move, he and Boss went for a walk to the park to watch the sunset. Jack informed Boss of his intentions as the sun was sinking below the horizon. Jack was moved once again by the great dog's pleasure as he watched the colors play across the sky.

Boss was happy Jack had finally made up his mind.

"I've known this was coming for a long time."

"Do you think it's wise of me to ask her to move in? We'll always have the threat of Colonel Meyer hanging over us. I'd like to ask her to marry me, but I'm not sure it's fair to do that when at any moment, he could come back to haunt us.

"She's going to be with us most of the time anyway. It would be wonderful having her live with us. I think you should ask her how she feels about it. It's been over six months since our run in with the Colonel. We all could still be in danger, but I think if he hasn't done something by now, he never will."

"I've been putting off asking her until you and I could find the right time to talk. I believe she'll accept the risk, the same way she has accepted everything else about us."

"I think you should be upfront with her about our concerns."

"It's not just that. If she was any other woman, I might be worried about her being jealous of you. Some people get upset with how much attention their spouse gives to a pet. This situation is way more complicated than that."

"I've been your friend and partner for years, but I'm not a pet. I am a dog, but I don't believe you should ever think of me as a pet."

"I couldn't agree more, boy. You're so much more than that. You're the best friend I've ever had and nobody could ask for a better partner. It will certainly be different from an average man asking his sweetheart to move in with him and his dog, won't it?"

"I know. I'm going to enjoy watching you squirm when you ask her."

"You would, you devil. You're going to have to do your part to help me. You want her to be with us as badly as I do, don't you?"

"I do. I love her too, Jack. Let's don't wait. Call her and ask her if we can come over."

Jack pulled the phone from his belt and spoke her name.

∞ ∞ ∞ ∞ ∞ ∞

Heather greeted them both warmly when they arrived at her apartment and listened intently as Jack asked her to share their home with them. She had never returned to Washington. She'd hired a moving company to bring her belongings to Baltimore where she'd rented an apartment from a company that provided around the clock security for tenants.

"Why didn't you ask me before now? I've wanted to be with you."

"We didn't want you to get hurt and we weren't sure we could always be there to protect you. We're both still worried that Colonel Meyer might have his people try to kidnap you."

"I understand that, but, if we had to be apart, I think you should have talked to me and let me help make that decision."

"I know. I should have. I thought you knew we were more worried about your safety than we were our own. You know how much I've, no, we've come to love you. We've wanted you to be at home with us for a long time, but we haven't wanted to put you in any more danger than you were already in. If you were with us and the Colonel tried to kidnap us again, he couldn't very well just take us and leave you behind to tell about it. Boss and I are his real targets. That's why we thought you shouldn't live with us. We've been thinking, though, if he was going to try something, he would have by now. I know this is a heck of a way to ask, but would you consider maybe, beginning to plan a wedding? Our wedding?"

She laughed and took his right hand into both of hers and kissed him.

"I've been wondering how long it was going to take you to ask me."

"So, you'll do it?"

"Of course I will, you big lug. I've loved you since the first I saw you in Washington and how could anyone not love Boss? I'll be the first woman in history to marry a man with a dog who can talk to him. It's too bad I'll never be able to tell anyone about it. Jack, I just thought about something. What will we do when we, you know, when we….?"

Boss looked uncomfortable. He whined and shook his head.

Jack laughed. "I've thought about that. Boss and I can break our connection anytime we want. I'm sure he'll be enough of a gentleman not to intrude on our private times."

Heather blushed and smiled. "I can see we're going to have to adapt to some situations that regular people wouldn't have to deal with."

Chapter 16

There were many wedding plans to be made. When Governor Thomas received word of the approaching nuptials, he asked to be allowed to take part in the wedding ceremony. Jack and Heather told him they would be honored to have him there when they were married. Since Heather's father had been dead for many years, when the Governor asked to give the bride away, she agreed to his request. He asked if he could inform the media. When they gave him permission, he had his office make the announcement. The media eagerly sent reporters to cover the story.

During the wedding ceremony, only one reporter and cameraman was allowed inside the church. The lucky pair would share the story and video with the other members of the press who would be waiting just outside of the building.

Captain Harrison stood as Jack's best man as Governor Thomas gave the bride away. Mayor Pembroke delivered the words of the wedding ceremony. Boss sat proudly beside his partner as Jack and Heather made their solemn vows to each other.

Chief of Police Hampton and members of the K9 Department provided an honor guard as Jack, Heather and Boss left the church and entered a limousine for the short ride to the reception. The three men who had taken part in the ceremony and their wives rode in the Governor's limo. The press was ecstatic.

At the reception, Jack and Heather presided over the duties of a newly married couple. Boss stayed quietly at their side as dinner was served. The big dog was served his own plate of prime roast beef while the wedding party and the rest of the guests ate.

After the wedding cake was cut, it was time to open gifts. The Governor asked for the members of the media to be allowed into the reception hall as he made his presentation. The entire wedding party smiled and stood patiently as reporters and photographers crowded into the room to ask questions and take pictures. The Governor beamed as he and his wife stood beside the happy couple and presented them with the gift of a week in the Governor's suite at the finest hotel in Maryland's Ocean City. He also provided a limousine for them to use during their honeymoon. Arrangements had been made so Boss could stay with them. He'd be able to see the sunrise over the ocean every morning from the balcony of their suite.

Boss, as always, was the perfect gentleman.

Chapter 17

A year passed by quickly. During that time, Jack, Heather, and Boss continued to make sporadic public service appearances. Another media storm erupted when it was announced that Heather was carrying their first child. Soon after, she ceased making appearances as her body grew larger.

A few months into the pregnancy, a sonogram indicated the baby would be a boy. Heather broke the news to Jack and Boss that evening when she arrived home after a late afternoon Doctors appointment. A quizzical look appeared on Jack's face.

He said, "I'm happy that everything is going so well with the baby. What will we name him?"

Heather said, "I don't think we should consider any name except, John Junior. We'll call him, Little Jack. Maybe we should call him Little Boss instead of Little Jack. That would work."

Jack spoke for Boss. "Boss says to tell you, whatever we want to name the baby is fine with him."

She looked down at the dog.

"You make me love you more every day, boy."

She attempted to bend over to hug him, but the bulge caused by the baby she was carrying prevented her from doing so. He licked her hand and gazed into her eyes.

She said quietly to him, "With both of my big guys around, I know our little boy will always be safe and happy."

∞ ∞ ∞ ∞ ∞ ∞

The big day finally arrived and it was not a moment too soon for Heather. She was a small woman and the pregnancy had not been easy for her. Jack was by her side in the delivery room when their son was born. Boss was not happy that he couldn't be allowed to go to the hospital with them. He was forced to wait impatiently with Captain Harrison until they returned.

Jack brought Heather and the baby home the day after delivery. When Heather was made comfortable on the big sofa, Boss stood silently for many moments while gazing into the eyes of the new arrival that she held in her arms.

Finally, he looked up at Jack.

"Please tell Heather I said this to you. You know that I love you and Heather beyond all others, but it's hard for me to describe what I'm feeling right now. I've never seen anyone or anything that has caught my heart like our little boy. My heart is breaking. I love him so much."

"I know, boy. I feel the same way. I'll tell Heather exactly what you said."

Jack told Heather what Boss had just said to him. She reached over and placed her hand on the huge head. Boss returned his gaze to the face of the baby until he felt her touch. He moved closer to her and put his head across her arm as tears filled her eyes.

"Boss, you are so sweet. I don't know what we'd ever do without you; you big gorilla."

∞ ∞ ∞ ∞ ∞ ∞

Not long after the baby was born, Jack was promoted to Lieutenant and began spending more hours working behind a desk when on duty. From now on, he would be assigned to permanent day shift. Except for the brief times when he and Jack had to be out on the streets together, Boss stayed home with Heather and Little Jack.

Jack's mind was always connected to Boss, even at a distance. He took comfort in knowing that no matter what happened while he was away from home, Boss was watching over his wife and son.

Little Jack grew rapidly. As he began to crawl, then take his first toddling baby steps, Boss was there to support him. He very patiently put up with the eye gouging and the ear pulling that all dogs must endure when they live with little children. Rather than being upset about it, he took great joy in knowing the little boy loved him so much. By the time Little Jack reached his third birthday, he and Boss had become inseparable. He was everything to the boy; a friend and companion as well as a protector and guardian.

Jack missed having his friend constantly at his side, but he was happy knowing that everything was going so well with his family. Almost every evening when weather permitted, he and Boss would go to the park so Boss could watch the sunset. They had almost forgotten about Colonel Meyer and the secret program that had locked their minds together.

Chapter 18

Jack's phone buzzed. He tapped the screen and Heather spoke.

"Honey, would you please stop by the grocery store and pick up some milk and vegetables on your way home? I need them to make dinner this evening. We're out of both."

"I'd be happy to do that. Do you need anything else?"

"No, that should about cover it. Be sure to get enough veggies to last us a few days, though. I think we have enough of everything else to make it through the rest of the week."

"Ok. I'm leaving early today, so I'll have plenty of time to run by the store. I'll see you when I get home. Love you."

∞ ∞ ∞ ∞ ∞ ∞

Jack was making his way down the fruit and vegetable isle in the grocery store when his head suddenly began to swim. An overwhelming sense of foreboding slammed into him as he began to black out. He fell to his knees.

A store employee rushed over to help him sit on the floor before he completely collapsed. Slowly, his mind began to clear.

He reached out, *"Boss, where are you, boy?"*

Boss was not there. Within moments, his phone buzzed. He reached to his belt and pulled it out of the case and touched the screen.

"Jack, it's Heather." There was fear in her voice.

"What is it?"

"It's Boss. He just collapsed."

"I felt it. It knocked me off my feet. What happened to him?"

"I don't know. He and Little Jack were romping and suddenly he fell over. I can't wake him up. He seems to be breathing normally, but something is very wrong with him. Where are you? Can you come home right away?"

"I'm at the grocery store. I'll be there in five minutes."

Jack was still groggy. He shook his head back and forth to try to clear the cobwebs from his mind. With the help of the store employee, he rose to his feet and began to make his way out of the store. He felt better when he walked into the sunshine.

He ran across the parking lot and jumped into his police cruiser. In minutes, he was sliding to a stop in front of his home. He slammed the gear shift lever into park and dove out of the car and rushed into the house. He had begun to feel the connection again just as he was approaching the driveway.

Boss was lying on his side in the middle of the living room floor and attempting to get up. Little Jack was crying and sitting between his legs and stroking the long black hair on his side. Heather was kneeling over them and wringing her hands.

Jack rushed to his side. *"What is it boy, what's going on?"*

"Don't---know. Don't remember. Just---woke up and ---tried to sit up, ---can't.--- Haven't felt---just right---for a-----all--day."

"Don't try to get up. I'm going to get you to a doctor. Just lie still. I'll carry you."

Jack struggled under the weight of his friend and with Heather's help, managed to carry him outside to the back seat of the car.

"Jack, where are we going to take him? Let me get Little Jack and my purse. I'm going with you."

"I'm not sure you should. We shouldn't upset Little Jack any more than he already is. Do you mind if I take him by myself? It may not be anything serious. I'll be as close as the phone and you'll know how he is at all times. When I get him settled in, I'll call you and the two of you can come to where we are in your car."

"You're right, of course. Where are you going?"

"To the emergency room at the hospital."

"You can't waste time doing that. They won't let him in because he's a dog. You'll have to take him to the animal hospital. It's not far from here and it's run by a man named Edwards who is supposed to be a very good veterinarian."

Jack hadn't had time to think about what to do. When he left the grocery store, he was still dizzy. The meaning of Heather's words finally began to sink in.

"My gosh, you're right. I wasn't thinking clearly. I haven't considered him to be a dog for such a long time. To me, he's a person."

"He is to me, too. Get him to the vet as quickly as you can. While you're on the way there, I'll call Captain Harrison to see what he can do to help. Call me as soon as you get to the vet. If I get off the phone first, I'll call you. Are you alright to drive?"

"I think so. Why?"

"You're as pale as a ghost."

"The sudden shock hit me hard. When Boss passed out, I almost passed out too."

"Then, don't drive fast in case Boss loses consciousness again. Just drive steadily and make sure you can get safely stopped if you have to."

"Ok. I can't wait any longer. I'm getting him to the vet."

Jack jumped into the car and pulled out of the driveway. He spoke to his dash computer and asked for directions to the veterinary hospital.

He turned his head toward the back seat. *"Hang on, Boss. I'm going to get you some help. Stay with me, boy."*

"I--- think I'm feeling--- better. Something is wrong--- with my legs---on---my left side. I'm going to try---to---to--get up."

"No, don't do that. You might make whatever is wrong with you worse. Just hang on. We'll be at the vet's office in a couple of minutes."

Moments later, Jack drove into the parking lot at the veterinarian's office. He was glad it was not later in the day when the office would be closed. It was not quite 3 P.M. He put the car in park and shut off the engine.

"Wait here, boy. Don't try to get up. I'm going to run inside and tell them I need help bringing you in."

Jack ran into the building and told the receptionist his dog was in the back seat of his car and there was an emergency. He insisted the veterinarian would have to see his dog right away.

146

She rushed into a side cubicle to get Doctor Edwards. Edwards turned the cat he was examining over to another veterinarian and called for an assistant to accompany him. The three men hurried outside to the car.

They gently picked Boss up and carried him inside. They took him into an examination room and laid him on his right side on a stainless-steel table. Edwards began taking Boss's vital signs as Jack told him what had occurred.

Jack pleaded with the doctor. "You have to help him. Do you have any idea what could be wrong with him? Nothing like this has ever happened before."

"It could be a lot of things. How old is he?"

"He's not even nine years old."

"He's past middle age. It's probably not his heart, although the beat is a little irregular. He seems to have no strength in his left legs. I don't want to frighten you, but he may have had a stroke. There's no way to tell for sure until I get some pictures of what's going on inside his head."

"It can't be. He's way too young to have had a stroke."

"You may be right, but he's showing the symptoms. I need to do a scan right away."

Jack thought about the implants.

"Just be careful with him, please. Doc, I don't care what this costs. You've got to make him better."

"The money doesn't matter; I know who you are. I've seen you and this dog on television. His name is Boss and you're Lieutenant Jack Randall. It's an honor to have you in our office. Don't worry, we'll give him the best care that we possibly can. I'm going to have to take him into a back room to do the scan. Please take a seat in our waiting room while we do that and I'll let you know as soon as we're done so you can come right back to him."

"I don't want to leave him."

"You won't have to for very long. Just bear with us for a few minutes while we do this."

"Ok, but let me know the second you're through."

"I will. Now please, let us do what we need to do. As soon as I find what's wrong with him, you'll know, too."

"Thanks, Doc. You have no idea what he means to me. Please do your best."

"I promise you, I will."

"I'll call my wife and let her know we're here."

"That's the best thing you could do right now."

Jack walked out of the room and closed the door behind him.

"Boss?"

"----Yes?"

"Don't be afraid. They're going to put you into a machine for a few minutes to see if they can find out what's wrong. It won't hurt at all. Just lie still when they put you in there. I'll be in the next room and I won't leave you. I'll come back to you as soon as they take you out of the machine."

"I heard---what he said. I--think--- you're more afraid--- than I am. I'm not in--- pain. My legs don't hurt, --- just won't--- move."

"I'll call Heather. I hope she's gotten in touch with Captain Harrison."

"Good. Do that---now. Don't----worry."

Jack pulled the phone off his belt to call Heather.

She answered almost instantly.

"Heather."

"Are you at the vet's?"

"Yes. I'm at Doctor Edwards' office. He just took Boss back to do a scan of his head. Did you get the Captain?"

"Yes. He said you've done the best thing you could do for Boss right now. I told him where I thought you had gone and he's making some calls. He wants us to get him to the best veterinarian the P.D. uses as soon as possible. He said he'll do whatever it takes to get a regular doctor for him if it's necessary. He said not to worry about the bill; the city will take care of it. I know you're not worried about that right now, I just thought you'd like to know what the Captain said. Does Doctor Edwards have any idea what's wrong with him?"

"He suspects a stroke. He can't be sure, that's why he's doing the scan. It's not just his legs; his heartbeat is irregular."

"Jack! What if it's the implants?"

"That's exactly what I'm afraid of. I don't think the scan will see the sensors. If it does, I'll explain it, somehow. I don't want to put Doctor Edwards in any danger."

"You're right. We need to get Boss to the police department's veterinarian in case the Colonel hears about this."

"I'm afraid for him, Heather. He can't talk to me clearly. He says he's not feeling any pain, but he still can't move his left legs."

"Just do what's best for him. I'll call you back when I hear from the Captain again."

"Ok. I'm going to get off the phone. I want to be ready to go back to him as soon as Doctor Edwards calls me."

"Jack, I love you. Please tell Boss that Little Jack and I love him, too."

"I don't have to; he heard you when you said it to me. We love both of you."

∞ ∞ ∞ ∞ ∞ ∞

Ten minutes later, Jack was back in the cubical with the veterinarian and Boss.

"*I'm here, boy.*"

"*I---know. --- Good.*"

"Doc, did you find anything?"

"I'm pulling the pictures up right now."

He touched his computer screen several times as he studied the images.

"I think I see the problem."

"What is it?"

"There appears to be a small spot, no, two small spots, here and here. Do you see them?"

He pointed at the dark smudges on the image of Boss's brain.

"I do. What are they?"

"I'm not sure. They don't look like aneurysms or leaking blood vessels or clots. I'm not exactly sure what they are. They appear to be some type of lesion."

"What's that?"

"A lesion is like a sore, a raw spot. They're usually caused by an infection or some kind of irritation. They're in exactly the right place to be causing the kind of problems he's having."

"It's hard to believe something that small could do this to him. They're so little, I can barely see them."

"There's something else here, too. There are some tiny straight lines coming from the top of his head and leading toward his neck. I've never seen anything like them. If I hadn't zoomed in on the pictures so much, they'd be invisible. I don't think they're anything to worry about, though; they're too straight to be biological. It must be some kind of electrical static that happened during the scan."

"What can we do about the lesions? Will his legs be permanently disabled?"

"I suggest a strong antibiotic. I'd like to get an I.V. line in him and get the drip started right away. We're going to have to keep him here until we see if he has a positive reaction to the medicine. If he doesn't, we'll try something else; maybe a combination of two different antibiotics. At this point, it's about all we can do for him. If they are lesions, they may clear up without causing any further damage. If they don't, we may need a surgeon to go in to see what can be done about removing or cauterizing them. As far as permanent damage, it's too early to tell if his legs will be disabled, but it's possible they could be. The first thing we need to do is use antibiotics to try to clear up the lesions. Then, we'll worry about his legs. If we can get the lesions to heal, the problem with his legs may just go away."

"Doc, I don't want to hurt your feelings, but as soon as I left the house with Boss, my wife called my Captain. He wants us to get him to a police department veterinarian. Do you think moving him would make him worse? My concern is entirely about him."

"I think for right now, it's best not to move him at all. I'm sure you know that brain tissue is very delicate. If you want to take him to your police department's animal treatment center, it's your call of course, but I wouldn't suggest moving him unless you absolutely must. We should see if the antibiotic is going to help him. If your veterinarian would like, he can come here and we can consult on what the best treatment would be. If you'll get me the contact info, I'll email the scans to him so he can look them over. If it's alright with you, I'm going to put in the I.V. line and get the antibiotic going into him. I'm also going to give him a mild sedative. It will make him sleepy and help keep him calm. We don't want him to try to get up."

"I understand. Let's get it started. Doc? I can't leave him. I hope you don't mind, but regardless if you do or not, I'm going to stay with him until he can go home or be moved. Is that alright with you? If I can't stay with him, I'm going to take him to the police department's veterinary hospital where I can."

The veterinarian talked as he worked to insert the I.V. line. "Under normal circumstances, it wouldn't be, but you're a police officer and he's not a regular patient. We have a cot you can sleep on. We'll put him and the cot in a bigger room in the back of the building so you'll have privacy. We have a refrigerator and a microwave back there in our kitchen in case you'd like someone to bring food to you. We'll put a pad on a table for him so he'll be more comfortable and put guard rails around the sides so he doesn't fall off if he gets restless. If you're staying with him, we won't have to put him in a cage."

"How long will you be here?"

"I usually go home at 6 P.M. when we close."

"What if he needs help during the night?"

"We have someone who comes in before I leave and she'll be here most of the night. Her name Doctor Shelly and she's one of our best vets. One of our other vets will come in at 3 in the morning to relieve her. They'll check the I.V. drip from time to time to make sure the line stays open and Doctor Shelly will replace the antibiotic and sedative bags around midnight when they run out. Other than that, they'll leave you alone unless you ask for assistance."

"What if we need you?"

"There's really nothing more I can do for him until we know how the lesions react to the antibiotic. I should tell you, I don't like what I'm seeing. One of the lesions is very close to the area of the brain that controls the heartbeat. That's almost certainly why his heart isn't beating normally. We could have a surgeon go in right away to look at the lesions, but because of where they're located, trying to remove them could kill him. We're going to have to see what the antibiotics do for him before we try anything else. If the infection keeps spreading......."

Chapter 19

Captain Harrison arrived within the hour to see if Boss was improving. He had stopped by Jack's house on the way to the veterinarian's office to pick up Heather and Little Jack. Boss was drowsy from the sedative and was content to have his friends with him.

When the Captain arrived, he immediately called the K9 Department veterinarian. He'd already seen the scans that Doctor Edwards had sent to him and agreed that Boss should not be moved. They both felt the antibiotic drip should continue for twenty-four hours to see if there was an improvement in his condition before making any further decisions.

Doctor Edwards gave a door key to Jack when he closed the office at 6 o'clock. There was nothing more he could do, but he stayed until 7:30 before going home to his family. He told Jack to call him at home if he thought it necessary, no matter what the hour.

Captain Harrison stayed with them until 8:30 when Heather said she needed to take Little Jack home. He had fallen asleep in her arms. She kissed Jack and Boss and left with the Captain. She was crying as she walked out of the clinic. Boss fell asleep soon after they were gone.

Jack slid his chair close to the table where Boss slept and put his head down on the edge of the pad that Doc Edwards had put on it to make Boss more comfortable. He placed his hand on his friend's shoulder and closed his eyes. The feeble connection with Boss's mind was still affecting him.

At midnight, Doctor Shelly came into the room and changed the plastic antibiotic and sedative bags that were feeding into the I.V. drip. A few minutes later, Boss woke up.

"Jack?"

"Yes, boy?"

"We need to talk. My mind is clearer now."

"*I know. I can feel it. What would you like to talk about, my friend?*"

Jack placed his hand on Boss's head and began to gently caress it. Boss's thoughts were coming to him stronger than before, but they were still weak.

"*I need to ask you some questions. I hope they won't trouble you too much.*"

"*Nothing you say could trouble me.*"

"*I hope not. I've thought about something from time to time, but I never thought we'd need to talk about it so soon. I thought we'd have many more years to be together.*"

"*What is it, boy?*"

"*What happens to us when we die?*"

"*What do you mean?*"

"*I've seen people on television talking about God and a place called Heaven. They said people have souls and that good people go there when they die. Do good dogs go to Heaven when we die?*"

"*Boss, I can tell you this much, if there is such a place as Heaven, it wouldn't be Heaven unless we had our dogs there with us. I'm sure, if I get there, you'll be there, too.*"

Tears began to trickle down his face.

"*I'm sorry; I was afraid I'd upset you.*"

"*I'm not upset about your question. I just feel so helpless because I can't do anything to make you better.*"

"*I know, but it's not your fault. I know you'd give your life to save mine, just as I would for you. Could I ask you another question?*"

"*You know you can.*"

"*I don't understand about God. If He loves us so much, why would He let people like Colonel Meyer do the terrible things he does to people and to dogs and the other animals? I don't understand why God allows that to happen.*"

"*I don't know, boy. It doesn't make any sense to me, either. You heard what Mayor Pembroke said. People like the Colonel have been around since the beginning of time. We do our best to* stop them, but some can't be stopped. If we do manage to get rid of one of them, another usually shows up to take his place."

"That's a shame. I hope that one day, something can be done about him. He's a very bad man."

"I know, boy. If I had the power to stop him, I would."

"There is something that's very important to me. My mind is not focusing well and I don't know how much longer we'll be able to talk, so I need to make sure you understand something in case I lose the ability to communicate with to you. You heard what the doctor said; the medicine might help me and it might not. If it doesn't, he'll want a surgeon to cut open my head to try to do something about the lesions. The sensors are probably causing the problem. You know that, don't you?"

"Yes. I'm so sorry, boy. It was my decision to have those things put into us. If I hadn't let them do it, you wouldn't be lying on that table."

"I wish you didn't feel that way. I'm not at all sorry. If you hadn't agreed to it, we would never have been able to understand each other the way we have and be as close as we've been. I wouldn't have missed what we've shared for any reason. In every way, the implants have been a wonderful gift to me. I want you to promise me something while my mind is still clear. If the medicine doesn't help me, I don't want an operation. Please promise me you won't let it happen. I understood what the vet said as well as you did. I might not be able to walk again even if he can get rid of the lesions. If he has a surgeon operate on my head, he'll find the sensors and take them out. If that happens, I'll never be able to talk to you again and never see another beautiful sunset. I wouldn't want to live like that. You understand, don't you?"

"I do, but I can't lose you."

"I know, but you wouldn't let them do the operation unless I could still talk to you and say it was alright, would you?"

"No, boy. I promise I wouldn't. Not unless you said it was ok."

"There's something else I want you to promise me. I heard what the vet said about the lesions being close to the area of my brain that makes my heart beat. If I don't make it, I want you to *get Little Jack a puppy that looks just like me. He should never be without a dog. I don't want you and Heather to be without one, either. Will you promise me you'll do that? If I can't be with you, he'll remind you of me. I don't want you, Heather or Little Jack to forget about me."*

Tears continued to flow down Jack's cheeks.

"We could never forget you, boy, not for any reason. I promise you I would do that, but that's something I'd have to do if you don't make it. You're talking like you won't ever be going home with me again. We're going to do everything we can to make you well. It may not be the sensors that are causing the problem. When we get the lesions cleared up, your legs will be fine again. You'll be as good as new."

"I hope you're right, but just in case that doesn't happen, there is one more thing I need to ask you. No matter what happens, if I die, don't let Colonel Meyer take me away from you. I don't want him to put electricity through me or cut out my brain, even if I am dead. Will you promise me you'll keep him away from me?"

"I promise you, Meyer and his people will never touch you again. I'll always keep you with me, no matter what happens."

"Thank you, Jack. I'm sorry, but I'm feeling so tired. I'm going to have to stop talking to you for a while. I'm so sleepy, it's hard for me to keep my eyes open. It must be the sedative that's making me feel this way. While I'm still awake, please tell me more about Heaven."

Jack's tears continued to flow. They were dripping off his chin and onto the table.

"I'll try, boy. It's hard because I don't know much about it. Nobody really does. It's supposed to be a beautiful and happy place in the sky where there's no pain and nobody ever gets old or dies. There's no sickness there. If there are things wrong with you when you die, when you get to Heaven, you are well again. Bad people like Colonel Meyer aren't allowed to go there."

"That sounds nice. If I don't make it through this, will you come to me there when you die?"

"I will. I'd look for you forever if I had to; until I found you."

"I'm glad. I wouldn't want to be there without you."

156

"I wouldn't want to be there without you either, boy."

"How would I find my way to Heaven?"

"There's supposed to be a bridge made of rainbows that will take you from here to there. You'd see it right away."

"I can almost see them now. I love to see rainbows. The colors are so beautiful."

"I know you do, boy. So do I. You would see the bridge and you'd cross over it. Your legs would be well again as soon as you saw the rainbows, so you'd be able to walk right across the bridge. The sun is always shining and warm and there's a beautiful field of flowers on the other side of the bridge. You'd see other dogs over there that have gone on before of you. Those dogs are waiting for the people they love to come be with them. They're all good dogs, so they'd be happy to see you. The ground is nice and soft so you would have a good place to take a nap whenever you wanted to. You would wait there for me until I could come for you. Time is different there. It would only seem like a couple of minutes to you before you'd see me coming across the bridge to find you. Then, we'd go on to Heaven together."

"I'd be waiting there for you, right at the end of the rainbow. I love you, Jack."

"I love you too, boy."

Jack continued to weep.

Boss's eyes slowly closed as the sedative in the I.V. once again took effect. Jack continued to stroke the big head as his friend drifted off to sleep.

Moments later, Boss whined quietly and his right feet began to twitch as if he were dreaming. His chest rose and fell heavily. Suddenly, he stopped breathing. Jack jumped to his feet as his connection with Boss's mind once again began to waver. Boss opened his eyes and raised his head from the table and began to breathe again. A single thunderous bark roared out. His eyes slowly began to close as his head fell back to the table. All movement ceased. The mighty heart had stopped beating. The big dog was gone.

Jack's knees buckled as the connection between their two minds slipped away. He'd never felt so alone. He gripped the railing and pulled himself back to his feet and bent over the table. He buried his face deep into the thick fur on Boss's neck.

Doctor Edwards arrived at 7 A.M. He'd come in early to check on Boss before beginning his regular appointments. He found Jack sitting on the table. He was holding Boss's head in his lap.

Chapter 20

Jack asked Doctor Edwards to have Boss's body removed immediately for cremation and to have it done that very day, if possible. The veterinarian made the necessary phone calls and assured Jack it would be done that afternoon. The ashes would come back to his office within forty-eight hours. He said he would keep them there until Jack came back for them. Colonel Meyer and his people would never touch the big black dog again.

Jack asked for a clipping of Boss's hair. The veterinarian removed a pair of shears from a cabinet drawer and took a large cutting off the long hair on the dog's shoulder and placed it into a plastic bag and handed it to him.

Jack caressed Boss's head one last time. He turned to the veterinarian and shook hands with him and thanked him for all he had done. He returned the key the veterinarian had given him the evening before and walked slowly out of the office. His feet felt as if they were made of lead. A gentle rain had begun to fall during the night. It seemed as if the sky was weeping for his lost friend. He opened his car door and slid wearily into the seat and drove home to break the sad news to Heather.

Little Jack was still asleep when he arrived, so he and Heather could share their grief without disturbing him. When he awoke, they explained that Boss had passed away during the night and wouldn't be coming home. The boy couldn't understand why Boss wouldn't be coming back, but he was old enough to know that both of his parents were terribly upset.

Afterward, Jack called Captain Harrison and told him Boss had died. When they hung up, Captain Harrison called Chief Hampton and informed him.

The Chief immediately ordered that all regular uniformed Baltimore City police officers place black bands around their upper left arms and trim their badges with black crepe while on duty for a week-long period of mourning. Every police dog would wear a black crepe covered collar. He then called his friends in the media and informed them of the passing of one of Baltimore's finest police officers.

∞ ∞ ∞ ∞ ∞ ∞

The public's attention was once more drawn to the great black dog. A large picture of Boss with the Medal of Honor around his neck was trimmed in black and hung on the Wall of Honor in the Baltimore City Courthouse. Pictures and videos of Jack, Heather, and Boss flashed around the world once again as the news spread of his untimely death.

Jack and Heather took comfort from the letters and sympathy cards that began to arrive at the K9 Department from across the nation.

Seven days after his passing, Boss's ashes were given a police escort to the courthouse, where a memorial service was to be held in his honor. Nothing the City of Baltimore could do seemed to be enough to honor him. The street in front of the building was closed to traffic as several thousand people and dozens of news reporters and cameramen gathered in the open area in front of the steps. A podium had been placed on the wide landing in front of the massive doors. The people were there to say goodbye to what they had come to think of as, their dog.

As the service began, twenty uniformed police officers lined the steps and stood at attention as Captain Harrison carried the urn containing Boss's ashes to a marble table beside the lectern. After placing the urn on the table, he snapped to attention and saluted it.

Many of the city's K9 officers and dogs stood at attention on each side of the podium. K9 officers and dogs from various police departments from across the State of Maryland stood with them. Each officer wore the traditional black crepe trimmed badge and a black armband. Each dog wore a black crepe collar.

The service began. Chief of Police Hampton was the first to speak. He thanked the people of Baltimore and the officers that had arrived from other communities for coming and asked for a moment of silence to honor Boss's memory. He then introduced Mayor Pembroke.

The Mayor spoke at length of his memories of the big dog and his sadness when he heard of his passing. When he finished speaking, he introduced Governor Thomas.

The Governor explained how, because of Boss and the other dogs and members of the Baltimore City Police Department, the streets were once again safe for citizens to walk without fear of becoming victims of crime. When he finished speaking, he returned to his seat beside Jack, Heather, Little Jack and Captain Harrison.

The Governor had decided to run for the Presidency of the United States. According to all the latest polls, he was almost certain to win the next election. As he sat down, Jack leaned over and asked him if he had a few minutes to talk after the service. The Governor nodded his head.

When the service concluded with a salute from the Honor Guard, Jack asked the Governor to accompany the Captain and him to the Captain's office where they would have privacy.

Three of the Secret Service agents who had been assigned to guard the Governor walked with them and stood beside the door as they entered the office. Captain Harrison closed the door behind them so the guards wouldn't be able to hear what was being said. Governor Thomas was given a seat in the big chair behind the desk.

Jack said, "Sir, it looks like unless something unexpected happens in the next few weeks, you'll soon be our next President."

The Governor smiled. "It's looking that way. Won't it be grand to have someone from the State of Maryland sitting in the Oval Office?"

"Yes sir, it certainly will."

The Captain spoke. "Governor, Jack and I would like to ask a favor of you. We would like you to investigate something once you take office."

"If I'm elected, nothing I could do would be too good for either of you."

"Good. We've uncovered something very wrong in Washington that we can't do anything about. We'd like you to have it investigated when you get there."

The Governor's face took on a more serious demeanor. "So, you want to talk police business?"

"Yes sir, we do. What if I told you there is a secret program in Washington with a certain Lieutenant Colonel Joseph Meyer in charge, where K9 police officers from across the nation are being lured under false pretenses and sometimes held against their will while researchers perform bizarre medical experiments on them and their dogs? Would you look into it?"

"I'd find that hard to believe. We don't do things like that in this country."

"Of course, you would, but I assure you, it is happening. What if I told you that not too long ago, Lieutenant Randall and Boss were part of that program and not always willing participants? What if I told you that Colonel Meyer and his people performed surgeries on them and put things into their heads and that one of those things caused Boss's death? What if I told you, that a few years ago, I had to stop this Colonel Meyer and two of his thugs at gunpoint, from kidnapping Jack and Boss in their own home and taking them back to D.C. for more experiments?"

"You're a Baltimore City Police Captain. Of course, I'd believe you, but you know how the system works. I'd need to see some evidence before I could do anything about it."

Captain Harrison took a large yellow envelope from the top of his desk that contained computer discs and paperwork. He handed the envelope to the Governor.

"There's evidence here, certainly enough to warrant an investigation. The Chief knows about this and so does the Mayor. They'll verify what I'm telling you. Unfortunately, it's out of our jurisdiction and we can't do anything about it. Colonel Meyer calls it "national security". In this file are the names of some of the researchers, the phone number of Meyer's office at the Pentagon and the address of the government research hospital where Meyer supervises the surgeries that are performed on the officers and dogs. You'll also find the address of the clandestine research facility where Jack and Boss were kept. Officers and their dogs are taken there before and after surgery. Horrifying experiments are carried out at that place. You'll find personnel records from our office that show the dates Jack was on temporary assignment to Colonel Meyer while the experiments were being performed on him and his dog. You'll also find the last names of the two men, Hamrick and Mullins, who along with Colonel Meyer, tried to kidnap Jack and Boss. You'll find the names of a Corporal Hamilton and his dog, Drake. They were with the New York State Police Department. They went into that research facility the same time Jack and Boss did and never came back out. The dog was killed and dissected against Hamilton's will and Hamilton was put through terrible pain while undergoing experimental procedures. He went mad because of the things they did to him and his dog. You'll find the contact information of Hamilton's supervisor in the envelope. I looked him up and called him in his office in New York. According to him, Hamilton "accidently" died while undergoing surgery in Meyer's research facility. Other officers and dogs have also disappeared there."

"How did you find out all these things?"

"From information Jack gathered while he was at Meyer's facility and research I've done. There are notes from conversations the Chief, Jack and I had with Meyer. Then, there's Heather. She used to be Meyer's secretary. That's how she and Jack met. She had a Top-Secret security clearance and can't tell us everything she knows, but you, when you become President, could override that restriction. We believe the CIA is also involved. There must be records about this somewhere in Washington, Governor. There are too many people mixed up in it and too much money being spent for there not to be. This file will help you get started with the investigation. That program has got to be stopped."

The Governor stared at the envelope in disbelief. Finally, he looked into Jack's eyes.

"You saw some of this happening."

"I did, sir."

"You met this Corporal Hamilton from the New York State Police Department?"

"I did."

"And they performed experiments on you and Boss?"

"They did."

"Captain, would you testify about the attempted kidnapping and what you did to prevent it?"

"I certainly would, with great pleasure."

"Jack, are you and Heather both willing to testify about this, even if it meant there might be danger involved for you and your family?"

"We are. We've been living under that threat for years, so another year or so wouldn't make that much difference. Governor, what they did to Boss caused his death. They did the same thing to me that they did to him. What took his life, could take mine tomorrow. We're used to living with threats, sir."

The Governor banged his fist on Captain Harrison's desk. "I'm making a promise to you, right now. If I'm fortunate enough to be elected President, I'll put the FBI on this and that program will be fully investigated and shut down, even if I need to call for Congress to do a formal investigation. This Colonel Meyer and anyone who has been helping him will be put away for a long time. This is the United States of America. I repeat; we don't do things like that in this country!"

Jack smiled. "I'm glad you feel that way, sir."

"I'm sure you're aware, Jack, before you and Boss came along, I was just a run-of-the-mill State Governor. The positive attention you, Heather and Boss have brought to the City of Baltimore and the State of Maryland has helped me get to the door of the Presidency. I'm not ungrateful. I promise you, if I'm elected, I'll get to the bottom of this and heads will roll. I feel I owe you, Boss and Heather at least that much."

"Thank you, sir," said Jack.

"There's something that might interest you that has been in the news for the past few days."

"I haven't had much time to keep up with the news, Governor."

"No, of course, you haven't. Since the media people became certain I'll be elected, they've been speculating on who I might have in mind for Cabinet members. Keep this under your hat, but if I'm elected, I'm going to appoint Mayor Pembroke as the Attorney General. He's a good and brilliant man. I'm sure you know he was a great Maryland State's Attorney before he was elected Mayor of Baltimore. If what you're telling me is true, he'll want to go after this Colonel Meyer and his program as badly as you want me to. If anyone can get to the bottom of this, Pembroke can. We'll shut Meyer's program down and put him and his people in jail, national security or no national security and no matter who is involved. We'll see if what they did to you can be undone. We'll also make sure any other officers and dogs that have been victimized by him will have proper treatment and we'll do our best to find out what happened to the officers and dogs that have gone missing."

"Thank you, Governor. That's how I hoped you'd feel. I wish my friend Boss could have heard what you just said. I believe it would make him rest easier. Maybe somewhere, he did hear you."

∞ ∞ ∞ ∞ ∞ ∞

After Jack left the Captain's office, he walked back to the podium to get Heather and Little Jack and to retrieve the urn that held Boss's ashes.

They took the urn home and carried it to a table in the living room where he and Heather had prepared a place earlier in the week. There was a large picture of Boss hanging on the wall behind it. They had put the clipping of hair that had been taken from Boss by Doctor Edwards under the glass in the bottom right corner of the picture frame. Boss's Medal of Honor and his other awards had been hung on the wall around the picture. The big dog would never be forgotten and would always rest in a place of honor in their home.

Epilogue

Jack waited almost two months for his grief to subside. Some of the pain would never go away. There were empty places in his heart and mind that time would never heal.

One afternoon, while Little Jack was taking a nap and Heather, was busy cleaning the house, he got into his car and drove out of the city. When he returned home, he walked inside with something hidden inside his jacket. He called Heather and Little Jack to the front room of their home. He still had a promise to honor.

"Guess what I got for us today," he smiled and said.

"What is it, Daddy?"

Jack bent down and took a small black male German Shepherd puppy from inside his jacket and placed it on the floor before his wife and son.

Little Jack squealed with delight and bent over to greet his new friend. Jack stood up and locked eyes with Heather for a long moment. He reached for her hand.

Jack looked down at his son. "So, what do you think we should call him?"

"He looks like a tiny Boss. I think we should name him, Little Boss," he said.

The End of Book One

The Rainbow Bridge

There is a bridge connecting Heaven and Earth. It is called "The Rainbow Bridge" because of its many colors. Just this side of the Rainbow Bridge, there is a land of meadows, hills, and valleys with lush green grass. When a beloved pet dies, the pet goes to this place. There is always food and water and warm Spring weather. Those old and frail animals are young again. Those who have been maimed are made whole again. They play all day with each other. But there is only one thing missing. They are not with their special person who loved them on earth. So, each day, they run and play until the day comes when one suddenly stops playing and looks up. The nose twitches, the ears are up, the eyes are staring, and this one runs from the group. You have been seen. When you and your special friend meet, you take him or her in your arms and embrace. Your face is kissed again and again. You look once more into the eyes of your trusting pet. Then, you cross the Rainbow Bridge together, never again to be separated.

(unknown author)

Baltimore Blackie

Book Two

BALTIMORE BLACKIE

Blackie was lying in his cage, alert, but calm and seeming unaffected by the noise the other dogs were making when Jack walked down the aisle between the cages. Blackie's head turned in Jack's direction. Suddenly, his eyes locked on the officer and he stood up. As Jack approached the cage, the dog yelped and jumped to the door of his enclosure. He pushed his nose against it and began to claw at the door.

Jack hurried to the door and pressed the palm of his hand flat against the coarse metal mesh so that his skin would touch the dog's muzzle. Blackie closed his eyes and began to make a low whining sound that was almost inaudible to Captain Harrison. The hair on the Captain's arms began to stand up. Jack stood there for many moments. After what seemed to Captain Harrison to be an eternity, Jack turned toward the window and nodded his head. He'd found a new partner. The Captain smiled...

BALTIMORE BLACKIE

Prologue

June 16, 2033

Colonel Robert "Bull" Baker was not happy. He was here to do a favor for a fellow officer and he didn't like to be kept waiting. He'd been cooling his heels in this little room for the past fifteen minutes; if something didn't happen within the next five, he was going to leave. He was only in town for ten days. He'd returned from the Iranian front lines the day before and had better things to do, like walking back up the hallway and making the acquaintance of that cute little WAC Lieutenant he'd met on his way through one of the Pentagon's security checkpoints.

The old hag sitting at the receptionist's desk was smirking. She seemed to know he was growing impatient and was enjoying every moment. The nametag on her blouse, Hattie Crutchfield, seemed to fit her well.

The buzzer on her desk went off.

"Hattie?"

"Yes, Colonel?"

"Please bring Colonel Baker in."

"Yes sir, we'll be right there."

She looked over at him. "Colonel Meyer will see you now, sir."

"It's about time."

Baker stood up from his chair and followed her into the office of Lieutenant Colonel Joseph Meyer. When he entered, she left the room and closed the door behind her.

Meyer and Baker had known each other at West Point. Baker had been the athletic type and had pursued amateur boxing while in the military college. He'd developed the habit of lowering his head and butting when he was fighting against a more skilled opponent, hence the nickname, Bull. After leaving West Point, he was ordered to combat school. He now was the commanding officer of a combat outfit in Iran.

Meyer had been known as an egghead. He was just tall enough to pass the Army's height requirement for an officer and had been assigned to Army Intelligence after graduation. Baker had been promoted to full Colonel the year before and Meyer hadn't been pleased when he'd heard about it.

Meyer stood up from his desk and extended his hand.

"How are you, Colonel Baker? It's good to see you again. Congratulations on your promotion."

"Thanks. I'm not so good, Joe. I stopped by to do you a favor and you kept me waiting for over fifteen minutes. If this was my office, I'd get rid of that old bat out there and find somebody better to look at. A prettier receptionist would have made it easier for me to wait."

"I'm sorry about that, Colonel. I was on the telephone with an emergency. The research we're doing doesn't always work out the way we want and I had to handle a problem right away. Hattie isn't very pretty, but she does her job well and she knows how to keep her mouth shut. I inherited her from the last guy that had this office and she only has a year or so to go before she retires. When she leaves, I'll find somebody more appealing to the eye."

"I won't take up much of your time. I saw somebody on the way down the hall I need to talk to. I'm only here for a few days before I go back to Iran."

"What can I do for you?", Colonel Meyer asked.

"I'm trying to do something for you. The last time I saw you, you asked me to keep my eyes open for anybody in my K9 unit that seems to have an unusual rapport with his dog. I think I have somebody serving under me that you might be interested in."

"Oh? Who is it?"

"His name is Sergeant John Randall. His buddies call him Jack."

"What's unusual about him?"

"He's an excellent soldier; the kind who constantly volunteers for duty that none of the others want. He had one dog that was shot and killed while they were on patrol and another was assigned to him. He and that dog meshed like two fingers on the same hand. They have this ability to work together that's hard to describe. My officers think it's almost uncanny. It's like each of them always knows what the other is doing and they've been extremely effective. Between the two of them, they've probably saved the lives of a dozen or more of the other K9 teams that they've worked with. You asked me to keep an eye out and let you know if I ran into a team like that."

"How long have they been together?"

"About nine or ten months. Randall's enlistment is just about up and he'll be going home in a few days."

"Is the dog going with him?"

"No. That's my doing. I need this guy, Joe. Before Randall came, the enemy was running all over us. When he got there, things began turning around and we started winning instead of being pushed back all the time. He's the kind of fighter who motivates other soldiers and I can't afford to lose him. I told his Lieutenant to make whatever kind of deal that was necessary to keep him with us. Randall refused. I even talked to him myself. I offered him a job in the K9 Division training dogs and soldiers in the States if he'd re-enlist and stay with me for another year. He turned me down flat."

"You can't make him stay if he doesn't want to."

"I know that, but if he won't play ball with me, I'm not going to give him what he wants. He can go home if he feels he has to, but the dog stays in Iran."

"Did Randall tell you what he plans to do when he gets home?"

"Nope. He said he'll think about that after he gets back. He's really into dogs though and he'll probably end up somewhere working with them. You know how these guys are, once they've been in combat, it gets into their heads and they can't stay away from the excitement. He'll probably find a job with a police department that has a K9 unit."

"Where is he from?"

"Actually, not far from here. He's from Baltimore."

"Colonel, we're doing some pretty important intelligence work. If this soldier and his dog have the kind of rapport you say they do, they could be very important for my research. Would you reconsider your decision and let the dog come home with him? I could approach him about helping us after he gets back."

"I would if he hadn't made me so mad when we talked. You know how I can get when somebody doesn't do what I want them to do. His Lieutenant says he's more of the thinking type of soldier and all the killing he's involved with gets under his skin. He says he's done his duty and wants to go home. That just seems downright un-American to me. I'm not going to reward him by letting him take the dog home with him, so I'm going to have the dog assigned to another soldier. I'm telling you about Randall so maybe you can get together with him after he gets back. Check out his service record. I don't know what's going on with your research, but if he's the kind of man you're looking for, just hook him up with another dog when he gets home and go from there. He worked well with the first dog until the mutt got himself killed and he did even better with his second. He'll adapt just as well to another one if you set it up."

"I wish it worked that way, Colonel, but it doesn't. I need the man and dog together. Maybe we can make some kind of deal. Can't we work something out between the two of us?"

"No! Drop it, Joe! The dog stays in Iran. You can do whatever you like about Randall."

"Well, if your mind is made up, I guess that's that. I appreciate you telling me about your soldier. Is there anything I can do for you before you go back?"

"No, not unless you're a female. Look me up if you get over to Iran in the next year or so."

"I can't help you much with the females and I hope I never have to set foot in Iran. If you wind up at the Officer's Club tonight, I'd be glad to buy dinner and set you up with drinks for bringing me this information."

Baker laughed. "Will you spring for two? I might just take you up on that if the young lady at Security is as friendly as I think she is. That's where I plan on taking her."

Meyer stood up and extended his hand. "I'll be more than happy to do that. Thanks again for your help, Colonel. I hope I see you there."

Meyer waited until he was certain Colonel Baker was well down the hallway before he called Hattie into his office. He had no intention of letting the matter drop. He'd just have to go around Colonel Baker and bring this Sergeant Randall and the dog into his program and hope Baker never found out about it.

"Yes, Colonel?"

"I need you to do something right away. Pull up the service record on a Sergeant John Randall. I don't have his service number, but it shouldn't be hard to find out what it is. He serves under Colonel Baker in Iran and his enlistment period is just about up. He's in a K9 unit. While you're at it, find out what Randall's Lieutenant's name is and get his contact information for me. I think I'll have to talk to him."

"I'll do that as quickly as I can, sir."

"And Hattie, what you're doing stays in office."

"Yes, Colonel.

∞ ∞ ∞ ∞ ∞ ∞

Colonel Meyer called the cell phone number of Lieutenant Turnbull and waited for the connection to go through. It was still early in the day; it should be evening in Iran. He hoped the Lieutenant wasn't out in the field. He'd have to be careful how he handled this. It usually didn't turn out well if you were caught going behind the back of a superior officer.

"Hello, Lieutenant Turnbull speaking."

"Hello, Lieutenant, this is Lieutenant Colonel Joseph Meyer calling from the Pentagon."

"How can I help you, sir?"

"I understand you have a soldier serving under you, a Sergeant John Randall?"

"That's affirmative, sir."

"I understand that he works with a dog and that the Sergeant's enlistment is up in a few days. Will the dog be returning to the States with the Sergeant?"

"No sir, he won't be. Our C.O. gave orders for the dog to be assigned to another soldier."

"Lieutenant, the last thing I want to do is cause problems between you and your Commanding Officer, but it is imperative to me that the dog is returned safely to the United States. I intend to reunite him with Sergeant Randall when he gets home. I checked your service record and understand that you will be leaving Iran within the next few weeks and I see that you have thirty days of leave coming. Will you be going to your next post right away or will you be going home for a while?"

"I plan on taking leave and going home to Connecticut for a few weeks. Then, I'll report for my next assignment."

"If I pull some strings here, can you make a request to bring Randall's dog home with you when you return? I'll see to it that it doesn't cost you anything to bring him with you and I'll also see to it that your plane trip home is paid for if you're successful. I'll need you to keep him with you for a few days when you get back until I can arrange to have him brought to Washington. I need Randall and the dog for some important undercover security work that I'm doing."

"I'll see what I can do, sir. Randall is a good man and I'd like to see him keep his dog. I'll try to get all the paperwork pushed through channels before Colonel Baker gets back."

"Good. I'll give you my phone number so you can call me if you run into problems. I need you to keep this under your hat. Don't even tell your C.O. about it. The program I'm working in is Top-Secret and I don't want word of our conversations getting out. Is that clear, Lieutenant?"

"Yes, sir. I'll do whatever I can on my end, sir."

"Thank you. I won't forget about you helping me."

∞ ∞ ∞ ∞ ∞ ∞

August 14, 2033

Colonel Meyer's office phone rang.
"Yes, Hattie."

"There's a Lieutenant Turnbull on the phone, sir. He says something important has come up."

"Put him on, Hattie."

"Yes, sir."

"Hello, Lieutenant. What's up?"

"Colonel, I'm at my home in Connecticut. I'm afraid I have some bad news for you. It's about Sergeant Randall's dog, Kelly."

"What is it, Lieutenant?"

"Sir, I don't know how it happened, but the dog got out of the house the night before last while my wife Molly and I were asleep. We weren't expecting anything like that; we thought he was happy here. Molly has a young female German Shepherd and she and Kelly were getting along very well."

"Is he lost?"

"No, sir. We've managed to recover him, but I'm sorry to tell you, he was hit by a car. We didn't notice he wasn't here yesterday morning when we woke up. We left home to do some shopping and saw that he was gone when we got back. All the doors and windows were locked while we were away, so we knew he had to have gotten out somehow during the night. We started checking and found where he'd pushed the bottom of a screen loose in a window we'd left open while we were asleep."

"Is he dead?"

"No sir, but he was hurt pretty badly. We called the Sheriff's Department and the Humane Society right away when we found out he was missing and asked them to have their people be on the lookout for him. We drove around for hours trying to find him. A Deputy called us about four hours ago and told us they found him. It's odd. He was almost twenty-five miles due south of here. I know there's no way he could possibly know where Sergeant Randall lives, but it does seem strange, doesn't it, sir?"

"Not if you're involved in the kind of research I'm doing, Lieutenant. I assume the dog is being seen by a veterinarian?"

"Yes sir, he is. We went straight to the veterinarian's office where he was taken as soon as the Sheriff's Department called us. He has a terrible concussion. The vet says he thinks he'll be ok, but he'll never be a military dog again. Also, two of his legs are broken. They're not severe breaks; the vet says they're simple fractures that will heal. It will just take some time."

"That's a shame. I guess I won't be able to use him in my research program after all. I don't want Sergeant Randall to find out about this. Lieutenant Turnbull, I want you to stay in touch with me. I'll see to it that the vet bills are all paid by my office. Do you want to keep the dog after he comes back from the vet or will you need me to find another home for him?"

"We'll keep him, sir. Broken legs or not, he's a very special animal. Molly will look after him when I return to duty and he'll always have a good home with us."

"Thank you, Lieutenant. I need to ask a favor of you. You work with the K9 troops and their dogs. Will you let me know if you run into another team like Sergeant Randall and his dog? It would mean a lot to me."

"Of course, I will, sir."

"Thank you. Don't hesitate to call me at any time if you think there's something I need to know. Will you do that?"

"Yes, sir, I will."

∞ ∞ ∞ ∞ ∞ ∞

February 19, 2034

Colonel Meyer reached for his buzzing cell phone.

"Hello, Lieutenant Colonel Meyer speaking."

"Colonel Meyer, this is Lieutenant Turnbull. How are you, sir?"

"I'm very well, Lieutenant. How are you doing?"

"Very well, sir. I volunteered to go back to Iran. I'm there now and things seem to be winding down. I'm calling to tell you about something that's happened. You probably won't think it's important, but I thought you might like to know."

"What is it?"

"It's about Sergeant Randall's dog, Kelly. I believe I told you my wife had a female German Shepherd. Her dog and Kelly mated and there is a litter of puppies. It's her first litter. I haven't seen them because I've been over here, but Molly tells me they are some of the most beautiful pups she's ever seen. They're almost 8 weeks old and I was wondering if Sergeant Randall might like to have one of them. Would you know how I can get in touch with him?"

"This is very interesting, Lieutenant. Perhaps I can use Sergeant Randall after all. Please let me handle this. Your wife may have to keep the puppy for a while, but you can be sure I'll get it to Randall."

"When you find Sergeant Randall, I'd like for him to have the biggest one. He may turn out to be just like Kelly. Molly says he's about twice the size of any of the rest of the litter and has pretty much taken control of things around the house. She said because of that, she named him, Boss."

BALTIMORE BLACKIE

Chapter 1

March 4, 2044

Border Patrolman Grant Davis was fighting to stay awake. He was a giant of a man who spent many hours each day in the gym. He was proud of his well-toned body and the hard muscles that bulged in his arms and shoulders.

What a way to spend a shift, Davis thought to himself. The Sergeant must have been out of his mind when he assigned this job to me. One of the newer men should be guarding this creep.

Normally, he'd be home with his lady friend at this late hour instead of babysitting some fat drug-smuggling big shot at the Imperial Beach Border Patrol Station. All he had to keep him awake as he stood watch was a three-month-old outdoor magazine. He could see the scowling prisoner behind the bullet proof window as the man paced back and forth in his small cell.

Fortunately, Davis's supervisor had allowed him the comfort of a heavily padded office chair as he maintained his lonely vigil. It was almost 4 A.M. when he leaned back in it and drifted off to sleep. He wouldn't wake up for almost a week.

The latch clicked quietly behind him in the outer door. Two men in hooded sweatshirts slipped silently into the room. Each wore thin latex-lined leather gloves that would prevent them from leaving fingerprints or DNA behind. One carried a short wooden club. The business end had been drilled out and filled with lead to make it into a more effective weapon. Using most of his strength, he swung the club at the sleeping officer's head. The blow would have instantly killed a lesser man. The guard thudded to the floor as his chair spun across the room.

Using the same master key that they'd used to enter the outer room, the two men quickly unlocked the inner cell door and moved to the prisoner's side. He was happy to see them. He spoke quietly to the tallest of the pair.

"I've been expecting someone to come after me. I hope you killed that pig. How did you get in here?"

"Money pays for the entry through many doors, amigo."

"Good. Let's get out of here before more guards show up."

"I'm afraid you won't be going with us. Jefe Rodriguez said to tell you, adios!"

As he spoke, he pulled a razor-sharp knife from a sheath on his belt. Sudden understanding and fear appeared in the doomed man's eyes. Without warning, the shorter of the two men grabbed him from behind and pinned his arms to his sides. The steel blade slashed upward. Blood spurted from the gaping hole it tore in the prisoner's neck. Both intruders dodged the torrent as they fought to maintain their footing on the now bloody tile. As the smuggler's strength ebbed away with the last few ounces of his blood, the assassins lowered him onto the small cot in the corner of the room.

The tall man bent forward and pulled the dying man's mouth open. Using the tip of his knife, he pierced the end of the lolling tongue and pushed it through the ghastly slash in the prisoner's throat. Their assignment was finished. They wiped the bottoms of their shoes on the coarse bed sheets before leaving the cell.

Chapter 2

March 10, 2044

The past year had not been kind to Sergeant John "Jack" Randall of the Baltimore City K9 Department. He had lost his best friend and partner, Boss. With the dog's passing, the electronic connection between their two minds was broken forever. It had been more of a joining of souls than a technologically induced linkage between the brains of a man and a dog.

Boss's last request was for Jack to find a puppy that would grow up to look just like him. He knew that a puppy would help heal the pain that would occur in Jack's family when he was no longer there. Jack waited almost two months before he followed through on the request. He'd hoped the puppy, which his son had immediately named Little Boss, would help him with his own anguish. It didn't.

Since Boss's passing, Jack had experienced unending bouts of severe depression and deep emotional turmoil. The pain caused him to lose all the joy in his life; his wife, his son, his sobriety, his job; everything that mattered to him had become unimportant because of the pain that no one else could possibly understand. He could not find his way through the sorrowing fog that his life had become.

His wife, Heather, knew what he was going through, but her love and understanding had not been enough to pull him out of his misery. To cope with the hurt, Jack had begun stopping at a bar in the evening with some of the other officers after they got off duty at the police department.

The occasional evening with his friends became a habit as he sank further into the depths of despair. His relationship with his wife and his son began to suffer and within a few months, so did his devotion to duty. He was demoted from Lieutenant back to Sergeant. His supervisor, Captain Mark Harrison, had done everything he could to end Jack's slide into alcohol abuse, but the time finally came when he could do no more. Jack's work habits had become sloppy and he could no longer be trusted in criminal investigations where his testimony in a courtroom might be questioned by defense attorneys who knew about his drinking problem. He was given a desk job where his primary duties were to check the files of the other officers to make sure all their data had been entered correctly.

Heather did all she could to help her husband, but the time finally came when she felt their son, Little Jack, should no longer see his father arrive home late every evening and fall into bed in a drunken stupor. Jack was not abusive; he had simply become an indifferent husband and father.

She and Jack didn't argue when she told him she was going to find another place for Little Jack and her to live for a while. She'd hoped he'd disagree with her plan and want to get counseling, but his reaction had only been a nod of sad acceptance. He simply looked away from her pleading eyes and said it was probably for the best. He said he would provide for them and help them find whatever they needed for their new home. The only thing he asked in return was that Boss's ashes, the big picture of the dog and the honors he had won would remain with him when she and Little Jack moved out.

Captain Harrison was one of Jack's closest friends. Heather called to tell him of her plans and he agreed that what she was doing was probably for the best. He helped her find a comfortable home close to his own where he could make sure she and Little Jack would have a good place to live in a secure neighborhood. He hadn't trusted Jack to follow through on his promises. He understood more than anyone what Jack was dealing with and had been doing everything possible to help his friend. After many months of research, phone calls and emails, he thought he may have found an answer to the problem.

He asked the Desk Sergeant to tell Jack to come see him when he arrived at work.

When Jack received the message, he walked to the Captain's open office door and looked inside.

"You wanted to see me, Cap?"

"Yes, I did, Jack. How are you doing this morning?"

"Pretty well. I have a little bit of a hangover, but other than that, I'm alright."

"Have you seen Heather and Little Jack lately?"

"Yeah, I have. Heather has been taking him to visit her family almost every weekend, so it's been tough for me to see as much of them as I'd like. I see them as often as I can, though."

"Are you still stopping at the bar every evening?"

"Not quite as much as I used to, but way more than I should," came the answer.

"Jack, nobody is sorrier than I am to see what has happened to you since Boss died. You were one of the best officers I've ever worked with. I'd like to tell you I understand what you're going through, but I won't lie to you. No other man on this planet has been through what you have. There's no way for the rest of us to understand what you've had to live with since he died. The implants that Meyer's people put into the two of you allowed you to share something with him that almost no one has experienced. You volunteered for what was supposed to be a great service to our police department and what you received in return was a deep emotional pain."

"I wasn't the only person to receive the implants, Cap. Other good men and dogs received them, too."

"I know, but except for a very few, no other team was able to establish such a strong joining of the minds. Most of the teams had only minor connections if there was anything at all. You shared something with Boss that was unique and it lasted a long time. I can't imagine how horrible it was for you when he died and that tie was broken."

"It was and it still is. It's something I'm going to have to live with for the rest of my life. I'm just trying to handle it the best way I can."

"Drinking isn't the answer."

"I know. I've told myself that a thousand times. It isn't the answer, but it's the only thing I've found that dulls the memories that keep running through my head. I never drank much before Boss died and I hate what I've become since then. Not only have

I lost my best friend, I've lost my wife and son. I love both of them so much, but even that doesn't help. I feel like parts of my heart and mind have been torn out and I've felt that way every waking moment since Boss died. It's not just when I'm awake that I can't cope, it's also when I'm asleep. Every night, I dream he's still alive. I dream we're back on patrol together. I dream I'm watching sunsets with him; I dream about what we talked about just before he died, things like that. I can't get him out of my mind. The worst part is, I don't want him out of it."

"You've got to find a way to pull yourself out of this," said Captain Harrison.

"Nobody knows that better than I do, but even the police department shrinks haven't been able to help me. The anti-depression pills they prescribed helped for a while, but being dependent on pills is just as bad as being dependent on alcohol. Nobody has ever had to deal with something like this. I'm just going to have to work my way through it, Cap. I appreciate everything you've done to help Heather, Little Jack and me, but there's really nothing anyone can do. I've just got to live with it and hope the pain and depression eventually go away."

"There may be hope for you. You're not alone in this. Chief Hampton is just as concerned about you as I am and so is President Thomas. The President knows what you've been going through and he wants to help. He's told me some interesting things. Our old friend, Colonel Meyer, turned out to be even more devious than any of us thought."

"I'm not sure the President cares very much. He promised both of us right here in this very office that if he was elected, he was going to investigate everything Meyer was involved in. He said he was going to have him and all his people prosecuted to the fullest extent of the law. Well, he got elected and as far as I know, the only thing he did was have Meyer pulled out of the program. After that, he didn't want to talk about it anymore."

"There are good reasons for that."

"I can't think of any."

"Meyer was right about national security being involved. The President and I met a week ago, for almost three hours at the

White House. It wasn't easy for him to be able to free up that much time, but he remembers how much you, Heather and Boss were factors in him being elected. Are you interested in hearing what he had to say? You must remember, what I tell you can't be spread around. The President doesn't mind if Heather knows, but that's as far as our conversation goes. Ok?"

"Sure, Cap. It probably doesn't matter much, anyway."

"It might after you hear me out. When the President went into the Oval Office, he did what he promised. One of the first things he did was ask the Director of the FBI to investigate Meyer and the implant program. The inquiry turned up a lot of things we didn't know about. Meyer was doing some horrible things in that research facility, but his scientists were somewhat successful in finding out how to use technology to connect two minds. The way Meyer went about it was wrong, but the research turned out to be important for national security after all and the President didn't abolish the program. He put in a lot of safeguards to make sure it will be done properly from now on, but he didn't shut it down."

"What happened to Meyer? I never heard anything about him being prosecuted."

"It was kept away from the public and the media, but he's receiving his just dues. It wasn't just dogs that were killed in his facility. People were, too. He was put through a quiet Court Martial and was charged with several different crimes. First-degree murder, kidnapping, false imprisonment and embezzling funds from the program he was heading up were among them. Basically, he knew the FBI had him dead to rights, so he pleaded guilty and threw himself on the mercy of the three officers who tried him. He was lucky he didn't receive the death penalty, but he'll never see the outside of Fort Leavenworth again."

"What about the people who were helping him?"

"Some of them were hit with the same charges. They plea-bargained and received lengthy prison terms. It was decided by the President and his advisors that the program is producing vital information that the government needs, so the research is still going on, but it will always be closely monitored."

"I guess that's a good thing, but I don't understand why it would have any bearing on my problem."

"It might. Years ago, you told me about a dog that served with you in Iran. Do you remember? His name was Kelly."

"Sure, Cap. I may be depressed and live in my cups too much, but I'll never forget about him."

"Meyer was defiant at first when the FBI investigators began to question him, but when he realized just how much trouble he was really in, his whole attitude changed. He started spilling his guts and all sorts of little details came out. He was manipulating people and events far more than we originally thought."

"What about Kelly?"

"Meyer had a buddy named Baker who served in Iran. He mentioned him to me when he first began to talk about you and Boss being involved in the implant program. That buddy was your C.O. while you were over there and he wanted you to stay for another hitch in the Army. You had a meeting with him before you got out and refused to re-enlist. It made him angry and he made the decision you couldn't take Kelly home with you when you were discharged to punish you for not doing what he wanted."

"I thought at the time that was probably what happened."

"Baker told Colonel Meyer all about you and Kelly before you left Iran and explained his reason for wanting to keep Kelly over there. Meyer went behind his back and called Lieutenant Turnbull, your immediate supervisor. He had Turnbull make a request to take Kelly home to Connecticut with him when he took leave. Meyer used his contacts in the Army to help get it done. Kelly got back to the States about the same time you did. He was very happy with Lieutenant Turnbull's family. He died just a few months ago and he lived years longer than most dogs of his breed."

"That's good to know, Cap. He was a good dog and I'm glad he had a good life. He deserved it after all the hell he went through in Iran."

"Here's where it really gets interesting. Meyer wanted to use you and Kelly in his research. That's why he risked making a superior officer angry and had your Lieutenant bring Kelly home. He planned to reunite the two of you, but his plans went awry when Kelly was hit by a car. He mended well, but he'd suffered a severe concussion and Meyer was afraid to use him in the implant program. He also had two broken legs. Meyer paid all the vet bills and asked Lieutenant Turnbull to keep him with his family. It's weird how the accident happened. Kelly got out of the house one night shortly after he arrived with Lieutenant Turnbull. He was twenty-five miles from the house and headed south when he was hit by the car."

"That's strange."

"Lieutenant Turnbull's wife always thought that somehow Kelly knew where you were and was trying to get to you. There's more. She had a young female German Shepherd to help keep her from getting lonely while her husband was away from home."

"That's nice. They make wonderful guard dogs and they're good company."

"Let's go back to you for a minute. Because of what your C.O. said to him, Meyer looked you up and kept an eye on you after you got back. There's a history of K9 soldiers becoming K9 cops after they serve with dogs in the military. After a while, you joined our police department. You fell right into his plans by doing that."

"I don't see where you're going with this."

"Brace yourself. While Kelly was recuperating, Mrs. Turnbull's dog went into heat. Kelly mated with her and she had a litter of pups. One of the dogs was a jet-black male that grew much faster than the rest of the litter. He basically took over his brothers and sisters. Because of that, the wife named him, are you ready for this?"

"I guess so."

"She named him, Boss."

"No, Cap! You're not telling me..."

"I am. Turnbull called Colonel Meyer and said he'd like for you to have the puppy. Meyer asked Turnbull to have his family keep the pup for a while. When he was barely old enough, Meyer arranged to have him put into our K9 Training Center and somehow managed to get him assigned to you. Everything fell right into place and things couldn't have worked out better for him. He had long arms, a lot of patience and a long-term plan. That plan was what caused you to be teamed with Boss."

"I can't believe this. Do you mean to tell me, the man I've hated for so long is responsible for Boss and me being together in the first place?"

"That's exactly what I'm telling you. Meyer thought there might be more to making the implants work than just producing a technological connection. He thought it might also be very important for a strong mental rapport to exist between the man and the dog. Once he was told by Colonel Baker about the almost mystical bond you had with Kelly, he had to have the two of you for his program. When that became impossible because of the accident, he thought it might be feasible for the same rapport to develop between you and Kelly's son if you were put together as a team. His original plans were to use you and Kelly in his program, but those plans were ruined when Kelly was hit by the car and received the concussion. When Boss got old enough, Meyer managed to have him assigned to you after you joined our K9 Department and he was right back on track. He watched, through his contacts in our police department, as you and Boss built the strong mental relationship he was looking for and became our best team. When the new computer chips came along, he thought it was imperative that you and Boss be one of the very first teams to be implanted with them."

"As much as I knew about Meyer, I never dreamed he was that resourceful. So, Kelly was Boss's father. It's strange, Cap, but I felt like I knew Boss the first time I laid eyes on him and he accepted me like a long-lost friend. Knowing this just makes me miss him even more."

"I wasn't sure if I should tell you about it or not. My visit with the President clarified a lot of things. I found out more that might help you and could help our police department with an investigation we have going on. I'm going to hit you with something that might throw you, so if you feel like I'm treading where I shouldn't, just stop me. Lieutenant Turnbull, who is now

Major Turnbull, was questioned at length about his involvement with Colonel Meyer. That's how the President found out that even though they were both older dogs, Kelly and his mate produced another litter about three years before Kelly died. One of the pups was a big black male that outgrew his brothers and sisters very quickly. The President persuaded Turnbull to donate him to our K9 Training Center a few months ago. He thought you might want to work with him. I've been keeping tabs on the dog. He's very intelligent and learns quickly. Would you be interested in working with him?"

"Cap, I don't know what to say. I appreciate everybody trying to help me, but the sad thing is, there will never be another Boss. Even if there was, there's no way another dog and I could ever establish a mind connection like Boss and I had."

"Maybe there is."

"How?"

"If there is a great need, many things can be made to happen. The implant program is still going on with another man in charge. He reports directly to the President. If you want, Boss's brother will be assigned to you and the President says he'll be implanted with a device just like the one that was put into Boss. We'll see if the two of you can establish a connection like you and Boss had. You won't even need to have another operation because you never had your implant removed. Once you started drinking, you didn't want to be bothered with the procedure."

"Life wasn't very interesting to me after Boss died."

"Heather and Little Jack didn't stop loving you and they both need you in their lives. Maybe you and another dog working together would help your family get back together. Plus, you could get back to real police work and become useful again."

"I don't know, Cap. I hoped another dog would help and I tried that when I brought Little Boss home, but it didn't work. He and Little Jack hit it off right from the start. It may have been because I was always thinking about Boss and he could sense that, but he didn't bond with me. Maybe what I felt with Boss was so strong that I'll never care for another dog again. There's also something else to think about. Nobody wants my family back together more than I do, but the truth is, the implant killed Boss. I wouldn't want to be responsible for that happening to another good dog. I've looked back so many times and thought about how Boss would have lived a much longer life and would never have known what dying meant if he hadn't been implanted. So, there are many other things to think about than just my feelings."

"There's also the police work you used to be so dedicated to."

"I realize that has taken a back seat along with everything else I care about."

"Then, think about this. Our city is once again being overrun by drug pushers, gangs, and violence. It has gotten a lot worse in the past year. We haven't been as successful at fighting it as we were when we had you and Boss to help us. We're talking about drugs that are killing people every day and gangs that are killing just as many. We have a Mexican drug cartel that's operating here and we can't put a lid on it. I believe if we had you and another dog like Boss to help us, we could infiltrate the gang. We need you, Jack. If we can make another implant work, maybe we can stop the violence."

"There's still the fact the implant killed Boss. I won't risk that happening to another dog."

"The researchers discovered that one of the metals in the alloy the sensors are made of was chemically reacting with brain tissue in some of the dogs and causing lesions to occur. That's exactly what killed Boss. We've found out that scientists were working on the problem even before the lesions on his brain showed up and they're sure now that they have it licked. Evidently, it was an allergy thing that only happened if a dog had an unusual sensitivity to the metal. They've lengthened the time they leave the samples under the dog's skin when they test for allergies. To be completely safe, they leave them in for a month. The probability of the lesions attacking another dog's brain is remote now that better procedures are being followed. You've had your implant for many years and the doctors believe if you haven't already had a problem, you never will. Boss's brother will be safe too if he doesn't respond negatively to the metal. If he does, they'll use sensors made from a different alloy."

"What's the dog's name?"

"According to President Thomas, Major Turnbull's wife likes to watch old movies. There used to be a detective character in one of them called Boston Blackie. The pup was black and she's known for a long time that you're from Baltimore, so she named him Baltimore Blackie. It was a play on words from the movie. I've seen him. He looks so much like Boss, it's uncanny. He's had his training and we're ready for you to take him on as a partner. If you don't want to work with him, he'll be assigned to another officer. I hope you decide to accept him."

"I need to think about this before I make up my mind and I want to talk to Heather about it."

"You should. Your decision should involve her. She still loves you, Jack. That's never changed."

"I'll talk to her about it tonight if she'll see me."

"She will. Just call her first and don't stop for a beer on the way to her house so you'll both be clear headed when you spring this on her."

"I won't drink anything before I go. Before I leave your office, I just want to say thank you for not giving up on me. I know I've been a problem for you and I'm sorry for that."

"I'm only doing what any friend would do for another. That's what friends are for. If anybody ever had a reason for being depressed, you did. Maybe we can get you back on your feet again and the world will look a lot brighter to you."

"It already does, thanks to you, Cap."

Chapter 3

Heather was more than agreeable to Captain Harrison's plan. She and Jack talked long into the night. They decided they would keep their living arrangements as they were for a while until they could see if having another friend like Boss was possible. They didn't want Little Jack to get used to having his father around again, only to see him fall back into depression if the new dog didn't work out. The conversation was the longest one they'd shared since shortly after Boss died.

The next afternoon, Captain Harrison drove Jack to the K9 Training Center so he could observe what would occur at their first exposure to each other. Jack was understandably apprehensive about meeting the dog. The Captain made an excuse not to be with Jack when he entered the kennel area so he wouldn't be a factor in what happened when Jack and Blackie first saw each other. He opened a small window between the office and kennel and watched from a distance.

Blackie was lying in his cage, alert, but calm and seeming unaffected by the noise the other dogs were making when Jack walked down the aisle between the cages. Blackie's head turned in Jack's direction. Suddenly, his eyes locked on the officer and he stood up. As Jack approached the cage, the dog yelped and jumped to the door of his enclosure. He pushed his nose against it and began to claw at the door.

Jack hurried to the door and pressed the palm of his hand flat against the coarse metal mesh so that his skin would touch the dog's muzzle. Blackie closed his eyes and began to make a low whining sound that was almost inaudible to Captain Harrison. The hair on the Captain's arms began to stand up. Jack stood there for many moments. After what seemed to Captain Harrison to be an eternity, Jack turned toward the window and nodded his head. He'd found a new partner. The Captain smiled.

∞ ∞ ∞ ∞ ∞ ∞

Blackie was put into the back seat when they rode back to the police station in the Captain's unmarked car. Jack kept his left arm extended over the top of the front seat while Blackie kept his nose pressed into the palm of Jack's hand. When they arrived at the station, they walked from the parking lot to Captain Harrison's office. Blackie walked over to the older officer to get his ears scratched before stretching out on the floor at Jack's feet in the same spot where Boss always waited while Jack visited with the Captain.

It was an eerily familiar situation. It seemed as though a year had not passed and Boss was still with them. Neither man mentioned the similarity; it was as if they feared talking about it would break some magic spell.

The Captain smiled at Jack.

"I'm glad that turned out so well."

"So am I, Cap. It's almost as if I took a step back in time. The first time I saw Boss, I felt like I'd already known him for a long time. He didn't react exactly as Blackie did, but it was like he chose me to be his partner instead of the police department choosing him for me."

"Jack, I think I need to tell you a story. It's not about me; it's about a friend of mine and his wife. His name is Bob and he told me this story one night while we were drinking a couple of beers at his home and his wife verified it. It seems Bob had a cat that he and his wife dearly loved. He said he wasn't anything special, just an ordinary old gray cat that had been given to them when he was a kitten."

"What does this have to do with me?"

"I'll get to that and it won't be a long story, but I think I should tell it to you. Bob's wife Cathy decided she wanted to get a kitten, but Bob didn't want one. He didn't want to be bothered with having a litter box and cat odor in the house. He finally gave in and told Cathy he'd agree to get one, but only if it was Siamese. He had one when he was a youngster and liked them. Cathy told her friends that she was looking for a kitten and it would have to be Siamese. As it turned out, one of them had a kitten she wanted to give away, but it was solid gray and only half Siamese. She owned the pure-bred mother cat and the father was a neighborhood stray. There was only one kitten left from the litter and it was a male. Cathy went to look at it and fell in love with it. She told Bob about it. Bob wanted a chocolate point Siamese but finally gave in about bringing the gray kitten home when Cathy kept talking about. He immediately bonded with it and named it Smokey. After another couple of weeks, Cathy's friend told her she was moving to Florida to a place that didn't allow animals and needed to find a home for the mother cat. Cathy felt like it would be nice to reunite the mother and son and talked to Bob. She pushed hard and Bob finally gave in, since he had originally wanted a chocolate point Siamese and that's what the mother was."

"I don't see where you're headed with this."

"You will. When Bob was home, Smokey was always with him. Every night when they went to bed, he crawled onto Bob's chest for about ten minutes to be petted. Afterward, the cat would sleep between his feet. It became a nightly thing. Bob loved the cat and the cat loved him right back. Every night for ten years, the cat would come for his nightly loving. Smokey and his mother, who they just called Mama Cat, were very territorial; neither would allow any other cat within sight of their home. If another one came around, there would be a terrible fight. Bob said he and Cathy sometimes called Smokey, the old warrior. That's finally what killed him. He was bitten in a cat fight and caught feline leukemia. The vet couldn't save him and he died. It hurt Bob and Cathy very badly. They buried him in the backyard with a single artificial rose they had from their wedding day."

"I can understand how they felt."

"So can I. After that, they only had Mama Cat, since she wouldn't allow another cat on the place."

"At least they had her. I still don't know what this has to do with me."

"I'm getting there. They didn't want to get another cat. They felt that if they did, they'd have to deal with the pain of losing it and they didn't want that. They were also afraid if they got another kitten, Mama Cat would try to kill it when they brought it home. Now, I'll get to the crux of my story. A couple of years later, Bob and Cathy went on vacation in Florida. They had a friend check on Mama Cat every day while they were gone. On the way home, they stopped to visit Bob's sister. She lives about a ten-hour drive from here in the Carolinas. While they were there, Bob's sister asked him if he remembered the gray cat he used to have. Bob said he certainly did and would never forget him. The sister said her boyfriend had a cat with a litter of kittens and that one of the males reminded her so much of Bob's old gray cat, she couldn't believe it. She said he moved like Smokey, talked all the time like Smokey and was the exact same color as Smokey. She said it was uncanny. She told Bob they would have to visit her boyfriend so he and Cathy could see the kitten. Bob and Cathy liked her boyfriend anyway, so they went with the sister the next day to visit him. When they arrived, they walked into the living room and sat down. As soon as they began to talk, they heard a screech in the bedroom where the mother cat had the kittens hidden. Suddenly, this little gray kitten came running into the room, saw Bob and jumped all over him. The kitten acted as though he knew Bob and Cathy and would not leave Bob's lap the entire time they were there. He purred constantly and kept pushing his face into Bob's hand while Bob gently rubbed his face with his fingertips, just as he used to do every night to Smokey when he was still alive."

"I think I know where you're headed with this."

"You should by now, but there's more. Bob and Cathy went back to Bob's sister's house to spend the night. The next morning, they were going to go home. About 9 o'clock that evening, the boyfriend called. He said, after they left his house, the kitten went crazy. He said he would not leave the front door when they left and was clawing at it, attempting to get out; something he'd never done before. He said he thought the kitten wanted to get to Bob for some reason. He asked Bob if he'd like to have it. Bob, without even asking Cathy, said he'd love to have him and they would stop to pick him up after they left Bob's sister's house the next morning."

"I think you're trying to tell me the cat was Smokey, reincarnated. That's not something I'd believe, Cap."

"There's still more. Now they had the kitten, but it hit both of them when they were about halfway home that Mama Cat wouldn't allow it into their house. She'd kill it. They had the rest of the trip to think about it. They'd almost certainly have to find the kitten another place to live. Bob said, when they were about a mile from their home, the kitten suddenly went wild. He climbed onto Bob's shoulders and started yowling and running in circles around his head. The closer they got to their house, the worse it got. They decided the best way to introduce Mama Cat to the new kitten was to take him into the house, sit him on the floor by their feet and watch what happened when she saw him. They knew they'd have to be ready to snatch it away from her if she tried to kill it."

"What happened?"

"They didn't even carry in their luggage right away. They walked into the house and took the kitten to the kitchen where Mama Cat usually hung out and sat it down just inside the door. Mama Cat saw it and the kitten saw Mama Cat at the same instant. They dove headlong at each other. The next moment, they were rolling on the floor playing with each other and jumping around all over the place. There was never an occasion from the time the kitten arrived when there was a problem with Mama Cat. Cathy said it was as if Smokey had been reincarnated and Mama Cat recognized him the instant she saw him."

"There are explanations for things like that if you look for them."

"Of course, there are. It may have been the kitten just liked the way Bob smelled. It may have been that Mama Cat missed Smokey and mistook the kitten for him. But, you'd have a hard time convincing Bob and Cathy there wasn't more to it than that, especially when the first night they were home, the kitten climbed onto Bob's chest to get his head rubbed before going to sleep between Bob's feet. They can't explain what happened and they were glad their old cat accepted the new kitten, but they think there is also the possibility the kitten was their old Smokey coming home to them. I didn't try to talk them out of it; there are things that happen that we just can't explain. You, of all people, should know that."

"I think you're trying to tell me Blackie is Boss coming back to me."

"No, I'm not. But, I did see something happen today that was peculiar. People talk about racial memory and things like that. Maybe this is something similar."

"Maybe, but I'm not going to dwell on it. I've accepted the fact that Boss is gone forever. I've just been having problems living with the idea. I'm hoping Blackie will help me; when I first saw him, I felt that somehow, he will."

"Then, let's just leave it at that. Since you and Heather decided to go through with this, I guess we need to talk about what we'll be doing next."

"We do. Then I'm taking him to Heather so she and Little Jack can meet him. After that, I'll take him to my house so we can get to know each other better."

"I think that's a good idea. Would you like to hear more about what the President, the Chief and I have been talking about? We've been making some plans for you and Blackie after the implant is put into him."

"Yes."

"We'll have it put in as soon as possible. When he fully recovers from surgery, we'll need to put him to work right away, if it works and the two of you establish a mind connection."

"We'll take it one step at a time. There is one special thing I want to do if it does work. I'll take him for a ride. After that, we'll be ready to do whatever you want. How has the research been coming along?"

"Not as well as the government would like. When the implants were put into you, Boss and the other volunteer teams, only a very few could establish a mind connection the way you and Boss did. They're still having that problem. As hard as it is to talk about, when it did work and Meyer's people studied the brains of the officers and dogs, they learned a lot. But, they still couldn't make the mind connection happen every time they tried. To this day, only a very few experiments have been successful. I wish we could be certain an implant will work for you and Blackie."

"Why do they think it isn't working most of the time?"

"They believe the problem is the subtle physical differences in the brains of the dogs. I'm hoping that since Blackie is Boss's brother, Blackie's brain is like Boss's. There's a very good possibility it is. The only way to find out for sure is to have the procedure done and see what happens."

"Then, let's go ahead and set it up. There are some conditions I have to put on this. I want to be there in Washington when all the tests are run on him. I also want to be there during the surgery and when he wakes up so I'll be able to see what happens right away and I want to be at the other facility during the entire time it takes for him to recover. If I can't do these things, I don't want him to be implanted."

"Don't worry, you'll be there for all of it. If any of the scientists have objections, the President will see to it that they back off. This time it won't be necessary for a long stay at the research facility while the scientists are waiting to see if he's allergic to any of the implant materials. You can bring him home for most of the month. But, he should be there for a few days while they run their regular tests. They'll have to do blood tests and run brain scans so they'll know exactly where to put the sensors and things like that. Those tests and procedures shouldn't take more than a few days. After that, you can bring him back home with you. About three weeks later, you'll take him back to Washington so they can inspect his shoulder for allergy problems. If there are none, the implant will be put into place and you'll stay with him at the facility until he heals. Then, you can bring him home for good and we'll start working on our cartel problem if the implant works."

"I should know if it does or not just about as soon as he wakes up. This all sounds good so far. If you don't mind, I'd like to take him to see Heather and Little Jack now."

"That would be the best thing you can do. Come back here as soon as you get to work tomorrow morning and I'll begin explaining what we have in mind for our drug kingpin."

"Ok, Cap. Thanks again for everything you've done."

Chapter 4

Jack walked Blackie out to his unmarked police car and opened the door so the dog could jump inside. He started the engine and pulled out of the parking lot. As soon as Jack put the shift lever into drive, Blackie put his head on his lap. Jack laid his hand on the big dog's shoulder as he drove. A feeling of déjà vu washed over him.

He'd told Heather the prior evening that he would be meeting Blackie for the first time today and that he would stop by their home so she, Little Jack and Little Boss could meet the new dog if things had gone well. He shared with her what he knew of Blackie's family tree. Heather had worked for a long time for Colonel Meyer as his secretary, but even she was surprised at the twists and turns the Colonel had performed to further his research program.

Jack pulled up in front of the house and he and Blackie got out of the car and walked to the front door. Jack rang the doorbell. He felt as nervous as a schoolboy on his first date.

Heather must have been waiting anxiously for them to arrive. She opened the door within seconds and kissed Jack on the cheek as they entered.

Blackie placed his paw on her knee and stared up at her.

"Jack! He's a living picture of Boss!"

"I know. It really threw me when I first saw him. The strange thing is, it was almost as if he recognized me as someone he knew when he first saw me. I didn't know what to think."

"I don't, either. He immediately put his paw on my knee. Boss always used to do that."

"Well, he is Boss's brother so there are bound to be similarities."

"It's going to take me a few minutes to get used to this. I'll call Little Jack. He's out in the back yard with one of his friends and Little Boss. I hope there isn't a problem between the two dogs."

"So do I. I guess we'll just put them together and see what happens."

Heather walked to the open door and called to her son and his friend. The two boys came in and were followed by the black German Shepherd that Little Jack loved so much. The dogs saw each other and walked stiffly together. Blackie was the much larger of the two. They gave each other a thorough sniffing and then walked apart. The smaller dog walked to Little Jack's side and Blackie returned to Heather and Jack.

Heather smiled. "That went well."

"It could have gone bad. Little Boss is protective of both you and Little Jack. He's a smart dog too and must have sensed Blackie isn't a threat. Let's sit down and visit for a while and keep an eye on them."

"I think that's best. Little Jack, come here and say hello to your father."

Little Jack walked over and hugged his Dad. He took Jack's hand and pulled him to the sofa. He was growing fast.

"How are things going, son?"

"Good, Dad. Is Captain Harrison coming by?"

"No, he wants us to have some time alone so the dogs can get to know each other. Who is your friend?"

"This is Sammy. He lives over on the next street. His Mom will be here to pick him up in about half an hour. Can you stay for a while? I miss you."

"Yes. I miss you, too; both of you. Maybe your old Dad can be around a lot more, soon. I'll have to be away from time to time for work, but, if things go the way your Mother and I hope they will, maybe we can be together again permanently. What do you think of Blackie?"

The boy reached out to touch the dog. Blackie stood at attention.

"Little Boss likes him. He sure is big and he looks like Boss. Do you think he'll be just like him?"

"I doubt any dog will ever be just like Boss. He was special and we'll never be able to replace him. Maybe Blackie will help me get over some of the problems I've been having. I'm glad you like him. I love you, Son."

"I love you too, Dad. Can I go back outside with Sammy and Little Boss until Sammy's Mom comes to pick him up?"

"It's ok with me if it's alright with your Mother."

Heather smiled. "Of course, it is. Just don't go outside of the fence. I'll call you when she gets here."

The boys and the smaller dog walked back outside. Jack turned to Heather.

"Is it alright if we stay a while?"

"I'm way ahead of you. I was hoping you would. Don't you use your nose? I bet Blackie knows I've been cooking all afternoon. I have a good dinner in the oven."

"I think from now on I'll be a different man, Heather. I'm sorry for the way I've been acting for the past year, but I just couldn't shake the despair. I know it's probably too quick to be saying so, but I feel like something has changed inside me. I felt it as soon as I saw Blackie. You and Little Jack should have been everything I needed, but you know how it was and what Boss and I shared. It was as if part of my soul was gone. Now, I feel like some of it has come back."

"Nobody blamed you, Jack. What was troubling you was worse than even an addiction problem would have been. We knew you still loved us, but there was no way Little Jack or I could replace what you lost when Boss died. All we could do was hope that time would heal all of us. Now, thanks to Captain Harrison, maybe we can put our family back together and things will be even better than they were before."

"I'll do my part and I know you and Little Jack will, too."

"Then, let's stop talking about it and you can help me put dinner on the table. Sammy's Mom will be here soon. By the time she picks him up, we'll be ready to eat. Does that sound like a good deal to you?"

"Absolutely! What do you want me to do?"

"If you put the dishes on the table, I'll start cooking the vegetables. I think there should be roast left over so Little Boss and Blackie can have some."

Chapter 5

The next morning, Jack and Blackie were waiting in Captain Harrison's office when he arrived at the station. The Captain smiled when he saw them.

"So, how did things go last night?"

"Way better than I deserve, Cap. Blackie and Little Boss got along well. There was no trouble between them at all; they accepted each other right away."

"I was hoping that would happen. There were only a couple of things I've been worried about since I started putting all this together. One is that the dogs wouldn't like each other; the other is that the implant might not work."

"Weren't you worried about what Heather might think about all this?"

"No. She'd do just about anything to have the man she married back."

"I think she has me."

"Good. Then I know you'll help us take care of our city's drug problems and skyrocketing murder rate. Are you ready to hear about them?"

"I sure am."

"Have you ever heard the name Ernesto Carlos Immanuel Rodriguez?"

"I may have been a drunk, Cap, but I haven't been deaf. Every cop in the country has heard that name."

"Then you know what we're up against. He runs the biggest drug cartel in Mexico and the United States is his best market. He's been shipping tons of cocaine, heroin, meth and other drugs into the country every year and a huge amount of that is coming straight to Baltimore. He has organizations in most of the larger cities across America, but for some reason, he has fixated on ours. So, he's one of the biggest problems we're facing right now. We take out a shipment occasionally and from time to time we'll catch some of his smugglers, but we've never been able to put our hands on any of his big people."

"Are they that good or are there too many cops who aren't doing their jobs?"

"Maybe it's a little bit of both. If someone does manage to capture one of his supervisors, they usually don't last three days in jail. They turn up dead and there's never anyone around who saw anything. The U.S. Border Patrol intercepted a drug shipment a few days ago that was going into the Southwest and caught one of his top men red-handed. The very next morning, he was found dead in his cell with his throat cut. The killers pulled his tongue out through the hole in his throat. It's usually done when Rodriguez has someone killed. It was called a Sicilian necktie in the old days. Rodriguez loves the idea and uses the symbol as a warning to anyone who might be thinking about betraying him."

"Didn't security cameras record what happened?"

"They would have if they hadn't quit working just before the man was knifed. Somehow, the killers must have jammed the signal that was coming from the cameras. They started working again about fifteen minutes after the guy was killed. It was done very early in the morning when most of the staff wasn't there. Everybody who was on duty is being questioned, but I doubt the investigators will find out anything. They're trying to find out why the camera stopped working and why there weren't more people assigned to watch the dead man. The only guard they had on him was hit on the head with a club and was in a coma for a week. We're dealing with some very clever, vicious people."

"There are payoffs going on, Cap, there have to be."

"Of course, there are. Rodriguez is making so much money, he can pay off just about anybody. When a prison guard is only making sixty thousand dollars a year and somebody puts fifty grand into his hand to look the other way for a few minutes, it's hard to turn that kind of money down. Rodriguez has everybody so afraid, we can't get anybody to talk about him. We can't even figure out how he gets back and forth across the border. The wall has been up for a long time and there are cameras everywhere, but we can't seem to get a glimpse of anyone we think could be him. His people must be paying off border guards from both countries to look the other way while he passes through."

"How deeply has he embedded himself into our Hispanic community? There are so many people of Mexican descent in this country; it should be a huge market for him. Maybe we could get a recovering addict to talk."

"He's very clever. He throws a lot of money around in the Hispanic community. Some of them even think of him as a folk hero, sort of like Robin Hood. He spreads the word that he loves "his" people and he doesn't want "his" people using hard drugs. He doesn't worry about the cheap marijuana that he ships here and lets them know it's okay if they smoke it. It's the same with the rest of the country."

"I don't understand why he even bothers with smuggling pot. It's been legal across a lot of the United States for years. How is there any money in that?"

"It costs next to nothing to grow in Mexico, so he has very little out of pocket expense to produce it. The money he gets for it in this country is almost all profit except for shipping costs. Plus, there's no tax paid on what he sells, so he can set his prices at half of what legal pot sells for and still stick a lot of money into his pocket. Legal production of marijuana in the United States is constantly monitored and security must be maintained. That means grower's costs here are much higher. It has high sin taxes added to the price, like alcohol and tobacco when they're sold. It's like illegal whiskey production in some of our southern states. There's still a good bit of profit to be made when manufacturing costs are low and no taxes are paid. When you buy a legal bottle of rum for say, $50, way over half the cost to you is the taxes that are added to the price of the rum. If you don't pay any taxes on cheap, illegal pot, you can make a lot of money by selling it and there are quite a few states where it's still illegal to possess or sell it. He probably pays most of his regular operating costs out of his marijuana business. If he can do that, every cent he collects from selling hard drugs is pure profit."

"What about people who grow their own?"

"Some states allow that where recreational use is legal. Most people don't bother growing it because it's sold in stores. You can make a limited amount of alcohol for your own use if you want, but most people don't. It's the same with pot."

"Ok, so he doesn't want his people using hard drugs. All of them can't like what he's doing."

"Most Hispanics believe he doesn't target them or their children, so they protect him, or at the very least, ignore him. They have lots of drug money coming into their communities and they don't have as many of the addiction problems that the rest of the country faces. If someone in the Hispanic community starts talking bad about Rodriguez, he's told to shut up. If he doesn't, he turns up dead. It's as simple as that. We believe at least one hundred people are killed every day across this nation because of the violence that's associated with his cartel and that's not counting the people who are dying from drug overdoses. Rodriguez is said to have murdered quite a few people with his own hands, but we can't get any evidence on him to prove it."

"Why isn't our State Department working with Mexico? We have some of the finest people in this country watching our borders and inspecting foreign shipments that come here, we have drug sniffing dogs and security camera's everywhere and we have drones watching everything from the sky. Surely, if our two governments worked together, we could make short work of him and his cartel. We've done it before. We used to have this kind of problem twenty-five or thirty years ago, but the wall, technology, and good police work helped get rid of most of it."

"Corruption has become just as bad in Mexico as it used to be. The Mexican government looks the other way because of all the U.S. dollars that come into their country. It helps their economy and a lot of that drug money finds its way straight into the pockets of their crooked cops and politicians."

"Where did Rodriguez get his start? It takes a lot of time to build up a big organization like he's running."

"He's supposed to have inherited a small organization from an older brother when the brother was killed in a shootout with Mexican police many years ago. He cultivated relationships throughout North America as he gradually took over the drug trade from most of the other criminal organizations. He's smart. If he wasn't involved in this business, he'd probably be successful at just about anything else he wanted to tackle."

"What does he look like? I don't believe I've ever seen as much as a picture of him."

"He's smart about that, too. The man is like a shadow. Not many people know what he looks like and so far, no branch of law enforcement has been able to get even a blurred picture of him. He has a very small group of people, his board of directors if you will, that answers directly to him and he gives them instructions about exactly what he wants them to do. Not many people know what any of them look like, either. He makes payoffs to politicians, judges, and cops all over Mexico and we believe he's done pretty much the same thing in this country and Canada. His board members all live in Mexico and he's been clever about picking his top organizers from people who don't have police records. If any of them had records, he paid off the right people and had them taken out of the computers."

"I would think that's impossible."

"Nothing's impossible if you have enough money. This guy is swimming in it."

"There has to be a weak spot in his organization. We need to find the right person and get to Rodriguez through him."

"He doesn't have many weaknesses. Some of the old Mafia bosses used to have this thing about wanting the public to know who they were and so did some of the earlier Hispanic cartel operators. They liked the notoriety. This guy isn't like that. He has very carefully kept his own and his board member identities hidden. In each city he operates out of, there are only one or two people at the top of the local organization. He assigns each board member to a couple of cities and only the top cartel people in those cities know the board member that is assigned to them."

"He's planned things pretty well."

"He has. This is a man who controls the biggest cartel in the history of North America, a man who would cut your throat and twist the knife and laugh at you while you were dying. He's unbelievably vicious and he's trained his board members to be the same. The board, in turn, trains the top people in their cities to practice the same methods. Rodriguez has planned well and he wants to be around a long time to enjoy his ill-gotten gains. If nobody knows who he is, he can stay in business until he's ready to retire. We've decided that we'll have to overlook his top people for a while and go directly for him. If we can get him, we believe all his board members will start fighting amongst themselves for control of his organization and get sloppy. If that happens, between us, the F.B.I. and the Mexican government, we should be able to take them out and shut down the rest of the cartel. As a matter of pride, I'd like for us to take Rodriguez down before anyone else gets their hands on him."

"This job sounds almost impossible, Cap. We're looking for a man who could be anywhere and we don't know what he looks like. On top of that, we don't know who his top people are and what any of them look like."

"I didn't say the job was going to be easy; I just said we have to do it."

"What do we know about him that we can use? Does he like women, does he gamble, does he do his own drugs? What?"

"As far as we know, he doesn't do any of those things to the point where they've become a habit for him. We do know that he travels under an alias, he likes luxury waterfront hotels and he keeps his head down."

"That won't make it any easier to find him. Sorry, Cap, just thinking out loud. What else do we know about him?"

"Not a lot. We've been trying to infiltrate his gang here in the city and we finally have a couple of our people in place. We've only been able to find out a couple of things that might help us."

"At least we have something."

"For some reason, he likes to come to the City of Baltimore occasionally when the board member, who oversees this area, meets with his top local people. We've heard that he's stayed at the Harbor House Hotel and he likes to hobnob with rich people from time to time so he can act like a well-heeled gentleman."

"That should narrow it down slightly, but not much."

"There are a few other things we've been able to find out about him."

"What are they?"

"He's tall and thin and supposed to speak English with only the slightest hint of an accent. He always wears the best custom made suits money can buy and he likes high-dollar handmade western boots. It's also said that he loves dogs, especially German Shepherds. He breeds them and is very proud of the ones he's produced. It's believed he has two or three that live inside his house that are beloved family pets. We don't know where his home is, but it's supposed to be surrounded by high walls that are patrolled twenty-four hours a day by specially trained men and his German Shepherd guard dogs. We've heard that he goes to his kennels every day when he's home and visits with his dogs. That's just gossip, but maybe it's something we can use."

"Why didn't I see that coming?"

"I know it's not much, but when you don't have much to go on, you grab at every straw you can find. If we can put an undercover officer with a beautiful German Shepherd into the right situation, we might be able to draw him out. If he sees Blackie, he may just slip up. They don't come much more handsome than he is."

"So, what do you have in mind?"

"We'll keep trying to get more information as we infiltrate more of our people into his organization. While we do that, we'll send you and Blackie to Washington so we can begin the process of having Blackie implanted. It will be many weeks before he'll be ready for this assignment, if he's not allergic to anything and if the implant works. You'll be working on your relationship with him until we get information about when Rodriguez will be coming for a visit. You'll be living a dual life for a while. You'll be spending a lot of time with your family, but once Blackie is ready, he'll be given a name that's not filed with our police department and so will you. You are going to become a lonely, independently wealthy gentleman who is going blind from Retinitis Pigmentosa. We'll have people that train service dogs to work with both you and Blackie. He will be trained to be your Seeing Eye Dog. You'll begin staying at the same hotel where we believe Rodriguez stays when he's in town, so it won't be unusual for you to be there when he shows up. There are a lot of Hispanics working there and we want them to get used to you and Blackie being there. We're hoping when he and his Board member comes around, you might be able to set them up. We're going to use one of his own methods against him; you're going to be a man with a lot of money who doesn't want anyone to know who you really are when you travel. We'll be able to slip that little bit of gossip to hotel management and the housekeeping staff, so it will become your cover. If you're blind, you'll seem less threatening to him and it would give you the perfect reason for traveling with a Seeing Eye Dog that's one of the breed he loves."

"It sounds like there's been a lot of planning going on, already."

"There has been. The Chief, the President and I have been talking about it off and on for months. The President hasn't told any of his advisors. Rodriguez has influence in so many places; the President can't completely trust any of them where he is concerned. Only the Chief and I know about the plans here at the police department. We can't trust everybody who works here, either."

"I guess I can handle the job if you can."

"This is not a typical assignment and you're free to refuse it if you want. I don't have to tell you how dangerous it will be. Ideally, we would want someone without a family to tackle it. You're going to be away from home sometimes for days on end and you may have to travel out of the country while you're undercover."

"We have a lot to do and think about, don't we? Are you sure you can trust me to handle all this? After all, I have been a heavy drinker for quite a while."

"I believe in you, Jack. You had a reason to drink. If the reason is gone, the problem should also be gone. You were one of the most dedicated officers I've ever known. I have no reason to believe you won't handle this assignment as well or better than any other man or woman on the force."

"Thanks for saying that, Cap. I won't let you down. But, what if the implant doesn't work?"

"Two things come to mind. First, we can try again with another implant. If that doesn't work, you'll still have Blackie. Trying to make it work a couple of times won't hurt him very much and if it doesn't happen, he's still Boss's brother. He's more like him than any other dog on the planet. Let's have faith that it will work and do our part to make it happen."

Chapter 6

The next six weeks were a busy time for both Jack and Blackie. They were instructed to report to a police education center in northern Baltimore where a mock apartment had been set up. The only breaks they received were on the evenings and weekends they spent with Heather and Little Jack as they continued to strengthen their bond. Jack was taught how a blind person took care of himself as Blackie learned the duties of a Seeing Eye Dog.

It was a difficult process. The trainers gave Jack a white cane to help him feel his way around and insisted he keeps his eyes covered as he learned to change clothes, cook and eat meals and bathe and groom himself. He had to learn to do everything a man with badly deteriorated vision would be expected to do. After cutting himself many times while shaving, repeatedly burning himself on the stove and constantly spilling food on his clothing as he ate, he became frustrated. Learning to be sightless had not sounded so difficult when Captain Harrison explained what he would be doing. Now he understood the problems the visually impaired had to cope with every day of their lives.

Blackie was put into a special harness with a handle at the top of his shoulders and taught to be Jack's eyes. If they ever met Rodriguez, they would have to persuade him that Jack was blind and that Blackie really was his Seeing Eye Dog. They would need to be more convincing than any Hollywood actor.

Almost immediately, for the first time since he and Boss were implanted many years before, Jack returned to the clandestine research facility in Washington D.C. where he and Blackie would remain for almost a week as specimens were placed under the dog's skin and other tests were performed.

During one procedure, Blackie was put to sleep so a tiny piece of his hip bone could be surgically removed. Jack insisted on the anesthetic because he remembered how painful it was when it was done to him. It was immediately put into a freezer where it would be held until it was needed. During the implantation procedure, it would be necessary for surgeons to drill small holes in his skull. While that was being done, the bone fragment would be ground up and combined with a non-toxic adhesive. The mixture would be pressed into the cavities after the sensors were put in place. It would quickly harden and lock them into position. Because the adhesive contained bone from Blackie's own body, almost instant healing would occur.

The microscopic sensors would barely touch his brain. They were connected to tiny wires that would be threaded under his scalp to a small transmitter/receiver positioned under the loose skin of his upper neck. That device would be tuned to the same frequency as the transmitter/receiver that had been placed into Boss's body many years ago.

After Blackie awoke from the procedure, they returned to the education center in Baltimore where Blackie received further training and Jack put the blindfold back on. Time passed quickly until the day finally arrived for the surgery. When it did, Jack said goodbye to Heather and Little Jack and drove Blackie to the small government hospital in Washington where the operation would take place. It was only a few miles from the secret research facility.

Hours would have to pass from the time the dog was taken away until he was brought to the recovery room. Jack was now impatiently walking the floor while he waited for that to happen. It was the first time in two months he thought a cold beer might be necessary to soothe his jangled nerves. He'd brought a couple of magazines along to read, but he couldn't keep his mind on them. The "what if's" kept running through his head. What if the procedure didn't work? What if it did? What if Blackie didn't make it through surgery? He finally gave up and walked outside, hoping some fresh air would help. It hadn't, so he made his way to the recovery room. Blackie was no longer just a dog; he had become his best friend.

Jack was astonished when Captain Harrison walked into the room. The President had given directions that only a very few visitors would be allowed inside the hospital or research center while Jack and Blackie were there. The Captain was one of them.

"Cap, I'm surprised to see you here."

"I wanted to be with you when Blackie wakes up. If he isn't able to communicate with you, you should have a friend with you when you find out. If he can, I want to be here to see what happens."

"I'm glad you came. I've been sitting on pins and needles."

"I thought you would be. When I went to the office this morning, I tried not to think about it, but I couldn't help myself. I knew I should be here, so I came on down. How long will it be before he's brought in?"

"It should be just about any time now. I'm not a nail-biter, but I'm about to become one."

Just then, two men in green hospital gowns and surgical masks pushed a gurney bearing the sleeping dog into the small room. One of the surgeons, Dr. William Bailey, followed close behind.

Jack didn't wait for either of the orderlies to speak; he turned to the doctor.

"I'm so glad the operation is over; how did it go?"

"Everything went well and he should be fine. Hopefully, we'll have some idea if he can communicate with you shortly after he wakes up. The few dogs we've successfully implanted could usually communicate with their handlers right away. If they couldn't within a couple of hours, the procedure was almost always a complete failure. He's beginning to move; let's watch him as he comes to."

Blackie was beginning to stir. It seemed to Jack that time stood still as the dog opened his eyes and looked around.

For a long moment, nothing happened. Suddenly, Jack felt the familiar, almost imperceptible tingle inside his head. He smiled and nodded to the Captain.

"*Jack, is that you?*"

"*Yes boy, it is.*"

"*Where am I?*"

"*You're in the research hospital recovery room with Captain Harrison and me.*"

"So, the Colonel finally caught us. What is Captain Harrison doing here? Is Heather here too?"

"I don't know what you mean, Blackie. The Colonel is in jail. Captain Harrison came so he could see what happened between us when you woke up and Heather is at home. I can't believe you're able to talk to me so fast."

"Blackie? Who is Blackie?"

"It's you, boy. I know this is a lot for you to understand, so I'll try to explain it to you. You were given something called an anesthetic that made you sleep while the doctors put a device into your head. It connects your mind to mine and we'll be able to talk to each other through it from now on. You'll learn more as the sedative wears off."

"Jack, don't you know me?"

"What do you mean, boy?"

"It's me; Boss. What am I doing here? Did you decide I should have the operation to remove the lesions? You promised me you wouldn't do that. What if my legs don't get better?"

"Boss? You're not Boss; you're Blackie."

"No, I'm not. At least I don't think I am. I'm not sure I understand all this. I'm very sleepy."

Jack turned to the surgeon.

"Doctor, something strange is happening."

"What do you mean?"

"The procedure seems to have worked. Blackie is communicating with me, but he thinks he's Boss, my dog that died."

"What? That shouldn't be happening. Actually, it's impossible. A dead dog can't communicate through another dog's mind."

"As my dead dog once told me, if it's happening, it must be possible."

"There has to be an explanation. Ask him why he thinks he's Boss."

"Why do you think you're Boss?"

"Because that's who I am. I heard what you and the doctor just said, but I'm not dead."

"Boss died, Blackie. It broke my heart when he left me. If I'd known this was going to happen when you were implanted, I wouldn't have let it be done."

"I don't know anything about more implants, but I do know who I am. I'm Boss."

"No. I don't know why you think you are, but Boss died over a year ago. You're Blackie, Boss's brother. The anesthetic must be confusing you. It should be wearing off in a little while. Maybe then, you'll realize who you are."

"My brother?"

"Yes. Boss was your brother,"

"No, I'm Boss and I'm asking you about my brother. I didn't know I had a brother named Blackie."

"If you're Boss, what are some of the last things you remember before you woke up on this gurney?"

"I remember being in Doctor Edwards' office and not being able to walk and I couldn't talk to you very well. I remember you telling me about Heaven and a bridge made of rainbows as I went to sleep. Then, I woke up and you and Captain Harrison were here."

Jack felt his knees begin to weaken. Could it be possible?

"Whoever you are, hang on for a minute. I need to talk to the doctor again."

"Doc, Blackie insists he's Boss. I just asked him what his last memories were and he told me the exact thing we talked about just before he died. I haven't told another living soul what we said to each other. I can't believe it, but I think Boss is talking to me."

"Mr. Randall, it's just not possible. A dead dog can't do that. I don't know why this is occurring, but there must be a logical explanation for it. He might think he's Boss, but he's not."

Jack's head tingled again.

"Jack? I'm Boss and I know it. The anesthetic is wearing off and my mind is getting clearer every second. I think there's something else going on. I think I'm Blackie, too!"

"What do you mean?"

"You came to the kennel one day while I was there. I saw you and it was as if I had known you for a long time. You took me with you when you left and we've been together since then."

"Blackie, is Boss still there or is he gone?"

"I'm still here Jack, but so is Blackie. I'm confused."

"Hang on; I have to talk to the doctor again."

"Doc, now he says he's Blackie, too. How can he be both dogs?"

"I don't know. We've never had anything like this occur. Maybe it's because you have an implant that was put into place when Boss was implanted. Or, it could be there's something strange going on with the electronics that we haven't seen before. Let's not do anything to upset him"

"Your people tested my implant a few weeks ago when they were checking out Blackie. Everything is supposed to be fine with it. How could it be causing this to happen?"

"I don't know. I'm going to have to think about this for a while and speak with some of the other scientists. Maybe one of them will have some insight."

"I'm going to talk to him some more."

"Tell him we're going to move him to a room where the two of you will be comfortable."

"Blackie, did you hear what he said?"

"I did. So did Boss."

"You need to stay calm so you don't hurt yourself. We'll be here for a couple of days before we go back to the research center. We'll have plenty of time to talk while you recuperate."

∞ ∞ ∞ ∞ ∞ ∞

Three days later, the surgeon who had spoken to Jack at the hospital came to their room at the clandestine research facility where Jack and his dog were transferred two days after surgery. They would stay there for at least a couple of weeks until the scientists were ready to release Blackie. Jack had many questions for the doctor.

"Hi, Doc. I'm waiting for an explanation."

"Is your dog still telling you he's both Boss and Blackie?"

"Yes."

"I've talked to several of our scientists and we think we know why."

"Ok."

"This is just theory mind you, but we believe it's the only possible explanation. We put the implant into Blackie, so Blackie is communicating with you."

"Then, why does he think he's Boss?"

"This may not make any sense to you, but in a very real way, he is."

"How can that be?"

"When you and Boss were implanted, your minds were connected. You both shared every memory that was stored in them and every thought that either of you had from then on. That happened right up until the moment Boss died. When Blackie was implanted, all the thoughts and memories you and Boss shared were immediately transferred to him by your implant, when he woke up. The anesthetic caused him to become confused as he was waking up. He thought that he was Boss and for all practical purposes, he became and still is, Boss. But, he is also, Blackie. Blackie has all the thoughts and memories he had before the surgery, so, he is still Blackie, but, he is also Boss. Does this make any sense to you?"

"I'd begun to suspect that was what had happened. I guess I had to hear you say it to believe it. Boss is back inside my head and Blackie is there, too. Blackie's memories are also in my mind, so I'm convinced that's what occurred. It all seems to be coming together. I think we'll be able to sort this out, it'll just take a while."

"We've been discussing you and your dog for the past seventy-two hours. Some of us have barely slept. Our brains are funny things, Mr. Randall. We believe you and your dog, or I should say dogs, will adapt to this. Your minds seem to be recognizing three distinct personalities that are in communication with each other. There will be you, Blackie and

Boss. There's the possibility that both dog's minds will meld into one, but we don't believe that will occur."

"Won't that be confusing?"

"It may be at first, but you should be able to keep the three personalities separate. I wish our program wasn't Top-Secret so we could share this information with the rest of the world. It would give psychologists many things to think about."

Jack laughed. "Yes, I believe it would," he said.

"I'm pleased to see you're taking it this way. Many people wouldn't be able to."

"Dr. Bailey, maybe they'd be afraid of what has happened, but I'm not. I'm happy it did. You have no idea what I went through when Boss died. It's as if I'm hearing his voice again."

"You are. What you and Boss used to be is still there. It's just that Blackie's voice has been added to the mix."

"Do you think we'll be ok?"

"It's impossible for us to know. Mr. Randall, I'm going to ask a favor of you. After you and Blackie leave here in a couple of weeks, will you please give me a call from time to time? In all the years I've been practicing veterinary medicine and doing research, this is one of the most interesting things that has ever occurred. I'd like to know what happens to you and your dog in the coming years."

"I'll be happy to if you give me your phone number. Right now, I have to call my wife and tell her about this. I didn't want to until I'd talked to you about it."

"I'm sorry, but I have to ask you not to do that. All of our research is Top-Secret."

"It's ok, Doc. I have the President's authorization to tell her about anything that happens to me or my dog where this is concerned. He said she's one of the few people I can talk to about it."

"I didn't know that. In that case, I'll leave you alone so you'll have privacy while you speak with her."

"Before you leave, you asked a favor of me and now I need to ask one of you. As soon as you think it will be ok, I'd like to take Blackie for a ride one evening about an hour before dark."

"I think that will be alright in a few days if you don't let him become too excited. If you don't mind me asking, where do you want to take him?"

"We'll go to a park down along the Potomac River that faces to the west. I have to show him a sunset."

Chapter 7

Three weeks later, Jack and Blackie were back at work and in training for their assignment. It had become much easier for each of them. Now that Blackie could access Jack's mind and Boss was there to help him, he could easily understand all the trainer's commands. It was just a matter of a few hours before he knew all that was expected of him. Jack's training in how to be a blind man became just as effortless. As long as Blackie was at his side, he could be blindfolded and still see through his dog's eyes.

Since Jack and Blackie no longer needed weeks of training, they could spend more time with his family, but Jack didn't feel it was safe for them to live together right away. That would have to be delayed until either Rodriguez was apprehended or the local pursuit of him was abandoned.

Now it was just a matter of waiting until the undercover police officers who had infiltrated the gang down at the docks could get information about when the cartel leader might be making a visit to Baltimore. Captain Harrison thought it best that Jack and Blackie begin spending a few nights at the hotel where they thought Rodriguez would be staying when he visited with his upper management. Jack was sent to a police makeup artist where his hair was streaked with gray and he was shown how to use the cosmetics that would make him appear to be a much older man. Little Jack thought it was amusing the first time Jack visited with gray hair. He laughed and said his Dad now looked more like a grandfather.

∞ ∞ ∞ ∞ ∞ ∞

Jack was driven to the Harbor House Hotel by a hired driver in a black limousine. He'd made reservations at the hotel under the name of Elwood James. The limo driver held the door for him as he stepped out of the back of the car with Blackie at his side and the white cane in his hand. He was wearing a costly dark blue suit that had been tailored to fit his body so he would give the appearance of being a wealthy older man with very expensive tastes. He was also wearing a pair of dark glasses to cover his supposedly diseased eyes. A doorman immediately sent an attendant to the back of the car to take the luggage out of the trunk and move it to the rooms that had been reserved on the top floor of the hotel.

Jack was accompanied by an undercover officer who would act as his valet. Corporal Silas Jones, who had been assigned the name of Edwin Bishop, had been a member of the Baltimore City Police Department for several years. Captain Harrison had revised the plan to include him. The Captain rightly assumed that a man of great wealth, who was losing his vision, would travel with an assistant as well as a Seeing Eye Dog. A rumor had been spread through the hotel staff that he was staying under an assumed name for reasons of privacy and security while undergoing treatment for his vision problems with a local eye specialist.

Within minutes, Jack, Blackie, and Silas were whisked to adjoining rooms. Their accommodations overlooked the Inner Harbor area of downtown Baltimore. It was not a view that room attendants thought Mr. James would be able to enjoy, but they were lodgings a wealthy traveler would be expected to occupy. They'd stay for a week to become familiar with the hotel staff, leave for a few days, then return. The cycle would be repeated until an opportunity to meet Rodriguez might occur. Almost three months would pass before Captain Harrison received a tip from his officers at the docks that the drug lord could arrive at any time.

∞ ∞ ∞ ∞ ∞ ∞

Jack was eating dinner at the hotel when two men walked into the dining room and were seated at a nearby table. One was tall and extraordinarily handsome while the other was short and swarthy. The tall man carried himself in a way that said he was accustomed to having his wishes carried out as soon as they were made known. He wore expensive western boots and a tailored charcoal colored suit. The shorter man was dressed in a rumpled brown suit and shoes that needed polishing.

Silas was seated next to Jack to appear to be helping him with his meal. Blackie was in his Seeing Eye harness and lying between their chairs as they ate. Jack and Silas were both wearing special contact lenses that would send audio and video messages by radio to a disguised police van that was always parked two blocks away from the hotel when they were in residence. The signals were scrambled to prevent anyone from monitoring their transmissions. They were brand new technology; criminals shouldn't even know about them yet.

They continued with their meals. Jack knocked over his water glass to draw attention to their table. A waiter came immediately to his side to wipe up the spilled drink as Jack apologized for being clumsy. The two unknown men looked in their direction as another waiter brought a clean glass and filled it with water. Jack noticed the taller man's eyes seemed to be drawn to the huge dog that was lying at his feet.

They ate slowly so they would end their meal just before the two strangers were getting ready to leave. When they finished their drinks and dropped their napkins onto their plates, Jack rose from his seat. He reached for the handle on Blackie's harness and moved in their direction. As he hoped, the tall man stopped him. He spoke in perfect English except for a barely discernible Spanish accent.

"Good evening, sir. May I compliment you on your beautiful dog? I am particularly fond of German Shepherds."

"Why, yes. Thank you. I'm rather proud of him. I've been told many times that he is very handsome."

"I don't believe I've ever seen one that is as big as he is and entirely black. Have you had him for a long time?"

"No. He's only been with me for about six months."

"He is a Seeing Eye Dog?"

"Yes, he is. My sister insisted that I get him. I didn't believe he would be necessary since my man Bishop is always with me; I thought he would be all the help I need. But, since my dog has been with me, I've come to depend on him more all the time. He's become a friend. I've never owned a dog and had no idea how attached you can become to them."

"I noticed he ate nothing as you dined."

"He's been trained not to accept "people" food since that would be a problem in dining rooms when we travel. He'll have his meal when we go back to our rooms."

"Are you staying just for the night or will you be here longer?"

"I'll be here for a few more days unless my plans change. I am being treated by an eye specialist for my vision problems. I always stay at this hotel when I'm in Baltimore."

"I am sorry for your affliction, sir. May I say hello to your dog?"

"Yes, of course. He's a good fellow, although he won't appear to be overly friendly. He's wary of people he doesn't know. He's not just a Seeing Eye Dog; he's been trained to protect me."

"I understand. I have German Shepherds that patrol the grounds of my residence. I have taken three of the most devoted inside my home. I love them almost as much as I love my own children. I believe your dog will like me. Hello, boy."

The man moved his hand cautiously toward Blackie's head. The dog didn't move as the man gently patted his head and scratched behind his ears.

"He is magnificent. What is his name?"

"I don't use his pedigree name, it's too long. I just call him Champ."

"He looks like a champion."

"I agree with you. From what I can see of him, he is a beautiful animal."

"So, you still retain some of your vision?"

"Yes, but almost none. My night vision went away some time ago. The rest has slipped away to the point that I'm almost blind. The doctor I've been going to here in Baltimore may be able to help me keep the slight bit of vision I have left. I was hoping for retinal implants. Unfortunately, the optic nerve has deteriorated and my doctors have told me I'm not a candidate."

"From what do you suffer?"

"I have a condition called Retinitis Pigmentosa. There is no cure."

"I will say a prayer that it does not worsen. God can do all things."

"Thank you, sir. I believe that. Are you staying at the hotel very long?"

"No. I will only be here for two days while I attend to business. However, I will be here tomorrow evening. Will you do me the honor of dining with me?"

"I would like that. A blind man doesn't receive many dinner invitations when he's away from home. May I ask you, what is your name?"

"My name is Manuel Garcia. This is my business associate, Jose Malenia. May I ask yours?"

"I am Elwood James."

The tall man offered his hand.

"Mr. James, I will see you tomorrow evening at seven, if that is agreeable to you."

Jack put out his hand and bumped Garcia's. It appeared that he hadn't seen Garcia's hand.

"It certainly is. Thank you again for your kind invitation. Good evening, sir."

"Good evening to you. Good evening, Champ."

Garcia patted the dog's head once more as Jack and Silas moved away from the table.

Garcia turned to the short man who was seated beside him.

"Jose, see what you can find out about him."

Jose left the table and walked to the bar in another area of the hotel. Bartenders were always good sources of information. It would help that he was also from Mexico; they could converse in Spanish. Jose was not completely comfortable with the English language.

∞ ∞ ∞ ∞ ∞ ∞

Jack and Silas left through a side entrance of the hotel and went to an area on the grounds near a waterfront sidewalk. It was something they did every evening so the hotel staff would become accustomed to them leaving the hotel to walk the dog. They could talk without the risk of anyone overhearing their conversation. Silas didn't know Jack could communicate with Blackie.

"What do you think, Silas? Could he be our man?"

"It's the closest thing we have to a lead so far. We'll have to assume he is, at least until we find out differently. He sure fits the description."

"We'll walk along the water for a few minutes and then go back to our rooms. After we're there for a couple of hours, I'll go to bed. You wait until I should be asleep, then go out for a walk around town and stop in a bar for a drink. While you're there, call the Captain and tell him what's going on. I don't want to call him from our rooms or talk about this while we're in the hotel; someone could hear what we're saying. He should already know we may have contacted Rodriguez because of the monitoring of our contact lenses. He might want to tell us if he thinks we're on the right track."

"Right, Jack. That guy sure looked the part, didn't he? He had the nice suit and the boots and he was attracted to Blackie."

"He did all the right things. From here on in, we can't be too careful. While we're at the hotel, there can't be any more Blackie or Jack. He's Champ, I'm Mr. James, you're Bishop and that guy we met is Manuel Garcia. If that was Rodriguez, he'll have his people check us out and they'll probably be watching what we do. He didn't get to where he is by being stupid. We'll have to do whatever he suggests from now on and hope the Captain follows along through our lenses. I hope we can pull this off."

"I understand, Mr. James. That won't happen again."

"If the Captain has instructions for me, write them on a piece of paper and slip it under my pillow when you get back. I'll pretend to be asleep. I don't want to risk talking about this in our rooms. If anyone is watching, they'll think you're just checking to make sure I'm alright. I'll read it after you go to bed and flush it down the toilet. I want to try something tomorrow evening. Listen closely. I'll tell you what I want the Captain to do..."

Jack waited for almost two hours before going to bed. Silas had gone to his room through the connecting door after helping "Mr. James" change into pajamas. They would have to adhere to their deception every second from now on. After Silas left his room, Jack spoke through the implants.

Jack- *"What do you think, boys?"*

Boss- *"I think he's our man. I could sense something deadly about him."*

Blackie- *"I could feel that too, but there was something else there. I think he has a good heart."*

Boss- *"Blackie, you're young and inexperienced, but you can tap into what Jack and I know about people. Couldn't you tell he's a very evil person?"*

Blackie- *"I could feel that as well as you could, but there was something I liked about him. He likes dogs, so he can't be all bad."*

Boss- *"You need to search Jack's memory for everything Captain Harrison said about Rodriguez. He may like dogs, but that's the only thing that's good about him. If he is Rodriguez, we're going to have to take him out. We can't let your feelings get in the way."*

Blackie- *"I know we have a job to do. I'll get over the way I feel."*

Jack- *"Boys, Boss is right. If he's Rodriguez, he has to go down. People are dying every day because of him. Boss, if you think he's our man, he almost certainly is. It may take us a while to get him, but if anyone can do it, we can. Tomorrow evening, I'll make an excuse to leave our table while we're eating. Maybe you'll overhear something while I'm away that will help us. If you do, I'll also hear it and that will give us more to work with. Ok, Blackie?"*

Blackie- *"Of course, Jack. There'll never be a time when you can't rely on me."*

∞ ∞ ∞ ∞ ∞ ∞

Jack arrived in the dining room promptly at seven the next evening. He saw that Garcia was already seated with Jose in a dimly lit area in the back of the room where a casual observer might not even be aware of their presence. A bandage was wrapped around Garcia's left hand. Jack noticed he was wearing a lighter colored suit and a different pair of western boots. Both men stood as he arrived at their table with Silas and Blackie at his side.

Garcia spoke first. "Ah, Mr. James. I am happy to see you and your beautiful dog, once again. Will you please sit here beside me? Your dog can take a place on the floor between us. May I ask a favor of you? In my country, we do not have dinner with our servants. Would it be too much to ask to have your man sit at another table? I have made arrangements with the waiter that he be seated nearby in case you should need him."

That would fit in nicely with Jack's plans. Silas already had his instructions. Sitting at another table would make them easier to carry out.

"That's fine with me, Mr. Garcia. I'm sure Bishop won't mind. I'm not so blind that I can't eat without his help if our dinnerware is placed in the customary positions. Bishop, will you please sit where the waiter takes you?"

"Yes, Mr. James."

"Good."

They sat down as the waiter led "Bishop" away.

"Mr. Garcia, how is your visit coming along? Is your business going as expected?"

"It is, but unfortunately, as in any business, there are always problems."

"I hope you can take care of them successfully."

"Thank you, I already have. Our attendant is coming back. Do you know what you would like to have for dinner? The seafood is wonderful."

"I do. I've almost memorized the menu. I had Bishop read it to me the first time we came to this hotel. I try to eat things that won't drip onto my clothing."

"Then, we'll go ahead and make our order. Please go first, sir. Would you like to order something from the bar so we can have a drink while our meals are being prepared?"

"No, thank you. I have to keep my wits about me. Since my vision began to fade, I can trip over something as small as a ripple in the carpet. Please don't let that prevent you from having a drink."

"Thank you. I never have more than one glass of wine with dinner. I agree with you; it dulls the mind and sometimes makes us forget ourselves."

The three men made their orders.

Garcia remarked several times as they were eating about how much he admired Champ. He said he'd never seen a dog quite so beautiful. Jack could feel the pleasure emanating from Blackie. As planned, toward the middle of their meal, Jack's phone buzzed. He pulled it from his jacket pocket and pretended to fumble with it until he found the oversized off button. Within minutes, a waiter came to Silas and told him there was a phone call for Mr. James at the front desk. He rose from his table and walked over to Jack's side.

"Excuse me, gentlemen. Mr. James, there is a phone call at the front desk for you. Would you like me to tell the waiter to transfer it to this table?"

"Thank you, Bishop. Is it my sister? She probably just called me. I turned off my phone so our meal wouldn't be interrupted."

"Yes, sir. The waiter said it was her."

"I should have called her before we left our rooms. She'll want to talk my ear off about how my treatments are coming along. Gentlemen, will you please excuse me for a few moments? I don't want to bore you with our conversation, so I'll go to the front desk to speak to her. I'll have to take her call or she'll be angry with me."

"Of course, Mr. James. I hope you don't need your dog to accompany you. Please allow him to stay with me while you're gone. Can your valet escort you to the telephone?"

"Certainly. I didn't realize you were enjoying Champ's company so much."

"I am. He reminds me of my dogs at home."

"Then, I'll leave him with you. I'll be back as soon as I talk to my sister. Bishop, please take my arm. Champ, stay! "

Jack let Silas lead him away from the table. As they left, he saw that Garcia had dropped his hand onto Blackie's head. They walked to the front desk where he was shown into a small office. A policewoman, who had already been given instructions by the Captain to act like a worried sister, spoke with him for several minutes on the telephone. As they talked, he listened through the implants to everything that was being said at the dining room table.

Jose leaned close to Garcia and spoke quietly in Spanish. "So, Jefe, what do you think we should do about the next shipment?"

"Speak only English, Jose. You need the practice. We'll go ahead with it. I'll be here with you when it arrives. I hope your new Baltimore supervisor understands what will happen to him if he ever double crosses me. He should after he saw what I did to his cheating boss last night. Things will go very badly for him if he ever tries to steal from me."

"I could have handled the problem for you."

"I know, but there are times I need to take care of something like that myself. You shouldn't have a boss who is afraid to get his own hands dirty. Your people now know you have someone that you have to answer to and it's good for you to be reminded of it occasionally."

"You don't have to do that. I would never do anything to harm you."

"For your sake, you'd better not ever try. Your friend was trying to tell me he wouldn't last night, even as I was pushing his lying tongue through the hole I made in his throat. I wanted to be sure there was plenty of blood in the water to attract sharks to his body when I threw it off the number seven pier. He caused me to cut my own hand. I got so much of his blood and my own on my clothes; I had to throw them away when I got back here last night."

"I tried to tell you, I don't think there are any sharks this far away from the sea."

"Then the other fish can eat him."

"Ok, Jefe. I hope they eat him before somebody finds him."

"They will. Even if they don't, there's nothing that will tie him to either one of us. Do I have to remind you again to speak English?"

"No, boss, I will remember."

"Good. I'll set up our next delivery when I get home. I'll have it come in on a ship from Canada, so even if there are people on the inspection team who aren't on our payroll, it won't be searched very well. There will be almost fifty million dollars' worth of cocaine and heroin on that ship."

"Won't it have to go a long way to stop in Canada before it comes here?"

"It will be worth it. The ship will be carrying other cargo from Mexico that will be offloaded in Canada. It will then be reloaded with Canadian goods and make a stop in Baltimore on the way back to Mexico. Some of the Canadian freight will be taken off, along with our goods. Since it's coming from Canada, the inspectors won't think it will be carrying anything illegal. We control the Customs supervisor here and he can manage the details. There shouldn't be any problems."

"That is a good idea. When will it get here?"

"If everything goes as it should, in three weeks. I'll tell you the name of the ship just before it docks. It will come to one of the piers that we control. I'm not usually in a city when one of my shipments arrives, but because I've had to appoint a new supervisor, I'll have to make an appearance."

"Will we be staying at another hotel? It is not good for us to always be staying at the same one."

"Why should we? I like it here and many of our people work here. They know how a Mexican gentleman expects to be treated when he is away from home. No, Jose, we'll be staying at this hotel. If Mr. James should also happen to be here, I'll buy his dog from him."

"I don't think he's for sale. I found out last night that Mr. James is from a very wealthy family that lives in the middle part of the United States. They made most of their money many years ago with their steel factories and oil wells. James isn't even his real name. For security reasons, he doesn't want anyone to know who he is when he travels. If he is as attached to the dog as he says he is, he won't sell him."

Garcia laughed. "Then, I'll take him. How hard can it be to steal a dog from a blind man? I get what I want, when I want it, Jose."

Jack waited until he was certain Garcia and Malenia had finished speaking about business before he had Silas lead him back to the table. He apologized when he returned.

"I'm sorry, gentlemen. It was unfortunate I had to leave you during our meal. My sister worries about me when I travel because of my fading vision."

"Think nothing of it, Mr. James. It is good to have a family that cares about you."

"Did Champ behave himself while I was gone?"

"Yes, he did. He is very well trained. May I ask something of you? I am returning to my home tomorrow and I admire your dog very much. Would you be interested in selling him to me? I'll pay you very well. I'd like to breed him to one of my dogs. I have a beautiful female German Shepherd that would make a superb mate for him. They would produce magnificent puppies."

"No, Mr. Garcia, I'm afraid I couldn't do that. I've become very attached to him in the short time he's been with me. I wouldn't want to part with him. I'm sorry, but I can't sell him."

"I was afraid you would say that. He would make a wonderful addition to my family. But, I understand how you feel. If he was mine, I wouldn't let him go."

"I'll need him even more as the last of my vision fades away. I'm sorry you have to leave so soon. I get lonely when I have to be away from home and I've been enjoying your company. I need to come back to Baltimore in a few weeks for more eye treatments. It would be nice if you were here."

"You may see me again, Mr. James. What is your schedule?"

"I'll be here in three weeks."

"This is a good thing, sir. I will also be here in three weeks for a business engagement. Will you be staying at this hotel?"

"I always stay here. A man with my condition needs to be in familiar surroundings."

"Then, we should meet again. I'll be hoping that you'll change your mind about selling your dog to me. If you haven't, perhaps other arrangements can be made about breeding him to my dog."

"It's possible. We can always talk about that when we see each other again. I'm sorry, but I'm afraid I'm going to have to leave you now. By the time I take my evening walk with Champ and Bishop, it will be time for me to go to bed. My eye treatments are vexing and I've had a very long, difficult day. Thank you for the wonderful dinner and your fine company, gentlemen. I wish you a safe journey home and I do hope to see you on my next trip to Baltimore."

"It has been a pleasure, Mr. James. I'll look forward to seeing you again you when I return. Good evening, sir."

∞ ∞ ∞ ∞ ∞ ∞

Jack and Blackie left the room with Silas and walked outside to the waterfront sidewalk. When they were far enough away from the hotel, Jack spoke quietly.

"Silas, I need you to get a message to the Captain as soon as I go to bed tonight. Go back to your bar and have a drink. Call him and tell him to very discreetly have a dive team go to pier seven and search under it for a body. He'll have to sneak the team into the water in another area. When they find the body, they'll have to bring it out where they went into the water. If anyone around pier seven sees them, they'll blow this whole thing."

"How do you know there's a body?"

"You'll have to trust me on this; there is. There are a few other things to tell Captain Harrison. Tell him to get hold of all the trash from the hotel and to try to figure out a way to do it without anyone at the hotel knowing that the police want it. Hopefully, it won't be picked up until tomorrow morning. If it's already gone, maybe it hasn't been burned yet and he can look through it at the incinerator. He's to search for a bloody suit and a pair of western boots with bloody soles. Tell him, if he finds them, to check them for two different blood types. There should be some from the body that's in the water and some from a cut on Rodriguez's hand. If he finds the clothes, we should have enough evidence to put Rodriguez away for first-degree murder. Have you got all that?"

"I do. I wish I knew how you got all that information."

"I'm sorry. Maybe one day I'll be able to tell you, but I can't right now."

"That's ok, just as long as we can bust this guy. Do you think he really is Rodriguez?"

"I'm certain he is."

"Then, why don't we go ahead and arrest him?"

"As it stands right now, we don't have anything on him. We need the dead body and the bloody clothes before we do anything else and we might not be able to find them. There's a big shipment of drugs coming here from Mexico, by way of Canada, in three weeks. He'll be here when it arrives. If we can get those drugs and arrest him at the same time, we can tie him to them. Before we do anything else, we have to find that dead body in the harbor. If we do that and get lucky and find his clothes in the trash, we'll be able to send him to prison for the rest of his life."

"How do you know he'll be here in three weeks?"

"He will be. If something happens to blow our case and he's not here, at least now we know who we're dealing with. If the contact lenses did what they're supposed to, we'll have video recordings of his face and voice. I slipped his butter knife into my pocket, so now we have his fingerprints. If we don't get him, somebody else will. It'll be just a matter of time before he goes down."

"That all sounds good to me. He's supposed to be the most bloodthirsty cartel leader in the past fifty years. I want to be with you when he's arrested."

"You will. Let's get back inside. I'll go to bed and you can call the Captain."

∞ ∞ ∞ ∞ ∞ ∞

After Silas left to call Captain Harrison, Jack directed his thoughts to Blackie.

Jack- *"Well boy, what do you think about Rodriguez, now?"*

Blackie- *"It looks like I was wrong about him. He seemed like such a nice man. It's hard to believe he could talk about killing someone so brutally and throwing the body into the harbor for the fish to eat and be willing to steal a Seeing Eye Dog from a blind man. I've never been around anyone who would do those things."*

Boss- *"Jack and I have met too many people like Rodriguez, Blackie. Up until now, you've only been around good people. There are some very bad ones out there. You'll just have to accept it and learn how to tell the good from the bad. It's not always easy."*

Blackie- *"You were right. I won't doubt you again."*

Boss- *"Good. Now, stop fretting about it. We have too many other things to worry about while we're taking this guy out. What's the next step, Jack?"*

Jack- *"All we can do is wait while the Captain looks for the body and the bloody clothes. Then, we'll come back here to help make the arrest when Rodriguez gets back."*

Boss- *"He won't be here for three weeks. Let's go home for a few days. We can spend some time with Heather and Little Jack. I miss them, so much."*

Jack- *"We will, boy. Let's go see our family. We'll leave here in a couple of days."*

Chapter 8

Captain Harrison wanted them to stay away from the office so Jack wouldn't be seen with his gray hair. He was afraid Rodriguez had people there working for him. So, they could spend as much time with Heather and Little Jack as they liked.

When Blackie received the implant and went back to Heather's house with Jack, the Boss part of his mind had been surprised at the difference in Little Jack's size. Even though he shared Jack's memories, Boss's recollection was of a toddler that was just three years old. Little Jack had grown. However, he still smelled the same. Boss was overcome by emotion when Blackie nuzzled up to the boy. As love for the child crashed through him once again, the joy he was feeling caused Blackie's body to quiver uncontrollably. Boss was happy to see that Jack had followed through on his promise to get Little Jack a puppy and pleased that the new dog not only looked like him but was named after him, too.

Boss also loved Heather. Since he and Blackie now co-existed in the same body, Blackie's love for Jack's wife and son was reinforced. Little Boss could sense the feelings the bigger dog had for the people he cared about, so there was no animosity between the two of them. They became close friends.

Heather knew the all-consuming depression that had haunted Jack was now gone. He was once again the gentle and caring man with whom she had fallen in love. They made plans to unite their family in one home as soon as the Rodriguez case was concluded.

Rodriguez had been carried away by his blood lust and forgot to use his normal animal cunning while discarding the evidence that could be used against him. He'd simply shoved the bloodstained clothing into a plastic bag and tossed it in a hotel dumpster. The hunt for it was rewarded within twelve hours. The trash had already been taken away from the hotel and hauled to the Baltimore City Incinerator, but fortunately, was not burned. The suit and boots were soaked with the two types of blood Jack predicted would be there. When the suit and boots were sent to Washington D.C and tested by the FBI, two sets of DNA were isolated. One came from the body that had been pulled from the Baltimore Harbor and the other would certainly match blood that would be collected from Rodriguez when he was arrested.

The mangled body Rodriguez had thrown off the pier had not been as easy to locate. After two nights of searching blindly through the cold, murky water, divers finally located it almost a quarter of a mile from where it was thrown into the harbor. It had been carried away by the tide that changed several times each day. It was brought to shore in an unmarked police boat and taken to the morgue where it was autopsied. Blood and tissue samples were collected. The Baltimore City Coroner's Office was trying to identify the corpse.

The murder would be tied directly to Rodriguez when he came back to the city. Jack had seen the bloody clothes. He'd be able to identify them in court as the suit, shirt and boots the drug lord was wearing on the first night they met at the hotel. He would also be able to testify he'd heard Rodriguez say he had injured himself while cutting the murdered man's throat. There would be a scar on his hand to verify that testimony.

Captain Harrison was doing research on ships going from Mexico to Canada with a stop in Baltimore on the way back to their home port. So far, he'd found three that would be arriving at the expected time. One would be docking at pier number seven. Unless they received better information, it was the ship that would receive most of their attention.

Three special Customs inspectors were sent to Baltimore as a safety measure to supervise the search of the ships. Each was advised to be meticulous as they were unloaded. The Customs inspector that the police department thought to be on Rodriguez's payroll would be closely watched as he went about his job.

It appeared that all that remained to be done was for police and Customs agents to concentrate their efforts on the ship that would dock at pier seven. Rodriguez would be arrested at either the pier or the hotel when the drugs were found. A case that Jack and Captain Harrison had thought would be almost impossible to solve might not be so difficult after all.

∞ ∞ ∞ ∞ ∞ ∞

Jack, Silas, and Blackie checked into the Inner Harbor House three days before they expected Rodriguez to return. They wanted to be there in the event he arrived earlier than anticipated. As usual, the same rooms and dining table were reserved so it would appear that an almost blind Mr. James would be in familiar surroundings. They didn't expect to see Rodriguez until shortly before the ship arrived. They were correct. Almost forty-eight hours would elapse before he appeared. They were seated at their regular table when Rodriguez and Jose walked into the dining room. The two men walked in their direction. Jack stood up and offered his hand.

"Hello, Mr. Garcia. It's nice to see you again."

Garcia looked puzzled.

"I'm sorry, do I know you, sir?"

"Yes, I'm Elwood James. I've been hoping to see you for the past couple of days. I heard Jose's voice and knew you must be with him."

Jose quickly thrust his own pudgy paw into Jack's hand.

"Hello, Mr. James. I'm glad to see you again, sir. Mr. Garcia, I'm sure you remember Mr. James. He was staying at this hotel the last time we were here. Remember?"

"Oh, yes. I do, now. I'm sorry, Mr. James. Sometimes my mind is occupied with so many things, I forget people I've met in my travels."

Blackie- *"Jack, it's not the same man!"*

Jack smiled. "That's quite all right. I thought for a moment I had said hello to the wrong person. My fading vision sometimes causes that to happen."

"It's good to see you again, sir. You'll have to forgive us, I've only just arrived in your city on business and I have much to talk about with Jose. I hope I see you again before I leave."

"That would be nice. Perhaps we can have dinner again."

"I'll try to set aside the time. Good evening, sir."

"Good evening."

Garcia had not appeared to notice Blackie. When Garcia and Jose were seated at their table, Silas whispered to Jack.

"What the heck was that all about?"

"It's not the same man. Don't say anything else about it; we'll talk later," whispered Jack.

After finishing his meal, Jack reached for the handle on Blackie's harness and stood up. He and Silas led the dog to the side entrance of the hotel for his evening walk. None of them noticed the short, powerfully built man who followed them as they made their way to the waterfront sidewalk.

Silas spoke first.

"What did you mean, it wasn't the same guy?"

"It wasn't. Did you notice the difference in his Spanish accent?"

"Yes. I thought it was more pronounced. I also thought his voice was a little different."

"The accent wasn't real; he was faking it. Rodriguez has a ringer. We've got to get word to the Captain before he and the Customs agents search the ship tonight. If this fake Rodriguez is there, they'll charge him with smuggling drugs and first-degree murder. The DNA evidence we got off the clothes won't match his blood and we won't be able to connect him to the body. The murder charge will be thrown out and maybe the smuggling charges along with it."

"Are you sure? This isn't a good time to be making mistakes."

"I'm sure. I don't know why Rodriguez sent an imposter, but he may have gotten suspicious and did it because he's afraid of being set up. He's supposed to be wilier than a fox. He's probably still out of the country, so he won't be in any personal danger while he waits to see what happens to his body double. If we arrest the phony, the real Rodriguez won't be coming back to Baltimore for a long time. We may never get him."

"What do you want me to do?"

"Go back to my room with me so it looks like we're settling in for the night, then go straight to the bar and call Captain

Harrison. We can't be sure he'll get the message through these contact lenses. They're just not reliable enough. Regardless of what else happens, we must get that shipment. We can't have those drugs hitting the streets. Tell the Captain not to arrest the imposter if he's there when they search the ship. The Customs people have to act like they only know about the drugs and don't suspect him of being involved. We'll have to let him go so the real Rodriguez won't be afraid to come back here at another time. We'll get him sooner or later; it just won't be tonight."

"What will we do about the fake?"

"We'll let him be, for now. He may not even know what's going on. If he did, he probably wouldn't be here. He's small fish, anyway. I don't believe the real Rodriguez suspects us of anything, so if we ever see him again, we'll still have a chance to pick him up. We'll just keep up our act and try to get info on when his next visit will be."

"Ok. The surprise inspection isn't supposed to happen until after midnight when the ship docks. I should have plenty of time to tip off the Captain."

"Good. Let's go back inside."

They went to their rooms. Silas waited a few minutes before leaving. He would be gone for nearly an hour. Jack would have to wait until he returned to find out what the Captain wanted them to do next.

∞ ∞ ∞ ∞ ∞ ∞

The hour passed and Silas hadn't come back. Just as Jack rose from his chair to look out of the window, he became aware of a quiet hissing sound coming from the air vent in the ceiling of his room. Blackie let out a low growl and ran toward the door as Jack slumped to the floor.

∞ ∞ ∞ ∞ ∞ ∞

Jack slowly opened his eyes to try to find the source of the roar that was buffeting his ears. A strip of black cloth had been tied around his eyes and he was lying on his right side. He tried to roll onto his back, but couldn't. His hands were bound behind him by stiff nylon straps and they were firmly attached to something that wouldn't move. As he came more to his senses, he realized he was aboard an aircraft that was moving swiftly through the sky. He reached out unsuccessfully with his mind to try to find Blackie and Boss. Where was he and how long had he been unconscious?

Almost an hour passed before he felt the toe of a shoe being thrust into his abdomen.

"Hey cop, are you awake yet?"

"What do you mean, cop? Where am I?"

The man laughed.

"You don't have to keep up the act. I know you're a cop."

"I don't know what you're talking about. Where is my dog? I can't get around without him."

The man laughed again. He seemed to be taking pleasure in Jack's questions.

"I just wanted to see if you were awake. We'll be landing in a few minutes. If you promise to be a good boy, I'll put you into a seat and put a seatbelt on you. If you don't, you can take your chances down there on the floor. We'll be landing in some bad weather and the ride may get a little bumpy."

Jack felt it was better to maintain the act of being blind for the time being until he had more information.

"I'll be a good boy, as you say, but I have no idea why you think I'm a policeman. I'd appreciate it if you'll be kind enough to put me into a seat and give me my cane. Where are we going? Am I being kidnapped? If I am, my family has money and will pay you whatever is necessary to have me taken home."

"You can stick to your story if you want to. All I'm getting paid to do is deliver you. I was told you were a cop and to make sure you didn't get hurt while I was making the delivery. I was also told not to answer any questions when you woke up. Maybe somebody will answer them when we get to where we're going and maybe they won't. After you're on the ground, this plane will be headed somewhere else and I'll be on it. That's all I know. I just go where I'm told and do what I'm told to do. You might want to think about doing the same thing when we land."

The man released the bindings that were holding Jack's hands to the side of the plane. He refastened them behind his back before lifting him to his feet and placing him into a seat. Jack felt the seatbelt being tightened around his midriff. Within moments, the engines became quieter and he could feel the airplane begin to settle toward the ground. He felt a sharp jolt as the plane's wheels touched the ground, rebounded off the pavement and finally settled onto the wet runway. His stomach was queasy and he felt lightheaded. Whatever they used to knock him out was still affecting his body.

The plane moved along the runway until he heard the engines shut off. Seconds later, he felt the slight change in air pressure as the cabin door was opened and the steps were lowered to the ground. He could hear the heavy footsteps of someone walking toward him and his unseen escort. The new man spoke with a heavy Spanish accent.

"I see you have brought my package. Has he made any trouble for you?"

"No. He was as good as gold. He just woke up a few minutes before we landed."

"Do you know anything about him?"

"Only that he insists he's a blind man and his family will pay a ransom if he's being kidnapped. I was told not to talk to him, so I didn't."

"That is good. We're not supposed to let him know where he is. I think there are some special plans for this one. You and the pilot are supposed to take the plane back to where you came from and keep your mouths shut. Do you have any questions?"

"I don't. I don't ask questions, I just do what I'm told."

"Then, adios amigo, until we meet again."

The man who had entered the plane unfastened the seatbelt. He pulled Jack to his feet and led him toward the door.

"Amigo, there are four steps to the ground. They are slippery because it is raining. We have a long ride ahead of us. If you don't cause any trouble, you will ride in the back seat of the car with me. If you try to talk to me or the driver, my orders are to place you into the trunk. I do not wish to do that because it gets very hot in there and you may suffer. Will you keep quiet until we get to where we are going or do you want to ride in the trunk?"

"Of course, I will. I just want to tell you something before you put me into a car. My family has a lot of money and will be very grateful to anyone who helps me. I promise you a large reward if you help me find my dog and see to it that we get back home. Will you please do that?"

"Money is of no use to a dead man. That's what I would become if I helped you. I suggest you speak no more or you will be placed into the trunk. Do I make myself clear?"

"Yes, you do. I'm sure this can all be worked out if my dog and I are not harmed. Where is he?"

"I know nothing about a dog. Whether you are harmed or not, is not for me to decide. Lower your head and bend down. I am putting you into the seat now."

The man helped Jack get into the back seat and then slid in beside him. The door closed and the car began to move. Almost two hours passed before it stopped again. When they reached their destination, Jack was pulled from the vehicle. He and his captor walked for several minutes across the rough bare ground before he was led into an overheated room and placed into a wooden chair. The humidity was very high and the air smelled of the jungle and rotting vegetation. They must be somewhere in the tropics; probably southeastern Mexico.

"I am supposed to tell you, I can release your hands, but when I leave, the door will be locked behind me. Many people have tried to leave this room without permission. None of them have ever succeeded. You will remain here until someone comes to talk to you. Under no circumstances are you to remove the blindfold. Meals will be brought to you when it is time for you to eat. If you remove the blindfold or try to get out of the door, you will be punished and from then on, you will not eat so well. I will know if you take the blindfold off or try to get out of the room. There is a camera in the ceiling and you will be watched at all times."

"The blindfold won't bother me, I can't see. If I did get out of here, I wouldn't be able to go anywhere. Will you please tell the person who has taken me prisoner, that I'm ready to negotiate for my release and will do whatever he asks of me?"

"The man who ordered you to be brought to this place is not here. When he arrives, I'm sure he will want to talk to you. I do not know how long it will be before he comes. Until then, cause me no problems and I will see to it that you are well taken care of."

"You won't have to worry about me doing anything wrong. Will you please bring my cane to me and tell me where I can go to the bathroom?"

"The banyo is right behind where you are sitting. I cannot let you have anything that you could use as a weapon, so a cane will not be brought to you. You will have to feel your way to the toilet. Do you have any other questions?"

"Since I'm to be held prisoner, will you bring me some food and let me have something to drink? I feel ill. I don't believe I've eaten for many hours."

"I am sorry you are not feeling well, but I cannot do anything about that. I will have food and drink brought to you. Do not try to talk to the guard. If you do, the meal will be taken away. There is a small opening in the door where he will pass meals to you. I assure you, the door and the lock are made of very heavy metal. It will do you no good to try to escape."

"I won't do anything to make a nuisance of myself. I'm only interested in my family paying whatever ransom is asked so I'll be released."

"That will not be my decision. I hope your stay with us will be a happy one."

The man left the room. Jack could hear the door being closed and locked. Rodriguez must have ordered his people in Baltimore to use some type of gas to knock him out and take him to the plane. That would explain the hissing sound he'd heard just before he passed out. He could only hope Blackie was still alive. For the time being, he felt it would be better to maintain the subterfuge of pretending to be blind. It probably wouldn't do him any good when Rodriguez arrived, but perhaps the man who brought him here would let down his guard and he could somehow make his escape.

He reached out with his mind for Blackie, in case he was nearby. There was still nothing, not even the slightest tickle in his head that would indicate he was in the area. Rodriguez may have sent orders for the dog to be killed, but Jack didn't believe he would have done that. He'd spoken of his great admiration for the dog.

He felt his way around the tiny cell and found a cot and a small table and chair where he would eat his meals. All three were fastened to the floor and there was nothing else in the room he could possibly use as a weapon. While he was using the bathroom, he reached under the blindfold and removed the contact lenses that had become almost glued to his eyes. Since they were supposed to be cleaned every day and he had no way to do that, he would have to leave them out. He stuck them underneath the filthy sink that was in the room so their transmissions could be picked up by anyone who might be searching for him. It would have to be soon. The minuscule energy cells would die within a few hours after the lenses were removed. Once they were taken out, the electricity from his body would no longer maintain the charge. He'd flush them down the toilet in a day or so.

Afterward, he stumbled to the hard cot where he'd sleep whenever his overworked mind would let him. The bed reeked of sweat and mold. Several days later, he felt a slight tickle in his head that lasted only a few seconds. Blackie must have been brought to somewhere in the vicinity. Many more days passed by without incident before Rodriguez finally made an appearance. Jack was almost happy to hear his voice outside the door. The tumblers clicked in the lock and the cell door opened.

"Mr. James, it is good to see you again. I hope you've found your room to be to your satisfaction."

"Who are you, sir? I don't believe I recognize your voice."

"Come now, Mr. James. Do you wish to continue this charade? You must know by now that I have discovered your true identity."

"Am I speaking to Mr. Garcia? I believe I recognize your voice from the hotel in Baltimore. I thought you were a gentleman, sir. It shouldn't have been hard for you to find out who I am. It usually becomes known after a while that my name really isn't James in most of the hotels where I stay. My family must be worried sick about me. Have you tried to arrange for my ransom?"

Rodriguez laughed.

"I haven't tried to contact your family, Mr. James. Or should I say, Sergeant Randall? Why Sergeant! Your hair is dark where it is growing out and your beard is not gray!"

Jack realized his cover had been blown. He hoped Rodriguez didn't know the murder of the drug lord's supervisor had been tied to him by his bloody clothing or that Jack had any way of knowing about the drug shipment. He might also be unaware that Jack knew his true identity.

"Ok, Garcia, I assume if you know who I am, then you must know what I was doing at the hotel. I was trying to find out about money laundering that we believe is going on there. I wasn't aware it had anything to do with you."

"Is that why your police department tried to have me arrested when my drug shipment was seized?"

"I don't know anything about a man named Garcia being involved in drug shipments and I certainly wasn't expecting you to be tied into the money laundering scheme. When I met you, I was trying to cover all my bases. I wanted the staff to believe I was just a lonely traveler who had met a stranger and was enjoying his company. I thought that's what you were."

"I'm not sure I believe you, Sergeant. I do believe that somehow, you have caused me a lot of trouble. People who make trouble for me are not allowed to live. The undercover officer who was working with you at the hotel found that out the hard way. You'll be happy to know he had two smiles when he died. The man I sent to kill him was instructed to pull his tongue through the hole in his throat after it was cut. He wasn't very pretty when your police department cameraman took his picture."

Jack shuddered. Silas had a wife and two children.

Rodriguez continued, "I still haven't decided what to do with you. You are very brave and I like you, but I believe you may have caused a man who looks like me to be arrested and charged with murder and drug smuggling. That man was very important to my business. I also believe that you may have caused me to lose a shipment that was worth a great deal of money and along with it, my board member, Jose. Because he would have told your police department everything he knew about me to save his own neck, I had to have him silenced when he was arrested. I'll find a way for you to make these things up to me if you were involved. Until I find out from my people exactly how your Customs inspectors got their information about my shipment and how your police department found out about my dead Baltimore supervisor, you will stay in this room. I'm not certain you could have known about those things and I want to be fair with you. I don't know why I like you Sergeant, but I do and I don't want it to be said that I killed someone I admire for something he didn't do. It's possible that some of my own people told the authorities in Baltimore about my shipment. If they did, I will find out and they will be punished. You will remain here while I investigate."

Jack could hear the controlled fury in the man's voice. He realized Silas hadn't been able to contact Captain Harrison and warn him not to let the false Rodriguez be detained when the ship was searched. Malenia must have been apprehended at the same time. After the lookalike was charged with drug smuggling and murder, it would have been quickly discovered that his DNA didn't match any of the samples that were taken from the bloody clothing Rodriguez had worn, but that wouldn't matter. By now, law enforcement agencies across the nation would know that the real Rodriguez looked exactly like the man who had been arrested. He had good reason to be angry.

"Since I'm going to be your prisoner for a while, maybe you could answer some questions for me."

"Like what?"

"How did you find out who I really am? Do you have people working in our police department?" Jack was hoping that like most criminals who seem to have been dealt a winning hand, Rodriguez might like to gloat.

"It doesn't matter what you know; you aren't going anywhere. Of course, I have people working there, but that's not how I found out who you really are. I owe that discovery to my youngest son, who is only twelve years old. Whenever I travel and make the acquaintance of people who are interesting to me, I have my people take pictures of them. I also have them find out everything they can about the person. They couldn't find much information about "Mr. James" and that made me curious. I pulled up pictures of us having dinner together on my computer several days after I returned home. My son loves our dogs almost as much as I do and the picture of your magnificent animal attracted his attention. He said you looked like a K9 police officer named Jack Randall from Baltimore who used to work with a black German Shepherd. He told me he'd seen this officer many times on his computer and our television and that the dog had died. I pulled up pictures of the officer and his dog and saw that while the man in my pictures appeared to be older, the dogs looked alike. When I compared my pictures of you to pictures of the young police officer, except for your gray hair, they looked almost the same. I suspected then that you were not the blind man that you pretended to be. I had my people at your police department send me copies of your fingerprints. I already had the ones taken from the silverware you used at the hotel. When I compared them, they were an exact match. At that time, I didn't believe you had any way of knowing about my shipment, so I let it be sent."

"Ok, Garcia, you found out who I am. Do you mind if I take off the blindfold now?"

"You are a worthy adversary, Sergeant and you seem to have a great love for German Shepherd dogs, as do I. A man like that can't be all bad. Maybe that's why I didn't have you killed right away, along with your friend, Silas Jones. You can take off the blindfold. I'll allow you that luxury while I'm deciding if I should kill you. I made you wear it all this time because you deceived me and pretended to be blind."

Jack removed the blindfold.

"Maybe you'd answer a couple of other questions for me?"

"What are they?"

"Why did you have Silas murdered?"

"The night we met, he left his room after my people thought you were asleep. He was followed as he left the hotel and was observed making a phone call while he was at a bar. I thought that was odd since he could have had a drink at the bar at the hotel if that's what he really wanted. Unfortunately for him, he spoke a little too loudly and the person I had following him overheard some of the conversation and suspected he might be working with law enforcement. After I returned to Mexico, I sent orders to have my people at your police department look at pictures that were taken of him and he was recognized as being a police officer. I was notified. At almost the same time I received the report about your friend, I discovered who you were. A man in my position can't allow things like that to continue, so I ordered my people to send you and your dog to me and to eliminate the other officer as soon as you went back to the hotel again and the opportunity presented itself."

"I'm assuming that you live in Mexico and I'm a prisoner somewhere near your home. If you're a big-time drug smuggler, how are you able to slip into and out of our country without getting caught?"

Rodriguez laughed.

"Only a very few people in my organization knew that I used a body double to do that. It was not hard to arrange. The man who looks like me is a citizen of your own country who knows very little about my business. I took the precaution of sending him to Baltimore when my shipment arrived instead of going there myself. I'd been told by my people that several new Customs officials had been sent to Baltimore and thought I'd better send him in case you knew more about me than I realized. I had to be seen by my people so they wouldn't start believing I wasn't watching my business very closely and begin cutting in on it like my last Baltimore supervisor. That could just as easily be accomplished by sending my body double if nobody knew about him except Jose. By doing that, I could remain safely here in Mexico while my business was still being carried out. It's a good thing I did that, wouldn't you agree?"

"Who is he and how did he get involved with you?"

"I'm sure the people at your police department have found out his identity by now, so it will hurt nothing if I tell you who he is. His name is Lawrence Turner and he's from the State of Arizona in your country. One of my people saw him and realized he could be very valuable to me. He's a poor man with no police record who wished to have a better life. I paid him very well for his silence and cooperation. He knows only that I am a wealthy businessman who likes to travel without being recognized."

"He must know what you do. If he didn't, how would he be able to help you maintain your cover and go in and out of the United States?"

"He knows very little. I supplied him with a military satellite telephone from my country, which has a scrambled signal, so we could communicate with each other. It is the same method I use to communicate with the rest of my people. He welcomed the opportunity that I offered him and didn't ask many questions. I paid him to get a passport from your government and to make himself available to me when I needed his services. As I said, he was a very poor man, but he soon learned to enjoy the luxury of traveling in the best suites on cruise ships and staying in fine hotels, just as I do. Whenever I wanted to enter your country, I simply paid him to arrange travel on a ship that docked in Cozumel. I would go there. He would leave the ship and I would go back aboard in his place later in the day with his identification papers. I carried aboard the papers which also identified me as Manuel Garcia in my pocket. He would stay in my hotel room in Cozumel while I disembarked in a port in your country when the voyage ended. When I wished to fly to different cities in your country, I bought a ticket in Mr. Turner's name. When I wanted to return to my home, I purchased a ticket on another ship, also in Mr. Turner's name, and left it in Cozumel. Mr. Turner would go back aboard and return to the United States until I needed him again. So, you see, he didn't need to know anything about what I do. Mostly, he lived in excellent hotels and traveled on fine ships and kept his mouth shut, which is exactly what I paid him to do. He didn't even know my real name."

"But, wasn't he acting as your agent in Baltimore?"

"No. All I needed for him to do there was to be seen by my people so they thought I was keeping an eye on them. I used Mr. Turner as a stand in whenever I needed to be in places where there might be risk involved if I was there personally. Since he knows nothing about my business, when he was detained in Baltimore, I allowed him to live. Until he was arrested for smuggling drugs and for a murder he did not commit, I'm sure he was very happy with our arrangement. Of course, he has told the authorities in your city about our arrangement by now, so he is of no further use to me. My precautions worked out well, don't you think?"

"I have to admit, you thought of just about everything and covered your bases pretty well. Garcia, I miss my dog. What have you done with him? I hope you didn't have him killed."

"As angry as I am with you, I would never have allowed that to happen. He was as much affected by the gas that was sprayed into your hotel room as you were. I had him brought out of your country and he is now living at my home. He is treated as well as my own children."

"Would you bring him to me?"

"Sergeant Randall, I have not yet decided what to do with you. I may keep you in this room until you are an old man. That would be a severe punishment since you are like me, a man of action. I will have to see how much trouble you have caused me. If I find out you were responsible for the loss of my shipment, I will give you to my men and their knives so you can entertain us with your screams. They are very good at making a man shriek for hours, without killing him. Then, I will cut your throat with my own hands. I will not allow you the courtesy of having your dog come here at this time. When you see him again, you will be a prisoner and he will not. He will always come and go as he wishes. I enjoy his company much more than I am enjoying being in this filthy room with you."

"How long will it be?"

"I won't tell you that. It might be next month, or it could be a year. I promise you will see him again, but I will not tell you when. You may leave the blindfold off. Other than that, you will remain my prisoner and that is the only luxury you'll be allowed."

"I guess that's more than I should expect from someone like you."

"I don't like your tone of voice, Sergeant. You will be very sorry if you make me angry. I'll give you some advice before I go. You should pray that you don't see me again right away. If you do, that would mean I have found out that it really was you who caused me to lose my shipment and you will suffer a very painful death. You should thank God that I haven't already killed you myself or had one of my people do it, instead of bringing you here. I am a very busy man and our conversation is growing tiresome. Goodbye, Sergeant Randall, for now."

Rodriguez left the room. Jack didn't fully understand why the drug lord hadn't ordered his death while he was still in Baltimore. His good fortune could change. Rodriguez was a psychopath and could change his mind about keeping him alive. He must be ready to attempt an escape at any moment if the opportunity presented itself.

∞ ∞ ∞ ∞ ∞ ∞

Weeks crawled by. His personal comfort depended upon the mood swings of his jailers. The building was made of solid concrete block with a reinforced cement floor, so breaking out of the cell was impossible. There was a fan in the ceiling that helped with the worst of the tropical heat that radiated from the metal roof and the room became extremely warm when his guards decided to turn it off, which they were prone to do upon the slightest provocation. The only window in the room was the small opening which the guards used to pass food to him. It was shielded glass and had been painted black so that no light would pass through. The only way he had of knowing what time of day it was depended upon the good will of guards who seemed to enjoy keeping him isolated from all human contact.

Finally, he felt the slight tingle in his head that indicated Blackie was nearby. The sensation became stronger.

Jack- *"Blackie? Boss?"*

Blackie- *"Jack! It's you!"*

He could feel the joy in the dog's mind.

Jack- *"It's me, boy! Where are you?"*

Boss- *"We're coming. We heard Rodriguez talking to one of his men on the telephone this morning. He's bringing us to you. He isn't going to let us stay, though. He's not going to let you do more than see us. He thinks it will upset you."*

Jack- *"It will. Do you know how long you're going to be here?"*

Boss- *"No. He's coming to see someone else that he has imprisoned. After that, he's going to come to your cell and talk to you for a few minutes before he takes us back to his home. We've been riding in this car for well over an hour. Do you know how we're going to get away from him?"*

Jack- *"I've had a lot of time to think about that. I don't have a lot of ideas. I've only been able to come up with one and whether it works or not will depend on you. Rodriguez has to leave home on business from time to time and he may let you stay with me. If he does, you'll be allowed to come and go whenever you want, but I won't. I'll need you to do something for me."*

Blackie- *"We'll do whatever we can to get us all away from here."*

Jack- *"I know you will, boy. You have to find something small that has a pocket in it, or at least something that has a place to hide a small object. You'll have to act like it's a favorite toy; something like any other dog would play with. If the time comes that he'll let you stay with me, you'll have to pick it up and bring it along with you. You doing this might be our only way to escape."*

Blackie- *"I see what you have in mind. We'll do it. I think we're getting close to you. I can see large buildings ahead of us through the trees. It looks like the buildings are camouflaged. There are trees all around them that are bigger than any I've seen except for the ones at Rodriguez's home."*

Boss- *"We're stopping. There's a gate and there's a tall chain link fence that's topped with barbed wire. It runs all the way around the buildings. Now we're going through the gate. There are guards everywhere and there's a big building with a lot of people in it that has a metal roof over it. It has canvas walls that are rolled up and there are several people inside."*

Jack- *"I know. I can see it through your eyes. We must be at one of the places where he gets his drug shipments ready to go. We've hit the jackpot."*

Boss- *"Hitting the jackpot won't do us any good if we can't get you out of here alive."*

Jack- *"I think we can do it if you can find the right kind of toy to bring with you the next time you come. After that, we'll make our own luck. I'll watch as you go with Rodriguez."*

Blackie- *"Ok, Jack. I hope we see you before we go."*

Jack- *"Me too, boy."*

He watched through Blackie's eyes as Rodriguez stepped out of the car. The tall man held a leash that was attached to the collar the dog was wearing. The men who were guarding the compound could be seen coming out from under the tall trees that shaded much of the area. They were carrying automatic weapons and all of them were being extremely attentive to the drug lord.

Rodriguez spoke to a guard who seemed to be in charge. He was taken to the end cell in the long building that Jack assumed housed him and other prisoners. Rodriguez entered and spoke briefly with the heavily bearded man inside who was dressed in rags. The man must have been imprisoned for a long time. That did not bode well for Jack.

Rodriguez left the cell and made his way to the room where Jack was being held. He banged on the metal door.

"Sergeant Randall!"

"I'm still here."

Rodriguez laughed.

"I'm certain that you are. How are you? Do you have any complaints that you'd like to share with me?"

"I have many, but I doubt telling you what they are would do any good."

Rodriguez laughed again.

"I'm afraid you're right about that, my friend. My people have been instructed that you should not be treated as well as you would be if you were staying in one of my country's finer hotels."

"None of them could be accused of doing that."

"You shouldn't be so negative, Sergeant. I brought you a gift."

"What is it?"

"I am going to open your window so you can see."

The portal opened.

Jack took the five short steps that were required to cross the small cell to the door. He knew he should appear to be surprised when he looked through the opening.

"You brought my dog to me! Hey, how are you, boy?"

He reached through the narrow window to touch the dog. Blackie knew he had to act as if he hadn't known Jack was inside. He barked excitedly and jumped toward the opening as Rodriguez cracked Jack across the knuckles with the short riding crop that he was carrying. He pulled Blackie away from the door and slammed and locked the window. Jack could hear him laughing as he stepped away from the door.

"You were too eager, Sergeant! Maybe next time I will allow you to pet your dog. Then again, maybe I will not! I hope you are enjoying your stay with us."

Jack watched through Blackie's eyes as Rodriguez walked to the car, entered the back of the vehicle and instructed his driver to leave the compound. The tingle in his head began to weaken.

Chapter 9

Time seemed to stand still as the unchanging days crept by. Keeping track of them was almost impossible. The only way he had of estimating how many months he had been imprisoned was by placing his finger into his mouth and using saliva to make a mark for each passing day on a grimy wall in his cell. He tried to count the days by the number of meals that were handed to him through the small opening in the door. When he had first been locked in the room, he was usually given three small meals each day, but sometimes there were only two and at other times there were four. Occasionally, the meals came during the day, but mostly, they came at night. Jack suspected this was being done intentionally so he would have no way of knowing how much time was passing. It was a form of psychological torture he knew Rodriguez enjoyed inflicting upon him. The small portal in the door sealed so tightly, it allowed no light to pass into the cell unless it was open. His cell was illuminated by one small light fixture that hung just barely out of reach. It glowed night and day.

When he had first been imprisoned, he promised himself he would stay in good physical and mental condition by practicing a daily regimen of calisthenics and by counting the thousands of steps he took while walking back and forth across the tiny room. He maintained his routine faithfully, but as the months dragged on, he began to miss a day from time to time.

When there were no further visits from Rodriguez and Blackie, it became harder to maintain the positive outlook he'd clung to when he was first locked away. Finally, there were days on end when he did little or no exercise at all. Every day, it became harder to focus on what was real and what was not. An unexpected noise from outside would sometimes cause him to leap across the room, while crashes of thunder from the numerous storms hardly bothered him at all.

More than anything, not being able to see sunlight began to fill his mind with an intense feeling of anxiety that increased with each passing day. It became almost impossible to sleep. What sleep he did get was broken by nightmares of being imprisoned for years in unending darkness. He would awaken from the dreams only to see the same dirty light burning dimly over his sweat-stained bed.

Just as he was about to give up all hope of rescue, he felt the familiar tickle under his scalp. Blackie! The sensation became stronger until the dog was once again with him in his mind.

Blackie- *"Jack! We're coming back. We're almost there!"*

Jack- *"I know, boy. Thank God. I was beginning to think I was never going to see you again."*

Blackie- *"Rodriguez is going away on business for a few days. He's having a problem with one of his drug factories somewhere in southern Mexico. Boss and I did our part. As soon as we left you, we began to pine for you. I started lying around, acting as if my heart was broken. It wasn't hard, we really did miss you. Rodriguez didn't pay any attention at first, but after a while, he began to talk about it. He talks to me like I'm another person. He'd tell me I'd forget about you in time and that it was best if I never saw you again, things like that. I kept it up. He began to tell me a couple of weeks ago, he was going to bring you to his house and keep you locked in a cell where I can see you every day. He's going to do that to keep me happy."*

Jack- *"That could help us get away from him."*

Boss- *"I doubt it. We can't be sure of anything where he's concerned. He changes his mind whenever his moods swing. He's a walking time bomb."*

Jack- *"I won't do anything to provoke him when he comes to my cell. It looks like he's coming straight here. I see you brought the toy."*

Blackie- *"We did. I've been playing with this thing since the last time we saw you. It has a nice big pocket in it."*

Jack- *"That's good."*

Boss- *"We have a lot to tell you. We've been listening to every meeting he's had at his home with his board of directors and almost every call he's made on his satellite phone. He even took us with him a couple of times when he inspected some of his drug* factories. *If we escape, we'll be able to shut down his entire operation with what we've found out!"*

Jack- *"That's wonderful, but unless we can get away from him, that knowledge won't do anyone any good."*

Boss- *"We'll do it. Jack, we can feel that you're very depressed. You have to pull yourself out of it if we're going to be able to get you away from here."*

Jack- *"Don't worry about that, I've been depressed before. Just knowing you're back, even if it's only for a few days, makes me feel better."*

Ten minutes later, there was a rap on the door.

"Who's there?"

"It is I, Sergeant. Were you beginning to wonder if I was ever coming back to see you?"

"I was hoping someone would come to see me, Garcia. I was beginning to get lonely. After all, what has it been, ten months since you locked me up?"

Rodriguez laughed.

"Something like that, Sergeant. I'm coming in. This time, I really did bring you a visitor."

The lock clicked and Rodriguez entered the cell with Blackie. The dog raced across the small room and jumped into his arms. Jack fell to the floor; the big dog had knocked him off his feet. He rolled across the room with the dog as he rumpled his ears.

"How are you, boy?"

Rodriguez looked unhappy, but not angry.

"I could see I was doing something very cruel. Not to you, to the dog. He missed you very much. When I took him away the last time I was here, he began to grow listless. He wouldn't play with me or my sons and he lost his appetite. He would lie with his head on his paws for days on end and I could only get him to eat the finest cuts of my best beef. All he seemed to be interested in is this chew toy that he picked up and brought with him today. I began to see he was never going to adapt to his life with me unless he could be with you. So, I had a special room constructed in a building on the grounds of my home, where I will have to take you so he can see you every day. Unlike him, you will be kept in chains. How does that sound to you, Sergeant?"

"I doubt I have any choice in the matter."

"You don't. I won't be able to do it right away since I have to go away on business for almost a week. I want him to be happy, so, while I'm gone, I'm going to allow him to stay with you here in your cell. As I said many months ago, when I told you I might do that someday, he'll be allowed to leave your cell whenever he desires. I'll tell my guards to be sure he is regularly exercised and that he will have full run of my compound. I'm also going to tell them to clean this room so he has a decent place to sleep. This is not a fit place to keep pigs. You stink, Sergeant."

"I'm sorry, Garcia. If I had known you were coming, I would have taken a bath. I haven't had a chance to freshen up this morning." Jack had not been allowed to shave or bathe since he'd been imprisoned.

"That is very funny. You will be taken to another building where you'll have a shower and you will be given clean clothing to wear. You can shave while you're there. After that, you'll be brought back here. I'll have your cell cleaned and fresh bedding brought for you and the dog while you are bathing. I hope you don't believe I am doing this to make you happy; I'm doing it so my dog will be comfortable."

"I never thought otherwise."

"Good! I'm going to give my men instructions and then I will be leaving. When I return in a few days, you will be taken to my home. Buenos Dias, Sergeant."

Rodriguez left the cell. The lock clicked behind him."

Boss- *"At least we'll be together for a while."*

Jack- *"Yes, unless he changes his mind. We're going to have to put my plan into motion as soon as possible. One chance might be all we get. As soon as he's gone, I'm hoping his men will get lazy again. Did you see how they jumped to attention when he got out of his car?"*

Boss- *"Yes, we did. Except for his children, there's fear in everyone. Even his wife seems to be afraid of him. He's an evil man."*

Jack- *"We'll give his men a few hours to get used to you being here. Then, we'll have to see what we can do when it gets dark. When the guard brings us our evening meals, we'll eat. When he comes back for the dishes, I'll tell him you have to go out. Since Rodriguez said he'd leave instructions for my cell to be clean and for you to have full run of the place, it shouldn't be a problem. You'll take your toy with you. I doubt Rodriguez allows any of his guards to bring regular cell phones onto the grounds. Once you're outside, watch for one of his supervisors to get careless and leave a satellite phone lying around. If he does, slip it into the pocket of your chew toy and bring it here. If you get one of the phones, I should be able to call the Captain on it. I used satellite phones when I was in the Army. I shouldn't have a problem making a regular call on one, even if the signals between his phones are scrambled. As soon as I'm through using it, I'll yell through the door that you want to go back outside. You'll take it back to where you got it. If the man who laid it down is looking for it, you'll have to put it on the ground near where you picked it up. He'll think he just dropped it."*

Blackie- *"It'll be easier when it gets dark. The hard part will be getting the phone into my toy. I don't have hands."*

Jack- *"Just do the best you can. It will be too big to hide inside your mouth."*

There was a knock on the door.

Jack - *"Here comes the guard to take me to the shower. While I'm gone, walk around the compound and make as many friends as you can. It'll be easier to get a phone if the guards aren't afraid of you. You are one scary looking dog, you know. I want them all to think you're as gentle as a lamb."*

Blackie- *"That should be easy. We won't be scary until we have to be. Do you have a complaint about any guard in particular? Maybe one day we can get even for you."*

Jack- *"There aren't any that really stand out. They're all bad. I'll see you when I get back."*

∞ ∞ ∞ ∞ ∞ ∞

Three days passed before the opportunity presented itself to act on Jack's plan. On the third evening, just at dusk, Rodriguez called one of the supervisors on his satellite phone to see if Blackie was being well taken care of. The man had only been on duty for a short time. He'd managed to slip a bottle of tequila into the compound to help him pass the night. After he finished talking to Rodriguez, he laid the phone down on a small table and walked outside of the building and looked around to see if anyone was watching. Then, he strolled around to the back of the building into the darkness and urinated as he drank from the bottle. Afterward, he lit a small cigar and walked across the compound to another building to talk with a friend. As Jack had anticipated, the men were careless when they knew Rodriguez wasn't expected at the compound for a few days.

Blackie picked up the phone, put his foot on the end of the toy he'd been carrying and pushed the phone into the pocket with his nose. As soon as it was inside, he picked up the toy and walked across the compound and scratched at the door to Jack's cell. A guard unlocked the door to let him enter. He relocked it after the dog was inside and walked away.

Jack took the toy from Blackie and walked over to the commode in the corner of the room, pulled down his pants and sat down on it. Blackie stood in front of him and blocked the camera's view. He hoped the guard watching the feed wouldn't be interested in what he was doing. He removed the phone and punched in Captain Harrison's cell phone number.

The Captain answered immediately.

"Hello, Harrison speaking."

"Cap, this is Jack. Quick, get a trace going on this call before you do anything else!"

"Jack! Where are you?"

"That's what I'm trying to find out. All I know is that I'm somewhere in Mexico near Cozumel. Get the trace going! I'm on a satellite phone and I don't know how long I'll be able to talk!"

"Ok, give me a second to push the right button. There, it's working."

The Captain's police issue phone had a button on the side that would begin an immediate tracking of a call from any other phone. It would work if the caller hadn't been able to set up a system that would hide his location. Rodriguez had almost certainly done that.

"I'll talk fast while you're tracing the call. From what I'm seeing in Blackie's mind, we're in Mexico, maybe two hours southwest of the Cozumel area. We must be close to the west coast of the peninsula. We're in a compound where drugs are being packaged. It's camouflaged and surrounded by a high fence. I'm guessing it's probably five or six acres in size. I'm locked up in the middle of a long building on the west side of the compound. The building has a corrugated metal roof. I believe it runs north and south, but I'm not certain of that. The fence is chain link and it's topped with barbed wire. There are about a dozen or so guards here and they're all carrying automatic rifles and pistols. There are workers that come here during the day to package drugs. Most of them must go home at night, but there are always guards here. Is your phone signaling a successful trace?"

"Not yet. We thought you and Blackie were dead. We found Silas a few blocks from the hotel in an alley with his throat cut. It looked like he was taken from behind. We couldn't see who jumped him through his lenses when he was attacked. We lost the signal from both of your sets of lenses just before you finished eating. A component burned out and our receiving equipment went down. We couldn't get it running again for almost two hours. By then, Silas was dead and there was no signal from you. It couldn't have happened at a worse time."

"I must have been on the plane by then. If Rodriguez hadn't taken such a liking to Blackie and wanted to pay me back over a long period of time for being a cop and deceiving him, he would have killed me already. He's away right now. If he hadn't left Blackie with me, I wouldn't be calling you. Blackie stole a phone from a guard. Cap, you've got to get us out of here. Rodriguez has kept Blackie with him since we've been gone and Blackie has heard almost everything Rodriguez has said regarding his business. He's filled my head with it. If you can get us out of here, we'll blow the lid off his entire operation. We know the names of most of the top people he has working for him. How's the trace going?"

"There's nothing, yet. You have no idea how good it is to hear your voice. Heather and Little Jack have been going crazy. We've been searching everywhere for your body. We've had divers all over the harbor, we've had people searching every woods and swamp that are anywhere near the city..."

Jack interrupted him. "We can talk about that later. Rodriguez will be back in three or four days. When he gets here, he's going to have me locked up in a building behind his house. If you don't get me out of here by then, you're going to have to look there. Getting me out of there will be a lot harder. It must be somewhere close to Cozumel, but it's on the mainland. I've seen the place through Blackie's mind. It looks like a fortress. It sits on about twenty acres that are surrounded by a stone wall. It must have cost a fortune just to build the wall. The house is huge. It's three stories high and there are several outbuildings around it. He slips in and out of the country on cruise ships, or at least he used to when he was using his body double. Because of that, he lives close to a port. Do you have anything on the trace?"

"It's still working. If I don't get one, at least we have some idea of where you are. We arrested the man we thought was Rodriguez, but we couldn't figure out what was going on. His fingerprints didn't match the ones on the knife you got from the hotel and his blood didn't match the blood on the clothes. When he told us his name and we checked him out, we knew we had an imposter. We had no idea what happened to you. Since we thought you were dead, we didn't even consider searching in Mexico. Now that we know where to look, we'll find you, even if I don't get a trace on this call."

"You probably won't be able to get one. Rodriguez uses military satellite phones he got from the Mexican government. They're all scrambled. Some of the biggest politicians in Mexico and in the U.S. are in on this with him, Cap. I have many of the names and the locations of several of his drug factories in my head. He'd kill me in a second if he thought I had any of that information. How's the trace going?"

"There's nothing, Jack. If it hasn't found you by now, it won't. Just sit tight and don't worry. I'll call the Attorney General as soon as I get off the phone. We'll have his best people going over satellite images of every inch of southeastern Mexico. We'll also send up drones to look for you. We should find out where you are within hours. We'll send people to get you as soon as we can. Just be watching for them to show up, in case you can do something to help us get you out of there."

"I won't be able to do anything. I've only been out of this cell once since I've been here. How long have I been away? I've lost track of time."

"You've been gone for over nine months. A couple of more days won't hurt now that you know help is on the way."

"I thought it was longer than that. Rodriguez is a mad man, Cap. He may come back and take me to his home or he may just decide to kill me. When you talk to Pembroke, tell him to make sure the people who start looking over satellite images of Mexico are watched every minute. Tell him not to let them make any phone calls without supervision until you send somebody to get us."

"I'll do that. Don't worry, Jack, we'll get you out of there, if I have to come get you myself."

"Tell Heather I'm still alive, but tell her not to let anyone else know, not even Little Jack. Rodriguez knows who I am and he might have people watching them. He has people working in our police department like we thought. Whatever you do, don't let anyone know about this that might run to the press."

"Don't worry. Nobody will know anything until you're back in Baltimore."

"Great! Do you have the trace?"

"I'm sorry, there's nothing."

"Then, you won't be able to track the call. I'm getting off this phone before the guy who owns it starts looking for it."

"We'll get our best people down there as soon as we find out where you are. God bless you, Jack."

Jack turned the phone off. *"Ok, boys, we're on our own for now. You heard everything he said. Let's get this thing back to the guard."* He slid the phone back into the toy and gave it to Blackie. It was returned without incident.

∞ ∞ ∞ ∞ ∞ ∞

Three days slowly passed by. Blackie spent much of the time outside so he could overhear anything that might be useful. Just at dusk on the third day, he made his way back to Jack's cell and scratched at the door. A guard walked over to let him inside.

Blackie- *"Jack, we have a problem."*

Jack- *"What is it, boy?"*

Blackie- *"The men are saying they think Rodriguez is home. If he is, he'll probably come and get us tomorrow. If the Captain is sending help, it'll be a lot easier getting us out of here than where Rodriguez lives. He spends a lot of money on security at that place. There are hidden cameras everywhere. There are two men assigned to watch the video screens at all times and there are guards with automatic weapons everywhere. To get onto the property, you have to pass through an iron gate that has a heavy machine gun mounted on each side. There's a guardhouse in front of the gate. There are a couple of low towers built into the corners of the walls on the back of the grounds that are also topped with heavy machine guns."*

Jack- *"I've seen it all in your mind. He lives in a fortress."*

Boss- *"He does. He'll have you heavily guarded and he'll leave orders to kill you if there's any sign of an attack."*

Jack- *"Then, we'd better hope the Captain sends help tonight."*

∞ ∞ ∞ ∞ ∞ ∞

Just before dawn, Jack heard whirring sounds that seemed to be getting louder. Suddenly, explosions erupted all around the compound. He and Blackie could see nothing of what was occurring outside of their cell, but they knew Captain Harrison was making good on his promise. They could hear screams and automatic weapons being fired. There was the momentary rattle of bullets hitting the walls of their building; then, all was quiet. An eerie silence swept through the compound.

A fist pounded on the door.

"Sergeant Randall, are you in there?"

"Yes. Who's out there?"

"Sergeant McCall of the United States Marine Corps. Are you alone?"

"I am, except for my dog."

"Do you know who has the key to the door? I don't want to blow it open. You might get hurt."

"I thought they usually just left it stuck in the lock. One of the guards must have it. You'll have to ask them which one has it."

"Not all of them are still alive. We'll find it. Just sit tight for a couple of minutes. If we don't, I have a small shaped charge that should blow the lock off without hurting anything except your ears."

"Take your time, Sergeant. Now that you're here, I'm not in a big hurry."

"I am. The Mexican government doesn't know we're here. We want to get out of their airspace as soon as possible."

"In that case, blow the door open."

"Wait a second, here comes a man with the key. It looks like he wants to cooperate."

Jack laughed. It was the first time he'd felt like laughing in many months.

"Cooperating with angry Marines is a wise thing to do."

McCall smiled as he turned the key in the lock.

∞ ∞ ∞ ∞ ∞ ∞

Fourteen hours later, Jack was back in Baltimore. He was wearing a clean set of military fatigues that had been given to him on the rescue helicopter. He was about to be debriefed by Captain Harrison and Special Federal Agent Ronald Strong.

Strong was a former Maryland State Police Colonel who had followed Governor Thomas to the White House when he was sworn in as President. He had been one of the President's closest friends and advisors throughout his political career. Because of his unwavering loyalty and impeccable service record, the new President immediately appointed him to a supervisory position at the Department of Justice. He answered to no one except the President and Attorney General. He'd been with the Marines during the raid on the compound.

Jack was telling Captain Harrison about how the attack had taken place.

"That was a well-planned operation. There was a brief flurry of explosions and gunfire which ended almost before it began. Within minutes, the Marines were hustling us into a chopper and getting us out of there."

Agent Strong helped describe the incident. "We sent in a couple of drones that were armed with rockets and took out the strong points. As soon as the rockets hit their targets, Marines began dropping down ropes from stealth helicopters. Rodriguez may have had the best guards his money could buy, but they were no match for our Marines. It wasn't much of a battle. We only had one man who was slightly wounded."

"Won't there be problems with the Mexican Government?"

"There may be, but not many. We did invade their airspace, but it was to rescue a kidnapped United States citizen from an ongoing criminal enterprise. We rescued some of their people while we were getting you out of there and you weren't the only U.S. citizen that Rodriguez had locked up. There might be a few grumbles from their President, but for political purposes, he'll probably make a show of thanking our government for helping him rid his country of organized crime. We don't believe he's involved with Rodriguez, so he may even say he asked us to go in. Our Marines destroyed a lot of dope while we were picking you up. Captain Harrison says you have sensitive information about Rodriguez and his contacts all over Mexico, as well as people in this country. I know you're exhausted, but I need to know everything you learned. I'm going to start recording our conversation if that's alright with you."

"It is. The sooner Rodriguez and his people are stopped, the better. Start your recording and you better hang on to your hat. The names of some of the people on his payroll are going to rattle a lot of cages."

"Then, we're going to have to keep you under wraps for a while. If the word gets out that you've been rescued, some of them may go underground. We'll have to keep our conversations secret until the Justice Department is ready to act. Nobody in this room will talk to the news media about any of this. From now on, we're all sworn to secrecy until the Attorney General gives us the official word to begin making arrests."

The agent began his recording. The interrogation ran long into the next morning. Just as the sun was rising, Agent Strong grimaced and turned off the recorder.

"You're right, Jack. This is going to shake our country right down to its roots. I didn't realize you only saw Rodriguez a few times and that he has no reason to suspect you know these things. When Captain Harrison called the Attorney General, he thought you had personally seen how the Rodriguez organization operates. He didn't know you'd only seen it through Blackie's eyes. Rodriguez believes you don't even know his real name."

"So, what's next?"

"Rodriguez doesn't know about your ability to talk to Blackie. I can barely believe it, myself. I'm going to call the Attorney General and see what he thinks. If he agrees, we'll tell the media that you were kidnapped for ransom by a Mexican drug gang and finally rescued. Since nobody but the three of us and the President and Attorney General will know you've given us this information, you'll be safe. We'll put security around you until we get Rodriguez in case he wants revenge for your escape, but other than that, he has no reason to bother you."

"I hope he does come after me."

"I just don't think that will happen. He doesn't know you contacted Captain Harrison on one of his satellite phones. If he checks call records, he'll see the call and believe one of his own men squealed to get a reward. We'll keep you under wraps until the Attorney General makes a decision. If he says it's ok, we'll make the announcement to the press about your rescue. Then, there'll be reporters for you to dodge for a few days until something else makes bigger news. We'll get Rodriguez as soon as he goes back home. He doesn't realize we know where he lives. We located his home with the info you gave Captain Harrison while you were still in Mexico. He skipped out when the Marines hit his drug factory, but he shouldn't stay away for very long. We'll keep a drone flying over his house twenty-four/seven and it will see him when he comes back."

"There are a couple of glitches in your scenario. If Rodriguez thinks one of his men has talked, he may not go back to his main home. He has several others, so it may not be as easy to find him as you think. Another problem is, the man is a psychopath and there's no good way to predict what he'll do. I'm ready to go back to my regular duties right away. It may be a good way to draw him out. He considered Blackie to be one of his finest possessions and he went to a lot of trouble to kidnap me. I don't imagine he's very happy I escaped and took Blackie with me. I think he may just come back to Baltimore again. I think he'll come after me, personally. I don't believe his ego will let him rest until he does."

"If he does, what's your plan?"

"I don't think he knows I'm married and I want it to stay that way. If he has his people look up my address, I want it to be different from the place where my family lives. I'll stay at my own house with Blackie and go back to work after the press coverage dies down. I want you to put some of your best people around my wife and son twenty-four hours a day. I want them to be handpicked by you and they'll have to come from your agency, not from ours. That way, I'll be able to concentrate on Rodriguez if he shows up in Baltimore. He had Silas Jones brutally murdered. My family thought I was dead. He kidnapped me and held me for the better part of a year in solitary confinement in a filthy, stinking, stifling-hot cell and went out of his way to make me miserable. He took Blackie from me and kept him away during all that time. He's a psychopath who likes to kill people with his own hands and gets a kick out of ordering the murder of others that he can't get to personally. He peddles death through the tons of drugs he ships into our country every year. I can't forget about things like that. I want him, Ron. I want to take him down and put handcuffs on him, myself."

"I think we'll get him when he goes back home. I'm happy to have your help, though. He's eluded us for years. It may take everybody we have to bring him in."

"Don't forget, we also have a couple of aces up our sleeve. He doesn't know what Blackie and Boss can do. In the end, that could make all the difference."

"I'm sorry, Jack. I guess I was forgetting about them."

"There's no apology necessary. We know about their abilities and Rodriguez doesn't. That may be his undoing."

"I hope so. I don't know what you're going to do right now, but I need some rest. I'm going to call the Attorney General to tell him I'm sending this recording. Then, I'm going to get some sleep. When I wake up, I'll call him back to see what he thinks after he and the President have had a few hours to talk.

∞ ∞ ∞ ∞ ∞ ∞

Captain Harrison drove Jack and Blackie to a nearby hotel that the police department used to house visiting lawmen. They stumbled into a room and collapsed onto the bed. When Jack woke up hours later, he saw that Blackie was still lying beside him. He gave his friend a gentle shake and the dog opened his eyes. The telephone Captain Harrison had given him buzzed. He touched the screen.

"Hello?"

"Jack? This is Captain Harrison."

"Good morning, Cap. What time is it?"

"It's almost 10:00 A.M. You slept completely around the clock, twice. I tried to call you about an hour ago, but you didn't answer. I figured you were probably still sleeping."

"I was. What's going on?"

"I got a call from Attorney General Pembroke a couple of hours ago. The President gave his approval to what you and Agent Strong want to do. There's going to be a press conference tomorrow morning and you'll have to be there. A spokesperson from the State Department will also be there to give a song and dance about how you were kidnapped while you were doing undercover police work. You were taken to Mexico and held for ransom. The media will be told that the President of Mexico asked our government to send some of our drug gang specialists down there to help train his federal police. They went along on a raid to destroy a drug factory. While they were there, they stumbled across you and sent you home. We don't want it to be any more complicated than that. If we give out more information, some of the people we're going after may start covering their tracks."

"I understand, Cap. What will I be doing until tomorrow?"

"I'm sending a man over with some new clothes and shaving supplies for you. I called Heather. She'll be joining you in about an hour. She'll bring you and Blackie something to eat. You'll have to explain to her what's going on so she'll know to stick to the story about you and her being separated in case the press tracks her down. I doubt that will happen, but she'll need to be ready in case it does."

"I understand about that and so will she. Little Jack may be another story. He thought everything was going to be alright between us and then he thought I was dead for almost a year. Now, he's not going to have his father come back home. This is going to be hard. I haven't seen either of them for a long time."

"I know. It's just until Rodriguez is caught. I'm going to come over and get Blackie after she's there for a while. I'll bring him back to you in the morning. I want you to take some time off after the press conference and spend it with her, Little Jack and Little Boss. You and Blackie should take them with you and leave Baltimore for a few days and get to know them again. I'll get the police department to cover the bill. My wife and I will look after Little Jack and the dogs tonight so you and Heather can have some private time. You'll have to tell Little Jack about the three of you being apart for a while longer the best way you can. Once we get Rodriguez, then you can put your family back together."

"Ok, Cap. This just makes me even more determined to get him. He's destroyed enough lives."

"That's the spirit. I'm going to hang up now and send the clothes and the shaving gear over. We'll talk more about Rodriguez in morning, after the press conference."

"That sounds good. I'll see you in a couple of hours."

He touched the screen and broke the connection.

Jack- *"I guess you heard that, boys."*

Boss- *"We did. It will be wonderful to see Heather again. We both understand why you need some time alone with her. We want to get Rodriguez as badly as you do and we'll make whatever sacrifices we have to, to get him. Silas was a good man and didn't deserve to die the way he did. It's terrible that his family will never see him again. Having to be away from Heather and Little Jack for a while longer seems like a small price to pay, when you weigh it against that."*

Jack- *"You're right, boy. Thanks. You just helped make this a lot easier for me. Let's get this press conference behind us. Then, we'll have some time to visit with our family."*

Chapter 10

Several weeks passed without incident. Jack was beginning to think Agent Strong had forgotten him. He was surprised when his phone buzzed one morning almost an hour before he usually got out of bed.

"Hello. This is Sergeant Randall speaking."

"Jack?"

"Who's this?"

"This is Ron Strong. Sorry about the early call. Would you like to take a ride with me?"

"It depends on where you're going and if I can take Blackie along."

"You can. We need him, too."

"Where are we headed?"

"We're going on a little trip down to Mexico with a few Marines to see if we can find our friend, Rodriguez. You said you wanted to personally put handcuffs on him and I wanted you to have your chance to do that. We're going to raid his home. We believe he slipped back there early yesterday evening."

"Won't the Mexicans be upset about that? We'll be invading their country, again."

"President Thomas called the President of Mexico directly to tell him we'll be doing it. He threw a fit at first, but he calmed down when he was told about half of his foreign aid would be cut off if he didn't give us permission. He was asked to keep quiet about it until after we're through. When we get Rodriguez, he can say anything he wants to the press, but he'll probably say he helped plan the raid."

"It may cost President Thomas some votes in the next election. There are a lot of people in this country with roots in Mexico."

"Right now, he's more concerned about drug-related crime than he is about politics."

"He's a good man. I wish we had a hundred more like him in the House and Senate."

"So do I."

"I appreciate you taking me along with you."

"We need you. You know Rodriguez better than anyone else. You're also a combat veteran with a head full of details that Blackie put in there about how the house and grounds are laid out. We're going to put a set of fatigues on you and give you a weapon. You and Blackie won't be going in with the Marines when they hit the ground; you'll be in a backup chopper with me. Once the heavy machine guns are knocked out, we'll set down and help take Rodriguez."

"I'm looking forward to spitting in his eye and telling him I'm partly responsible for the lifetime in prison that's ahead of him. I wish Maryland hadn't done away with the death penalty. He deserves it for what he did to Silas."

"We won't be taking him back with us. His life won't be worth five cents if he comes straight to the States. When we get him, there'll be a lot of politicians both here and in Mexico who won't know you already gave us all the information we need to get them. They'll do their best to silence him. The President says we're to take him to Guantanamo for questioning and safekeeping. We'll keep him there and take him to Baltimore when it's time for his trial."

"It sounds like a good plan, but we'll have to catch him first."

"We will. How soon can you be ready to go?"

"As soon as I talk to my Captain. I'll need to call my wife to tell her Blackie and I won't be around for a few days. I won't tell her where we're going."

"I'm going to send a car tomorrow morning to pick you up at nine o'clock sharp at the police department. I'll see you as soon as you get to D.C. You'll meet with me and a Colonel Sharpe from the Marine Corps tomorrow afternoon. He'll want to know the layout of the inside of the house and you can tell him where the heaviest guns are located. We'll compare your info to satellite and drone pictures. Then, we'll fly down to Key West tomorrow evening and lay over until the Marines finish making their plans.

When they're ready, we'll take choppers at night to just east of Cancun, where we'll meet an air tanker and refuel. We'll hit Rodriguez a couple of hours before dawn when most of his guards are asleep."

"It sounds like you've planned this mission out well. Let's just hope it's that easy. We thought we had him once before, in Baltimore."

"It should be. I'll see you tomorrow morning. You won't have to bring more than one change of clothes to wear when you go back home. We'll take care of everything else."

"Ron, thanks again for including us in this raid."

"No thanks are necessary. Let's get Rodriguez."

∞ ∞ ∞ ∞ ∞ ∞

Jack and Blackie could hear machine gun fire on the ground over the engines of the stealth helicopter that was carrying them. Drones had been sent in ahead of the strike force to neutralize the heavy machine gun positions and to punch holes in the stone walls with rockets before the first Marines slid down ropes onto the huge lawns.

The light from the explosions dazzled Jack's eyes. The entire ground attack force was equipped with night vision contact lenses to help them cope with the darkness of the moonless night, but he wasn't wearing the set that had been given to him. The lenses would darken momentarily whenever a burst of bright light hit the wearer's eyes. They would immediately become clear again when the light faded, so night vision would be maintained. They were easier to wear than the old-style night vision goggles that were used until a few years ago. They were new technology that was only available to the military.

The guards in the towers were taken out by the rockets, but others on the grounds that surrounded the mansion were putting up a stiff resistance. Tracer fire could be seen raining from the attacking helicopters to answer the bullets that were coming from the windows of the main house and surrounding outbuildings. The Marines on the ground were well trained and protected from all but the worst injuries by body armor. Except for a few minor cuts and bruises, they were taking no casualties. The men had been ordered to do everything possible to ensure the safety of the wife and children of Rodriguez. Jack hoped they were being protected by the thick walls of the house.

Only ten minutes elapsed from the beginning of the attack until the first men and women could be seen coming from the buildings with their hands held high over their heads. Captain Diaz, the officer in command of the raid, ordered all the helicopters to land. He had been chosen to lead the attack because of his combat experience and the fact that he spoke fluent Spanish. He was one of the first to slide down the ropes. The officer met them on the manicured lawn in front of the house.

"Sir, the guards are telling us that Rodriguez and his family are not here."

"Keep looking, Captain. Check all the buildings. They could be curled up in a spider hole somewhere on the grounds. It's possible there could be an underground bunker under one of the buildings that we don't know about."

"Can we use the dog? He's supposed to know exactly what Rodriguez looks like."

Ron turned to Jack.

"Do you and Blackie want to go with us while we search? It could be dangerous."

"We're not worried about that. Let's go."

Captain Diaz spoke again.

"He may have been warned we were coming. My men are telling me there are almost no civilians here except for a few female members of the house staff. Everyone else took part in the gunfight. We caught four men who had been loading a truck, sir. You need to see what they were putting inside and tell me what you want to be done with it."

"What is it, drugs?"

The Captain smiled. "No, sir. It's money."

"How much?"

"There's a lot."

"Let's go see."

The three men and Blackie walked around the mansion to where a large covered truck was parked close beside a rear door. Captain Diaz had ordered two Marines to stand guard at the back of the truck. Another guarded half a dozen prisoners who were sitting nearby with their hands bound behind their backs.

Jack gasped. The truck was loaded almost to the top of the metal roof with bundles of money that were wrapped in clear plastic. Another Marine climbed from the back of the truck as they approached.

Diaz walked up to the man.

"How much is in there, Sergeant?"

"There's too much to count, sir. It looks like there are tens of millions of dollars. From what I can see, it's mostly fifty and hundred dollar bills. We'll have to unload the truck to see if anyone is hiding underneath it. There's a lot more in the basement of the house."

Captain Diaz turned to Strong.

"What do you want me to do with it? If we take it with us, we'll have to bring in a couple of more choppers to carry it."

"We don't have time for that. Just have your men throw it all into a pile in the middle of the house. They'll have to unload most of it anyhow to see if anyone is hiding behind it. After they do that, have the rest brought up from the basement and put it into the pile. See if your men can find a can of gasoline or diesel fuel. If you find some, we'll pour it over the pile just before we leave and set fire to it. I want one of your men to count out five thousand dollars for each member of your attack force. They deserve it for a job well done. Don't forget your own share, Captain. Afterward, count out a thousand dollars for each female member of the house staff and send them packing. It won't hurt us to spread a little bit of Yankee good will while we're down here."

"That's a lot of money to waste, sir. Shouldn't we take it with us?"

"No, Captain. It's all drug and blood money. We don't have enough time to call in more choppers and we can't leave it behind. We'll blow the house up along with it just after we clear the area. If we can't find Rodriguez, we don't want him to come back here and start over again. We'll put explosives in all the outbuildings and blow them, too. Just make sure your men don't stuff their pockets with cash before we go. Let's get busy and see if we can find out where Rodriguez is hiding."

"What do you want me to do with the guards who weren't killed?"

"See if you can find out which ones are the leaders and we'll take them with us for questioning. Make sure the rest are unarmed and put handcuffs on them. Have some of your men take them out into the woods far enough so they won't be hurt when the house blows. Cuff them all together in a circle around a big tree so they can't go anywhere. We can't take them all with us, so we'll leave them for their own government to worry about. I'll make sure law enforcement down here knows where they are. Take all the guard dogs that weren't killed out into the woods and tie them to trees close to the prisoners. We'll have to move the people who were killed out there too, so their families can claim the bodies. While your men are doing that, have them put a thousand dollars into the pockets of each dead man. It will help the families with funeral expenses. God knows the people are so poor around here, they can use the money. On second thought, put $5,000 into the pockets of each dead man. If they weren't so poor, maybe they wouldn't have been involved with Rodriguez in the first place. Don't give any money to the prisoners that we leave behind."

The men searched for almost an hour before Agent Strong told them to stand down. Jack and Blackie, along with Agent Strong, Captain Diaz, and six Marines, had searched through all the buildings and over the vast lawns that surrounded the house. Rodriguez and his family were not there. An armory containing almost three hundred automatic weapons and hundreds of metal boxes of ammunition was found along with another huge room containing millions of dollars' worth of customized guns and jewelry. The walls of the palatial home were covered with works of art. Except for the artwork, jewelry, and guns, everything was left as it was found. The artwork and jewelry were carried hundreds of feet away from the buildings and covered with tarpaulins to protect it from the weather and the explosions that would follow. It could be recovered by Mexican authorities. The munitions were placed in the big room in the center of the house along with the money.

Explosives were placed in the outbuildings and around the outer walls of the house and in the huge living room where the money and munitions were piled. Jack sat by the window of Ron's helicopter as it lifted off and watched as all the other aircraft departed from the recent scene of battle. They were more than two miles away when explosions began to brighten the dawn sky. The huge home and all the outbuildings were almost leveled. What remained would soon be consumed by the fires the explosives and gasoline had produced.

Agent Strong was seated beside Jack; Jack spoke loudly so his voice would be heard over the noise of the engines and rotors. They were no longer running under stealth conditions.

"Ron, I'm not sure I'd want to be the one to tell Rodriguez about what happened this morning. That person might not live to talk to anyone else."

"He'll be like an angry tiger from now on. He'll lash out at anyone he thinks had a hand in this. I wish we'd caught him. There'll be a lot of blood spilled because we didn't."

"Hopefully, it will all be criminal blood. Do you think he was told we were coming?"

"I don't think the President of Mexico tipped him off. President Thomas believes he's an honest man. He probably made the mistake of telling one of his crooked advisors about what we were going to do and the advisor warned Rodriguez. President Thomas has the names of the Mexican politicians Blackie told you were involved with Rodriguez, but we may not know who they all are."

"Didn't President Thomas tell the Mexican President who he shouldn't talk to?"

"I believe he just said not to trust anybody. He didn't want to take a chance on him jumping the gun with arrests and upsetting the entire Mexican government before we got Rodriguez."

"Well, we didn't get him. I guess we're going to have to go back to square one."

"People like him always have a backup plan. You said Blackie told you he has other safe houses and may even have one in the States. We're going to have to hit all of them. The President of Mexico may not be so eager to cooperate from now on."

"Rodriguez would have him killed if he thought that would stop us."

"I know. President Thomas may tell the press we didn't have his have permission to enter the country."

"He'll have to do that if he wants him to stay alive. What do we do next?"

"Maybe we can get some useful info from the prisoners we took this morning. I'll send them to Gitmo to be interrogated."

∞ ∞ ∞ ∞ ∞ ∞

None of the men who were taken prisoner knew of other locations where Rodriguez might be hiding. Months passed as Ron, Jack and Blackie continued the pursuit of the drug lord. Each time they thought they were closing in on him, he would slip through their fingers once again.

The President of Mexico continued to cooperate with the investigation, but he knew his life was becoming more endangered with each passing day. Rodriguez sent warnings to him to stop allowing investigators from the United States to enter the country, but the President ignored them. He was a patriot who wanted what was best for his nation. He was aware Rodriguez would not let him live, so his only possible course of action was to let the raids continue until the fugitive was either captured or killed.

Agent Strong, Jack, and Blackie led assaults on strongholds that Rodriguez had set up in the western mountains of Mexico. Each foray came up fruitless except for the destruction of the lavish homes, money and other possessions Rodriguez had hidden away. With each attack, more of the criminal's associates decided it was no longer profitable to do business with a man who had such unwavering enemies.

Rodriguez had been told that one of his most determined pursuers was the police officer who he had once held prisoner. He instructed his shrinking board of directors to spread the word he would pay a one-million-dollar reward to anyone who would kill Sergeant Randall and bring the huge black dog that was always at the officer's side to him. When more weeks passed and two more of his safe havens were annihilated, he decided he would have to take a more personal approach to the problem. If he and his criminal empire were going to be destroyed, at least he'd have the satisfaction of taking his enemy along with him when he died.

Chapter 11

Jack's cell phone buzzed; he spoke into the screen.

"Hello, Sergeant Randall speaking."

"Jack, this is Captain Harrison."

"Hi, Cap, what's up? I was just getting ready to go to work. It's only 6:00 A.M. Are we going on another raid? It's been almost a month since the last one."

"No, not this time. I hope you don't mind the early call. I had to come into the office at four this morning because of another case I'm working on. I have a couple of bits of information I thought you'd like to know about. First, you've been promoted back to Lieutenant. It's already official."

"That's good news, Cap. Are you sure I deserve it? After all, I did let you and the P.D. down in a big way."

"It wasn't your fault and the Chief and I know it. If you don't deserve a promotion, nobody does. Just accept it and don't worry about it. You have other things to think about. I just got a call from one of our men down at the docks. We believe Rodriguez is on his way back to Baltimore."

"He's running out of places to hide. If he's on the way here, there's only one reason. I knew sooner or later he'd want to personally take me out. Actually, I thought he'd come sooner. I knew he wouldn't want to pay that million dollar reward we heard he'd put on my head to someone else."

"You said he'd eventually show up."

"I did. He's not right in the head. He'll believe he can get all the way to Baltimore, kill me, then get safely back home. He'll want to take Blackie with him."

"He's more dangerous now than he's ever been."

"I'd be more worried if Blackie and I weren't implanted with the electronics. That gives us a huge advantage."

"Still, we're dealing with a cold-blooded murderer who has only one thing on his mind. You've been out to get him since last year and he knows it's personal because of Silas. He may think if he kills you, the raids will stop. In his mind, it's either you or him."

"It won't be me, not while Blackie and Boss are with me."

"I just called to give you a head up. As soon as I get off the phone, I'm calling Ron Strong and telling him what we have found out. I'll tell him to alert the agents who are with Heather and Little Jack. I'm going to put some officers back around you. You said to pull them off a few weeks ago."

"I don't need them. Blackie and Boss are better security than having a dozen people around me. When is he supposed to get here?"

"We're not sure. All we know right now is, the word is out that he's coming. He could already be here, for all we know."

"I'll keep my eyes open. The only people I want around me are people I can trust, like you and Ron. If Ron has a couple in D.C. who he knows are reliable, he can bring them along. Other than that, I'd just as soon do this without any other assistance. I think we'll have a better chance of getting Rodriguez that way."

"I understand. I'm going to get off here and call Ron."

"Ok, Cap. I'll talk to you later. Call me if you get any more information about when to expect Rodriguez to show up."

Blackie- *"We're going to have to be ready, Jack. We've helped ruin him and his entire corrupt world. He won't take you to Mexico this time. He'll kill you."*

Jack- *"I know, boy. We'll just have to hope he gets careless."*

For some reason, a chill ran down Jack's spine when the phone buzzed again.

"Hello, Lieutenant Randall speaking."

"So, it's Lieutenant Randall, is it? You have been prospering while you were trying to destroy me."

"Rodriguez!"

"And now, you've decided to use my real name."

"Where are you?"

"I'm sure you'd like to know where I am, Lieutenant, so you could call your friends at the police department and tell them. Let's just say I'm somewhere nearby and I want you to come visit me."

"How would I do that if I don't know where you are?"

"You won't have to know. I'm sending two of my men to bring you here."

"What makes you think I'll go anywhere with your men?"

"Do you remember when we had our conversation while you were my guest in Mexico about how I found out who you really are?"

"Yes. You told me your son had seen a picture on your computer of me and the dog I used to work with."

"You have a good memory. I didn't tell you some of the pictures on my computer also held the image of a woman. She is your wife, Lieutenant. I had my people find out more about her. It seems that not only did you marry the beautiful woman, you are also the father of a fine young son. They are now my guests, just as you were a few months ago! I believe you will be happy to come to visit me. If you don't, you will never see either of them alive again. One of my men is holding a knife to your wife's throat right this second. If I tell him to cut it, he will. Then we can talk about what I will do to your son!"

"Rodriguez, I swear, if you hurt either of them, I'll…"

The man's voice became icy.

"Shut your mouth and listen closely. Two of my men will be arriving at your front door at any moment. You and your dog will get into the car with them and you will not cause them any trouble. I'll be on the phone with them every second while they are bringing you to me. If you try anything, I will have my man cut your wife's right hand off. I'll let you listen to her screams on the telephone while I'm doing it. If you cause any more problems, I'll have him cut off your son's right hand. Do we understand each other, Lieutenant?"

"I won't do anything until I hear my wife's voice. I don't believe you have them."

"Certainly. I wouldn't think of not allowing that. I'm putting the phone up to her ear right now. It is such a beautiful ear. I might cut it off, just to help you understand the situation. Would you like to say hello?"

"Jack?"

"Yes, Heather, it's me."

"Jack! He's crazy! He's going to kill all of us..."

Rodriguez spoke again in the same sinister voice.

"Was that enough, Lieutenant?"

"That was enough, Rodriguez. I know you want to kill me. If I come peacefully, will you agree to let them go?"

"I'm not agreeing to anything. We'll have to decide what to do about that when you get here, won't we?"

"You're holding all the cards right now, but I'm promising you, if you hurt either of them, I'll kill you."

Rodriguez cackled maniacally.

"You talk very bravely for a man who is so helpless! My men are now at your home. I will make one promise to you; we will have a very nice visit."

The connection was broken. Jack raced to his bedroom and hastily grabbed his uniform belt from a hook in the closet. He pulled a small, flesh-colored adhesive strip from one of the leather pouches. It held a tiny electronic tracer that would be nearly impossible for Rodriguez to find. He unbuttoned his trousers and dropped them to his knees. He yanked the backing from the strip and pressed it into place on his inner thigh. It activated and began to emit a radio signal the instant the adhesive touched his bare skin. He pulled his trousers back up and was taking a uniform shirt from his closet when the front door burst open. Two wild-eyed men rushed into the house. Both were holding semi-automatic pistols.

Jack yelled to them, "I'm in here putting my clothes on. Stay with me, Blackie."

The men ran into the bedroom and saw that he was putting on his uniform. The taller of the two men was holding a phone to his ear. He lowered it and spoke in a low growl.

"You will not need your police uniform. Take it off and put on ordinary clothing. Then, you and your dog will come with us."

The men waited until he had put on a regular pair of slacks and a pullover shirt. One of the men shoved him toward the front door. Blackie snarled.

"Calm your dog. If you do not, I will shoot him."

"Settle down, boy. Heel!"

Blackie came to his side as he walked toward the door.

"Is your boss still on the phone?"

"Yes."

"Tell him I'm coming along peacefully. I don't want him to do something we'll all regret."

The man spoke into the phone. Within seconds, he laughed.

"He said to tell you that you are doing the right thing."

Jack walked outside to the car. One of the men opened the rear door and pointed to the back seat. He and Blackie slid inside; the taller man sat down beside them. The heavier of the two men closed the door and grunted his way into the front seat behind the steering wheel.

Jack- *"Blackie! I don't know where we're going, but as soon as we get there and the door is opened, I want you to bolt from the car! Run as fast as you can and hide! You'll have to stay away from me until I need you!"*

Boss- *"No, Jack. Rodriguez may try to kill you as soon as you get out of the car! If we're not there to stop him, you could be dead before we get back to you!"*

Jack- *"We can't worry about that. I believe he'll want to gloat for a while before he does anything to me. That's the kind of evil maniac he is. You and Blackie may be the only chance we have to save Heather and Little Jack. I'm hoping I can bargain with him. I'm the one he wants. If he has me, he may let them go."*

Boss- *"There is no reasoning with a man who enjoys hurting people. He's worse now than he was when we were in Mexico. We could hear the madness in his voice when you were talking to him on the phone. Losing his empire has pushed him over the edge. He won't make any deals."*

Jack- *"I know, but we'll have to risk it. He'll probably want to put a leash on you right away. If he does, your movements will be restricted. Just get away from the car as fast as you can and make it look like you've panicked. I'll call you back the instant I need you. Run away! Then come back to me when it's safe and stay out of sight, if you can."*

Blackie- *"Ok, just don't take too long. I promise you, if he hurts you, Heather or Little Jack, he won't get away with it. I'll tear his throat out!"*

Jack- *"I hope I can keep him from doing anything to them until the tracker on my leg brings the Captain to us. If I can't, at least he'll know where to find our bodies. Just stay calm and maybe we'll all get out of this alive. We'll try to save them without any of us being hurt. If it comes down to them or me, you do your best to save them. They come first! You let me go! Is that clear, boys?"*

As he was communicating with the dogs, the man beside him pulled a wide strip of cloth from his pocket and tied it around Jack's eyes. He then pulled a strong cord from the same pocket and tied Jack's hands behind his back. When he was finished, he pushed the officer onto the floor of the vehicle. The car began to move. The two men had no idea Jack was watching everything through Blackie's eyes as they were leaving the neighborhood.

Thirty minutes passed before the car pulled to a stop in front of a huge rusted steel door. They were sitting at the entrance of a deserted warehouse near the Baltimore waterfront. The driver looked around to see if they were being observed. The gunman in the back seat exited the car and struggled to open the heavy door. When the corroded hinges finally yielded, the driver pulled the car into the warehouse and stopped. The door closed behind them. The only light inside the building came from a small barred window beside the main door and a dim glow from the open door of what was left of an office in the center of the dilapidated structure. There were tiny holes in the walls of the building that allowed small shafts of light to penetrate the gloom.

The driver turned off the ignition as the taller man opened the rear door. Blackie yelped and dove headlong out of the car to disappear into the depths of the dark warehouse. The gunman dragged Jack from the vehicle and onto his feet.

Rodriguez appeared at the door of the office and raced across the cement floor. His reddened eyes showed that he had not slept well for many days. He backhanded the tallest kidnapper across the face.

"You fool! I told you to watch the dog!"

The man touched his bruised jaw with his left hand and groveled.

"I'm sorry, Jefe. He seemed to be calm when we put him into the car. I didn't know he would run away."

"You should have looked around the Lieutenant's home and found a leash to put on him! Now we'll have to catch him before I can leave! Both of you; go find him before I get angry! See if you can find some rope to tie around his neck!"

"Si, Jefe."

As the two men trotted into the darkness, Rodriguez pulled a semi-automatic pistol from under his jacket and ripped the blindfold away from Jack's eyes. He pushed the end of the gun's barrel into the middle of Jack's back and shoved him toward the office.

As they walked through the door, Jack saw his wife and son. They were standing back to back with their wrists bound together. Both had strips of dark cloth tied over their eyes and mouths. A rope had been thrown across a steel beam directly above the partially collapsed ceiling of the office. One end was tied around their wrists. Little Jack had been lifted onto a rusted folding chair so that his hands were at the same level as Heather's. The only light in the room came from a dim portable electric lantern that hung from a hook on the wall.

Jack turned around to face the drug lord.

"So, where's the piece of crap that was going to cut my wife's throat?"

Rodriguez's voice lifted to a high-pitched, sadistic whine.

"That was just a little joke between friends! I only said that so you would come to visit me!"

"Ok, Rodriguez, I'm here. Let them go and I'll do whatever you want."

The voice changed to a snarl.

"I'm sure you will, even if I don't let them go. Perhaps we can have some fun before I kill you."

"I told you, if you hurt either of them, you're a dead man."

"You aren't in a position to threaten anyone! I'm surprised you are still so arrogant. Before we talk, I'll tighten the rope. It will make our conversation more interesting!"

Jack needed to stall for more time until Blackie could make his way to the room.

"Where are all your people? I thought you'd have a dozen of them with you."

The whine returned to Rodriguez's voice.

"I don't have many people left. They are abandoning me. Most of them left because I don't have enough money to pay them. It is all because of you. I lost my factory in the Yucatan because of you. I lost my home there, once again, because of you. Most of my other homes and factories are gone, too."

"You were peddling poison!"

Anger returned to the drug lord's voice.

"Everywhere, my people have told me the same thing. Each time your country's soldiers come to destroy what belongs to me, a tall man with a huge black dog is leading them. I haven't seen my wife or my sons in months. You have taken everything from me. While I have had to endure these things, you have prospered. So, I came to punish you while I still can. I discovered where you had hidden your wife and son and sent my men to get them. They broke into your safe house last night and killed the two men and the dog that tried to protect them. Now, I have used your wife and son to bring you here to me. It is time for you to suffer, Lieutenant! You have caused me to lose everything that was dear to me, so now my friend, I am going to take everything you love away from you! Then, you too, will die!"

"Rodriguez, you don't have to do this! If you let them go, I'll help you escape! There are ways I can get you out of the country!"

"Escape? To where? I have nowhere left to go. No, I will kill you and your family! You must pay for what you have done to me! Then, I will take your dog and return to Mexico."

During their terse conversation, Jack could see through Blackie's eyes as the almost invisible dog continued to elude the two men who were searching for him. He was making good use of the shadows behind the empty cardboard boxes and other debris that littered the warehouse floor. He had carefully made his way to the dimly lit office and was preparing to leap through the door.

"Not yet, boy!"

Suddenly, Rodriguez slammed his fist into Jack's stomach. Jack gasped and doubled over in agony as the unexpected blow caused all the air to rush from his lungs. Rodriguez shoved him toward a broken metal chair in the corner of the small room. He then turned and walked to the center of the office. He grabbed the loose end of the rope and gave a hard yank. Heather was pulled onto her toes. Little Jack lost his footing on the chair and shrieked behind his gag as he was left dangling on the end of the rope.

The boy's muffled screams galvanized Blackie into motion. With a horrific snarl, he threw himself through the open door and locked his jaws around Rodriguez's neck. The stricken man attempted to cry out as the dog slammed into him, but no sound emanated from his crushed larynx. He began to beat frantically at the huge head with his pistol. Little Jack dropped back to the chair and fought to regain his footing as Rodriguez fell to the floor. The crazed man's frenzied struggles began to weaken as his life gushed from the ghastly wounds Blackie's teeth were tearing open in his throat. He tossed the gun aside and clutched at the dog's mouth in a last desperate attempt to force the grinding jaws apart. The hands gradually became still and then fell away. He rolled onto his back as the final drops of blood trickled onto the stained cement. The last throat to be torn open during the drug lord's life of crime had been his own.

Jack pulled himself back to his feet. He was struggling to draw air back into his burning lungs.

Jack- *"Blackie, he's finished! Let him go and chew these ropes off my hands before his men get back!"*

Blackie jumped away from Rodriguez and quickly moved to bite through the bindings on Jack's wrists. The heavy cord fell away. Jack picked up the pistol that Rodriguez had been holding.

He was still fighting to catch his breath. He smashed the lantern with the gun butt. The light sparked, then went out.

Jack- *"Quick, boy, get back out there! See if you can find out where the other two men are! Stay out of sight until I need you! Be careful!"*

Blackie darted back through the open door into the warehouse. After grabbing the rope and pulling the dangling end over the beam, Jack shoved Heather and Little Jack onto the floor in the darkest corner of the room. He yanked the dark strips of cloth from their faces as he knelt beside them with his gun pointed toward the door. He whispered to them to remain silent.

Bullets began to explode through the crumbling sheetrock walls of the darkened office as the roar of gunfire echoed through the huge warehouse. The stunned gunmen had stared in horror as Blackie leaped through the office doorway and seized their boss by the throat. They stood immobile as Rodriguez lost his one-sided battle with the dog. The sound of the gun butt smashing into the lantern jolted them back into action. Within seconds, they opened fire on the officer who now had a weapon and was between them and the only exit from the building.

Neither gunman saw Blackie as he disappeared back into the warehouse. Both continued to fire into the office as the almost invisible dog crept up on them. Suddenly, a scream tore through the air just as one of the guns fell silent. The shorter man had not seen Blackie spring from behind a pile of crumbling cardboard boxes. The already bloody jaws were now clamped around the wrist of his gun hand. The weapon clattered to the floor.

Jack dove through the door and rolled across the discolored cement until he could find cover behind one of the thick metal stanchions that supported the roof. His eyes were quickly adjusting to the gloom. Fifty feet away, he could see Blackie as he fought with the gunman. Without warning, the taller man appeared from behind a stack of empty boxes and pointed his gun at the dog's side. Jack aimed his own weapon and quickly fired twice. The man slammed to the floor with two bullet holes in his chest. He was already dead when his body touched the floor.

Jack ran to Blackie and the other gunman. Blackie was loosening his grip on the man's wrist and preparing to go for his throat. Jack could feel the dog's hot rage boiling through his own mind as he struggled to control himself. His entire body was shaking as he spoke to the furious dog.

Jack - "Let him go, boy. I can take it from here."

Boss- *"Let's finish this now! He helped Rodriguez hurt Heather and Little Jack!"*

"No, boy. Rodriguez and the other man are both dead. You can stand down. None of these people will ever hurt any of us again."

Blackie- *"They killed Little Boss! He tried to protect Heather and Little Jack and they killed him!"*

"I know, boy. He'll pay for what he's done. He also helped kill two Federal officers. That and the kidnapping and assault of Heather and Little Jack will send him to prison for the rest of his life. Let him go. We'll take him back to the office and see how they're doing."

Blackie gave the thug's arm another violent shake before releasing his grip. He backed away and stood in front of him, growling ferociously. The man clutched his mangled wrist with his uninjured left hand in an attempt to staunch the flow of blood. He was confused by what he believed to be the officer's one-sided conversation with the dog.

Jack quickly walked over to the dead gunman and picked up the pistol that had dropped to the floor. He moved back to retrieve the second weapon from where it had fallen when Blackie attacked the other shooter. He shoved the whimpering gunman toward the door of the office. When they entered, he pushed the swarthy face against the closest wall.

"Watch him, Blackie."

"Please amigo, I am bleeding. I don't think I can stand here very long. Please don't let him get at me again. He is no perro, he is un diablo negro!

"You're right! He's not a regular dog. He's a black devil and he'll tear your heart out and eat it if I tell him to! He won't hurt you if you don't move. If you do, I might just let him do whatever he wants to you. What's your name?"

"I won't move, amigo. My name is Chico Morales."

Jack turned to Heather and little Jack and untied the knots in the rope that bound their wrists together. Tears from Little Jack's eyes had traced their way through the dust that had fallen onto his face when the sheetrock walls were shattered by the bullets. Jack pulled his wife and son into his arms.

"Are you both ok?"

"I'm alright, Dad. Mom?"

"I'm not hurt. I'm just so scared. Jack, are you sure you and Blackie got all of them?"

Jack- *"You don't smell more of them, do you, boys?"*

Blackie- *"No, Jack. If any are outside, they would have come in by now."*

Jack- *"Good."*

"There aren't any more of them around, Heather. Let's try to find a couple of these old chairs that are strong enough to sit on while I call the Captain. You've both been through enough today."

He turned toward the man who was leaning against the wall.

"Chico, do you have a phone on you?"

"Si. It is in the top pocket on the left side of my jacket."

Jack walked over and felt through the man's clothing until he located the phone. As he was searching for the phone, he also looked for hidden weapons. He found a razor-sharp switchblade knife with a six-inch blade in one of the front pockets of the man's trousers.

"You wouldn't happen to have had anything to do with the murder of my friend, Corporal Silas Jones, would you?"

"No, amigo, I have never heard of that man."

Blackie- *"He's lying, Jack! His heart began to pound the instant he heard the name. He's beginning to sweat harder."*

Jack- *"What do you think, Boss?"*

Boss- *"I agree with Blackie. He did it!"*

Jack grabbed Chico by his jacket collar and slammed him to the floor.

"Blackie, post!

Blackie stationed over the gunman and stood there snarling viciously with his huge teeth inches away from the sweating face. Saliva and blood from his gaping jaws began to drip onto the gunman's quivering cheeks.

"Chico, you have about ten seconds to come clean about what happened to my friend! If you don't, I'm going to let my dog tear your throat out! You've seen what he did to your boss and you've already felt his teeth on your wrist! He's just itching for me to let him have another go at you!"

"Please amigo, don't let him get me!"

"Five seconds, Chico! Blackie, get ready!"

Chico's face visibly paled as Blackie's body tensed and the snarling intensified. Jack touched the screen on the phone that would record Chico's words. He pointed the lens toward the man.

"Please, amigo, call your dog off me! I didn't want to kill your friend! Jose Malenia made me do it! He told me to follow your friend from his room that night and cut his throat after he left the hotel! He said I was to push his tongue through the hole in his throat after he was dead! I didn't want to do it, but when I refused, he said Senor Rodriguez would kill me himself if I didn't! I was afraid! I had to kill your friend or I would have been a dead man!"

Jack turned off the video recorder as the man began to sob. He turned to Heather.

"Did you understand exactly what he said?"

"Yes."

"I'm sorry you and Little Jack had to see that. I want you to remember every word you heard so you can testify when this piece of garbage goes on trial. Silas was a good officer with a wife and two kids."

"I know. I went to his funeral."

"I'm going to call the Captain. You can calm down, Blackie. We got what we wanted from him. He's through."

Jack touched the phone and made the call as Blackie backed away from the whimpering murderer.

"Cap, this is Jack."

"Jack, are you ok? We got the signal from your tracker. I just got here with half a dozen officers and we were about to move in."

"Come on in. The big door is unlocked; just push it open. It's all over. We're in the office, or what's left of it."

Within seconds, the huge entry door opened as half a dozen uniformed officers pushed from the outside. The Captain walked in behind them. He looked around the huge building and saw the dead man on the floor in the distance. He walked toward the office. When he stepped through the door, he saw Rodriguez lying in a pool of blood and the injured gunman lying on the floor close beside him.

"What happened here, Jack?"

Jack briefly explained what had occurred since he'd spoken with the Captain earlier that morning.

"That explains why Ron couldn't get an answer when he tried to call his people at Heather's house. Good work, Jack. Thank God Blackie was with you. I guess we don't have to worry about Rodriguez anymore. I'll have a medic help Little Jack and Heather. We'll send them to the hospital to be checked out after she gets done. When she's sure they're alright, I'll have her look at this other piece of crap."

Chapter 12

Six months had passed and the once mighty Rodriguez drug cartel was now little more than a memory. When their leader was eliminated, as Captain Harrison had predicted, the remaining members of the board of directors began to fight among themselves over the scraps of the organization. One by one, they had either been captured by law enforcement agencies from Mexico or the United States or were killed by other members of their own organization who wanted what was left of the cartel for themselves. All that remained was for the raid to take place on the last board member's hidden center of operations in southern Mexico.

Ron and Jack were seated toward the front of the stealth helicopter that would not land until the Marines had eliminated the worst of the resistance. Blackie was on the floor beside Jack. Without warning, bullets began to rip through the lower side of the fuselage. There were hidden men with machine guns in the jungle below that surrounded the drug factory. Some of them were firing armor piercing bullets. They should not have been there; they must have been warned an attack was imminent.

Jack was immediately struck on the right side where he wasn't completely shielded by his body armor. He hadn't tightened it because they didn't anticipate such a vicious ground fight. Blackie jumped onto a seat beside him to use his body to prevent more bullets from striking his friend. Jack began to sink into blackness.

Boss- *"Stay with us, Jack, don't let go!"*

More bullets tore into the helicopter. One struck Blackie behind his right front leg. He was thrown across the aircraft by the impact.

Ron yelled into the microphone that was attached to his helmet. "Pilot! Get us out of here and find a hospital! Lieutenant Randall and his dog have been hit!"

Jack heard no more.

He slowly opened his eyes. Heather was sitting beside his hospital bed with Blackie at her feet. The instant he moved his hand, the dog jumped toward the bed and placed his paw on his arm. Heather immediately tossed the computer scroll she was reading onto a bedside table and stood up to lean over him. She pushed aside the medical drip tubes that were attached to his arm and kissed him on the forehead.

Blackie- *"I'm glad you're finally awake. We thought we had lost you."*

Jack- *"I thought you did, too."*

Heather spoke in a trembling voice.

"Sweetheart, I've been so worried. I was afraid you weren't going to come back to me."

"That seems to be the going opinion around here. What happened?"

"Don't you remember? You, Blackie and Agent Strong were in a small helicopter near the factory in Mexico when you were hit in the side. The bullets were coming into the helicopter at an angle. A fragment from the bullet that hit you damaged your lung and nicked your heart. If a small hospital hadn't been nearby, you would have died. There wasn't even a doctor present when you arrived. A combat medic came in right behind you on another helicopter and did everything he could to save you. You were given blood transfusions and stabilized until a heart surgeon could be flown in to begin repairing the damage the bullet had done. Agent Strong insisted that surgical supplies and equipment be airlifted to the hospital to supplement what they already had on hand. You couldn't be moved for nearly a week. You've had two operations to repair the damage from the wound. The impact from the bullet did most of the damage. Agent Strong said it was slowed by a metal support and the outer skin of the helicopter, but it was deformed and broke up when it hit you. It was like you were hit by a small explosion. That wasn't the worst of it; you picked up a terrible infection before you could be brought home."

"Where am I?"

"We're at Walter Reed. You were sent here on the President's orders."

"How long have I been here?"

"Almost a week."

"I don't remember much of anything. I seem to remember Blackie being hit."

Blackie- *"I was, but my body armor stopped the bullet. My side was sore, but I wasn't badly hurt."*

"He was, but the K9 armor he was wearing stopped the bullet."

"He just told me. Is Ron alright?"

"Yes. He wasn't wounded. He and Blackie never left your side unless you were in surgery until you got here. The President sent a specially equipped hospital plane to bring you home and they came back with you. Agent Strong had a meeting with the Attorney General today, so he couldn't be here."

"Where's our son?"

"He's staying at Captain Harrison's house until I can go home. He and his wife have been wonderful since you were hurt. I wasn't going to leave you until I knew you were going to live. After that, I decided to stay until you woke up. The nurses had a cot brought to your room and I've been sleeping on it."

"You didn't have to do that."

"I needed to. The world can wait until we're ready to catch up with it, Jack."

"Did the Marines take out the factory?"

"They did. They captured the last board member. Agent Strong says he's sure he's the last one. He was taken to Guantanamo for questioning and he'll be brought to Washington in a few weeks for the trial."

"That's good. I'd hate to think we didn't get him after we went to all that trouble."

"The FBI will be rooting out what's left of the cartel in this country for a while yet. Basically, they're all done for. Agent Strong says Mexico may be a different story. There are a lot of corrupt politicians and police officers in that country who were involved with the cartel. Many of them probably won't go to prison, but at least they're out of business."

"We'll have to put away many of our own people. There was a lot of drug money being used for payoffs in this country. We've got information that's going to stir things up from top to bottom. Now that we've caught the last board member, we can go ahead with our own prosecutions. Bribery and corruption have been running rampant. When everything hits the fan, you'll be hearing about people you would have thought could never be bought. They'll all be lawyering up, but they'll start ratting each other out when they realize they've been caught with their hands in the cookie jar. They'll want to save their own skins. Many very powerful people are going to be charged with conspiracy to commit crimes and some will be charged with actively taking part in them. The President and the Attorney General will have to be very courageous to see this through to the end."

"They will be. Blackie and I don't want you to worry about it. You need to rest so you can regain your strength."

"I heard that. I don't know how I could have slept for two weeks and still be so tired."

"The doctors kept you medicated so you'd sleep. I'll push the call button so the nurses will know you're awake."

"Ok, go ahead. Do you know we have Blackie to thank for me being alive? He jumped into the seat beside me after I was hit and protected me with his own body. If he hadn't, I believe the bullet that knocked him away would have hit me in the side of the head."

"Agent Strong told me about it. Before that, he saved all of us at the warehouse. We've been so blessed. Boss helped bring us together and watched over us before Blackie came into our lives. He came back to us through Blackie after we thought he was gone forever. Little Jack grieved over losing Little Boss and they were there to help him get through that. I don't know what we would have done without them. Our lives would have been completely different."

"I know. It's good that they both know how much we love them and how much we appreciate what they've done."

"There have been many times when I've wished I could have been implanted so I could be a part of what you've shared with them."

"I've wished for it too. You never know what the future might bring. I guess it's possible to have it done if the President could be convinced it's necessary. Here comes the nurse."

∞ ∞ ∞ ∞ ∞ ∞

The next afternoon, Ron walked into the room.

"Hey, flatfoot. How are you feeling?"

"Like I got shot out of a helicopter. How are things going?"

"I've been tying up a lot of loose ends. I've been so busy since we got back, I haven't been able to get here to see you more than a few times. You were always sleeping. All in all, things have been going well. I've got some news for you."

"Good or bad?"

"It depends on how you look at it. It has to do with your job. After what you've been through, I wouldn't blame you if you decided to get out of the law enforcement business forever."

"I guess I'm getting too old to change."

"That's good to hear. I can use a sidekick from time to time. Are you interested?"

"I'm always interested if I can bring Blackie along."

"I wouldn't have it any other way."

"So, what's your news?"

"The Attorney General and I have been making plans regarding how we're going to put away the bad guys who were involved with Rodriguez in this country. How soon do you think you can come back to work?"

"The doctors are telling me I'm beating the infection. I should be able to leave here in a few days and do the rest of my recuperating at home. I don't think I'll be out of commission for more than two or three more weeks. I'll have to take it easy for a while until my heart and lung are completely healed."

"I've been hearing about that infection the whole time you were milking it and lying around asleep. You're one of the laziest men I've ever worked with!"

Jack laughed. "Are you going to tell me the rest of your news?"

"Oh, yeah, I almost forgot. It's not very important. The President really appreciates what you've done. He wants you and Blackie to meet with him and the Attorney General after you get well. How would you like to become a U.S. Marshal? He wants to make you a Captain. Would you be interested in that?"

"I might be if I can get the BCPD to let me take Blackie along."

"I think that's exactly what he has in mind. I don't know how many times this has been done, but he wants you to stay with your police department and also be a Marshal. I think he's going to fix it up so you can draw two paychecks. Since you seem to have all this pull, maybe you can talk him into doing the same kind of thing for me. I'm always broke."

Jack laughed again. "I'll see what I can do when I talk to him. Seriously Ron, why does he want to do that?"

"I think it's because he's a smart guy and knows a good man when he sees one. He said people like you are hard to find. You always put aside everything that matters to you, to respond to the call of duty. He says you've always looked out for your country first, even when you've known you were going to suffer for it. I believe he wants you to keep your day job, but he wants to be able to call on you whenever he requires special help. That's about all I know. He can tell you the rest when he talks to you."

"I hope I can live up to his expectations."

"You will. He knows we're only men, Jack. All we can do is our best. You have this wonderful dog to help you. A team like the two of you will always be needed. If Blackie had a use for money, I'm sure the President would put him on the payroll."

"Thanks, Ron. We both appreciate you saying that. How soon does he want to see us?"

"He says it'll be whenever you're completely healthy. I'm sure he'll have someone call you when he thinks you're ready."

Epilogue

November 15, 2046

Blackie had been bathed and brushed until his hair glistened and Jack was clad in his best dress uniform. President Thomas and Attorney General Pembroke stood as the officer and his dog entered the Oval Office. Both men extended their hands in welcome. Blackie insisted on shaking the President's hand. After the exchange of goodwill, the President moved to the big chair behind his desk.

"Have a seat, Jack. Can I have something to drink brought to you? Coffee? Cola? Water?"

"No, thank you, Mr. President."

"What about your dog? Would he like some water or a dog biscuit? I'd be happy to have a hamburger or even a steak brought to him."

"Thank you, he's fine, sir."

Blackie groaned and shot him an evil look.

President Thomas chuckled. He and the Attorney General sat down. He could see Jack was ill at ease. He knew the officer understood that much of the nation's history had been put into motion in this very room.

"You shouldn't feel so intimidated by being here. After all, you're one of the people who helped put Arnold and me into these chairs. We wanted to meet with you to thank you for your service and to tell you how concerned we were when we heard you were so grievously wounded."

Jack laughed, nervously. "Thank you. I believe you both would have made it here anyway, sir, with or without my help. I've been watching a lot of news while I've been recuperating. It's good to know the polls are showing support for almost everything you're doing. Our country needs more men like you and Attorney General Pembroke. I'm glad you sent for me. I wanted to thank you for appointing me as a U.S. Marshal."

"You are very welcome, but there's more involved in the appointment than just rewarding you for your service in helping shut down the Rodriguez cartel. In the future, you'll need greater jurisdiction. We have jobs for you, Blackie and Agent Strong that will require you to be a Marshal. You'll be helping him as he makes the arrests of some of the more powerful people in this country who were associated with Rodriguez."

"Still, thank you; both of you."

"We would have come to visit you in the hospital except for one thing; we don't want the press to know we're so personally concerned about your health. From now on, we're going to try to keep you under their radar as much as possible. It's necessary for what I have in mind. I've appointed you Marshal for more than one reason. When I was still Governor of Maryland, I didn't know about the special relationship you shared with your dog, Boss. Once I became President and appointed Mayor Pembroke to be the Attorney General, he told me about it. I learned more as the investigation of Colonel Meyer progressed. I was startled when I found out what happened to Blackie when he was implanted. It seems he has within his mind, all the thoughts and memories you shared with Boss. For all practical purposes, Boss still lives inside him."

"That's correct, sir."

"That has to be a great comfort to you and your family. I know it was a terrible loss to each of you when Boss died. I'm sorry Jack, my time is not my own, so please forgive me. We have a lot to discuss and not much time to do it. I have to get right to the point."

"I understand, Mr. President."

"As you know, the research program has been going on for many years. As hard as they've worked and regardless of the time they've spent, the scientists in the program have not been able to duplicate what happened with you and your dogs. They've had limited success, but nothing like what occurred between the three of you. As I dug deeper, I learned that your dogs are as intelligent as any human being and are mentally, our equals."

"That's true, Mr. President. I don't know that I would have put it exactly that way, but they are certainly my equal."

"I understand now, just how important the three of you are to law enforcement and to our country. I've spoken with Agent Strong and read every one of his reports. Without Blackie and Boss's unique abilities, we would have never been able to defeat the Rodriguez cartel."

"That's also true, sir. People are very careful what they say when they're around other humans, but they'll speak freely around a dog and never suspect he could be an eavesdropper. Rodriguez made plans in Baltimore with his board member, Jose and with his board of directors in Mexico, while Blackie was lying at his feet. He talked to his people on a scrambled satellite phone without knowing Blackie could understand everything he was saying. He didn't know a dog could pass all that information to me through an implant when we were together again. He also took Blackie along on visits to his drug factories. It was only the distance between us when I was locked up in the cell that kept me from seeing everything through his eyes, but when we were finally back together, he passed all that information to me. The implants let that happen."

"I didn't know that was possible when I became President, but I do now. It's another reason I was so concerned when I learned you had been badly wounded and might not survive. Your country can't afford to lose either of you."

"What do you mean, sir?"

"There will be times in the future when this country needs special operatives like you and your dog. When that happens, you'll have to be available. If both of you had been killed during one of those operations, we would have lost a very valuable resource. We can't take chances like that again. You should never have gone on those missions with Agent Strong. We have other men who are trained to do those sorts of things. We need to protect you and Blackie as important assets to our national security."

"I think I know where you're headed with this, sir. I need to say, respectfully, that I'm not sure we want to be thought of in that way. If we don't have the freedom to do what we do best, we won't be able to accomplish much of anything."

"You're misunderstanding what I'm saying. There will be times, very special times, when I, or possibly another American President, may need to call upon you and Blackie for some very dangerous missions. Until that happens, we can't afford to risk your lives in situations where another officer or agent could do a job just as well as you can. There will be more specialized assignments for the two of you. Would something like that interest you? As I said, there are reasons I appointed you a U.S. Marshal. I might have to appoint you to other positions from time to time if the occasion should call for it."

"I believe we'd be inclined to serve in that way, Mr. President."

"Good. I have one more item to talk to you about while you and Blackie are here. It's why I asked our Attorney General to be present. I want him to be aware of everything I'm planning, in the event something unexpected should happen to me and I wouldn't be around to call the shots. He'd have to inform the next President about you. As I read through the records of Blackie's procedure, I came upon the notes of a Doctor Bailey. He is the surgeon who implanted the communication device into Blackie's body. You had a rather curious conversation with him before you left the research facility."

"I did, but I haven't had much time to think about it."

"I gave it a lot of thought while you were lying in the hospital and none of us knew if you were going to live or die. I began to think more about what unique assets you and Blackie, and Boss, of course, are to this government. I thought about Doctor Bailey's notes and had my secretary call and ask him to come here for a chat. It seems he mentioned the possibility to you of our government being involved in clone research."

"He did."

"He told me if clones were produced of you and Blackie, he believes there's every possibility that all of your thoughts and memories could be transferred to them if those clones were implanted with identical devices. What if I was to tell you that our government has indeed been involved in a research program that has been very successful and that most of the difficulties of producing healthy, long-lived clones have been eliminated?"

"I wish I could say I'd be surprised, but I really wouldn't be. After what has happened in the implant program, it would be hard to surprise me about anything our government is doing."

"You're being cynical, but I guess I should expect that after everything you've been through. I like to believe that our government does such research for the good of all of our people."

"I certainly hope so, sir."

"I've had to think about a couple of possibilities. Jack, there may never be another successful implant, at least with the degree of success that we've have had with you, Boss and Blackie. The other possibility is, we should be able to repeat that success with healthy clones of you and your dog. I'm asking for your permission to take tissue samples from both of you, so we can begin producing them."

"Does it make any difference if I say no?"

"I can't force you to do this, but I'm hoping you'll volunteer to go through with it. I'm still thinking about what would have happened if both of you had died on that helicopter in Mexico. We wouldn't be having this conversation right now and the possibilities of what you could do in the future to help our country would be moot. We need both of you. What if we'd lost you and didn't have your clone available for an implant? By the time we brought one to maturity, Blackie might not be alive to transfer all of your memories. Dogs don't live as long as we do. But, if we already had an adult clone of you, Doctor Bailey believes we could have implanted it and awakened it with Blackie at its side and it would be the same as if you'd never been harmed. If we had a mature clone of Blackie and he had been killed, we could have implanted it and awakened it with you at its side. Do you see where I'm going with this? It's not just me, as the current President, that's asking you to be available for service; I'm asking you for future Presidents who will hold this office. You, Blackie, and Boss may be badly needed by any one of them. Your country needs you, Jack."

Jack sighed. "It seems like I've heard that a lot."

"You have and you've always answered the call."

"Yes."

"Then, please answer it again. With the world as it is today, there are never enough dedicated men like you to call upon. There are plenty of big talkers around and there always will be, but intelligent men of action with partners like Blackie and Boss may never again be available. I'm sure that every person who follows me into this office will have to deal with the same sort of problems I face, but some will have to cope with challenges we can't even imagine. If history has taught us anything, it has shown us that there will always be wicked men who will cause all forms of carnage to further their evil plans and schemes. Future Presidents may be able to cope with some of them if you and your dogs are there to help. Cloning will make that possible. It's regrettable, but if we go ahead with our plan, no one except Arnold and I and future Presidents and their closest advisors will ever know about what we set into motion today. I understand that I'm asking a lot from the three of you, but I do have to ask it of you. In return, you'll always be well compensated for your services and you'll have an opportunity that most men only dream of. You'll become almost immortal. There's that and the fact that you'll always have Blackie and Boss at your side. Will you help me, Jack?"

"But sir, if we agree to do what you ask, it could go on forever. Would we be allowed to end it if we ever decided we didn't want to go on being reborn?"

"I can only answer by saying that I would allow it to stop, but I can't foresee what a future President might decide. If you agree to what I'm asking, you must understand, there will be much heartache in store for the three of you. You will have to, in time, see everyone you care about grow old and die, while you remain young and healthy. Heather, Little Jack, your friends, you'll see them all wither away. You'll have to become accustomed to situations in the future that we can't foresee. It's impossible for us to know what could lie ahead for the three of you if you give me permission to proceed. It may not even be possible for the human mind to exist over such an extended period of time without breaking down. We can only guess at what might happen with Blackie and Boss. The only way we'll ever find out is if the three of you actually do it."

"There are a few conditions I'll need to ask of you if we decide to go ahead with this. I'll have to talk them over with Blackie and Boss. Can we have a few days to think about it?"

"Of course. I'll agree to anything that's reasonable."

Blackie put his paw on Jack's knee. *"He's right, Jack. Together, we can take on problems that no one else can handle."*

Boss- *"I agree with Blackie. It's what we do. What more is there to think about?"*

Jack- *"There's Heather and Little Jack."*

Boss- *"We thought you already decided what to do about them. We can't leave them behind. We'll have to find out if they can be successfully implanted and cloned."*

"Mr. President, we don't have to talk about it. Blackie and Boss both agree that we can't say no to your request. If you'll go along with a couple of ours, you can take your tissue samples and start preparing the clones. I guess we'll have to find out what the future has in store for all of us."

THE END...

About the Author

Born and raised in Maryland, after traveling the country, Richard now lives in S.W. Florida with his wife, Martha, of thirty-three years. They spend their days enjoying the Florida sunshine with their three loyal canine companions. They also have a houseful of aquatic pets, sugar gliders and the Queen, a very bossy cat named Moxy. Boss and Blackie, are a combination of every dog he has ever had the pleasure of loving and caring for.

These books are intended to appeal to people of all ages and to anyone that has ever felt the love and loyalty of a four-legged companion. As an avid reader, Richard has been able to sink all his knowledge and imagination into his writings. Besides Boss & Greater Love Hath No Man, Richard has also written a historical fiction called Gray Island.

Richard and Martha have two daughters, six grandchildren, and a great-granddaughter. Richard has included his family in the publishing of his books; Wife, Martha, edited Gray Island and Boss; Daughter, Melissa Fisher, edited Greater Love Hath No Man and contributed to layout, design and interior art; Granddaughter, Michelle Carver, did the cover artwork for both Boss and Greater Love Hath No Man.

www.ingramcontent.com/pod-product-compliance
Lightning Source LLC
Chambersburg PA
CBHW030019180626
46810CB00001B/108